**MAX RETURNED WILLA'S SMILE.
"HOW IS IT THAT OF ALL THE PLACES
YOU MIGHT HAVE ENDED UP,
YOU LIVE IN PLEASANT VALLEY,
WITH THE HOFMANS?"**

"You should smile more, Max. You're quite handsome when you do."

Then she focused on something behind him. Based on the sudden change in her mood, it must be Dan.

"You'd better get back, before his head explodes." She turned, but only halfway. "I hope we'll run into one another again . . . so that I can answer the rest of your questions, of course."

Of course? Max didn't know how to interpret that, but he watched until she turned from the jobsite's gravel drive onto the road.

"Oh, we will run into one another again, Willa Reynolds. You can count on it."

D0391925

More Amish romance from Loree Lough

All He'll Ever Need

Published by Kensington Publishing Corporation

HOME TO STAY

LOREE LOUGH

ZEBRA BOOKS
KENSINGTON PUBLISHING CORP.
www.kensingtonbooks.com

ZEBRA BOOKS are published by

Kensington Publishing Corp.
119 West 40th Street
New York, NY 10018

Copyright © 2020 by Loree Lough

This book is a work of fiction. Names, characters, places, and incidents
either are products of the author's imagination or are used fictitiously.
Any resemblance to actual events or locales, or persons living or dead,
is entirely coincidental.

All rights reserved. No part of this book may be reproduced in any form
or by any means without the prior written consent of the Publisher,
excepting brief quotes used in reviews.

To the extent that the image or images on the cover of this book depict
a person or persons, such person or persons are merely models, and are
not intended to portray any character or characters featured in the book.

If you purchased this book without a cover you should be aware that
this book is stolen property. It was reported as "unsold and destroyed"
to the Publisher and neither the Author nor the Publisher has received
any payment for this "stripped book."

All Kensington titles, imprints, and distributed lines are available at
special quantity discounts for bulk purchases for sales promotion,
premiums, fund-raising, educational, or institutional use.

Special book excerpts or customized printings can also be created to fit
specific needs. For details, write or phone the office of the Kensington
Sales Manager: Attn.: Sales Department. Kensington Publishing Corp.,
119 West 40th Street, New York, NY 10018. Phone: 1-800-221-2647.

Zebra and the Z logo Reg. U.S. Pat. & TM Off.
BOUQUET Reg. U.S. Pat. & TM Off.

First Printing: May 2020
ISBN-13: 978-1-4201-4924-1
ISBN-10: 1-4201-4924-5

ISBN-13: 978-1-4201-4926-5 (eBook)
ISBN-10: 1-4201-4926-1 (eBook)

10 9 8 7 6 5 4 3 2 1

Printed in the United States of America

Home to Stay *is dedicated to my husband,*
whose steadfast love and encouragement gives me
strength and the determination to keep working;

to my daughters,
best friends who never make fun of me
when countless hours of research, interviews, writing,
and editing sometimes means
"Mom spent all day with her hair in a tangle
and in her PJs again";

to my "grandorables,"
who are the living, breathing examples for the
"brighter than average" kids who appear in my books;

to my readers,
whose praise-filled letters motivate me
to continue writing;

to Kensington's talented editorial staff
and art department;

last but not least,
to God,
for blessing me with an Idea Factory brain

ACKNOWLEDGMENTS

My heartfelt thanks to my new Amish friends, who generously taught me about their way of life and, by doing so, helped me build legitimacy and accuracy into this story. (I wasn't kidding, was I, when I said I'd be back . . . often!) Thanks, too, to Jody Teets, longtime resident of Oakland, Maryland, who provided details about the Amish community and surrounding areas that even frequent visitors don't know about!

Chapter One

The work was hard, but Max liked it that way. The more demanding the job, the faster the hours passed. If he had a complaint, it was his partner's unpredictable moods.

"Where is Samuel?" Dan bellowed.

"Unloading the truck," their foreman said, pointing.

Max watched Dan's frown become a scowl as he stomped toward the flatbed, where Sam had just handed a two-by-four to Jonah. "You two . . . !"

"Who?" they asked.

"Your feet do not fit a limb, fools."

The Miller brothers—taller and broader than Dan—flinched as he used the roll of blueprints as a pointer. When he'd finished taking them to task for leaving the office trailer unlocked, he made his way back to Max.

Sensing Dan's mood today was more foul than usual, Max's mutt cowered and trotted closer to his master.

"You are not afraid that beast will get hurt on the job?"

"I never let him get near anything dangerous. Besides, I like his company. He *smiles* from time to time."

The sarcasm was lost on Dan, who said, "Your dog, your decision." He stepped onto the porch and smacked

the roll against a support post. "There is good reason for
my frown." He shook his head. "Do not marry. Do not
ever, *ever* take a wife."

Max had grown tired of listening to the man's criticism
of his wife. Squatting, he plucked sawdust from Rascal's
fur, and hoped Dan would move on to another topic.

He did not.

"You cannot satisfy a woman. Build her a house, she
wants to fill it with children. And if the doctor says she
cannot bear them, there will be no consoling her. So much
for accepting all things as part of God's will!" He kicked
at the post, missed, and issued a low growl. "I will gladly
work to provide for children of my own. But to endure
blisters and gashes and a sunburnt neck for a young'un
born of another man's loins? I think not! And instead of
appreciating my honesty, Anki punishes me with cold
stares and never-ending silence. Two solid weeks of it
now!" He kicked again, and this time, made contact.

Rascal pressed closer to Max. "Thank God for steel-
toed boots, eh?"

That joke, too, fell on deaf ears.

"Take my advice, boy. A wife is for cooking and cleaning
and not much more. Learn to do those things for yourself
and save your sanity!"

Boy, indeed. Max had been doing for himself since the
fire—six long years ago now—that had taken most of his
family. The women in his life had contributed far more
than belly-filling meals and clean laundry. They'd tended
gardens, stitched quilts, crocheted sweaters and afghans,
and managed shops that kept the Englishers coming back,
year after year. Oh, what he wouldn't give to be with
them again!

"Lord give me patience," Dan was saying.

"Ask for patience, and you will get it by way of trials and tribulations. Be smart, m'friend. Pray for endurance, instead."

Dan waved away the advice and focused on something across the way. Max followed his line of sight, and saw a young woman walking toward them. Walking fast enough to kick up clouds of dust with every purposeful bootstep. The brisk October wind pressed her gray skirt against long, muscular legs that told him she didn't spend her days lounging about. It also mussed shiny curls that had escaped the confines of her black cap . . . curls the color of the chestnuts his grandmother had once roasted at Christmastime.

Was she a visitor here, or new to Pleasant Valley?

"That," Dan said, pointing, "is the *second* thorn in my side." He thumbed the hard hat to the back of his head. "Anki's live-in helper."

"Helper?" Max met Dan's eyes. "I hope Anki is not sick."

"Hmpf. In the head, maybe. Dr. Baker says she is depressed, because she cannot have a baby." Using his chin as a pointer he said, "And that one? She pops out a child that she did not even want." He harrumphed again. "Are *all* women crazy?"

The young woman didn't look crazy to Max, but then, he was paying far more attention to eyes so big that he could tell, even from this distance, that they were bright green.

"You forgot your lunch," she told Dan. Thrusting a black dome-topped lunch pail at him, she added, "Again."

"You would forget, too, if you had to deal with Anki's nonstop whining."

From her facial expression alone, Max decided she didn't approve of the way Dan belittled his wife any more than he did. So far, she hadn't made eye contact with him. A good thing, since he'd probably fumble and stutter and stumble over his own boots, the way he always had around pretty girls.

Just then, she zeroed in on him. "Don't tell me *this* is your business partner. Why haven't I seen him before?"

"Maybe because, like most women, you are interested only in yourself. And maybe because he is a hard worker."

She clucked her tongue. And then, in a sad attempt to emulate Dan's deep voice, said, "Nice of you to deliver my lunch, Willa. Be careful walking through the construction site *on your way out*. And tell Anki I'll be there . . ." Eyes narrowed, she said through clenched teeth, "When *will* you be home?"

"I will get there when I get there." He clutched the lunchbox to his broad chest. "Now go. *We* have work to do."

Ignoring the insinuation, she inspected Max, starting with his well-worn work boots, stopping when their eyes met.

"What's your name, *partner*?"

He shifted the hammer from his right hand to the left. "Max. Max Lambright."

"Short for Maxwell?"

"Maximillian."

"Well, Maximillian Lambright, I feel very, very sorry for you, having to spend your days with *this* . . ." She glared at Dan. ". . . with this ungrateful, two-legged porcupine." She started walking away, stopping long enough to say, "And in case he hasn't already told you all about my pathetic past, I might as well do it myself. I'm Willa Reynolds, the reformed drug addict and unwed mother who would probably be in jail—or dead—if not for Anki's kindness and generosity."

And without another word, she jogged away.

"Close your mouth, boy, before a horsefly buzzes down your throat."

Max clamped his teeth together. "She . . . she lives *at your house*?"

"Believe me, it was not my idea. But anything to keep Anki's complaining to a minimum. Too bad it doesn't quiet Willa's baby. That child contributes nothing to the household but noise and poop and drool."

"And Willa's husband?"

"You were not listening when she said '*unwed mother*'?" An exasperated puff of air passed his lips. "*Genoeg* lollygagging! We can't make any money if we stand around, *te gapen*."

Max hadn't realized he'd been gaping. "Where is she from?"

"Baltimore. Philadelphia. Deep Creek." He shrugged. "She's a bit of a gypsy, if you ask me."

"Ah, so that is why she does not speak like us."

"*Jij oet wel een genie zijn*."

If Max was a genius, he wouldn't have said, "But her dress and cap, even those boots—"

"Hand-me-downs, given by the ladies in Anki's quilting circle. As long as Willa looks the part, people will tolerate her and the child. The pair of them get free room and board at my place. She gets a paycheck, too, in exchange for housekeeping, cooking, doing laundry and yard work . . . things Anki would do, if she wasn't . . ." He rolled his eyes. ". . . *depressed*."

Dan's mockery wasn't lost on Max. He pictured the

Hofmans' modest cottage and wondered how they'd found space for another adult *and* a baby.

Just get back to work, he told himself. *What goes on under their roof is none of your concern.*

Max decided to concentrate on the fact that today was payday. As bookkeeper of the business, he'd recently discovered that Dan had added to his regular salary reimbursement for what it had cost him to travel to the outdoor market in Grantsville. When Max had questioned going that far for jams and jellies, breads, and pies that were readily available in Pleasant Valley, Dan told him that Anki believed the Grantsville goods far surpassed those here at home; once she figured out the ingredients and duplicated the recipes, Dan added, she intended to sell them in her own shop. She hadn't, thanks to bouts with depression. Would Anki have been happier if she *had*?

"*Dunner uns Gewidder!*" Dan muttered. "*Guck emol do!*"

It wasn't like Dan to preface any statement with "confound it." Max followed his gaze again, this time to the path Willa had taken.

"The *simpele zielen* girl has dropped her apron."

The apron, like everything else she'd worn, didn't fit properly. It hardly seemed fair to call her simpleminded because it fell off.

"She probably did it on purpose."

"Why would she do such a thing?"

"Because she is a *vrouw*. And women want attention, no matter what it takes to get it."

"I'll fetch it, save you having to do it later."

Max didn't wait for Dan's agreement. He half ran toward the spot where he'd last seen Willa, slowing long enough to scoop up the apron. Shaking it free of gravel and grit as he made his way to the road, Max wondered what he'd say once he caught up with her.

She whirled around to face him. "Why are you following me?"

"I'm not." He held up the apron. "You dropped this."

Her expression softened a bit as she took it from him. "Thank you. This was really nice of you." She glanced toward Dan. "How long have you worked with Mr. Prickly?"

Rascal had followed, and now sat, smiling up at her. "Seven years," he said as she stooped to pet the dog. "One year as an employee, the rest, as a partner."

She exhaled a long, whispery sigh. "Seven years."

The way she said the word, it might have been seventy.

"I've only been with the Hofmans for a month. How do you do it!"

"You learn to let a lot of things slide," Max admitted.

Willa stood. "What's his name?"

"Rascal."

Her grin lit up her whole face. Her pretty, freckled, green-eyed face. Then she tied the apron around her waist. Her long, slender waist.

"Go ahead," she said, securing its bow. "I can see that you have questions. Ask away. I'm honest . . . when I can be."

A strange qualifier, he thought, and said, "How old is your baby?"

"Frannie is one. She isn't walking yet, and Dan believes it's because I was still taking drugs before I realized I was pregnant. I was *not,* but since the Great Hofman knows all . . ."

He spared her the ordeal of defending herself by saying, "According to my mother, I did not walk until I was well into my second year. Her theory was that I hadn't found a reason to get to my feet. She also said that such things are different for each child."

"That's exactly what Dr. Baker told me, just the other day!" She tilted her head slightly. "Next question?"

"How did you get here?"

"On the train. You didn't think I walked, with a baby on my hip, did you?"

Max returned her smile. "No, I just meant, how is it that of all the places you might have ended up, you live in Pleasant Valley, with the Hofmans."

"You should smile more, Max. You're quite handsome when you do."

Then she focused on something behind him. Based on the sudden change in her mood, it must be Dan.

"You'd better get back, before his head explodes." She turned, but only halfway. "I hope we'll run into one another again . . . so that I can answer the rest of your questions, of course."

Of course? Max didn't know how to interpret that, but he watched until she turned from the jobsite's gravel drive onto the road.

"Oh, we will run into one another again, Willa Reynolds. You can count on it."

Willa filled the tip of the tiny spoon with applesauce and held it near Frannie's lips.

"I tried to get her to eat," Anki said, "but the child only wants her mother today, it seems."

"Nonsense. She adores you. Who has the gift for quieting her when she cries? Who knows which toy she wants, even before she reaches for it? And who gets her to cooperate when we need to put a bonnet on her head? You, Anki, that's who!"

When the woman smiled that way, it lifted her entire being. It made Willa want to find ways to encourage Anki's smiles.

"May I be honest with you, Anki?"

"Of course."

As usual when she felt out of place, uncomfortable, or displeased, Anki stared at the floor and fiddled with her apron ties. Honesty, Willa realized, was the last thing she wanted to hear, thanks to her belligerent, overbearing husband.

"It's natural for Frannie to prefer me. I'm her mother, after all, and she knows it. But she's grown very fond of you in a very short time. And as you know, she's a very discerning li'l gal."

Frannie chose that moment to pound on the wooden highchair tray, one of the many items on loan from Anki's neighbors. "Mama!" she squealed.

"Aw, you want more applesauce, don't you, beautiful girl."

Frannie's wide smile revealed six tiny whiter-than-snow teeth, four on top, two on the bottom. "You're the best thing that ever has happened to me. I'll never love anyone more. Ever."

Anki stood at the kitchen sink, staring into the back-yard. "The human heart can hold much love, Willa. One day you will see for yourself that this is true."

It seemed beyond unfair that the poor woman so desperately wanted a child and couldn't carry one to term. Much as she'd like to blame Dan for his wife's depression, Willa suspected other factors were at work. For one thing, Anki didn't eat enough to keep a sparrow alive, and night after night, she'd heard the woman pacing the squeaky wood floors, muffling her tears with a linen napkin. Willa didn't know how long she'd be welcome to stay with the Hofmans, but while she was here, she intended to do everything she could to ease the woman's suffering.

"Guess what . . . I just met the most interesting man."

That, at least, made Anki turn around. "Oh? Here in Pleasant Valley?"

"Yes. When I delivered Dan's lunch to the jobsite, I met his partner."

"Ah yes. Max." Affection softened her features.

"He seems nice. Smart, too. And oh, that handsome smile!"

Cupping her elbows, Anki pressed herself against the back door. "It is difficult to believe he smiles at all, considering . . ."

"Considering what?"

Eyes closed, Anki bit her lower lip. "When he was a boy, his father and brothers were killed when a drunken driver crossed the center line of the highway and crashed into the Lambrights' buggy. He and his mother moved in with the grandparents. His grandfather began suffering memory lapses. Forgot how to run the farm machinery. Got lost walking from the barn to the house. And one night, he loaded up the woodstove and forgot to close the door. The fire killed them all and destroyed the house."

"How horrible! Where was Max?"

"He had delivered a load of firewood to the hardware store in Oakland. It was too dark to drive home, so he'd slept in the buggy."

That explained the sadness in his blue eyes. But why did *Anki* seem so shaken, relating the information? Had she witnessed the fire? Or perhaps she was related to Max . . . an in-law, a cousin once removed . . .

Willa fed Frannie the last of the applesauce, then let the baby bang the spoon on the empty bowl. Giggles rippled from her as she gnawed its rubber-sheathed tip. If only Willa could transfer some of that joy into Anki!

"How long ago was the fire?" she asked.

"Oh, six, maybe seven years ago?"

Willa had never known her father and didn't have siblings, but her relationship with her mother had been deep and abiding, and when cancer took her a decade earlier, Willa's life spun out of control.

"How many were . . ." It seemed heartless to say *killed,* so Willa said, "How many did he lose that night?"

"The grandparents, of course. His mother. And a sister. His father was an only child. So . . ."

"He never married? Has no children?"

Slumping onto a kitchen chair, Anki sighed. In place of an answer, she said, "Max is a lovely young man. He invested in Daniel's business when no one else would help him. The only person in all of Pleasant Valley who can control my husband." She smirked. "I wish I knew his secret."

"So do I." Willa shivered involuntarily. "Every time that temper of his flares, I'm reminded of Joe." She shivered involuntarily.

Anki leaned in close and drew Willa into a sideways hug. "Now, now, do not let his behavior—or my husband's, for that matter—remind you of bad times. Your life here can be good and fulfilling. It will take time, but I believe you will be happy here. It will be good for sweet Frannie, too, to live in a place where she is safe from people like your Joe."

Her Joe? Willa supposed she deserved that. She hadn't

been an impressionable child when he came into her life, and he certainly hadn't held a gun to her head. Everything she'd done, everything that had happened to her after meeting him . . . that was on her. And she admitted it every time she looked into Frannie's perfect, beautiful face.

"Max has not taken a wife."

Willa translated the woman's mischievous smile to mean he was eligible, if marriage was on her radar.

"It's time for Frannie's nap," she said, and lifted the baby from the highchair. "Once she's quieted down, I'll start supper. Did Dan demand—I mean, request—anything special for tonight?"

Anki shook her head. "No, but I'm in the mood for venison roast, with potatoes and carrots, green beans." She blinked, like an innocent schoolgirl. "If it isn't too much trouble."

"Consider it done." She gave her boss's shoulder a light squeeze. "Say nite-nite to Anki, cutie pie."

The baby opened and closed her chubby fist three times, then snuggled into Willa's neck.

"I will pray for sweet dreams," Anki said as they headed for the stairway.

Upstairs, in the room she and Frannie had shared for the past month, Willa pulled down the green roller blind to block the bright afternoon sun, changed the baby's diaper, and snapped her into a clean onesie . . . another hand-me-down from her Pleasant Valley neighbors. Leaning into the borrowed crib, she whispered, "I'll pray for sweet dreams, too." She kissed her daughter's cheek, then lifted the crib's guardrail until it snapped into place. "One day, we'll have a place of our own. I'll work hard and save every penny, and find us a place where you'll have a room and I'll have a room—with sunshine streaming through the windows—and a big front porch with rocking chairs and hanging plants and—"

But Frannie had already closed her eyes. *Best baby in all the world,* Willa thought, heart thumping with love.

Willa stood at the window and lifted the shade just enough to peek outside. How odd, she thought, that some of the community's women decorated their homes with curtains and tablecloths, while others, like Anki, did not. What would she say about the ruffled Cape Cods her mother had hung in every window . . . yellow in the kitchen, white in the bathroom, pale blue in the living room . . .

Plainness. Here at the Hofmans', it started with the white clapboards that hugged the house, then slid inside, where the only bright color was found on the pages of the calendar in the kitchen. If not for its counting-days usefulness, Anki had explained, it wouldn't be there, either.

"In *our* house, baby girl," she whispered, "there'll be curtains in the windows, puffy throw pillows on the couch, landscapes and still lifes on the walls, and thick rugs under our feet!"

In the yard below, Willa saw the white sheets, pillowcases, and patchwork quilts rising and falling on the breeze. If she closed her eyes, she could almost hear them, snapping and flapping to bring her attention to steely clouds that hung low on the horizon, warning of an oncoming storm.

The roast would have to wait.

Since her arrival in Pleasant Valley, the weather had been balmy and dry, and everyone had been praying for rain. Willa looked up, past the angry gray billows. "Just don't go overboard, okay, God? The crops and gardens and wells need water, but not a deluge." She could almost see her mom, pretending to look annoyed, shaking her forefinger, saying, "You talk to Him like He's one of your schoolmates. Show some respect!" They'd gone round and round about it, and because Willa hated seeing her mom the least bit upset, she'd taught herself to make every prayer sound a little more . . . formal. But in the privacy of her mind, she continued speaking to Him as a friend. Because that's exactly how she saw Him.

Until she met Joe . . .

Frannie exhaled a sweet baby sigh, and Willa tiptoed over for a closer look, taking care not to step on the creaky third board beside the crib. Oh, but she was adorable. "Thank you, Lord," she said softly. And she meant it.

As soon as the pregnancy test came back positive, she'd stopped drinking. Stopped taking drugs. Stopped delivering them to Joe's "customers," and started making plans to get as far from Philadelphia as possible. Her mom had left a small inheritance. If Joe had known about it, she never could have withdrawn every dollar . . . or taped the bills to her torso, then hidden them beneath thick, over-sized sweatshirts.

Leaning both forearms on the crib rail, she said, "Did you feel those big, hard bundles bouncing against you that day? Man, I sure hope not!"

She'd thanked God back then, too, for blessing her with the good sense to deposit the money in a major Philly bank—and giving her the strength to leave it there—despite a thousand temptations to spend it on pills or pot that promised to dull the pain of being completely alone in the world.

"But I'm not alone now, am I?" she whispered. "I'll never be alone again, thanks to you, sweet girl." Willa sighed. "Remember how much you hated walking with me?" A soft laugh punctuated her question. "Oh, what a fuss you kicked up in my belly, and you didn't let up until I found us a place where you could be born and a proper babysitter to keep an eye on you while I worked."

Outside now, Willa slid two-pronged clothespins from the line and made quick work of folding Dan's socks, handkerchiefs, and work clothes into the wicker basket, remembering how she'd walked west, stopping in town after town, washing dishes, cleaning motel rooms, babysitting, cooking and cleaning her bosses' houses . . . anything to earn a few dollars to add to her mother's savings. Her intended destination? Deep Creek Lake. She'd read all about the resort in a free brochure, found at the travel agency next to one of the diners where she'd waited tables. There, she believed, she'd find steady work, a place to live, and babysitters who worked for the lodge to care for Frannie.

Of course, she'd been just Baby, not Frannie, back then. Tears stung Willa's eyes, as she remembered how she'd dreamed of seeing the beautiful, white cloud–cloaked Allegheny Mountains in person. Sniffling, she dried them with the corner of her apron. The one she'd almost lost on Dan's jobsite. *Correction. Dan and* Max's *jobsite.*

It had taken months, and she'd taken a lot of risks, alternately hitchhiking and walking to get there. But they'd only made it as far as Baltimore, where she hired on with a resort-type hotel in the Inner Harbor. Her coworkers had taken a liking to her, but none more than the manager. Martha's kids lived on the West Coast, so she'd more or less adopted Willa. And when Frannie came along, it seemed the most natural thing in the world for Martha to step into the surrogate grandma role.

Everything was going great, Willa thought, carrying the basket inside, until someone filed a complaint with the Department of Child and Family Services. *But God . . . He was watching out for you, even then, baby girl.* It was thanks to Alice from DCF that Willa ended up in Pleasant Valley, working for cranky Dan and his sulky wife. Willa refused to complain, because here, it was calm and quiet and clean, and she didn't fall exhausted into bed at the end of each workday.

After putting the laundry where it belonged, she returned to her room, where Frannie still slept. She eased fingertips through Frannie's dark curls. "Oh, how I worried before you were born. I thought . . . what if the garbage I put into my system in the days before the pregnancy . . ."

At the window again, Willa cupped her elbows as the tears flowed freely. *Get hold of yourself, Will. That venison won't roast itself while you stand here feeling sorry for yourself.*

In the small bathroom across the hall, Willa blew her nose and dried her eyes. She looked into the mirror—hung for the sole purpose of helping Dan shave his mustache and groom his beard—and for the first time in a long, long time, she didn't hate the woman looking back at her.

"And that's all thanks to You, Lord."

She didn't deserve such a perfect, sweet-tempered baby. Living in this tiny house with the Hofmans was a challenge, but they paid a fair wage. More important than the money, Frannie was safe. That, too, was thanks to the Almighty.

Willa wasn't fooling herself. He hadn't done it for *her*. Not after all the sins she'd committed before Frannie came into her life. "I'll spend the rest of my life proving how grateful I am that You overlooked it all . . . for her sake."

She took a deep breath, exhaled it slowly, and once

again met her own eyes in the mirror. "If you don't quit talking to yourself, it's gonna become a habit. And if . . ."

The thought inspired a nervous snicker, which ended quickly. Because something told her that if Dan ever heard her behaving this way, he'd send her packing. "Wearing one of those hug-yourself jackets!" she said, still smiling.

Willa hurried downstairs, set the dial on the propane-fueled cookstove for 375 degrees, and rubbed butter into the sides and bottom of the heavy black pot. After arranging scrubbed potatoes and carrots, sliced onions, and green beans around the roast, she poured a quart of beef broth over everything and finished it off with salt and pepper.

While the roast cooked, she'd make sure the chickens were safe in their coop, the goats in their pen, the milk cow and horses in their stalls. It was as she removed the hanging baskets from their hooks on the covered porch that the first fat drop plopped onto her nose.

It made no sense, no sense at all, that Max Lambright came to mind just then. Was he outside, too, rushing around to finish up some construction chore before the rains came? Maybe he was in the work trailer, those intense blue eyes poring over blueprints or supply lists . . . eyes that had seen far more suffering than she had.

He probably had no idea that she'd heard his parting words. But she had. And since that afternoon, Willa had replayed them in her mind a dozen times.

She'd met taller, more muscular men, but none who'd aided a friend by investing his own hard-earned dollars into a flagging business, and helped turn it into a profitable enterprise. How had he managed, despite his youth, despite his many personal losses, to maintain his . . . niceness? It was an admirable trait, to be sure. One that proved he had the makings of a good friend.

Willa had something new to pray for now: that Max was old enough and wise enough to handle the truth about her past.

The whole ugly truth.

Because despite her blessings—and there were many—something was missing in her life.

Friendship.

Chapter Two

"Will I see you on Saturday?"

Max had vivid memories of three-legged races, lively games of stickball, and an array of mouthwatering foods that attracted locals and tourists alike. But as the only remaining Lambright, he felt out of place at the annual festival. To admit it out loud would make him sound like a self-pitying child, so he said, "No, too much work to do."

The bishop shook his head. "It is not wise to close yourself off from the community."

Not so much closed off as distanced, Max thought, looking into his toolbox.

"Some things in life are more important than work, you know."

Yes, he knew. Oh, how well he knew. He shouldn't have to tell Micah Fisher of all people. The man had read Scripture over the graves of everyone he loved. Surely he understood that work *was* his life now!

"Maybe I will stop in once I have finished for the day, have a slice of pie."

Micah smiled. "I am glad I stopped by your workshop today, and I am glad to hear this, son."

Respect for the elder's age and position in the community kept him from saying *I am* not *your son*. He added a hammer to the box's top compartment.

"What are you working on these days?"

"New contract. Extending the rear of the Bakers' house."

"Ah, yes. God's will is not always easy to comprehend. Never would I have expected Emily to so easily blend into our community."

Max nodded in agreement. "Her love for Phillip is boundless, that is for sure."

"And for Gabe, too. And . . . I forget the youngest child's name." Micah chuckled. "God is working overtime in that household!"

Despite being a newcomer to the community, Dr. Emily White—now Mrs. Phillip Baker—had thrown herself into the Amish ways. She hadn't just helped find a solution to her adopted son's heart-related problems, she'd also turned the boy's father from a stoic, sad-eyed widower into a boisterous man who smiled easily and often. On several occasions, Max and Phillip had discussed their many losses, and agreed that accepting painful losses as part of God's will was easier said than done. Much easier. But Phillip had something Max didn't: a life partner who'd dedicated herself to him and little Gabe, and who, using money inherited from her brother, had turned an abandoned house into a free clinic that catered to Pleasant Valley residents, young and old.

Micah straightened his black hat, gave the brim a jaunty pat, and said, "Is there news of a new addition to the *family*?"

The question brought Max back to the here and now. If so, it was yet another thing to ask forgiveness for . . . because oh, how he envied Phillip!

"If so, they did not share the news with me."

"Will the addition include extra bedrooms? A bigger kitchen, perhaps? A workshop for Phillip?"

He'd drawn plans for a two-story add-on that would span the width of the house. On the first floor, Phillip had asked Max to build a large windowed room with a door leading to the back porch, and a bathroom. His mother, Sarah, was getting up in years, he'd explained, and although she was alert and spry, Emily worried about her, living alone in a house with two steep staircases. Upstairs, Max's instructions were just as simple: two spacious bedrooms, each with windows that overlooked the valley and the mountains beyond.

If the Bakers wanted to answer the questions, that was their business, but Max had no intention of providing the information, not even to the well-respected Bishop Micah Fisher.

"I can see your thoughts are everywhere but on this conversation. . . ."

The bishop chuckled quietly as Gabe and his cousins raced up to Max.

"Hello, Max," the boy said. He pointed at his cousins Ben and Marcus. "We are going fishing."

They looked content, happy, excited about their little outing, as young boys should.

"Reminds me of when I was a boy," Max said. "When my brothers and I walked over to the farm on Landon's Dam Road. We always filled a creel with trout. Better check with the farmer first, make sure he is still willing to share his pond."

"You have brothers? I did not know this!" Ben said.

Marcus leaned closer. "Shh, *deibel*!" he said from the corner of his mouth. "They died."

Ben shot his brother an angry glare. "I am *not* a moron!" Then, looking at Max, he added, "I am sorry, Max."

"It's all right," Max said. "It happened long ago."

"Were they sick, as Gabe was before his operation?"

"*Deibel!*" Marcus repeated.

"No. They . . ." Max swallowed. "They died in a buggy accident."

The boys were curious to learn details about that day, and he could almost hear the thoughts tumbling around in their young minds: Where had it happened? When? What caused the accident?

Gabe put himself between the brothers. "It is a long walk to Landon's Dam. If we want to catch fish for supper, we should go." Then, smiling up at Max, he added, "Will you work on our house today?"

"Yes, just as soon as I finish gathering up my tools." He looked at each boy in turn. "Sit on the boulder," he told them. "You'll be able to see them swim right up to your fishhook from there."

"Good tip!" Gabe said.

The bishop chose that moment to pat the brim of his hat again. "How long since you have gone fishing, Maximillian?"

"Too long." And it was true. But . . . he rarely made time for such things anymore. His life was work, work, and more work. For the most part, it helped distract him from all he'd lost. These days, though, Max told himself it was because he had his eye on a new piece of equipment. In a matter of weeks, he'd pay cash for the skid loader: auxiliary hydraulics, vertical lift, two speed, manual coupler, with a sixty-six-inch bucket . . . It would make quick work of preparing the ground for foundations.

"You should go with them."

The boys smiled, first at the bishop, then at Max. "Yes!

Come with us. Then you can show us the sweet spot you and your brothers found!"

He'd grown fond of these three, thanks in no small part to their fascination with construction. When possible, he allowed them to watch as he worked, sometimes letting them pound nails or pick up board scraps. Max enjoyed having them around, asking questions, trying to emulate his every move, and to repay them for their help—and their companionship—he'd bought them kid-sized leather gloves, hard hats, and boots.

"Will you, Max?" Gabe asked. "Will you show us how you filled your creels with fish?"

"Thank you for the invite, but I have too much to do today."

"Another time, then?" Ben asked.

And Max nodded.

Micah nodded, too. "Will you do something for me, son?"

Max lifted one shoulder. How could he answer without knowing what the man would ask?

"Promise to come to the festival, at least for a little while."

"Yes! There will be ice cream!" Marcus said.

"And chocolate cake!" Ben added.

"And cherry pie!" Gabe chimed in. "Mama Em baked dozens of 'em yesterday!"

Their wide-eyed, expectant faces made it impossible to say no. "All right. But only if you promise to save me a slice of that pie."

"I will," he promised. Gabe wiggled his pointer finger, and Max bent to hear whatever secret the boy planned to share. "I will save you a whole pie!"

Chuckling, Max straightened. "We'll see how your Mama Em feels about that, all right?"

As the boys ran up the hill, the bishop started walking in the same direction. After taking only a few steps, he stopped and turned. "It would be wrong to disappoint those youngsters. You know this, do you not?"

Translation: You gave your word. Now you must keep it.

"I will be there, Bishop."

He wasn't looking forward to it, but he would be there. *Look at the bright side,* he thought. *You won't have to prepare your own supper or clean it up. Or eat it alone.*

"You are not wearing *that* to the festival, are you?"

Anki frowned. "Dan, why must you pick on her so?"

Willa tried to ignore his disapproving glare. She'd chosen the blue dress today. Her apron matched the collar and cuffs. And because it had belonged to a much taller woman, the hem almost touched her too-wide, beat-up boots. "What's wrong with what I'm wearing?"

"The hem is frayed. So is the collar. Those boots are scuffed, and the heels all worn down. You want everyone to think I do not pay you a fair wage?"

She could have pointed out that in addition to what she wore now, only a gray dress, two blouses, and a black skirt hung in her room's freestanding wardrobe. She'd carried an overstuffed suitcase into the house, but everything inside it would draw the attention—and very likely the disapproval—of her Amish neighbors, so it sat unopened on the cupboard's floor.

"I'm surprised that you care what people think of the way I look."

"I work hard. I bring home good money. Looking at you, no one would believe it!"

"My advice to you?"

He snorted. "Advice. From the likes of you?" Another snort.

"As soon as you get to the churchyard, look for the bishop."

"The bishop? Whatever for!"

"To ask forgiveness for your sin of pride."

He blinked a few times, and she would have sworn a blush colored his deeply tanned cheeks. Anki didn't help matters by snickering.

He turned his annoyance with Willa to his wife. "Are you ready to leave?"

She went to him, stood on tiptoe, and kissed his clean-shaven upper lip. "I will be in just a moment." She extended a hand to Willa. "Let's find something else for you to wear."

Once the door to the Hofmans' room closed, Anki opened her wardrobe and withdrew a pale pink dress. Its white collar and cuffs had been trimmed with matching pink blanket stitches. The same was true of the apron's pockets and ties.

"How beautiful! But . . . didn't you just finish these yesterday? Surely *you* want to wear them . . ."

Laughing softly, the woman held the dress up to Willa. "If I wore this, it would drag the floor."

Even without benefit of a mirror, Willa could see that its hem fell several inches below her knees. The sleeves, too, appeared to be precisely the length of her arms.

"A gift," Anki said, "from me to you."

"But Anki, you've already done so much for Frannie

and me, welcoming us into your home. And my wages are more than fair."

That's when Anki held up a tiny version of the same outfit.

"For Frannie," she said, "and look . . . new caps for both of you. Not hand-me-downs!"

Like the dresses and aprons, Anki had trimmed the bonnets with almost invisible pink stitches. Willa pictured her little girl in the pretty outfit, and grateful tears stung her eyes. "I . . . I don't know what to say. You . . . you've already done so much for us. Dan, too, of course."

"You do much for us as well. This house has never felt more like a home." She drew Willa into a hug. "Your greatest contribution has nothing to do with clean laundry or heartwarming meals." She held Willa at arm's length. "In a short time, I have come to see you as a sister."

If anyone had told her she'd grow weepy over a plain Amish dress, or a near-stranger welcoming her like family, Willa would have called them crazy. Yet here she stood, hugging the garment to her as if it had been trimmed in pure gold instead of pink thread.

"Won't Dan be—"

"If he questions it—and I doubt he will—*I* will answer him." She lifted her chin, as if to prove her intent.

The community's rules were simple, really: Trust the Lord in all things. Accept all things, good and bad, as His will. Wives and children should submit to the man of the house.

"What kind of friend would I be if I let you get in trouble on my account?"

"I do not mean this to hurt you, Willa, but I am your boss. As such, you cannot *let* me do anything. No one *lets* me do anything."

Willa could hardly argue with that. The woman could silence Dan's bluster and blow with a look.

Frannie started to fuss. "It's like she has a little clock in her belly," Willa said, opening the door. "She woke from her nap in *just* enough time to get her ready for the festival."

Anki followed her down the hall and lifted the baby from her crib. "I will get her ready," she said, taking the child's dress from Willa's hands. "You need to get *yourself* ready. And do not worry. I am aware that she can move quickly for one who has only just learned to take a few steps. If I put her down, I will hold tight to that chubby little hand!"

The woman bent over the crib and got right to work, removing Frannie's white gown, blowing kisses on the baby's bared belly. Suddenly, she straightened and looked at Willa. "That dress will not put itself on, you know."

By the time Willa had changed from the blue dress into the pink one, Anki had finished dressing Frannie.

"Oh, my," Willa sighed. "You look adorable. Precious. Like a doll baby!"

The width of Frannie's smile told her that she felt as pretty as she looked. *Careful,* Willa warned herself. The sin of pride didn't just apply to men who were concerned what the neighbors might think about an employee's appearance.

"What is taking you three so long?" Dan bellowed up the stairs.

"Hush, Husband," Anki bellowed back. "We are ready." She kissed Frannie's cheek, and after tying the new bonnet under her chubby chin, kissed Willa's cheek, too. "Don't be surprised," she said, opening the door, "if you're surrounded by every eligible young man at the festival."

Laughing, Willa propped Frannie on one hip. She'd

seen most of the so-called eligible bachelors, and only one had really captured her attention: Max.

"So you're saying that by the end of the day, I'll know how a flower feels when bees hover around it."

Anki giggled, and so did Frannie. At the bottom of the stairs they saw Dan, a faint smile on his usually stern face, gawking at them as if they'd all grown a third eye. But no wonder he looked confused; this was the first time since she'd moved into their house that the atmosphere felt warm and happy.

Willa decided to do everything possible to encourage more of it.

Chapter Three

With the Bakers' addition finally under roof, Max decided to call it a day. Dan hadn't shown up for work, but he wasn't complaining. The man's cranky disposition had a tendency to rub off on him, and in Max's opinion, life was tough enough without looking for reasons to complain.

While showering, Max let his mind wander to days when scrubbing away the day's work meant hiking back and forth to the stream, dumping bucket after bucket of water into the back porch trough-turned-bathtub, then delivering extra buckets and heating them on the wood-stove to make the icy liquid a tad more tolerable. To the trestle table where ten to sixteen Lambrights gathered to share roast venison, rabbit stew, chicken and dumplings. Now, in the small bedroom his sisters had once shared, a claw-foot tub and pedestal sink shone bright in the after-noon light.

Standing at the mirror, he coated his face with soap, just as his father had done, and his grandfather before him. As a boy, he'd stood, wide-eyed and fascinated, as their straight razors scraped the bristle from their cheeks and upper lips. "Papa," he'd asked once, "why do some of our men have beards and others do not?"

The blade's sharp edge had caught a glint from the overhead light, and it flashed in the mirror as his father delivered his typically quiet, measured reply: "When a man takes a wife, he is, according to *Ordnung,* a true man." He went on to explain how, "in olden times," soldiers wearing fancy mustaches had persecuted the Amish; determined not to emulate them in any way, their people decided that the sect would follow the precepts of the Bible, in which most spiritual leaders felt it vain—and therefore sinful—to shave their beards. Then he'd touched a dab of soapy foam onto Max's nose. "You will have one of your own soon enough. For now, enjoy being a boy!"

It was a fond memory, one that inspired a slow smile, and it reminded him of that day on the jobsite . . .

"You should smile more," Willa had said, "because you're very handsome when you do."

It was enough to erase the smile from his face. Pride in one's looks was sinful. *But hypocrisy is, too.* He needed to think on that, because his faith seemed as hazy as the plain curtains, fluttering in the afternoon breeze. Why was it so easy to go along with rules like that, and so difficult to trust that all things were God's will?

Max opened his closet, where every article of clothing he owned hung on hand-carved wood hangers: three shirts, trousers and a waistcoat for weddings and funerals, and the heavy wool coat that kept him warm even on the frostiest of days. On the shelf above, two pairs of neatly folded work jeans, two hats—one straw, one black. Spare suspenders. A sweater. Woolen gloves. And on the floor, black boots.

Snapping his suspenders into place, he walked into the kitchen. *Should have washed those up earlier,* he thought, frowning at reminders of his breakfast . . . dried-on egg yolk on the tines of a fork, on a plain white plate, and congealed butter covering the bottom of the black skillet. *No, much better to wait until evening.* Having something to do, like scrubbing day-old food from the dishes, would help him forget that while the rest of his neighbors were home, reminiscing with loved ones about the day's festivities, he'd be alone.

Max shook his head and stepped into the bright, brisk sunshine. He gave a thought to firing up his pickup, then decided against it. *The walk will clear the cobwebs from your head.*

Was self-pity also a sin? If not, he thought, it ought to be. Left unchecked, he'd learned, it could lead a man into a downward spiral that—

"Max!" Gabe shouted, waving as he ran closer. "You came!"

The boy's energy and enthusiasm were wonderful to see. Not so long ago, his heart condition would have made running impossible. Thanks to Dr. Emily, poor health was behind him now.

Max slowed his pace, to make it easier for the boy to keep up with his long strides.

"I said I would, did I not?"

"Yeah, but my dad said you'd probably change your mind."

Max had no better friend than Phillip. Since his marriage to Emily, Phillip had gone back to speaking like the rest of the community . . . for the most part. But Gabe's use of contractions proved that during those long, dark months when his father considered leaving Pleasant Valley, Gabe had picked up a few Englisher words.

Now, Gabe pointed at a group of young boys gathered just ahead.

"What's going on?"

"They're choosing up sides for the baseball game," Gabe said.

"Sounds like fun, so why the long face?"

"All the men are busy with other things, and we cannot find an umpire."

The hopeful expression on the boy's face left no room for doubt: He wanted Max to volunteer for the job.

"It has been quite some time since I played the game," he admitted. "Not sure I remember all the rules."

"You will remember enough."

Max watched him race ahead, straight into the crowd of boys. Within seconds, all of them turned, faces beaming. As he approached, he found himself surrounded by the happy mob. Shouts of "Thank you!" and "You are great!" blended with the din of community enjoyment that floated through the yard surrounding the meeting house, where handmade picnic tables and wooden chairs stood beneath ancient Wye Oaks. A plain white picket fence wrapped around the acreage like strong, protective arms, and at its base, colorful flowers bobbed in the breeze.

He looked toward the makeshift baseball diamond, saw two of the boys leaning on weathered bats. "One for each team?"

They nodded.

"How many of you are there altogether?"

"Seventeen," Marcus said, sulking. "One shy of two teams."

"The game is just for fun, so we can relax the rules. Six men per team."

Ben took a step forward. "What will we use for bases?"

Max pictured the empty burlap sacks in his workshop. If he half stuffed them with hay, they'd work out just fine.

"I have just the thing at home. While I am gone, you

boys find a stick and scratch the base lines into the dirt. A big square. Ninety steps for each side."

Gabe nodded. "The official dimensions of a field."

"Back soon," Max said, and jogged toward his place.

Head down, eyes on the road, he thought. Because if the bishop spotted him, no telling how long the conversation might sideline him.

"Where are you going in such a hurry?"

Though he'd only spoken with her once, Max recognized Willa's voice. Jerking a thumb over one shoulder, he said, "The boys need bases for their baseball diamond. I'm going home to make them."

"I'm not surprised."

He had a feeling that someone—Anki, probably—had been singing his praises. Max made a mental note to thank his partner's wife for that, because basking in the glow of her admiration felt good. Real good.

The baby on her hip tried to untie her bonnet, but Willa gently grasped the dimpled little fist. "This is Frannie," she said, love and pride glowing in her eyes.

Smiling wide, the child riveted her gaze to Max's eyes.

"Pleased to meet you, Frannie," he said.

"Can you say hi to Max, sweetie?"

The baby pursed her lips, blurted, "M-m-max!" then hid her face in the crook of her mother's neck.

"She favors you," he said.

"My mama always said that each fib paints a black spot on one's soul. I appreciate the compliment, but . . ." She winked. "Frannie is beautiful. Perfect in every way. But I'm afraid she looks a whole lot more like her father than me."

According to Dan, she'd run away from the man, so the buzz of jealousy that shot through him made no sense.

"Well, she is as cute as a baby duck."

Snickering, Willa kissed the baby's chubby cheek. "Did you hear that, sweet girl? Max says you're as cute as a baby duck!"

Frannie met his eyes again, and this time, she echoed, "Duck!"

He tried not to notice the music in Willa's laughter. Tried to ignore the way her pale pink dress reflected in her cheeks, and the gleaming tendrils of mahogany hair that had escaped her bonnet.

"Well, the boys are waiting, so . . ."

Fingers flicking in the universal *shoo!* sign, she winked. "Go then! We don't want to delay America's favorite pastime!"

Frannie mimicked her mother's hand signal, adding, "Bye!"

"Hope we'll see you later," Willa said.

Max hoped so, too. While stuffing the sacks with sawdust, he could almost picture Willa, seated across from him at one of the weather-beaten picnic tables. Better still, side by side.

Back at the yard, he made quick work of dropping the burlap squares into place. "They will probably slide," he warned the boys, "so take care when rounding the bases."

"Can we nail them down?" Thomas asked.

"We could, but I fear one of you might get caught on a nail head."

William grimaced. "That would not be good!"

Before long, onlookers gathered on all four sides of the diamond, encouraging the pitchers, the batters, and every bare-handed player in the outfield. It was all he could do to keep from laughing out loud when he heard Frannie doing her best to copy her mother's robust cheers. Her clothing was similar to other female spectators'. Why, then, did Willa stand out from the rest? Because unlike every other woman's honey-colored hair, Willa's gleamed like polished mahogany.

Samuel launched the last pitch, his quiet *oomph!* bringing Max's mind back to the game. Seconds later, the crack of Gabe's bat sent the tattered ball up in a high arc. Puffs of powdery dirt exploded from his feet as he sprinted toward first base, and as he shot toward second, Ben threw the ball to Marcus on third. Would Gabe make it home?

It would be close, Max thought, real close.

The catcher squatted, ready to tag his pal.

Gabe slid across home plate, and even before the dust cleared, Max yelled, "Safe!"

"Way to go, Gabe!" Willa hollered. Frannie's little fist shot into the air, too.

The look on Phillip's face as his boy scored the winning run said it all: *Good game!*

He shook Max's hand. "I admire a man who's willing to sacrifice a clean white shirt to ensure the boys' enjoyment."

Max looked down, surprised by the streaks of dirt that crisscrossed either side of the button placket. "Think the women will allow me to eat at the table?"

Phillip laughed. "I can count on one hand—and have fingers left over—those who weren't at the game. If anyone complains, we will say the dirt is the price of admission."

Dan joined them, looking every bit his gloomy self. "Where were you this morning, Max? Writing out paychecks?"

"No, I was at the Bakers', finishing the roof on their addition. Week or so more, I can hang siding, and then—"

"Where do we stand with them, payment-wise?"

When he'd found out that Max had accepted the job with nothing but some rough drawings and a handshake, Dan had flown into a rage: "If Baker welches on the deal, the loss will come out of *your* half of the profits!" Max was about to remind his partner that at the start of the last week, his friend had delivered a substantial down payment.

"If you two are short on cash," Phillip said, "I'm happy to pay the balance just as soon as the bank opens on Monday."

Max held up a hand. "No need for that. We will abide by the original terms. When you are satisfied with the work, you will pay the balance, and not a day sooner."

A moment of uncomfortable silence hung between the men. "I see Anki over there," Dan said. "Better make sure she is all right."

Phillip watched him walk away. "How do you work with him, day in, day out?"

"He does his fair share."

"But . . . does he *ever* smile?"

"He worries about Anki."

"Why?"

He could recite the short list: Moody. Withdrawn. Fatigued. Lack of appetite. Insomnia. Disinterest, even in her shop, which had once performed well. Max trusted Phillip with the information, yet felt it wasn't his place to provide it.

"You should ask him yourself."

"Yeah. Right." Phillip grinned. "Next time I'm in the mood for a good *mind your own business* tongue-lashing, that's just what I'll do."

The longtime friends shared a quiet chuckle over that.

"I haven't seen Emily. Is she at the clinic today?"

Phillip shook his head. "No, the baby is cutting teeth, so none of us got much sleep last night. I expect she'll be here shortly."

"I hope so. I'm looking forward to meeting the newest addition to the Baker household."

"Just take care if you ask to hold him. He has—how do I put this—a sensitive stomach."

Arms akimbo, Max said, "Maybe a little spit-up will camouflage the rest of this mess."

"You're a mess, that's for sure." He chuckled again. "But at least you don't smell like Parmesan cheese. Yet." Then, pointing over Max's shoulder, he said, "Looks like the ladies are serving the food. Want me to save a seat for you?"

"Sure. Thanks. I need to check on a few things, but it should not take long."

"Check on things? Not at my house, I hope. You've worked like a dog on our addition. Why, just this morning Em said she can't believe how much you've accomplished in such a short time."

Max waved off the compliment. He needed a few moments to shed the discomfort of being without a wife, children, without parents or siblings while surrounded by so much family love. "The weather has been cooperative."

Phillip shook his head. "You need to quit doing that."

"Doing what?"

"Shrugging off every compliment anyone pays you. You earn every word of praise that comes your way. It isn't a sin to acknowledge it."

"Thanks, friend. And yes, save me a seat at the men's table. Some pie, too."

As he left the churchyard, he wondered about what Phillip had said. Max had always felt that humility was a good thing, but had he carried it so far that it had become a source of sinful pride?

Just ahead, he saw a tiny girl, alone at the end of the

local pond's short pier. And not an adult in sight. Hollering "Stop!" might startle her right into the deep, cold water. Breaking into a full-out run, he covered the distance quickly, hoping with every step that he'd reach her in time.

She heard his boots, pounding over the weathered boards, and turned toward him. A slight motion, yet enough to disrupt her precarious balance. She leaned backward, forward, arms windmilling as tiny feet skittered left, then right. He reached out to grab her—a tick too late—for into the drink she went, plump legs kicking, arms flapping, eyes wide with terror as murky water filled her mouth, until all she could manage was a weak, choking gurgle.

Max jumped in, too, and within seconds, seized a handful of the pink skirt that bobbed like an unfurled umbrella atop the floating water plants. Clutching her to his chest and cupping one hand under her chin to keep her face above the surface, he sloshed toward the shore. Easing the girl onto her side, he gently pressed against her ribs to expel the water she'd swallowed. The impact with the water had been sufficient to dislodge her cap. It was as he brushed back her dark bangs that he realized whose child she was.

"Frannie," he whispered. Tiny fingers wrapped around his, and she began to whimper. He held her close, and with a strength that belied her size, she clung to him.

"You are all right, little one," he said, fighting tears of relief. "Thank God, you are all right."

He needed to find Willa right away. But first, something to warm Frannie. Max scrambled to his feet and hurried back down the pier. He scanned the churchyard, where checkered cloths of bright blue and red fluttered brightly on every picnic table. Paying no mind to the picnic basket and jug of lemonade that held down the corners of a colorful hand-stitched quilt, Max stooped, gave it a jerk, and quickly bundled Frannie into it.

"Where is your mother?" he wondered aloud.

As if in answer to his question, a woman fell to her knees beside him.

"*O, God sta me bij!*" she wailed. "*Wat heb ik gedaana?*"

It was Anki, not Willa. What had she meant by "what have I done"?

"She was . . . she was napping," Anki said. "I must have fallen asleep, too. . . ."

And then Dan appeared. "Get up, Anki," he scolded. "You are making a spectacle of yourself."

A small crowd had gathered. "What happened?" one woman said. "The child fell into the pond," said another. "Max jumped right in," a third added, "and saved her."

"I am sorry." Anki reached out to touch Frannie's cheek. "So sorry."

"Stop apologizing," her husband thundered, grabbing her wrist. "She is Willa's responsibility, not yours." He glanced right, then left. "Where is she!"

Anki sniffled into her apron's hem. "Frannie's fingers were cold," she cried, "so she went home to fetch a sweater." Fresh tears sparkled in her eyes. "She was going to bring Frannie, but the babe was sleeping so peacefully that I said not to disturb her, that I would mind the child."

Max saw Willa at the top of the hill, a small, knitted blue sweater draped over one forearm as she returned the friendly greetings of her neighbors. At first sight of the empty blanket, her smiled vanished, like the flame of a snuffed candle. Then, brow furrowed and eyes wide with terror, she whirled around, looking for her little girl. He couldn't stand to watch her suffer, not for one second more.

"Willa," he called out, waving an arm over his head, "we're over here."

She ran toward them. In one instant, relief washed over her lovely features. In the next, the fear returned. He could almost hear her thoughts as she took it all in: *Why are you holding my daughter? Why is Anki sobbing? Why does Dan look so furious? Why is Frannie soaked to the skin!*

He put the child into her arms, tucked the quilt under Frannie's chin. "I was walking by, saw her on the pier. Could not get there quick enough to stop her from falling in, but I got her out of there, fast as I could. No need to worry. She's cold and wet, but none the worse for wear."

Willa's gaze traveled the length of him, from water-logged boots to still-dripping hair. Her lower lip trembled slightly as she said, "You . . . you saved her life." Eyes on Frannie now, she chanted, "Thank-you-thank you-thank you," punctuating each utterance with a kiss to the baby's face. She met his eyes, and he resisted the urge to wipe away her tears.

"How can I ever repay you?"

"No need for that."

"But Max, if you hadn't been there . . ." She held her breath, then shook her head, as if unable to complete her sentence.

"I am sorry. So, so sorry," Anki said, and tried to hug Willa and Frannie.

Dan held her back. "Did you not hear me, woman? She is not your child. This was not your fault. *She* is the mother," he said, jabbing a finger in Willa's direction. "If anyone is to blame, it is *her*." In response to the quiet gasps and shocked expressions of his neighbors, he tempered his tone. "Besides, Frannie is fine. Anyone with eyes can see that."

Without another word, he led his sobbing wife from the churchyard.

"I . . . I should go home, too," Willa said, "get Frannie into warm, dry clothes."

After hearing Dan's scathing accusation, Max could only imagine what he might add behind closed doors.

"I will go with you."

"That isn't necessary. Dan's right. Frannie is fine—thanks to you."

The look on her face reminded him of a conversation he'd overheard once, while in town. Two men, facing a wall of screws and nails, spoke in low tones: "Sometimes I feel like the meat in a gone-wrong sandwich," said one. And the other replied, "Yep, sounds like you're between a rock and a hard place, all right." The discussion ended as soon as they noticed Max. He had no idea what had prompted the disquieting exchange, but didn't think he'd ever forget their troubled expressions. That's probably how Willa felt right now, forced by circumstance to live with Dan's stern, judgmental nature . . . and Anki's uncertain hold on stability.

She took a step closer and used a corner of the quilt to blot water drops from his cheek. Her voice was soft, her smile caring as she said, "You should get into dry clothes, too, before you catch a chill. I'll meet you back here when everyone is warm and dry."

"What if Dan thinks it is a bad idea?"

She kissed Frannie again. "Frannie loves people and parties. He'll understand."

And just like that, she walked away from him.

Max wished he could agree. Dan had always been a hard worker. Dependable. Honest. But *understanding* wasn't a word he'd used to describe his partner.

He caught up to her. "You are sure?"

For a second there, he thought she might say yes. Then Willa glanced toward the narrow road that led from the churchyard. Shoulders sagging slightly, he heard her soft intake of air. "Maybe . . ."

If Dan doesn't make the price to pay too high, he finished for her.

He walked with her to the Y in the path. Any minute now, she'd go right, and he'd turn left. But already, he felt alone.

Chapter Four

"Are you following me?"

Those had been the first words she'd spoken to him, the day they met. "No. Well, yes. But only until you are both inside." *And I can be sure Dan will hold his temper.*

Frannie leaned toward him, nearly throwing Willa off balance. "Max," the baby said, arms flapping, "Max!"

"No, no, Frannie," Willa said, "we need to go home, get you changed, and let Max do the same." She met his eyes, shook a finger under his nose. "It's fifty degrees, and you're soaked to the skin. So go home."

Her big eyes shone with kindness. If that was her idea of issuing a stern order, she needed a lot more practice.

The baby yawned and snuggled into the crook of her mother's neck.

"Looks like your little girl could use a nap."

"You're right." Willa started walking, and after a few steps, stopped and faced him. "Did you have a chance to eat at the festival?"

"No." Between umpiring the ball game and pulling Frannie out of the pond, there hadn't been time.

"Neither did we. Go home. Change. And come to the

Hofmans'. I'll fix us soup and sandwiches." She guided Frannie's hand. "Say bye-bye to Max!"

"B-bye, Max," the baby said.

He was smiling when Willa turned away from him. "We need to think of something really nice to do for Max," he heard her say, "to show him how grateful we are that he saved you."

She'd just turned up the Hofmans' drive when the wind kicked up, driving a shiver up his back.

Shaking his head, he started the short walk home, slowing when his house came into view. Four single-pane windows flanked the front door. Two more, gleaming from the second story, overlooked the porch roof. During reconstruction, neighbors often asked how he managed, driving an hour or more after eight-hour days on various jobsites, then working until dark on the once-dilapidated cabin. "Would have been easier to bulldoze the eyesore and start over," Dan once said. A time or two, as Max had dangled from the rafters or teetered on the rooftop, he'd agreed. He'd built all the cabinets, most of the furniture, installed electricity throughout and indoor plumbing in the kitchen, bathroom, and cellar. Now that the place was, for the most part, complete, it took concentrated self-control not to bask in the pride of all he'd accomplished, single-handedly. *Better to bask,* he thought, climbing the front steps, *than wallow in self-pity.* In Max's eyes, both emotions required confession, and there were few things he disliked more than admitting his failings to the ever-critical bishop, Micah Fisher.

Rising before dawn had long been a habit, one that guaranteed ample time to cook up a hearty breakfast and iron the wrinkles out of clothes he'd washed the night before. Now, he traded his white shirt for the blue one he'd pressed yesterday, and after swapping waterlogged boots for dry ones, clipped the spare suspenders to the waistband of his jeans. Since his hair was mostly dry, he only needed to run a comb through it. Max leaned into the mirror, frowning as his palm rasped over the day's growth of whiskers. He considered shaving, but remembering how Frannie giggled when his chin tickled her palm, decided against it.

When he arrived at the Hofmans', Willa looked so lovely, standing in the open door, wearing a pale green dress and a smile so sweet that he almost didn't notice when she stepped aside to invite him inside.

Max removed his hat, held it against his thigh, and followed her to the kitchen table. "Where is everyone?"

"Frannie's taking a nap, Anki's in her room, and only God knows where Dan is."

Her monotone made it clear the situation wasn't new to her.

What *was* new, he noticed, were the blinds, rolled up at the top of each window. Somehow, she'd taken down the rollers and covered the vinyl with pale blue fabric. The gray and white linoleum underfoot glistened, and every globe of the wrought-iron fixture above the table sparkled. Each shiny cup and plate on the hutch had been artfully arranged, and on the sideboard sat a basket of fruit that reminded him of a framed still life he'd once seen in the window of an Oakland art gallery. The faint scent of pine oil mingled with the waning sunshine, telling him she'd recently polished the wood cabinets, the grandfather clock, and the table and chairs. He'd been here dozens of times and didn't remember things looking tidier. Or more welcoming. This was Willa's work, he knew, not Anki's.

"Join me for some lemonade?" she said, standing in

front of the round-edged refrigerator. "Or, the water's hot. I can brew us some tea."

"Lemonade sounds good."

She pulled out a chair. "Take a load off, Aye-mish, while I set the table."

Aye-mish. Was that what she called Dan, too? Or had she reserved the nickname for Max?

Grinning, he stepped up to the sink. "I will do it." He began washing his hands. "It is the least I can do, since you are feeding me."

"I've never been one to turn down a little help." She turned up the flame under the stewpot, and pointed at the hutch. "You'll find everything you need on the shelves and in the drawers."

Max dried his hands and replaced the blue-and-white-checkered towel on the hook beside the sink just as he'd found it: folded three times, longways.

Frannie's voice floated through the heat grate, and Willa hurried for the stairs. "Make yourself at home. I won't be long."

His grandmother had spent hours teaching him and his siblings how to set a proper table. "We must do our best in all things big and small," she'd said, "to show our heavenly Father that we appreciate the many blessings He has bestowed upon us."

Max took his time, distributing blue-flowered bowls, and short, heavy-bottomed tumblers. After placing spoons and butter knives atop each cotton napkin, he slid Frannie's high chair close to the table, then draped a thick terry-cloth bib across the wooden tray. He took inventory: Salt and pepper shakers. Potholder for under the kettle. Butter dish. Nothing missing now, he thought, except the Hofmans, Willa, and Frannie.

A big ladle hung above the stove, and after lifting the pot's lid, he used it to give the stew a quick stir. Max had just bent to turn down the heat when Willa appeared in the doorway, holding Frannie on her right hip.

"Will you just look at this," she said.

Max smiled. "Would you like me to pour the lemonade?"

"I have a better idea. How 'bout while I slice the bread, you round up the lady and gentleman of the house?"

"Happy to."

And he was. For one of the first times since losing his family, Max looked forward to a meal. Now if only he could coax Dan into a cooperative mood. And talk Anki into drying her eyes long enough to eat.

He found the door to Anki's room open. She sat near the window, staring out at the lawn below. Doubling up his forefinger, he rapped on the doorframe.

"Anki . . ."

Except for a half-hearted nod, she didn't move. He entered and stopped several feet from the window seat.

". . . supper's almost ready."

"I am not hungry."

"No one asked whether or not you are hungry."

They both jumped a bit at the suddenness of Dan's voice.

"The food is ready and you *will* eat it." Arms crossed, he lifted his chin. "You know how I feel about waste." Almost as an afterthought, he tacked on, "And self-pity."

Shoulders slumped, she exhaled a weary sigh. "All right. Just as soon as I tidy my braid."

Dan growled under his breath and started for the stairs. "Are you coming?" he asked Max.

"After a quick trip to the bathroom." First, Max wanted

to speak with Anki. Perhaps he could help her understand that, despite his rough ways, her husband loved her.

He waited until Dan was out of sight, then turned the desk chair around and sat down. Arms resting on the chair's top rail, he said, "He cares about you, you know."

She met his eyes. "He told you that?"

"Not in so many words, but I work alongside him for hours at a time. I can tell that he is worried about you."

"Work beside him!" Anki shook her head. "You are on the road half the time, drumming up business in Oakland, in Martinsburg, in Cumberland."

She had him dead to rights, but Max couldn't let her change the subject.

"The man has a rough exterior—I will give you that. But he cares about you."

"Has he told you the reason for my . . ." She snorted. ". . . for my *depression*?"

This didn't seem to be the time to mention how long they'd tried—and failed—to have children.

"I know he wanted a son . . ." she went on. "That he would have settled for a daughter if he had to. It saddens me that I have disappointed him."

"I'm sure you haven't—"

"I cannot give him a family."

"But Anki, you *are* Dan's family."

She continued as if he hadn't spoken. "I am praying, day and night, asking for forgiveness."

"For what!"

"My disobedience." Hands clenched in her lap, she sighed again. "It should not be this hard to accept God's will."

Max had stayed behind to tell her that Dan cared about

her; if he could convince her that others believed that, too, perhaps it would be enough to shake her free of her ever-present sadness. If he'd had any idea things would go this far afield . . .

Should have learned by now what happens when you speak before you think.

He got to his feet. "Willa's stew smells delicious. We should eat now, before it gets cold."

"Yes." She stood, too. "Yes, you are right. And . . . and Dan would not be pleased if we missed the prayer time."

When they entered the kitchen, Willa avoided eye contact. He didn't know her well . . . just well enough to know that wasn't like her.

Dan, in place at the head of the table, waited for the rest of them to sit.

Frannie slapped both palms on her highchair tray. "Dan eat?"

Much to Max's surprise, his partner winked, leaned closer to the baby, and said, "Yes, sweet girl. Dan will eat. And so will Mama, and Max, and Anki . . ." He tapped the tip of her nose. ". . . and *Frannie!*"

Her giggles filled the room, and not even Anki could keep from smiling.

"We should pray," Dan said.

All eyes closed; all heads bowed. Peeking through the narrow slit between his lids, Max saw Frannie's lashes fluttering as she struggled to emulate the adults. She was an easy child to like, he thought. Very easy.

In the moment that passed as each silently prayed, Max wondered what kind of father would let go of a child so sweet? And what sort of man could let a woman like Willa slip away from him? If the Almighty ever saw fit to bless him with a wife and child, he hoped they'd be like Willa and Frannie.

The steady *tick-tick* of the grandfather clock kept time with his heartbeats, and then Dan cleared his throat. Willa looked up, as did Anki. And Frannie? Frannie's exuberant "*E-e-eat!*" inspired a round of laughter.

He looked at Anki, expecting to find her smiling, too. Instead, the woman balanced a slice of bread on one palm, using the other hand to wield the butter knife.

Max shook pepper onto his stew. "I will drive to Johnstown in the morning," he told Dan. "God willing, we will have a contract for a small housing development by this time tomorrow."

"Is our license renewed for Pennsylvania?"

"It is."

"How long a drive?"

"Hour and a half, if we leave early enough to miss rush hour traffic."

Dan bit off a corner of buttered bread. "A whole development, eh?" he said around it.

"Only ten or fifteen houses, if the developer can sell every lot."

"We will need the whole crew."

"If no one gets sick, I believe we can get by with four. Leave the other four to finish up projects closer to home."

"Where do you stand with the Bakers' addition?"

Max nodded. "Only a bit of trim to paint. Phillip said if we are pressed for time, he and Gabe will do it."

Dan harrumphed. "Have I ever *not* finished a job?"

"No, but . . ."

If the man paid half as much attention to his wife's well-being, Max thought, she wouldn't spend her days moping around the house. But then . . . Dan wouldn't have hired Willa to help her. . . .

Anki took advantage of the lull in the conversation to

say, "I saw you talking with Emily Baker today, Willa. Are you all right?"

Automatically, she blanketed the woman's hand with her own. "Yes, of course, and so is Frannie. Emily just stopped by to ask if I'd do her a favor."

Dan snorted. "What sort of favor?"

If Willa detected his disbelieving attitude, she gave no sign of it. Admirable, Max thought. He'd been on the receiving end of that caustic sarcasm and knew only too well that it wasn't easy to ignore.

"She needs some help with the bookkeeping, the appointments schedule, tidying up around the place . . . you know, things like that. Best of all, I can bring Frannie with me. She can play with little Rafe. That's short for Raphael. Just five more sons and they'll have all seven angels of God!"

Anki shrank back, no doubt asking herself why He'd blessed the Bakers with two sons, while she and Dan had none. For a second or two, no one spoke. Were Dan and Willa wondering the same thing?

"Don't worry, Anki, working for Emily won't interfere with my responsibilities around here. I promise."

Taking her seat again, Anki said, "I am glad, because I . . ." She looked at her husband. "*We* need you, don't we, Dan."

Wiping the butter from Frannie's bread from his face, he forced a stern expression. "I have no complaints about your work." He cleared his throat. "I would not object if you stayed." Now, he focused on Willa. "But it is more than a mile from here to the clinic. How will you get there?"

Willa sat up straighter. "I have two perfectly healthy legs, and . . . and comfortable shoes. I'll walk!"

Dan didn't look convinced. "Carrying Frannie?"

At the mention of her name, the baby said, "Dan!"

His features relaxed and he softened his tone as she wrapped chubby fingers around his thumb. "That might be fine when the weather is good. What will you do when it rains? When the snows come? You have not been here during the winter. It can get brutal, let me tell you!"

She hadn't considered that. Max could see it on her face, in her posture. And then he had an idea. . . .

"Do you have a driver's license?"

She gave him a look that said, *Sure.*

"Good, good. And can you operate a vehicle with manual transmission?"

"Hmpf. I'll have you know that my mom taught me to drive in an adorable little red pickup truck—"

Her hand floated in the air, mimicking the positions of the gearshift. If Max was a betting man, he would have wagered that under the table, her booted foot was pressing an imaginary clutch to the floor, too.

"That was a long time ago, though. . . ." Eyes narrowed, she asked, "Why?"

"I have an old truck out back. It is small, but reliable. I can give you a few lessons, if you like, to help you remember how to—"

"I appreciate the offer, Max, really I do. But I can't afford a vehicle right now."

"Never said I want to sell it."

Her brow furrowed with a confused frown. "I can't afford to rent it, either."

"It is not good for a motor to sit, unused that way. You would be doing me a favor, driving it to and from work."

If Willa accepted, he'd have to give the vehicle a thorough going-over, checking belts and hoses, topping off fluids, testing the tires' air pressure and the flexibility of the windshield wipers. He'd make sure the battery terminals weren't corroded, and because it had sat covered in the shed for months, it would need a good cleaning, inside and out.

She was considering the offer. Max could tell by the way she sat, alternately nodding and shaking her head, biting her lower lip. He searched his mind for the words that would convince her, because he wanted to help her, any way he could.

"Dan is right," he said. "Walking all that way with Frannie in tow will be difficult, especially when the road is covered by feet of snow."

"That much, huh? Well, I lived in Philly. And Baltimore. Chicago before that, so—"

"So you know all about below-zero temperatures, and mountain winds strong enough to overturn wagons . . ."

"Well, no, but . . ."

"I can hardly wait to hear what follows this *but*," Dan put in, chuckling.

To her credit, Willa didn't allow the comment to sidetrack her. Max didn't know how she'd respond to it, but he hadn't expected her to say, "What's in it for you, Maximillian Lambright?"

"I, ah, well . . ."

"Life has taught me that if something sounds too good to be true, it usually is. So . . . what's in it for you?"

He reminded himself that she'd been on her own for years, that she'd fled an abusive beau. Max could only imagine what she thought he'd demand of her if she said yes.

"I suppose you will just have to take me at my word: I expect nothing except . . ." Grinning, he winked. "Except that you drive the speed limit."

That inspired soft laughter. "Yeah, right. Like I could speed, even if I wanted to, in Pleasant Valley."

Now that he thought of it, the warning did sound a bit comical. The community's main road was paved, but hardly qualified as a raceway. "It's true that the truck is not registered. Has no license plates. No insurance. But that isn't the main reason I—"

"Now I get it," she interrupted. "If a cop stops me, you're in for a big fat fine."

"*Goeie genade*, Willa. You could at least *pretend* to feel grateful."

"Dan is right," Anki agreed. "Max makes a very generous offer."

Frannie, pounding on the high chair's tray, demanded a slice of bread, and Willa accommodated her. Now, with fingers and lips butter-shiny, she said, "Yum!"

When Dan laughed, she extended her arm. "Dan eat?"

He surprised them all when he leaned closer and allowed her to hold the bread to his mouth. After pretending to take a bite, he said, "Yum!"

But Frannie wasn't fooled. "Dan *eat*!" she scolded.

He took a bite, and in the ensuing quiet, Max focused on Willa. "So what do you say? Will you help me out and drive the truck for a while?"

It took a moment for her to say, "I suppose it makes sense. But let's get one thing straight." She scooted her chair closer to his, so close that their knees touched under the table. "First of all, I'll pay for the gas and oil."

She was close enough to kiss. If Dan and Anki hadn't been here, would he? As if she'd read his mind, Willa licked her lips. "And second?" he asked.

"When I think of a way to repay you, that's exactly what I intend to do. And you won't be allowed to object."

She sat back and, arms crossed, looked at Anki, at Dan. "You two are my witnesses."

Smirking, Dan said, "Oh, this is gonna be an interesting couple of months. *Real* interesting."

And Anki laughed, surprising them all.

Chapter Five

Dan rinsed his coffee mug and placed it in the drain-board. "Max is here," he said, turning from the window. "I thought he said eight o'clock."

"He did."

"It does not rile you that he is half an hour early?"

"Why would it? Breakfast is over and the dishes are done, your lunch is packed, and I'm ready." Willa patted her hair, which was finally long enough to twist into a thick, stubby little bun. Not that her hairstyle mattered. The minute she stepped outside, it would be hidden under a black cap. The clothes, the shoes, the hats . . . as someone who wasn't Amish, none of it was required of her. But blending in made life easier, and so since the day she'd arrived, when Anki had produced secondhand clothes from her friends, she'd worn them, always.

Dan opened the door, and in walked Max. Why hadn't she noticed before that he stood a good six inches taller than his partner? Dan's chest was broader, his shoulders and biceps more muscular. And yet somehow, Max seemed like the bigger man.

"Good morning," he said.

"Right back atcha." *What a stupid thing to say!* She felt

the heat of a blush creep into her cheeks and tried to hide it by fussing with her apron ties.

He shifted his weight from one foot to the other. "I am early, so if you have things to do, I can wait."

"No, it's fine. I'm ready." Facing Dan, she said, "Anki is in the parlor, reading. I fixed her some tea—with lemon, just the way she likes it—and put a plate of her favorite cookies beside the mug. So she's all set, probably for an hour or two."

"I know. I just checked." His smile disappeared, and in its place appeared a scowl. "I will be here for at least that long. There is a brush pile to burn, and more wood to chop for winter. We will go to her shop afterward. She has not been there in a while, and I am trying to talk her into going to check on things."

The shop, as he'd called it, sat forty or so yards from the house. According to Anki, the building had been a large shed when Dan's parents worked the land. Soon after their wedding, she'd said, she and Dan cleaned up the old tools, sold them, and used the money to buy paint and brushes, and install the shelves and counters where she displayed canned and baked goods. Willa pictured the shop's whitewashed walls, where Dan had hung Anki's paintings of buggies and horses, mountain vistas, and wildlife. Willa hadn't painted in years, and suddenly, she missed it. Later, she'd ask Anki about borrowing a few brushes and paint, and she'd find out if she still had a knack for it. Maybe the common interest would help them both deconstruct walls of sadness.

Willa scooped Frannie up from her highchair as Max said, "We will be back soon."

"No need to hurry." Dan started for the hall, but stopped in the doorway. "Think maybe you should wear a muffler around your neck?"

Max returned his partner's grin. "In fifty-degree weather? I will overheat and pass out, and Willa is not strong enough to pick me up."

"Your decision." He shrugged. "But if her first time driving the stick shift throws your neck out of joint, well, you were warned."

Dan's laughter followed him all the way into the parlor, and echoed in her ears as she walked after Max to the driveway. During her months with the Hofmans, Willa had witnessed more than enough to understand why Dan, at first, had seemed rigid and heartless. Seeing his smile, hearing his laughter, made her feel good.

"Well, there she is," Max said, gesturing toward the truck.

"She?"

He only shrugged.

Willa balanced Frannie on her left hip as her right fingertips traced the truck's left-side contours, from the strangely shaped taillights to the wood cargo box, and one of two vertical chrome smokestacks that rose behind the cab. "The only thing I've seen anything like this was on the highway, on eighteen-wheelers."

Another shrug.

When she reached the gold lettering on the driver's door, she faced him. "You named her?"

"No . . ."

"But this says 'Li'l Red Express.'"

"The manufacturer did that." He snickered. "Remember the old line, 'It was the best of times, it was the worst of times . . .'? Well, near as I can tell, the designer decided to foil some newfangled government restrictions that were written that year by building something of a hot rod, disguised as a pickup truck. She can go zero to sixty-five in under a minute."

"Really?"

"Really."

And then, looking like the proverbial boy caught with his hand in the cookie jar, Max shook his head.

"Relax, and quit lookin' all worried. Every time I'm behind the wheel, I'll have Frannie with me. No way I'm gonna put this baby to the test with *my* precious baby on board." She gave the smokestack a pat-pat-pat. "What a shame though, huh?"

He opened the door, and without warning, Frannie scrambled inside. Seated behind the steering wheel, she squealed happily.

"Have you made any changes to Li'l Red?"

"Nope."

"Well then, all I can say is, *some*body loved the color red."

He seemed hesitant. Had seeing Frannie bounce up and down, banging on the wheel, changed his mind?

And then it hit her: It wouldn't matter if he had!

"What's wrong? A spider? She doesn't get much attention out there in the shed." Max gently moved her to the right and stuck his head in beside Frannie. "I'll get it."

"Chivalry is alive and well in Pleasant Valley," she teased. "There isn't a spider, but if there was . . ." She flexed her bicep. ". . . I would have no problem mashing it."

"You know, I believe you." He straightened, leaned a forearm on top of the open door. "If not a spider, then what?"

"It's just, well, Frannie wouldn't be safe. How would I install a car seat—if I *had* a car seat—in there?"

His face took on that older-than-his-years look again, and rubbing his chin, Max said, "Let me give it some thought. Folks tell me I have a gift for jerry-rigging things. I'll figure out some way to make it safe for her."

"Newfangled? Hot rod? And now jerry-rigging?" She gave his shoulder a playful poke. "My grandfather used to say stuff like that. How old *are* you, Max?"

"Not quite thirty. Now, here is my idea: We will take a short ride to the dirt road that runs alongside Trout Run. I will drive until we get there."

"But . . . Frannie . . ."

"I will drive like your grandfather." He winked. "And you will hold her. When we get there, we will change places."

"Do you believe the folks who say you have jerry-rigging talents?" she asked, carrying the baby to the passenger side.

"Definitely."

Self-assured, hard-working, and serious as a judge. *And you should know about judges, since you've seen your share of them.*

Willa climbed in, thinking he was the oldest thirty-year-old she'd ever met. A symptom of being on his own for so many years? She sent a silent prayer of thanks heavenward. Life was tough enough without taking it so seriously.

The baby clapped. "Bye-bye?"

"Yes, sweet girl, we're going bye-bye." Now, Willa thanked God for Frannie, because without her, she might be as grumpy as Dan or as old-in-the-head as Max.

"All buckled up?" And when she nodded, he put the key into the ignition. Willa watched carefully as he grasped the choke nob and eased it out a bit. With his left foot on the clutch and the right on the brake, he drew the gear lever toward himself, then moved it up.

"First gear?"

"First gear," he echoed, and released the brake.

Once the speedometer registered fifteen miles per hour, he depressed the clutch again, and this time, moved the gear arm down a notch.

"Second gear," they said together.

"Okay if I ask a question?"

"We will be there soon."

"Oh. Good. But that isn't what I was going to ask."

Max grinned at Frannie, who babbled happily as she fiddled with the radio's station-selector buttons.

"I thought the Amish weren't allowed to have electricity and plumbing and . . ." She pulled Frannie closer, out of reach of the radio. ". . . and gas-powered vehicles. But you guys here in Pleasant Valley, well, you have all that stuff."

"You have been with the Hofmans since early spring and have not asked *them*?"

"I'll admit, it crossed my mind. Every time I opened the fridge, used the washing machine or vacuum cleaner. Guess I just never felt comfortable enough to bring it up."

"Because Dan can be . . . crabby?"

"Maybe."

He veered around a big rock in the road, and to his credit, she barely noticed.

"In my grandparents' day," he began, "*everyone* followed Old Order rules. These days, a few members of the community still abide by them, but most have shifted to New Order."

"Speaking of shifting, are you in third gear now?"

"Fourth, actually." He looked her way long enough to wink.

"Maybe I'll call you Mr. Smooth from now on," she teased. "What you said just now, about Old Order versus New . . . Was it difficult for those who exchanged long-standing traditions for more modern ways? It makes perfect sense. Changing, I mean. Because really, how could any of you compete with the service companies and businesses in town, doing things the older, slower way?"

"We could not. And yes, I can name one or two who believe their way is God's way, and that He disapproves of us."

"Now that *doesn't* make sense. Isn't pride one of the biggest no-no's for the Amish?"

Max chuckled. "Yes-yes."

So he *did* have a sense of humor. Willa liked that. Liked it enough to try to encourage more of it.

Max downshifted, then stopped and engaged the emergency brake.

"Did your mother teach you about using this each time you park?"

"Yes . . ."

"And that you should not let up on the clutch until it is fully engaged?"

"I don't remember *why,* but she mentioned that. Yes."

"Yes-s-s!" Frannie hollered.

He leaned close enough to rub noses with the child. "Ready?" he asked.

"Weddy!" she answered.

They traded places, and as she slid behind the wheel, Willa wondered if *she* was ready. Whether or not she accepted his generous offer depended more on his promise to make the truck safe for Frannie than her ability to drive it.

Gently, patiently, Max recited the step-by-step shifting process, and much to her amazement, she managed with very little lurching and gear-grinding. Every few minutes, he issued a challenge: Slow down. Speed up. Stop. Back up. Even more surprising, she met each with even less jerking and grating of gears.

So why, then, did he look so nervous?

Willa looked at him and, smiling, whispered, "Sleeping?"

Frannie exhaled a sweet baby sigh and snuggled deeper into his collar, and his heart thumped with fondness. "Mmm-hmm," he whispered back.

A few minutes ago, he'd noticed that the baby was struggling to keep her eyes open. So he'd turned her around and guided her head onto his shoulder. Within seconds, her soft, steady breaths were puffing against his cheek, and the feelings of fondness intensified. He liked knowing that she trusted him enough—already!—to fall asleep in his arms. If this was what fatherhood felt like . . .

Max stared through the windshield and tried to ignore the thought.

"We are coming up on Pleasant Valley Road," he said quietly. "When we get there, make a right."

"Where are we going next?"

"My place. And on the way, you'll see what it feels like when the speedometer needle crosses forty." Frannie stirred slightly. "Because this little one ought to be home, where she can stretch out in her own bed."

"Will you give me a tour?"

"Not much to see, really."

"Anki told me you built your house, all by yourself."

"Rebuilt is more like it, but true . . ."

"Then I'd love to see it, upstairs and down. The basement, even. The yard. The shed where Li'l Red lives. *Everything*."

He'd seen the difference her touch had made at the Hofmans'. Little things like hand-crocheted doilies protecting windowsills from the houseplants' overflow, the embroidered tablecloth that covered the wood kitchen table, a well-worn quilt, draped just so from the arm of Dan's favorite chair. She'd even found ways to pretty up the bathroom—quite a feat when the Amish goal was plainness—by folding bath and hand towels in half, then in threes, before stacking them on the open shelves. Max didn't know if he wanted a woman who paid that much attention to detail traipsing around *inside* his house. Had he washed the breakfast dishes and made up his bed? Swept up the kibble that always ended up on the floor beside Rascal's bowl?

"When do we turn?"

"In another mile or so. Just past the church, the road will jog right, then left. I'll let you know when to turn onto Carson Lane."

"That's where your house is?"

"Mmm-hmm," he said, absentmindedly stroking Frannie's hair.

"I just want to say . . . you're a very nice man, Max Lambright."

No doubt because he'd offered her his truck. He couldn't very well take credit for that. Not until he'd found a way to make it safe for Frannie.

"I appreciate your offer to loan me the truck," she said, "but that isn't the only reason I think you're wonderful."

Then maybe because Frannie's diaper had leaked, and he hadn't complained about the dampness that seeped through the thigh of his jeans?

"I heard what you said to Anki last evening."

How was that possible, when she'd been in the kitchen, and he'd been upstairs in the Hofmans' room?

"Then you must have ears like a hoot owl, to hear through carpet-covered floorboards."

"My ears work just fine, but not as fine as a bird of prey. No," she said, making the final turn off Pleasant Valley. The truck's gears protested as she slowed, but not much. "Sorry," she said, wincing. And then she continued, as though nothing had interrupted her. "There's a heat grate in the kitchen ceiling. On the other side of it . . ."

"The Hofmans' room," he finished for her. Max searched his mind, wondering what, exactly, he'd told Anki before going downstairs for supper. Something told him Willa would remind him.

"She seems fragile, but in my opinion, Anki is anything but. A person can't dig in their heels and stubbornly refuse to listen to anyone if they're delicate."

He'd thought the same thing on more than one occasion, with good reason.

"If that sounded harsh, or like criticism, I'm sorry. I wouldn't hurt her for all the world." She glanced at him again. "It's your fault, you know."

"*My* fault!" Max chuckled.

"If you weren't so easy to talk to, I would have kept my thoughts to myself." She pointed. "Carson Lane! I turn right, right?"

"Right."

When his house came into view, the familiar sense of accomplishment washed over him. Max unbuckled the seat belt, wondering how to ask forgiveness for his sin of pride while gathering Frannie up without waking her.

Willa braked the truck and followed every parking instruction to the letter.

"Oh *Max*," she breathed, her voice thick with admiration,

"it's . . . it's *beautiful*. Anki said it was, and she didn't exaggerate." Turning slightly to face him, she said, "I thought all Amish houses had to be white."

"I bought fifty gallons on sale and couldn't return it. The labels said 'white.'" He looked at the house. "The labels were wrong. And so is waste."

"Well, I've never seen a lovelier shade of yellow. Pale. Subtle. Like . . ."

". . . butter," they said together.

And then they laughed.

Together.

Again.

"Hey, this saying the same thing at the same time is getting to be a habit," she said, opening the driver's door.

He watched as she ran around to his side of the truck and opened the passenger door.

"Let me take her," she said, sliding her arms around Frannie, who grinned sleepily.

She was so close that he could smell the faint scent of bath soap. So close that he could feel the heat of her breath on his cheek. So close that if he turned his head, just a little, he could kiss her. If he wanted to. And oh, how he wanted to!

"Frannie! Oh my goodness," she said. "Oh my goodness. Max. I'm . . . I'm so, so sorry!"

Instinct made him lay a hand on his thigh, a futile attempt at hiding the damp spot. And when he remembered *why* it was damp, he withdrew it.

The baby's eyes, those big brown eyes, had dimmed. She looked sad. Hurt. Confused, because she had no idea why her mother seemed upset.

"She is only a baby." He reached up, stroked a fingertip across her pink, chubby cheek. "I will wash the jeans and forget all about it." He touched Willa's cheek now. "And you will, too."

She tilted her head, trapping his fingers between her cheek and shoulder. "But Max, you've been so good to us. *You saved Frannie's life!*" Willa looked around the truck's interior, at the keys still dangling from the ignition. "I don't . . . I can't . . . I'm not sure how . . ."

He couldn't stand to see her upset. Couldn't stand to see her beautiful eyes shimmering with unshed tears. Tears caused by feelings of gratitude . . . and wretched indebtedness.

"You have to listen to me, Willa."

She blinked, sniffed, nodded.

"You are listening?"

Nodding, she sent him the barest of smiles.

"You owe me nothing, except . . ." He put one foot on the ground, and when she backed up, put the other one down, too. They stood face-to-face, with Frannie looking from him to Willa and back again.

"Except friendship."

She'd developed a certain fondness for Pleasant Valley's residents, but so far, nothing beyond polite courtesies had developed. A rational, reasonable person would consider Max's simple words proof that God had answered her prayers for something more, something deeper. Why, then, instead of feeling grateful and satisfied, did she feel disappointed?

The baby reached out, grabbed his hair. "Max . . ."

He kissed the back of her plump little hand, and looking into Willa's eyes, said, "Would you like to see it now?"

"Oops," she said, gathering her composure, "you caught me daydreaming." She blinked. Forced a smile. "See what?"

"Everything," he said, reminding her of what she'd said, moments ago. "Everything."

Willa made quick work of changing the baby's diaper. She'd just finished slipping a dress over Frannie's shoulders when a medium-sized dog ran toward them, full throttle, and stopped just short of Max's boots. Its thick, multicolor fur gleamed in the sunshine. Lured by its doggy smile, Frannie struggled to get down.

"Here," Max said, taking her from Willa, "let me introduce them. And don't worry. He is as gentle as a newborn."

Her little girl went to him without a moment's hesitation.

Max got onto his knees. "Frannie, this is Rascal," he said, guiding her palm along the dog's forehead. "He is soft. Soft Rascal."

Frannie tried to make the *S* sound, and Max nodded. "Yes, soft. Rascal is *soft*."

Willa loved the way he'd emphasized the *S* and the *F*. If he kept this up, she'd be speaking like him in no time!

"Well," he said, standing, "if we are going to see everything, we had better get started!"

Frannie looked over Max's shoulder and waved at Willa. He whispered something that made her smile. "Mama come?"

"Yes, sweet girl, Mama is coming."

She followed them onto the covered porch, where two bentwood rockers faced Hoye Crest, the highest point in Maryland. A month from now, snow would blanket it, and the rest of Backbone Mountain, but even now, the view was magnificent. No wonder he'd chosen this west-facing site.

As he opened the wide Craftsman-style door, beveled

windows caused rainbows of sunlight to puddle on the entry floor.

She knocked on the door's center panel. "Did you make it?"

"I did."

"And the chairs on the porch?"

"Yes."

Nodding, Willa trailed behind him into the parlor where, straight ahead, caramel-colored leather love seats faced one another. A low table that matched the entry door stood between them. Centered on the left wall stood a huge woodstove. Directly across from it was a bookshelf, and to the right and left, tall, narrow wood-framed windows. He'd covered the floors with the same material.

"Black oak?" she asked.

"Wild cherry."

"It's beautiful."

His smile said what words needn't: *I know*. But, being Amish, Max couldn't admit pride in his home or his expert craftsmanship.

"Hungry?" he asked, leading the way to the kitchen.

"No, thanks. I have to make supper for Dan and Anki. And Frannie, of course." She stood at the sink and looked into the yard. Turning, she asked, "Why don't you join us?"

"I would not want to wear out my welcome."

Impossible, she thought. But then, it was the Hofmans' house, and Max knew them far better than she did.

She made her way around the room, admiring white cabinets that formed an L. Here, as in the parlor, light poured through tall, narrow windows. Unlike those in the parlor, though, he'd trimmed these in white. He waved her closer, so she could stand beside him and through the windowed door, at the deep covered porch and the vast lawn beyond it.

"Next time you visit, I will show you the workshop," he said, nodding toward a tidy, low-slung building. *He must love nature's light,* she thought, counting three windows on either side of its door.

"That's where Li'l Red lives?" she asked, pointing at a nearly identical building to its right.

"It is."

She could see that he'd built the double barn doors more than wide enough to accommodate the truck, with room to spare against the side walls.

Facing the cabinets again, she said, "Everything is so neat and clean. Does someone come in, help with the housework?"

"Someone like you, you mean?" Frannie had stuck a finger into his ear, and laughing, he removed it.

Someone like you, she repeated silently. "I wasn't always a live-in maid, you know. I earned a teaching degree from Philadelphia's Drexel University."

"Impressive."

She heard no rancor in his voice, and yet, the word annoyed her. *Maybe because you* wasted *your precious degree, running off with Joe and . . .*

Willa didn't want to think about the rest.

As though Frannie sensed her need for a reminder of the good things that had come after Joe, she reached out. "Mama?"

Willa gathered her close, blew kisses onto her neck.

"Is what Anki said true? You did all this—*all of this*—by yourself?"

He held out a hand, showed her his calluses. "Took the better part of a year, but I did not mind. Hard work and long days kept my mind off my problems."

Anki had provided just enough information about his

background to stimulate Willa's sympathy. And curiosity. She sat at the table, held Frannie on her lap. "What problems?"

He opened the fridge, slid a plate of ham and a wedge of cheese from the top shelf. "Sandwich?"

His way of saying "*I'd rather not talk about it*"?

"No, thanks. It's almost suppertime. If I don't clean my plate, Dan will launch into a 'why waste is a sin' lecture."

He placed the ingredients side by side, like components to be assembled on a factory assembly line: Bread. Cheese. Butter. Knife. Meat. "That does not happen . . . when you live alone." Max shrugged. "Do you want milk, then?"

"Sure." Until this point, he'd seemed so confident. Independent. Happy to live alone. "Just one glass, though. Frannie and I can share."

He opened a cabinet door, grabbed two stoneware mugs, and filled them to the brim.

"People say I'm a good listener, y'know."

Max handed her a mug, then went back to building his sandwich. By not responding to her offer, he'd underscored her earlier assumption that he preferred not to talk about his past. What kind of friend would she be if she didn't respect that?

After completing the sandwich, he cleaned everything up, then carried his plate to the table. Straddling the chair across from hers, he shook his head.

"I believe you *are* a good listener, but . . ."

"But talking about the past is painful." Frannie rested her head on Willa's chest. "It isn't easy, reliving hard times. But it isn't healthy, keeping it all inside, either."

"I have not heard you speak of your experience."

Was he challenging her to talk about her background,

or hinting that, as his friend, she should allow him to deal with the past in his own way? He was hurting. Deeply. Willa could see it glinting in his eyes. It was evident in the brittle edge to his usually smooth voice, too. A moment ago, Max had plainly said that he expected nothing from her but friendship. A good friend, she decided, would set aside curiosity in order to respect his need for privacy.

Forearms resting on the chairback, Max studied her face for a moment. She was tempted to crack the age-old "Is there spinach in my teeth?" joke when he said, "How did your father die?"

Although his question came as a surprise, Willa admitted, "I'm not sure that he *is* dead. He left before I was born."

His brows drew together, then dipped low in the center of his forehead. "I . . . Willa . . . I am sorry."

She'd heard the words before, but couldn't remember when they'd sounded as heartfelt.

"Must have been difficult for your mother."

Willa smiled, remembering how serene her childhood had been, thanks to her mother's sacrifices. "Yes, and I wish I'd figured that out sooner. A lot sooner, so I could have shown her how much I appreciated everything she did for me."

He blinked. Shook his head. And although he hadn't asked her to continue, she heard herself say, "Mom kept so much to herself, to protect me. My father's desertion, money troubles, her declining health—"

"Willa . . ." he interrupted, fingertips resting on her wrist, "shhh."

His touch was comforting, and might have moved her to tears, if Rascal hadn't chosen that moment to put a paw on her thigh. Seeing it, Frannie loosed a happy squeal, and bent over to press her forehead to his. Willa and Max laughed at the baby's affable actions. Then, squirming, she slid off Willa's lap. Breaking contact with Max, Willa got up and latched the screen door. In seconds, the pair stood side by side, Frannie babbling and pointing at something outside, Rascal looking on as if he'd understood every word.

Willa returned to her chair, and Max said, "Have some milk." He shoved the sandwich closer. "A bite to eat."

Rascal barked, drawing their attention to a bird that had landed on the porch railing. Frannie drew him into a sideways hug and, finger over her lips, whispered, "No-no-no!"

"I didn't understand, not fully, anyway, why Mom so willingly made sacrifices and kept things from me. And then Frannie came along." She met Max's eyes. "I know it probably sounds melodramatic, cliché, even, but I'd die for that little girl."

"What it sounds like," he said, "is the truth."

She'd fed morsels of her history to the social worker . . . but only because Alice threatened to withhold help if she didn't. When Anki's curiosity got the better of her, Willa added cursory tidbits. Joe asked about her past—once— but Willa had known he'd find ways to use it against her. She'd kept most of it to herself, believing people couldn't judge what they didn't know. What was it about *this* man that made her feel she'd be safe, baring her soul?

"Mom collapsed at work," she continued. "By then, she'd given up all but her easiest job, as a secretary for a law firm. Her boss called an ambulance, then picked me up at school." She described the scene as it flashed in her memory: her normally energetic mother lying still and quiet and nearly as pale as the sheets beneath her; a virtual parade of nurses and doctors and lab techs; hours of waiting as they put her mom through a succession of tests and scans.

"They diagnosed stage four pancreatic cancer. Sure as I'm sitting here, I know Mom would have tried to protect me from that, too, if the ER doctor hadn't asked me who would help me care for her until . . ." She shook her head, unable to say *until the end*.

"Were there any? People to help, I mean."

"Her boss and coworkers loved her. Everyone loved her. So they took turns, delivering meals, doing light housework, making sure she took her meds while I was in school."

"Good. They helped a lot, then."

"Yes. For a while, they came by once or twice a week." *Until they didn't anymore . . .*

"And when the good deeds proved more demanding than expected, you did it all, alone."

"Yes."

"What about your schooling?"

"It could wait. Mom couldn't."

"All that, while you were little more than a child."

Her childhood had ended when her mother got sick. Admitting it made her feel self-centered and shallow. Instead, she said, "Then her doctor suggested hospice."

Max folded his hands on the table, and after staring at them for a moment, said, "You are a remarkable, admirable woman, Willa Reynolds."

The list of her mistakes sped through her mind. "No, I'm not."

He opened his mouth, no doubt to disagree, but she stopped him with, "I could tell that she was holding on, to spare *me*. I had to make her realize that it was okay to let go of the pain and suffering, that I'd be fine without her."

"And were you?"

In place of an answer, Willa told Max how her mother's boss sat her down, explained the details of the will he'd written for her. "'Frugal living and wise investments of her own parents' inheritance,' he said, "allowed her to prepay the rent and my tuition. So I know what you mean, about working hard to keep your mind off . . . things. Mom went to a lot of trouble to make sure the plans we'd made for my future wouldn't change, just because . . ."

"Because she was not with you anymore."

Nodding, Willa said, "A few minutes before she died, she made me promise that I'd graduate high school, then college."

"And you did."

Willa nodded.

"Let me guess. At the top of your class."

That made her laugh a little. "No, but I held my own."

"And afterward?"

"Afterward," she said on a sigh, "I got a little lost. Made a lot of wrong turns that led to dangerous side roads and dead ends, and took me far, far from God. If my mother had known about any of that, it would have broken her heart."

For the longest time, Max didn't speak. *Should have kept your big mouth shut,* Willa told herself. He'd only listened this long because of his big, caring heart. Did he feel sorry for her? Or was he silently devising ways to avoid her now that she'd admitted her sins?

"Death is cruel."

Willa took a deep breath, released it slowly. If anyone knew about that, it was Max.

"Would you like to see the rest of the house now?"

"I'd love to, but I really should get her home, start supper, and finish my other chores while it's cooking."

"Next time, then."

Next time. His simple, matter-of-fact statement gave her hope that he wasn't just being polite, that he really wanted her to visit again.

The dog's cold nose touched her calf, and Frannie did her best to mimic him. *Children and pets, the perfect distraction . . . and mood lifter.*

Stooping slightly, she looked into the pup's face. "I just *love* that you have one blue eye and one brown!" Straightening, she faced Max. "What did his parents look like?"

"The mother is a border collie. Not a purebred, but she has all the traits: long black-and-white fur, stand-up ears, blue eyes. The father dog was a mysterious stranger, but my guess is Rascal got those brown splotches and the brown eye from him."

"How did you come up with his name? He's so well-behaved!"

"Not at first! As a pup, he got into so much mischief—chewing boots and work gloves and my tools' wooden handles, shredding newspapers, stealing food right off my plate—that one day, in the middle of a well-deserved scolding, I said, 'You are such a rascal!' It fit, so . . .'"

At the mention of his name, Rascal treated them to a doggy smile, and his bushy tail wagged hard enough to stir up a breeze.

"Funny thing, as soon as I named him, his behavior changed. The only time I need to discipline him now is when he barks at the neighbors' livestock."

"And birds," she teased. "I have to say . . . I know people whose faces aren't as expressive. Makes me wonder what he's thinking!"

"He is thinking that the sooner I bring you home, the sooner I can get to work, making the truck safe for our girl here."

"Can Rascal ride with us?"

"No, because until I make the improvements, he will not fit."

"Oh. True." But wait . . . had she heard correctly? Had he just said *our girl*? Willa tensed, and warned herself not to read too much into it. "I'm sorry we're so much trouble."

"Trouble?" He shook his head. "I have no family to spend my time with, so I enjoy it."

It seemed unfair, a real shame, that someone as good and decent as Max had no one to share his life with.

She carried his plate and their glasses to the sink. "We'll make it up to you. I promise."

He said, "Oh?" But she heard "*How?*" And as she searched her mind for the answer, Willa remembered that he still wore the jeans that Frannie's leaky diaper had dampened. "Would you like to change before we go?"

"No, it is fine."

Anki had told her that Max had spent his childhood helping his grandparents work their farm, so she supposed he'd contended with worse stains. Still, she felt obliged to let him take her home so that he could get out of the jeans sooner rather than later.

"I'll run a few repayment ideas past you during our ride home."

"For one thing, you should know that I do not like to repeat myself. It is a waste of time, one of the few things God granted us that, once gone, can never be replaced."

She didn't understand and said so.

"You owe me nothing. I am my own boss and do as I please. Got it?"

"Got it."

He stepped onto the porch. "And for another thing, I will not *ride*. You need more practice. Lots more." He held out his arms and added, "Come to Max, Frannie."

Yet again, he'd said one thing, and she'd heard another: *Come to Max* became *Come to Papa*.

Wishful thinking? she wondered, climbing into the truck.

Chapter Six

Emily walked in the back door, dusting her palms together. "Whew. Next time I try to carry *all* the trash out at one time, remind me that my name isn't Atlas, will ya?"

"You should've let me do it." Willa flexed her right bicep. "I'm taller than you, probably outweigh you by twenty pounds."

"You're stronger, I'll give you that, but unless you fibbed on your job application, that's a bunch of malarkey."

Willa loved working at the Baker Family Clinic, where her duties included taking calls and scheduling appointments, typing patient data into the computer, and tucking tabbed folders into the filing cabinets. She loved parking Li'l Red beside the big post-mounted mailbox, climbing the brick porch steps, and tucking Frannie into the playpen that stood beside Rafe's. Facing the exam room door, Willa looked into the waiting room, where two neat rows of blue upholstered chairs sat against pale yellow walls.

"I don't know what this place looked like before you bought it, but you've done wonders with it."

Emily grinned. "Most of the credit goes to Max. He moved walls, replaced floors, installed new doors and windows, painted, and helped Phillip find and refinish the shelves and filing cabinets."

"Don't tell me he designed the sign, too."

"No, I did that. But Max painted it."

"Anki said you spent most of your inheritance buying all the medical equipment."

"Close, but no cigar. I spent exactly what I had to and not a penny more. The rest? I took a page from Pete's book and invested what was left. God willing, we'll be solvent for another decade."

"Pete?"

"My youngest brother."

"He sounds like a wonderful man."

"Best guy on two feet. Except for Phillip, of course." A fond smile of remembrance lit Emily's face. "That Pete . . . he lived like a monk. Every penny he didn't need for food and rent went toward savings and investments. He left instructions for me to sell his house and car. Once everything was liquidated, I had more than enough to buy the house, make improvements, and furnish it."

"Sounds like you put years into planning the clinic."

"Nope. That happened pretty fast, actually. I met Phillip and Gabe, fell head over heels, as they—" The door *dinged,* and in walked Micah Fisher.

"I know I am early," he said, removing his hat. "I will sit right here until Willa has time to talk with me."

"What? Talk with *me*? But why? About what?" She looked at Emily. "I had no idea when he made the appointment . . ." She held out her hands, palms up. "He said it was time for a routine exam."

Emily picked up a clipboard, stuck a ballpoint under the clasp. "I'll be in my office." She glanced at her watch. "The bishop is our last patient for the day, so after the, um, exam, we'll close up."

After seventy-five grueling hours of studying and memorization, Willa was within weeks of becoming a certified nursing assistant. She'd learned a lot, working beside Emily: Injections. Blood pressure, temperature, and oxygen levels. Sutures. But to conduct a physical examination, all on her own, for someone as important as the bishop! If she had half the confidence in herself that Emily had in her, she might just make it through the next minutes with the bishop.

"Right this way, Bishop Fisher," she said, unpocketing her stethoscope.

He sat in the hard-backed chair beside the exam table. "No, no, Willa. You do not understand. I am not here to *be* examined. I made the appointment to ensure I would have enough time to *conduct* an examination. Of *you*."

"Of me?" A high-pitched nervous giggle popped from her lips. "You're right. I don't understand."

"Please have a seat. Looking up at you is giving me a pain in my neck." Fisher laughed at his own joke, and once she'd settled on the wheeled stool near the door, he cleared his throat. "I am here to talk with you about Maximillian."

She knew that Max spent half of his working hours driving the highways to secure contracts for the company, and the other half using power tools, or balanced at the top of a ladder.

"He's . . . he's all right, isn't he?"

"Yes, yes." The bishop waved her question away. "He is fine . . . physically." His features grew serious, and he regarded her over the wire rims of his glasses. "It is the state of his soul that concerns me."

Now she *really* didn't understand.

"I have spoken with the boy."

Boy? The word didn't come close to describing her do-the-right-thing friend.

"I have spoken with Daniel and Anki, as well."

Fisher slid a forefinger back and forth under his shirt collar. Willa tensed, wondering why the normally composed bishop looked so nervous.

"You see, Willa, Maximillian is Amish. And you? You are *not*."

Everyone in Pleasant Valley respected this man, and near as she could tell, he'd earned it. That alone was enough to prevent her from exhaling a sigh of frustration.

"I'm grateful to be here, living among you, but I assure you, Bishop, I'd never be so presumptuous as to pass myself off as one of you." It had never occurred to her to do such a thing, but even if it had? She'd never get away with it! Her clothes might fool tourists and casual visitors, but Willa was acutely aware that the moment she began to speak, everyone recognized her as an outsider.

"Yes, yes," he said again. "I believe this. But that is not what brings me here."

He drummed an arthritic fingertip on his knee. Tapped the brim of the hat balanced on the other knee. Tapped his foot.

"My eyesight is not what it once was, but *Godheid geprezen,* I still see clearly enough . . ."

Oh, how she wished he'd stop praising God and just *get to the point*!

"Maximillian is Amish, born and bred, and you . . ."

"I am *not*. Yes. We've established that." She got to her feet. If the exam room had been larger, she might have started pacing, too. "Max is a good man. I respect and admire him, and I appreciate him, too. But—"

"He is good, as good as they come."

"May I ask what Anki and Dan said? Do they agree that I'm not worthy of a man like Max?"

The bishop's fair complexion reddened. "It is not a matter of worthiness, dear Willa. It is a matter of faith."

Her mother had been a born-again Christian who'd raised Willa to believe in the mighty power of God. But why waste her breath, telling the bishop things that he couldn't accept?

"I am here to ask if you have considered living the Plain life."

She had, but mostly in passing.

"If your answer is yes, I can help you, as I helped Emily." He got up and, one hand on the doorknob, said, "I will leave you now, but before I go, I must ask something of you . . ."

Would he suggest that she get in touch with Alice, to see if the social worker could find her a job elsewhere . . . in a community that *wasn't* Amish?

"I ask that you pray on your place here. Pray, too, on your place in Maximillian's life."

My place as his friend? If she was just Max's friend, she ought to contact Alice. First chance she got. And ask the woman for help in finding a job in town. Any town. The farther from Pleasant Valley and Oakland, the better.

"At the risk of repeating myself," Fisher said, "I have seen things."

She wanted to ask what, exactly, he thought he'd seen. But the bishop had effectively put her back to the wall; she needed to make the best of her remaining days here, for Frannie's sake more than her own. She couldn't do that without the bishop's blessing.

"I have seen that he cares for you, and that you care for him." He put on his hat. "And this caring? It is much deeper than friendship. So yes, you must ask for the Lord's guidance. He will lead you to the decision that is His will, for all of you."

Willa was about to ask if he'd conducted a similar examination of Max when he hurried past, leaving her alone with her thoughts.

Thoughts of Max. Of Frannie. Of her place here in the community.

One thing was sure: She'd do exactly as the bishop had asked, and pray about everything he'd said. Because if he was right . . . if Max had said or done something to lead the man to believe he also wanted more than friendship . . .

On the other side of the window, she watched as a horse-drawn buggy rolled by. Inside was Simon Miller with his long white beard, and beside him, Rebecca, waving as Fisher made his way down the clinic's stone walkway. The couple had been born right here in Pleasant Valley. Had raised three sons and a daughter, also born right here, and like their parents, all four had married members of the community. Their children would do the same. Was their devoutness rooted in beliefs that had originated in Switzerland, centuries ago? Or simply a matter of habit, of going with the flow because this life was the only life they'd ever known?

Yes, she'd pray. Pray as she'd never prayed before. Because as Fisher had pointed out, her decision would impact Max. And Frannie. For a lifetime.

But what if the bishop was wrong? What if Max wasn't exhibiting feelings of fondness for her? What if instead, he'd consumed a plate of sauerkraut, or had just hit his thumb with a hammer?

She was snickering to herself when Emily walked in.

"Bishop Fisher is a lot of things," she said, "but *comedian* isn't one of them. Out with it. What's so funny?"

"Nothing really." And in truth, the idea that heartburn or pain had made it appear that Max was love-struck, well, that wasn't the least bit funny.

When Willa steered Li'l Red into the Hofmans' drive, she saw Dan out back, slapping paint onto the shed's exterior.

"Let's get you inside for a nap," she said, lifting Frannie from her car seat.

Yet again, she marveled at Max's talents. Not only had he extended the cab three feet into the truck's bed, he'd built an upholstered back seat that was deep enough to safely accommodate the baby seat. When she'd asked how he managed to sand the welds flat and perfectly match the paint and front seat carpeting, he'd grinned and said, "Trade secrets," and nothing more.

She and Frannie had adapted well to life here in Pleasant Valley. She now felt confident that they'd adjust to whatever difficulties they might encounter in the future. And she realized she was hoping that Bishop Fisher's perceptions about Max's feelings for her had been accurate.

Willa made quick work of washing up the dishes Anki had used throughout the day, and slid a chicken into the oven to roast. Boiled potatoes, spinach, and sliced carrots would round out the supper meal quite nicely. With both Anki and Frannie sleeping peacefully, she changed her clothes and walked across the backyard.

Dan had removed everything from the shed's shelves and piled the objects haphazardly on the lawn.

"You are home early today," he said as she began sorting them.

"Slow day," she replied, stacking buckets and baskets. "I had an interesting afternoon, though."

He met her eyes, briefly, then dipped the brush into white paint.

"Bishop Fisher came to see me. Made an appointment and everything."

"Oh? Is the old man sick?"

"Hardly," she said, laughing. "He wanted time to speak to me, privately, to make a few things clear."

The brush stopped, mid-stroke. "What things?"

"He said that he'd paid you and Anki a visit, to see if your opinions matched his."

"Sometimes, the man is as nosy as an old woman."

"So it's true then."

"If you are referring to his questions about you and Max, yes."

It's like that, is it? You're going to force me to pry the information from you, word by word.

"Did the two of you agree with him?"

He stuck the brush tip into the paint can again. "About what?"

"About whether or not I should dive in, headfirst, and become a card-carrying, badge-wearing Amish woman."

Dan laughed. "We do not carry cards. And badges, as you know, would be considered jewelry."

"Yeah, you're right on both counts. But my point was . . . my point *is* . . . do you agree? If I do everything that's required for baptism, could I pass for Amish?"

"Pass?" He moved the ladder, and after re-wetting the brush, climbed onto its first step.

"Dan, help me out a little here, will ya? You've gotten

to know me fairly well in the months I've worked for you—"

"If you do not know by now that you are more a family member than employee, you might not be smart enough to pass the bishop's tests."

She returned his smile, then finished organizing the tools that Dan would hang on the hooks screwed into the shed's walls: Rakes. Brooms. Shovels. Hoes. After tucking hand tools into one bucket, she lined up screwdrivers, pliers, wrenches, and hammers. Rooting in the pail that now held sandpaper, edging tape, and paintbrushes, Willa grabbed a narrow brush and dipped it into the paint.

"What do you hope to do with that?"

"I have a steady hand," she said, looking up at him. "If I paint the window frames and the doorframes, we'll be finished in time for supper."

"We? This kind of work is not expected of you. Besides, you will splatter your dress. Maybe even your shoes."

"I enjoy this kind of work." She showed him the threadbare cuffs and collar. "I can peel paint off the boots, and if the dress gets dirty, it won't matter much, now will it? And anyway, I've cut out all the pieces for a new one. To-morrow, since I don't have clinic hours, I'll see about borrowing Anki's sewing machine and stitch them together."

"I was wondering when you would make cleaning rags of that old . . . rag."

Again, Willa returned his grin, and as her brush slid alongside the right-side window frame, she said, "Planning to put your trousers into the rag bag?"

He glanced down at the dots and spatters that covered his trousers. "I will wear them next time I paint."

"I'm surprised you and Max don't have coveralls for this kind of work."

"We do." He snickered. "I was too lazy to go to the construction trailer to get them."

Using a fingertip, she pretended to write in the air: "'Daniel Hofman admits a moment of laziness.' Wouldn't that make a fantastic headline in *The Budget*!"

"No one pays any mind to that thing."

He knew very well that the newspaper provided for the Amish what the Internet gave the rest of the world. Community members looked forward to its delivery. Looked forward to sharing recipes, gardening tips, and items for sale found inside, too.

"You haven't answered my question."

"What question?"

She exhaled a frustrated sigh. "Do you think it's possible for someone like me to fit in here? Permanently, I mean?"

"Yes, I suppose you could."

She heard the unspoken *if* in his voice: If she vowed to abide by the *Ordnung*, which included baptism and so much more. Well, she had an *if* of her own: *If Emily could do it, why not me?*

Her next question wouldn't be as easy for him to answer, so Willa chose her words carefully.

"During our talk today, the bishop hinted that Max has feelings for me. Not just 'you're a good egg, Willa,' or 'you're kinda likeable,' but, you know, *feelings*. Is that what he told you and Anki?"

Dan climbed down from the ladder. She waited, thinking he'd reload his brush. But he didn't. Instead, he laid it crosswise on the can's lid. Then, one hand on each of her shoulders, he turned her to face him.

"Fisher implied as much with us, yes. But Max has not said such to me. At least, not in so many words. Since he has not, I do not feel as though I am betraying a confidence. And . . . this is only my opinion, you understand."

Willa stared into his eyes. How had she spent months working for him, sharing meals with him, without noticing the tiny black flecks that peppered the blue of his eyes?

"If it turns out that he thinks I'm a toad," she said, "I promise not to hold you accountable."

Stepping away from Willa, he used a stir stick to mix the paint. Then, one thumb behind a suspender, he said, "The life he has lived . . . it has made him old before his time. But when your name comes up, he changes."

"Changes, *how*?"

He mumbled something unintelligible. "Women," he said, shoving the brush deep into the paint. "Why do all of you demand specifics?" He wiped the bristles against the rim. "Just be satisfied that you are on his mind . . . in a positive way."

Willa supposed he'd made a good point. She went back to work, and repeated his words in her mind: *You are on his mind . . . in a positive way . . .*

"You and Max are friends," she began, "so if you don't want to answer this, I'll understand."

Dan whispered something like "*Goodness*" under his breath.

"There are quite a few unmarried women in Pleasant Valley. Has Max ever, you know, has he, is he . . . interested in any of them?"

"If Max confided such things in me, I would not answer your question."

Well, she'd asked for honesty . . .

"But since he has not, I can freely say I know of no one that he is—as you put it—interested in."

Relief swept over her.

"However, I cannot say the same thing for the young women." Dan used the brush as a pointer. "One in particular has let it be known that she is willing to begin the Bible studies, songs, and prayers that prepare couples for marriage."

Willa nearly dropped the paintbrush. Marriage! She hadn't expected to hear *that*!

"Does Max know? Is he aware that she has set her cap for him?"

"Cap. Very funny. But if you made a list of things that boy notices, you could roll it up and put it into a thimble."

Did it mean Max hadn't noticed? Or wasn't he interested?

She finished painting the window trim, then started on the doorframe.

"Sorry to have disappointed you," Dan said. "The Amish . . . we do not believe in flirtation, like you English do. This woman, she cannot flutter her eyelashes or giggle to let him know how she feels."

Willa decided not to ask how Dan knew so much about the pre-dating rules of Englishers.

"Is that how you and Frannie's father got together?" he asked.

She'd been completely up front about how she'd made ends meet before moving here, so it made no sense to beat around the proverbial bush. Still, she and Dan had been getting along well. Willa hated to throw cold water on the warm conversation, and decided to keep her answers short and sweet.

"No," she said, "Joe and I . . . we met quite by accident." *When I was looking for drugs, and he was selling them.*

"It took great faith to leave that life, to start over."

She half expected him to take her to task for the way

she'd escaped. Instead, he said, "I am glad, for your sake and Frannie's, and for Anki's sake, too, that you made that choice." He looked over his shoulder to add, "Do you regret it?"

"No." And she didn't.

"But this life is very different from your old one."

"That's just one of the reasons I don't regret the change."

"Mmm. And Max. He is one of those reasons?"

"Well, he wasn't . . . not at first, anyway."

"Do you think this Joe will try to find you, to demand his rights as Frannie's father?"

It would be a lie if she said the question had never occurred to her. "I can only hope and pray that he has moved on and forgotten all about us."

"Yes. I have said the same prayer."

"Why?"

"Anki and I, we . . . we do not want to lose you."

In response to his quiet admission, tears stung her eyes.

"I don't know what to say, except, I'm surprised."

"But why?"

Because I'm relieved. And touched to find out that you care about me.

"May I ask . . . is Max one of the reasons you want to stay here in Pleasant Valley?" Dan questioned softly. "I only ask because I think the bishop might be onto something, and I just wonder . . ."

He pursed his lips. Clearly, he'd decided not to complete his thought. Not that she could blame him. So Willa said, "I don't blame you for being concerned on Max's behalf. You're well aware of everything I did in the past, and how Max's background made him the man he is today. He's so good and decent. Vulnerable, too. So it's only natural that those who love him are worried."

"About what?"

"That I might hurt him." The words were hard to say. So hard that Willa bit her lower lip.

"Worry," Dan said, "is little more than a waste of time. Whatever happens, will happen. And it will be God's will. For Max, *and* for you."

For several moments, the only sound in the shed was the quiet *shhh-ing* of their brushes, stroking the plywood walls. Dan broke the silence with, "If he is looking for family ties, he could do worse, far worse than you, Willa Reynolds."

Coming from the no-frills Amishman, it was high praise indeed. Overjoyed, Willa crossed the space in four short steps and threw her arms around his neck. "Why, Dan, that's just about the nicest thing anyone has ever said to me!"

He was blushing when he peeled her off. "I hope that is not true," he said, returning to his work, "because if it is, you have lived a deprived life, just like Max. You will make a good pair, I think!"

Not even in her wildest dreams would Willa have thought Dan, of all people, might become a true and trusted friend.

Yes, with every passing day, she had a better idea why this place was called Pleasant Valley!

Chapter Seven

Max had stopped by to let Dan know he was driving into Frostburg, and to find out if he or Anki needed anything in town.

But he had another reason for his visit too. Mostly, he wanted to ask Willa if Li'l Red had been giving her any problems. Anki shushed him before he had a chance to knock.

"Frannie is napping," she said, "and Willa is out back, helping Dan in the shed."

He might have asked how Anki was feeling if he didn't already know. She'd sunk into another of her dark moods, as evidenced by the unemotional set to her face and her monotone words. After thanking her for the information, Max followed the flagstone path that led from the front walk to the shed. The flowers and precise cut of the grass that edged it were Willa's work. How she managed to keep up with meals, laundry, house- and yard work while caring for Frannie and working for Emily was anyone's guess. More amazing was the fact that long hours and hard work never seemed to dampen her pleasant spirit.

If he had to guess who'd arranged the yard tools in by-task order, he'd say that was Willa, too. Last summer, when Dan slipped from a ladder and sprained an ankle,

Max had volunteered to mow the lawn; it had almost taken as long to untangle the mower's handles from rakes, shovels, and broom handles as it had to get the job done. In the construction trailer, it never took more than five minutes for Dan to make a mess of blueprints, pencils, pens, and rulers. Yes, this systematic tidiness was Willa's work, all right.

Smiling, he approached the shed, planning to compliment her on her organizational skills, but something he heard stopped him: Dan, asking Willa if she thought Frannie's father might show up someday to claim what he believed was his. Max agreed with his partner. If she left Pleasant Valley, he, too, would be disappointed.

Their next few exchanges were too quiet and too murmured to understand. Something about the bishop. He took a careful step forward, leaned toward the shed just in time to hear her say, "He's so good and decent. Vulnerable, too. So it's only natural that those who love him are worried." Then, Dan's voice: "About what?" After a moment of silence, she replied, "That I might hurt him."

Max turned, headed back the way he'd come, intent on making a lot more noise as he approached the shed this time. When she saw him in the doorway, her smile brightened the newly painted shed. Streaks of white paint crisscrossed her cheeks, and she said, "Well hi! What're *you* doing here?"

It wasn't easy, tearing his gaze from hers to look at Dan, but he managed it.

"Going to town," he said, removing his hat. "Thought I would see if you or Anki need me to pick anything up while I am there."

Dan's eyes narrowed slightly. "Nothing that I can think of."

"But how nice of you to ask," Willa said. "Did Anki tell you that we're out of coffee grounds?"

"No." Because he hadn't asked what she might need. "But I will get some coffee and drop it off on my way home."

"You are going to Frostburg now? With a door in your truck?" Dan wanted to know.

"No," he said again. "I will stop at the Bakers', get it hung, and then make my way into town."

"Once you finish with the door, their job is done, yah?"

Max nodded. "Yah."

"They are pleased?"

Another nod.

"Why wouldn't they be!" Willa said. "I was there just yesterday, and Emily showed me around. It's beautiful, Max, just beautiful. My grandfather made furniture in his spare time and took great pride in his miters. He would have *drooled* over yours. Why, they're almost invisible!"

"Thank you." He spun the hat, like a steering wheel. "You need nothing else? Just coffee?"

"That's it," she said, taking a step closer. "What time do you expect to get back?"

He did the math in his head: an hour's drive to town, thirty, maybe forty-five minutes to meet with the developer, fifteen minutes at the hardware store, an hour back. And a quick stop at the grocery store for coffee. "Three, four hours, at most."

"Perfect. You'll have supper with us, then. There's just enough of a chill in the air that I thought chicken stew would be nice. With dumplings. And apple pie, afterward."

Max looked at Dan. He'd paid for the food, after all, and the meal would take place at his kitchen table.

Something between a grin and a smirk lifted the corners

of the man's mouth. "You are a full-grown man," he said,
and went back to painting. "The decision is yours alone."

"I hope you'll say yes." Willa wiped her brush's bristles
on a rag. "Because . . . *Frannie* would love to see you."

Max thought of what she'd said to Dan, just before he
made his presence known. Did he dare hope that she'd
accented her little girl's name to mask the fact that *she*
wanted to see him, too? Smiling, he put on his hat. "Yes,
that sounds good. Very good."

He started for the door, then stopped in the opening.
"But if traffic makes me late, please, eat without me."

Dan chuckled. "You need not worry about that, partner!"

Max left them, so eager about the chance to spend
time with Willa again that he nearly overshot the Bakers'
driveway.

As he hammered the nursery door's hinge pin into
place, Emily said, "Everything looks wonderful, Max, just
wonderful. Nicer, even, than we expected." She switched
Rafe from her left hip to the right. "You're such a good friend.
A talented one, too. Thanks so much!"

"Just doing my job."

And it was true. Other than adding a few hours to the
end of each workday to complete the addition ahead of the
deadline, he hadn't treated the Bakers' job differently from
any other.

"Gabe loves his new room," Phillip said. "Told me just
the other day how much he enjoys looking out those big
windows and seeing the mountains." He tweaked the baby's
nose. "Rafe will love his room, too . . . if his mother ever
lets him move into it."

"Now, now," she said, "he'll be a big boy soon enough. Let's not rush things, all right?"

Phillip met Max's eyes. "Women," he said, winking.

He heard love in the words and envied his friend. Just a mile or so up the road, he had a house, too. A good investment, he'd told himself during the building phase. Once, while wandering the nearly empty rooms, he'd remembered the welcoming touches his mother had given the old family home . . . tablecloths, doilies, flowers on the porch. Remembered, too, laughing and roughhousing with his siblings. *What were you thinking, building a house this big?* he'd demanded of himself. A one-room cabin would have been more than sufficient for a man such as he, who'd spend the rest of his days alone.

"I wonder if you could stop by the clinic in the next day or so," Emily was saying. "That last storm blew a few shingles off the roof. Phillip could do it, but he's swamped."

"One of those good things/bad things scenarios," her husband said. "I can't remember being busier, thanks to the rumor that's going around about an early winter. Farmers scrambling to harvest earlier than normal, everyone else determined to winterize everything with a motor."

Max understood, perfectly. "Extra business is a blessing. Especially when you have two healthy young boys to feed."

Phillip nodded toward the Alleghenies, where angry gray skies shrouded Backbone Mountain. "People are saying it'll be like the blizzard of seventy-eight. Thirty to forty inches of snow, with twenty-foot drifts."

"We will pray they are wrong. But just in case, I need to line up some indoor work." Facing Emily, Max added, "How about if I fix that roof tomorrow morning, first thing?"

"I'll be there by eight o'clock, so any time after that is fine."

Max returned the hammer to his tool kit. "Perfect. I can check out the roof and go straight to town from there."

"One of those inside jobs you were talking about?" Phillip asked.

"No, God willing, that contract will keep us busy through next fall. If the weather does not interfere, that is."

"Why's that?"

"The housing development is near Frostburg."

"Oh wow," Emily said. "Definitely not an easy trek on mountain roads . . . in snow and ice. And speaking of roads, Willa is on the schedule tomorrow." She smiled. "That girl is something else. Two jobs. A baby. Nursing classes. If I had half her energy, I might just complete a to-do list once in a while!"

Nursing classes? It was the first Max had heard about them.

Laughing, Phillip said, "Help me understand how one thing has anything to do with the other."

She grinned. "Well, thanks to Max's loaning her the truck, Willa will be on the road, going and coming to the clinic, anyway."

"Oh yeah. It makes complete sense now!"

When little Rafe heard the adults laughing, he threw back his head and joined in, which invited a hug from both of his parents. Yet again, longing closed in on Max.

"Which school does Willa attend?"

"She's enrolled in an online class. Once she passes the test, she'll work for me to finish up her hourly requirement. And then, our Willa will be a certified nursing assistant."

Not sure how he felt about that, Max pointed out several

faint scrapes on the door he'd just hung. "After I see about your roof, I will touch them up."

"No need for that," Phillip said. "You left paint out back. I'll take care of it, right now, before the sun sets."

Good, Max said to himself, because he did *not* want to be late for dinner.

He thought about Willa during the drive to Frostburg, and as he walked the aisles at the hardware store. It was all he could do to keep his mind on the meeting with the foreman in charge of the housing development, because the image of her happy, paint-spattered face seemed stamped onto his brain. She filled his mind at the grocery store, too, as he picked up a three-pound can of coffee for her, and on the way home, he could almost taste the chicken stew that would be waiting when he arrived at the Hofmans'.

"You will help with the dishes," he told himself. "And when the work is done, you will ask her to take a walk."

Max glanced out the driver's window and saw the female passenger in the car beside him lean forward, trying to look around him to see the person he was talking to. Chuckling under his breath, he stared straight ahead. "She thinks you are *krankzinnig.*" And maybe he was just a little crazy . . . over Willa.

The hour-long ride had felt more like four. Even the walk from the end of the driveway to the porch stretched ahead like a mile. Now, reaching over the console, Max grabbed the brown paper bag that held her coffee. And the box of fudge he'd bought on the spur of the moment.

"Hope she likes chocolate," he muttered, stepping onto the porch.

"Who *doesn't* like it?"

The quiet voice startled him. "Anki. I didn't see you there."

"I needed fresh air."

Threatening clouds had moved in from the mountains. A blast of cold wind spun new-fallen leaves into mini-tornadoes that skittered across the floorboards. She shivered as they hopped into the flower beds below.

Max put down the grocery sack. "How long have you been out here?" he asked, pulling the patchwork quilt higher on her shoulders.

"An hour? Two?" She shrugged.

He remembered the Anki who'd enjoyed life, who smiled and teased Dan, and loved visiting with the locals and tourists who browsed in her shop. When had she turned into this quiet, unhappy woman? The better question was *why*?

"I will go inside, see if Willa needs help setting the table. Can I bring you anything? Hot tea, maybe?"

She stared into the distance, looking as gloomy as the sky. If only he knew what to do or say to lift her spirits, for Dan's sake as much as hers.

Max opened the screen door, rapped softly on the windowpane.

"It's open," Willa called out.

Her voice was music to his ears, especially after listening to Anki's sad monotone.

He plunked the bag onto the counter. "Your coffee . . ."

"Oh, you're a lifesaver. Thank you. We'll thank you again in the morning!" She reached into the bag. "I'll put the can away, and then—"

A soft gasp escaped her lips as she removed the box of fudge.

"That is for you," he said. "A thank-you gift for inviting me to supper."

Before he knew what was happening, she was in his arms, punctuating every "Thank you!" with a tiny kiss, pressed to his cheeks.

All too soon, she stepped away, still hugging the box to her chest. "You're something else, you know that!" She slid off the curlicue blue ribbon that held the lid in place. When Frannie saw the bright color, she let out an excited squeal.

"Aw, sweet girl, you can't have this. It wouldn't be safe." Now, she opened the box and pinched off a corner of the fudge. "How about if we share a little of this, instead?"

Like a baby bird, Frannie sat flapping her hands, open-mouthed and waiting to be fed. Willa put a second small piece on the high-chair tray, then broke off a larger piece, and Max found himself watching closely, to see if she'd enjoyed it as much as her baby girl.

She surprised him yet again by walking right up to him. "Say ahh . . ."

He held up a hand. "No, no," he said, laughing. "The fudge is for you!"

"There's more than enough to share. C'mon now, open wide . . ."

. . . and for a reason he couldn't explain, that's exactly what he did.

She stood on tiptoe and fed him the candy, staying put until he closed his mouth. Nodding approvingly, Willa said, "My turn!" and bit into a piece. Then, eyes closed, she exhaled a dreamy sigh. "Oh. My. Goodness. It's . . . it's delicious."

They stood nearly toe to toe, and the closeness scared him. Because if she kept standing there, looking pretty and sweet, he might just kiss her. Max licked his lips just as she opened her eyes. Something—he couldn't define it—flashed across her lovely features. Affection?

Gratitude? *Willingness*? Whatever it was only made him want to kiss her *more*.

"Mmm-mmm," she said, crossing back to the stove, "can you smell those dumplings? I can't wait to taste them. It's a new recipe." Looking at him, she winked. "Do you mind being my guinea pig?"

"Small price to pay for a good meal," he said.

By now, Frannie had finished both pieces of fudge, and began impatiently slapping the tray. "Mo'e?" she said. "Mama . . . mo'e?"

Willa quickly handed her a cracker and told Max, "It isn't fudge, but it'll have to do. Can't have her filling up on candy when there's stew in the pot, right?"

"What can I do to help? Set the table?"

"You can let Dan know we'll sit down to eat in just a few minutes. He's out back, putting the tools back into the shed."

"Happy to," he said, meaning it. "What about Anki? Is she all right out there, all by herself? It's getting pretty cold . . ."

Just that fast, Willa's joy was replaced by a look of maternal concern. "I'll get her." She put the fudge onto a cupboard shelf and grabbed her shawl, and on the way to the door, she sighed. "Just between you and me? Tomorrow, I'm going to talk with Emily, see if she has any ideas. Because no one should go through life sad all the time."

"You might want to run that by Dan first. He is a very private man."

Willa, eyes narrowed and one hand on her hip, repeated, "Just between you and me? He had his chance. Years' worth of chances." She opened the door. "Will you keep an eye on Frannie while I talk Anki into coming inside?"

He glanced at the baby, who was staring at him and smiling.

"She won't be any trouble. Anki, on the other hand . . ." Willa sighed again. "If the baby starts to fuss, just pick her up. She loves being carried from window to window, so she can look outside."

The door had barely clicked shut when Frannie's lower lip jutted out and tears pooled in her eyes. "Mama?"

A baby. Alone, in his care. What had he been thinking! *You weren't thinking, Lambright.* Well, that wasn't entirely true. He'd been thinking all right . . . about Willa's long-lashed amber eyes, the reddish-brown bun that usually hid under a cap, lips that had parted slightly, as if she'd known exactly how close he'd come to kissing them . . .

"Mama . . ." Frannie was on the verge of crying now. Oh, how he wished he'd paid closer attention to where Willa had found that cracker!

"All right, little angel," he said, bending to inspect the high chair, "how do I get you out of this contraption, huh?"

She leaned right and left, following his movements.

"Ah-ha," he said, grasping the metal pulls on the tray's underside.

Frannie, sensing that soon she'd be free, giggled wildly. Max set the tray aside and unfastened the plastic belt around her belly.

"There we go," he said, hoisting her onto his hip. "Your mama tells me you like peeking out of the windows. Let us find out if this is true." He carried her into the parlor. "See there? See the big tree?"

Dimpled hands reached out, and she leaned forward, as if to grasp the fluttering leaves. As he tightened his grip to prevent her from tumbling from his arms, she faced him.

The eye contact lasted only a second, but it told him that she understood: He'd pulled her close to keep her from falling. As if to prove it, she pressed a dimpled hand to each of his cheeks and treated him to a baby-toothed grin.

"Max," she said, and rested her head on his shoulder.

Something stirred in his heart, and he found himself wanting to protect her, not just in this moment, but for the rest of her life, as any good father would.

"Ah, sweet Frannie," he whispered. "You are a blessing from God."

"God," she echoed, and sat up, pointing outside.

"Yes, He made the trees. And the sky and the clouds." Max moved from window to window, showing her the shed, the barn, and when he got to the chicken coop, she said, "Bawk-bawk-bawk!"

Laughing, he kissed her cheek. "Yes, sweet Frannie, that is what the chickens say."

The kitchen door opened and Willa led Anki inside. He thought surely Frannie would kick up a fuss, insist that he hand her over to her mother. Instead, in a voice barely more than a whisper, she said, "Max," and snuggled against his shoulder again. And again, that unfamiliar something moved in his heart. Aside from time spent with kids Gabe's age and older, Max knew little to nothing about children. He had a feeling that Frannie would put an end to his obliviousness.

He carried her into the kitchen as Willa said, "Anki! Your hands are like ice!" She settled Anki at the table. "The water in the teakettle is good and hot. I'll brew you a cup of tea."

Anki looked up, patted Willa's hand. "You are a blessing from God."

Frannie lifted her head and, taking his face in her hands again, forced him to meet her eyes. "God?"

"Yes, I believe you are right, little angel. He *is* here."

Willa smiled. "I knew you were a natural."

"Natural what?" Anki asked.

She placed the mug on the table. "Drink up, now, so it'll warm you, right down to your toes."

Willa was smiling when she said it. Smiling, and looking at *him*.

Frannie wiggled and whined. "Down," she said, aiming a fat forefinger at the floor. "F'annie down."

"Not yet, sweet girl. Mama needs to set the table, and you'd just be underfoot." She lifted the high chair's tray. "I'm sure your arms are tired. . . ."

"No, they are not." He nodded toward the row of wooden pegs on the wall beside the door. "Is that her wrap? I will bring her with me, to let Dan know supper is almost ready."

"You . . . you want to take her outside?"

"Unless you have a reason I should not . . ."

Willa grabbed the small pink cloak and quickly draped it around the baby's shoulders. She tied a matching hat under her chin, too. "You won't let her get down out there, right?"

"I will not," he said, and made his way onto the porch.

Instantly, the baby's mood brightened. "T'ee," she said, pointing at the maple that grew beside the porch. She said it again, this time pointing at the oak that shaded the shed.

Dan stood in the doorway, a rake in one hand, a hoe in the other, grinning like a fool. "What is this? You are a nursemaid now?"

"Just helping out. Willa said to tell you supper is ready."

"Where is Anki?"

"In the kitchen, sipping tea. She is fine." *Thanks to Willa.*

Dan disappeared into the shed long enough to hang the tools, then stepped up beside Max. He threw a thumb over his shoulder and knuckled Frannie's cheek. "Thanks to your mama, the place almost looks good enough to live in."

"Mama," the baby echoed.

Laughing, Max lifted her high, then put her onto his shoulders. She filled both hands with his hair and held on tight as delighted giggles rained down on him.

"Is my little angel *big*?"

"Big!" she echoed.

Dan climbed the porch steps beside them. Feigning a frown, he said, "I fear the net has been cast."

"What does that mean?"

Dan held the door as Max ducked so Frannie's head would clear the doorjamb.

"Something smells delicious!" Rolling up his sleeves, he stepped up to the sink, lathered his hands, and said over his shoulder, "Willa, you are a blessing from God."

Max tucked Frannie into her high chair, fastened the protective belt and slid the tray into place, then removed her hat and sweater and hung them up. Dan cracked his knuckles and took his place at the head of the table. Anki sent a weak smile his way. And Willa placed the big stewpot in the center of the table, scooted the high chair closer, and pulled out the chair opposite Dan's.

"Have a seat, Max," she said, sitting beside him.

With no announcement or fanfare, all eyes closed, all heads bowed . . . even Frannie's. As they each silently thanked God for the meal and other blessings that made it possible, Max thanked Him for the newly awakened feelings churning in his heart: He'd sat in this very chair, dozens of times, but he'd never felt *at home*. That, he knew, was Willa's doing. She'd warmed this once-stark house with rib-sticking food and the scent of fresh-baked pie. Potted plants lined the windowsill, and the bright blue-and-white tablecloth still bore the creases of her iron.

Was the awareness a sign? A message from God, telling him that with Willa at his side, *his* house, too, could feel like a home?

"Open your eyes, Max, or your first spoonful of stew is sure to miss your mouth."

Dan's voice brought him back to the here and now. More than ever, he wanted time alone with Willa. Time to see if she felt as he did . . .

. . . about the years that stretched out ahead of them.

Chapter Eight

"You certainly made that job fast and easy," Willa said. "Thanks, Max!"

"I have an ulterior motive."

"Oh?" She hung her apron on a peg near the door.

"Will you walk with me? Outside?"

"I wish I could, but I have to tuck Frannie in for the night, and sometimes, it takes a while."

"There are blueprints in my truck. I can look them over while you're upstairs."

She glanced toward the window, where darkness had made the glass seem like a black mirror. "Well, all right, if you're sure you don't mind waiting . . ."

"Not at all." He'd wait until midnight if it took that long!

A few minutes later, he'd spread the drawings on the kitchen table, and kept them flat by placing a big glass saltshaker on one corner, the pepper on the other.

"What is this?" Dan asked, leaning over the plans.

"Albertson gave these to me at our meeting today. It shows the layout of the homes that he wants us to build in Frostburg."

"Half-acre lots?"

"Quarter acre."

"Clever man, that Albertson, calling the development Royal Valley Overlook."

Max had to agree. The name drew a picture of expansive vistas, and while it was true that most lots would have views of Big Savage Mountain in the Allegheny range, buyers would live in very close proximity to their neighbors.

"Frostburg is a college town. Students cannot afford single-family homes."

"True, but Albertson believes their parents can."

Dan only shook his head.

"We will give them their money's worth. We always do."

"And make money ourselves?"

Max peeled back the top sheet and exposed the job's projected cost-to-profit numbers.

"Do these figures consider materials? Wear and tear on our vehicles? Time spent, driving to and from the jobsite?"

Max thought he understood his partner's lack of enthusiasm for the project: His unpredictable wife would be alone for a minimum of ten hours, every workday.

"Willa will look after Anki."

"She is a hard worker, I will grant you that. But she cannot be in two places at once."

In other words, she couldn't take care of Anki while working for Emily. He needed to find a way to ease his partner's mind, because this contract would keep their employees working for at least two years . . . important, since every man had a wife and children to provide for.

"We can alternate days, overseeing the job. And . . . and perhaps we can ask Willa to adjust her hours at the clinic. Or, I am happy to run the site while you manage the schedule, from here at our office. One way or another, we can make sure Anki will never be alone."

The man's fist hit the table hard enough to overturn the

salt and pepper shakers. Max righted them and dusted black and white granules from the drawings.

"If only she would stop behaving like a spoiled child!"

It wasn't the first time Max had heard such a complaint, and unless Anki's condition improved dramatically—and soon—it wouldn't be the last.

"Every day, I pray, Max. I have prayed until my knees are callused. Yet every day, she is worse, not better." Dan slumped into a chair, held his head in his hands. "I do not know what to do."

Max searched his heart, hoping God would deliver words to comfort and reassure his friend. A verse from Psalms came to mind: *O God, do not remain silent.* But memorized Scripture was the last thing Dan needed to hear right now. Max knew this because after the fatal buggy accident, after the deadly house fire, and a hundred times in between, he, too, had questioned God. The lesson—if he could call it that—wasn't terribly satisfying: Faith is the ability to trust that, in the end, the Lord will make things right; from God's viewpoint, heaven is *the end*. Not an easy concept for mere humans, who yearn for here-and-now physical and emotional comforts, to accept.

"Together," Max said, placing a hand on Dan's shoulder, "we will help Anki."

If the words sounded this trivial and hollow in his own ears, he could only imagine how empty they'd sounded to Dan.

Willa came into the room, and instantly, the atmosphere lightened.

"Frannie is asleep?" Max asked.

"Amazingly, yes." She glanced at the blueprints. "Your next job?"

Dan said, "It is. And we will need your help."

Laughing, Willa said, "*My* help? I can sketch a bit, but

I doubt I could draw house plans. And I don't know a thing about house building. Why, last time I tried to hammer a nail, it bent sideways, and I smashed my thumb!"

Max smiled. "Help with Anki," he explained. "Once we begin, our days will be long . . ."

"Oh. Right. I get it. And you don't want her to be alone." She met Dan's eyes. "I'm happy to step in whenever and wherever I'm needed."

He still looked troubled. "There are only so many hours in a day, and you are only one woman."

"Oh ye of little faith," she teased.

Her joke fell flat, and cringing slightly, Willa slid the salt and pepper shakers aside and rolled up the drawings. "Correct me if I'm wrong, but as far as I know, only one thing is written in stone." Snapping the rubber band into place on the tube, she added, "The Ten Commandments."

Dan's brow furrowed.

"If we're all willing to be flexible, things will work out. Emily won't mind if I ask her to make a few changes to my schedule. She's been an absolute doll, helping me with my classes."

"I do not want my private business spread throughout Pleasant Valley," he thundered.

"Don't worry, Dan, I promise to explain things in a way that doesn't give away too many details."

Interesting choice of words, Max thought, because in this case, a few details might be just enough to tell the bigger story.

"I suppose I have no choice but to take you at your word." Dan filled a glass with water, and after gulping it down, said, "There are many things to do in the morning. I am going to bed. And pray that sleep comes quickly."

"I'll pray for that, too," Willa told him.

"As will I."

Dan responded with a grunt, then fixed his gaze on Max. "You have many things to do tomorrow, as well."

The not-so-subtle hint wasn't lost on Max or Willa, who didn't talk as Dan's footsteps squeaked up the stairs and across the floor above them. When all was quiet, she whispered, "Lord, bless him with a good night's rest."

"Amen. If anyone needs it, it is Dan."

She opened a sideboard drawer and withdrew a clean apron. As she unfolded it, Max said, "What do you need that for?"

The rules were clear: Modest clothing honored the Lord and protected men from impure thoughts. He couldn't speak for others, but he had better things to think about than what might be hidden under dresses and aprons.

"I need the pockets." She clicked a switch on the palm-size receiver in her hand, and a dozen tiny red lights flashed. "I only use this when Frannie is in her crib, and I need to step outside. The transmitter is upstairs. If she fusses, even a little bit, I can hear it, and get to her before she disturbs Dan and Anki."

Willa held the unit to his ear, and he heard Frannie's steady, soft breaths. Oh, what a sweet, peaceful sound!

"Once she's down for the night, she rarely wakes up, but why take chances, right?" She dropped it into her pocket. "Dan and Anki have been good to Frannie and me, y'know? I don't want to disturb their rest if I can help it."

"Yes, of course."

Willa grabbed her shawl, and while draping it around her shoulders, said, "Where's your jacket?"

"In the truck." He picked up the roll of blueprints and opened the door. "The better question is, what about *you*? Is that flimsy thing going to keep you warm out there?"

"If it doesn't, we'll just have to come back inside, won't we?"

She said it so matter-of-factly that Max had to agree.

He eased the door shut behind them and led the way down the porch steps. "Looks like the clouds have lifted."

"I love nights like this, when the moon is *just* bright enough to make everything look . . . *creepy*. One of these days, I'm going to paint a scene just like this one."

"This is the first time I have heard anyone refer to moonlight as creepy." Grinning, he shrugged into his jacket. "I did not realize you were a painter."

"Not in the league of Rembrandt or Van Gogh, but I can hold my own with any kindergarten class in the state!"

"It has been my experience that when people say such things about their talents, it is because they *have* talents."

"Is Rascal home alone?" she asked, walking beside him.

"He is."

"I feel bad for the poor thing. He seems to love people. It's a shame that he has to spend so much time alone."

"He has the run of the house, and once I'm home, he doesn't leave my side."

"I'm not surprised."

Was she . . . was she *judging* him? For the way he cared for his *dog*? Max didn't quite know what to make of that.

"Dan is pretty worried about Anki, isn't he?"

"Seems so," Max said.

"I feel so helpless. I wish I knew what to do for her, what to say, to make her happy."

"As I told Dan, we can pray. There is little more we can do."

"I disagree. *Emily* could probably help her. There are hundreds of medications on the market designed to control depression."

"She is in God's hands."

"That's just silly, Max. God blessed Emily—and doctors everywhere—with the talent and know-how to care for people like Anki. Who's to say He isn't just waiting for one of us to use our heads for something other than to hold up our hats, and take the necessary steps to get her the help she needs?"

She wasn't afraid to speak her mind, that much was sure!

"I just have to think of a way to tell Emily, without telling her, you know, because—"

"Because Dan specifically told you not to."

"No, what he *said* was, he didn't want their business spread all over town. Emily is legally bound by doctor-patient confidentiality. And even if the oath wasn't in play, she's a good person. She'll keep things to herself for no reason other than it's the right thing to do."

"You should discuss it with Dan first."

"Mmm-hmm . . ."

Max didn't like this turn of the conversation. Yes, Anki needed help, and while it was possible that Emily could provide it, *Dan* was the head of the Hofman house, and such decisions should be his, and his alone. It didn't set well with him, knowing that Willa seemed bound and determined to interfere . . . even if it was for good reason.

She stopped walking and wrapped the shawl tighter around her. "Would you just look at that! If I had my paints and brushes, I'd do my best to capture that on canvas."

Max followed her line of vision, where moonlight skimmed the mountaintops, glowing bright on the highest peaks and fading as it slipped into rocky outcroppings.

"So you really are a painter?"

"Well, it's fun to pretend. Sometimes." Ducking deeper into the shawl, she said, "I'll bet the mountains are even more beautiful, covered with snow."

"Beautiful, yes, and dangerous."

"Dangerous?"

"Icy roads. Livestock trapped in snowdrifts. The weight of it making roofs collapse."

"Oh. Yeah. That's too bad. But . . . why not appreciate the beauty of it now, before all that ugly stuff happens, right?"

He had to agree. Why *not* focus on the good, rather than the bad?

They walked to the end of the drive, where Willa peeked into the mailbox. "Nothing," she said.

"You seem surprised. But why, when the mailman makes his rounds in the morning?"

"I keep hoping . . ." She closed the door. "See, when I first got to Pleasant Valley, Dan sometimes asked me to check the mail after supper, to see if a neighbor might have left a little note, asking Anki to set aside a jar of apple butter or preserves from her shop."

Max couldn't remember the last time Anki had spent any time in her shop. It was one of Dan's main complaints, because he didn't know what to do with the products that lined the shelves . . . shelves he'd built at her request.

"When was the last time he got a note?"

"A long time, I'm guessing. *I* never found one."

"Does Dan still ask you to check?"

Willa shook her head. "No."

Her voice had gone from lively and musical to quiet and dull. She spent a lot of time with Anki. It must be hard, he thought, watching the woman sink deeper and deeper into despair. Max slowed his pace, hoping words would materialize . . . words that might bolster her spirits. Unfortunately, none did.

"It's just all so . . . *weird*."

"How so?"

"I've been fooling myself, I guess. Here I was, going around thinking I've been a friend to her. Not just because that's part of my job, but because I genuinely like her. At first, I did *all* the cooking and cleaning. The yard work. The laundry. So that she could rest. Relax. Enjoy the weather. Or read. Bake. *Anything* that would shake her out of the doldrums. But even with all that extra time, she just . . ." Willa exhaled a breath of exasperation. "Then I thought . . . maybe by doing *too* much, I was making her feel useless in her own home. So I held back a bit. Found excuses to ask for her help: Frannie was teething; the wicker laundry basket gave me a splinter; I had a headache . . ."

"Did she help you?"

"Sort of. She put *time* into things, but if she finished a chore—which was rare—I had to redo it." Another sigh. "You have no idea how many times I've wished her parents were still alive. Maybe they could talk some sense into her."

She picked up the pace again. "I'm sorry. I didn't mean to ramble on and on. It's just . . ."

Willa kicked at a rock on the walk, sent it flying in a high arch. As it nestled into the dew-sparkled grass, she said, "I understand Anki had a sister?"

"Yes. A twin."

"What happened to her?"

"She was shunned. A little more than a year ago."

Willa gasped. Stopped walking. "I don't use the word 'hate' often, but I hate that word. *Why* was she shunned?"

"A fellow moved to Oakland. Englisher. Visited the shop, often enough to turn Abigail's head. She was told to choose . . . him or the Plain life." Max shrugged. "She chose poorly."

"Why do you say that?"

"You know what shunning *is*, right?"

"Of course I do. It's when the community boots a member out, lock, stock, apron, and *kapp,* and cuts off all communication with family and friends. She must have loved him a lot. Must have believed he'd make her happy enough to make the sacrifices worthwhile."

"Her choice did not make her happy."

"Oh really." She faced him, head on. "And just how do *you* know?"

She sounded miffed. Looked it, too, standing straight, arms crossed over her chest.

"If you weren't allowed to talk to her, weren't allowed to see her, how can you—how can *anyone*—know that he didn't make her happy?"

"Have you heard the old saying, 'Bad news travels like wildfire'?"

"Of course I have." She clucked her tongue. "The Amish don't have a copyright on adages, you know."

He bit back a chuckle. Did she have any idea how cute she looked, all fired up like that?

"Well? How did you find out?"

"The bad news reached us, delivered by the friend of a friend, just about six months ago."

"So . . . do you mean to say that Anki got the news . . . right before I arrived? Why didn't someone tell me!"

A beam of moonlight that had sneaked between the clouds lit her face, and seeing her wide, worried eyes, Max wished he hadn't brought up the subject.

"Well, you can't just drop a bombshell like that without finishing the story! What happened to her?"

"Abigail . . . She . . . took her own life."

Willa gasped again. "What! Why? How?"

"We will never know with any certainty *why,* but . . . she slit her wrists."

"Oh no. Poor Anki. No wonder she's such a mess. Twins are connected, heart and soul and mind. She probably feels as though part of *her* died when . . ."

She shivered, head to toe, and Max had a feeling the chill air wasn't the only cause. "And you know what? Suicide tendencies can be hereditary. I need to do a better job, a whole lot better job, taking care of Anki. I can't replace her sister—no one can—but I can be her friend. I can—"

"If you ask me, you are already doing far more for her than anyone in her life."

"No, no . . ." She shook her head. "In college, I took a few psychology classes, so I can make a few wild guesses about what she might be feeling. Guesses. Nothing more. Anki needs professional help. Which is why she needs to talk with Emily. Before it's too late."

"Too late? For what?"

Willa stopped walking again, pulled the shawl higher, and shivered again. Max slipped out of his jacket, draped it over her shoulders.

"Goodness, that feels wonderful," she said. "Thanks, Max. I'll give it right back, soon as I warm up a bit. We don't want *you* catching a chill. You have a big new job and can't afford to start off on the wrong foot . . . a sickly foot!"

"I appreciate your concern." And he did. "But . . . too late for what?" he repeated.

"Like I said, I'm not an expert. Far from it. But here's how I see it: Anki is like someone in a leaky rowboat. She only has one oar. And while the boat is filling with water, she's paddling in circles. If she doesn't get help . . ."

"She will sink." Nodding, Max said, "Now I understand. But Willa, she is Dan's problem, not yours."

Willa hid behind her hands, as if unable to believe he'd say such a thing. When she came out of hiding, her big eyes flashed with indignance, and unless he was mistaken, she intended to tell him *why,* right now!

But just as she opened her mouth, a cat bulleted past them. It startled him. Startled Willa more, and she practically leaped into his arms.

"What's chasing it?" she asked, clinging to him. "It's running like its tail is on fire!"

"I didn't see anything." But then, Max was only aware of Willa, pressed so close that he felt her heart, beating hard against his chest. His arms automatically went around her, and without thinking twice about it, he pulled her closer still. Eyes shut tight, he inhaled the faint scent of bath soap, clinging to her smooth cheek. In his mind's eye, he imagined pulling out the pins that held the loose bun in place and filling his hands with her hair. Would it feel as thick, as silky, as it looked? He'd seen it glisten in the sunlight. Would it shine as brightly in the moonbeams?

She ended the idyllic moment by stepping back, just enough to allow him to skim both palms from her shoulders to her fingers. "Willa! You're ice-cold. We should go inside, where you can get warm."

"Good idea. But . . ." She looked up, met his eyes, and smiled. "But let's not go inside just yet, okay? I'll grab that box of fudge. And a quilt. We can enjoy both, *and* the view, from the porch swing."

And just like that, she darted away, leaving behind nothing but the memory of her sweet-smelling warmth. He followed, and while waiting for her to get the blanket and the candy, Max sat alone, staring at the door, willing her to walk through it, and return to his side. She was gone all of a minute, and he missed her for every second of it.

"Hold this," she said, thrusting the white box into his

hands. Sitting beside him, she unfolded the quilt, gave it a flap, and tucked it around them. "There now. *That* oughta keep us warm!"

"Your energy alone will accomplish that," he agreed.

She reached across his chest, opened the box. "Fudge?"

"No, thanks. I am still stuffed."

"Which reminds me, before you leave, I'm gonna pack up some stew for you to take home. Pie, too. There's plenty. Don't worry, Dan won't mind. He isn't overly fond of leftovers, so he'll be happy the food isn't going to waste. And tomorrow, after work, all you'll have to do is heat it up, and voila, supper!"

"I have a question for you. . . ."

"I'm an open book." She took a big bite of fudge.

"How do you manage it? Caring for Frannie, running the Hofmans' house, looking after Anki, working at the clinic, studying to become a nurse . . ." Turning slightly, he looked into her face. "Two questions." He held up a forefinger. "When did you decide to go back to school?" The index finger joined it. "Do you ever sleep?"

"Nursing *assistant*," she corrected. "I decided the first day I worked with Emily. Such fulfilling work. I'll be able to help her so much more once I've earned my certification. And to answer your second question, of course I sleep. Although I'll admit, I've never needed the prescribed eight hours. What about you? I'm guessing six hours. Five, even."

"Close enough." He slept reasonably well . . . when nightmares didn't wake him.

"Hmm . . . Why do I hear a 'but' in that answer?"

"I, ah . . ."

"You sleep well, *bu-u-ut* . . ."

"But sometimes, I have dreams."

"Unhappy dreams?"

He looked toward the mountains, where the clouds now hid the peaks. Hid the moon, too. "You could say that, I suppose."

"I'm a good listener . . ."

"So you said."

"Okay. I can take a hint." She patted his hand. "No more sad talk. So tell me, what's your happiest childhood memory?"

Leaning back, he stared at the porch ceiling, where the white-painted beadboard reflected golden lamplight, glowing from the other side of the window.

"We did a lot of fishing, my brothers and I," he began, "using poles handcrafted by my father."

"Was your dad a carpenter, like you?"

"He was."

"Your brothers, too?"

"Taught us everything he knew. About woodworking. About fishing. About life. I miss him, still."

"Sounds like he was a wonderful man, a wonderful, loving father who left you with lots of wonderful memories. I sorta envy that."

The comment reminded him that, some time ago, Willa had told him she'd never known her father.

"I'm sorry you lost him, Max." This time when she patted his hand, she bumped the fudge box. "Give me that," she said, relieving him of it. "Holding it outside the quilt is making *your* hands cold." She put it on the low table on her side of the swing. "How about if I brew you a cup of tea?"

"No, but thanks." Because to make the tea, she'd have to leave him again.

She didn't question his response. Instead, she snuggled

close. "You already know that I was an only child. How many kids in your family?"

"Five. Two brothers, two sisters. I was the youngest."

"Five," she said, her voice softly thoughtful. "Wow. I'll bet the house was bursting with laughter!"

"We had our share of fun, but we had our share of squabbles, too."

"You squeeze that many personalities under one roof, occasional disagreements are bound to happen."

Usually, talk of his family made him sad, left him regretting all the years he'd lost to senseless tragedy. Tonight, with Willa at his side, the memories woke good feelings. She was a remarkable woman, all right!

He nodded at Li'l Red, parked beside his pickup. "Is the truck giving you any problems?"

"Nope. Not even one. I love her!" She turned to face him and, one hand on his forearm, said, "Have I told you lately how much I appreciate you?"

Max chuckled. "That is not why I asked about the truck. In truth, I should be thanking *you*."

She tucked her hands back under the quilt. "For what?"

"Let me put it this way: A good horse needs exercise every day. Food and water. A thorough brushing. Think of Li'l Red as a horse. By driving her, you're keeping her healthy."

"Hmm. If you say so."

"I say so."

The next moments slid past in quiet comfort, with neither of them feeling the need to speak. An owl hooted, hushing the cicadas' song. Soon, the bugs would hibernate, and the nights would grow silent.

"I wonder what time it is. . . ."

He didn't think it possible for Willa to move closer to his side . . . until she did.

"I don't know," she said. "Frannie is sound asleep and I'm enjoying myself, so . . ." She sat up suddenly. "What a selfish ninny I am! You have to get up early for—"

"Will you work here tomorrow, or at the clinic?"

"Both, but Emily won't need me until noon."

He got up then, and she darted inside.

"Where are you going?"

"To pack up the leftovers. What else?"

Leaning his backside against the counter, Max folded his arms over his chest, watching as she ladled stew into a deep bowl, and arranged three dumplings on top. Next, she positioned two wedges of pie on a saucer, and covered both with plastic wrap. After unfolding a big brown paper bag, she slid both into it and rolled down the top.

"There," she said, handing it to him. "Tomorrow's supper."

"I will return the dishes."

"Of course you will."

She followed him to the door.

"No need for you to go back out there. Stay here, where it is warm."

"You can't tell me what to do," she teased, "because you're not the boss of me, Maximillian Lambright!"

He had a feeling that would be just as true if *her* last name was Lambright!

Side by side, they followed the flagstone path to his truck. Willa stepped back when he opened the driver's door, waiting for him to lean in and place the leftovers on the passenger seat. Just as he prepared to slide in behind the wheel, she put herself between him and the seat.

"I meant what I said earlier," she whispered.

Max chuckled. "You said a lot. Help a guy out, will you?"

Willa laughed, too. "This was a good night. A very good

night. I liked talking with you. I hope we can do it again. Soon."

Oh, I hope so, too, he thought.

She shrugged out of his jacket, and hanging it around his shoulders, said, "Thanks for the loan of the truck. For the fudge. For the coffee. For the jacket. It really did the trick. Seems you're always looking out for me. One of these days, I'll find a way to show you how much I appreciate you."

"I like doing things for you." *I only wish I could do more!*

Then, she was in his arms again—her choice, and not inspired by a terrified feline—and again, he pulled her close. He stood, heart hammering, pulse pounding as those long-lashed lids drifted shut, as she stood on tiptoe, as she leaned in . . . and kissed him.

Max had never been lost in the desert, but right now, with his lips pressed to hers, he knew exactly how those disoriented wanderers must have felt as those first sips of water quenched their thirst.

"*That* isn't very romantic," she said, halting the perfect, satisfying moment.

"Really? I thought it was pretty good . . ."

"It was." She wiggled her eyebrows. "But you're supposed to *close your eyes* when you kiss a girl."

She sure didn't kiss like any girl he'd known! Not that he'd known many. His first experience consisted of a brief, chaste relationship that ended when the girl's family moved to Ohio to save her grandfather's ailing farm. With the second, things crossed the intimacy boundary, twice. But Max hadn't been her first beau, and as he soon found out, he wasn't her last: She left him to marry a wealthy widower in Lancaster, without even saying good-bye. In his mind, the heartache was penance enough, so he'd asked God's forgiveness in the privacy of his mind instead of the bishop's parlor.

"Next time," he said, "I will close them."

As if to test him, she stood on tiptoe again. He kept his promise, and quickly discovered how much more pleasant it felt when he wasn't distracted by her big, beautiful eyes.

"Good night, Max. Sweet dreams."

"You too."

Once she reached the porch, he slid behind the wheel and watched the lights go dark, room by room. Secure in the knowledge that she was safe upstairs with Frannie, he closed the driver's door and fired up the engine.

All the way home, strange emotions rolled through his mind. He thought about how effortless it all seemed to her . . . cooking, setting the table, filling deep bowls with steaming stew . . . Almost singlehandedly, she'd kept the conversation flowing, eliciting giggles from Frannie, chuckles from Dan, a genuine smile from Anki. He'd laughed, too. A man would have to be made of stone, he thought, *not* to react to her antics.

In his own driveway now, he threw the gearshift into park and let the truck idle as he stared through the wind-shield, remembering the scent and taste of her, the steady beat of her heart. He felt silly. Off-balance. Besotted. Grinning, he turned off the truck.

The instant he opened the front door, Rascal darted outside. "Good boy," he said. "Go. Do your business, and I will give you a treat."

The dog disappeared into the woods beyond the house. Max could hear him, digging and scratching for just the right spot to make his deposit. *The mutt can make a major project of the simplest thing,* he thought.

Rascal dashed toward him, tail wagging and dog lips drawn back in a jubilant, *welcome home* smile. It made

Max think of what Willa had said, about the dog being too sociable to be left without human companionship for very long. The pup was well behaved and obedient. Lately, he hadn't brought him to very many jobsites. But starting tomorrow . . .

Crouching to scratch his companion's head, Max said, "I am happy to see you too, buddy. Are you ready for your treat?"

The dog bounced along beside him, and once inside, sat statue-still while Max grabbed a biscuit from the jar on top of the fridge. Lifting a paw, Rascal tilted his head, and while waiting for his master to deliver the treat, licked his chops.

Max licked his own lips, mildly surprised that he could still taste the fudgy sweetness of Willa's kiss. *You are imagining things.*

As he hung the jacket on the hook near the door, he realized that her shawl still clung to its fleece lining. He pressed his face into the soft knit, inhaled deeply; her scent might not be there in the morning. He hung the wrap beside his jacket, then poured himself a glass of water. Carrying it to the parlor, he settled into his easy chair, thinking to read a verse or two of Scripture, just until he felt drowsy, before heading upstairs. Willa had wished him sweet dreams. She'd be in them. He was sure of it. So Max had no doubt that they'd be pleasant.

A disquieting thought popped into his head:

What if her ardent advances—welcome though they were—hadn't been motivated by feelings for *him*, but by feelings of *indebtedness*? She was smarter than most men he knew, smart enough to understand that the Frannie-inspired alterations he'd made to Li'l Red had lessened the truck's resale value. How many times since handing over the keys had he heard her say, "How will I ever repay you!"

Surely she didn't think to do it by . . .

Max shook his head. No. That couldn't be.

Unless . . .

Had he said or done something to make her believe such a thing? If so, how would he prove her wrong . . . and make it up to her!

She'd overcome hardship, without letting it harden *her*. It couldn't have been easy, moving here, working two jobs, trying her best to blend into life in Pleasant Valley . . . all while mothering Frannie and trying to help Anki.

A woman like that should never have to feel beholden to anyone, for any reason.

From now on, he'd do a better job of letting her know that she was enough. No strings attached. No reimbursement necessary.

Even if that meant *friendship* was all they'd ever share.

Chapter Nine

The damp, earthy scent of autumn filled the air as Max and Rascal made their way from the house to the shop. The dog zigzagged beside him, alternately barking and growling at the roof.

"Easy," Max said, "it is only acorns, falling from the trees."

A chipmunk ducked in and out of the woodpile, instigating a whole new yapping frenzy. "Get down from there, you crazy mutt. It took me days to make that perfect stack."

So far, he'd chopped two cords. Not enough to last the winter, but it would be, once he'd cut up the aspens that had fallen during summer's last thunderstorm. It wouldn't be easy, what with the jobs already on the schedule, but if he got up an hour earlier every day . . .

Willa had guessed he only needed five hours of sleep, and she'd been on target. He'd never met anyone more perceptive, or less afraid of sharing her insights, either. Her future patients didn't realize how lucky they'd be, having her looking out for them.

She'd looked out for Frannie. For Dan and Anki. If he could find a way to make her believe that she didn't owe him anything, and never would, she'd look out for him, too.

Max had given a lot of thought to her new warmth toward him. In his opinion, it could be explained in a word: fear. He didn't know how long she'd been with her ex . . . long enough to convince her that every generous act, however small, must be repaid . . . somehow. The fact that she'd escaped Frannie's father—and hidden where he'd never think to look for her—told Max all he needed to know about the man.

In time, she'd realize that Max was nothing like him. And until she did, he'd make sure to emphasize that he expected nothing from her.

Sawdust covered the workshop floor and coated the workbench and every tool on it. Few things irked him more than gritty hammers and plier handles. For now, he'd wipe down what he'd need for today's job. Tonight, he'd give the entire place—and every tool in it—a proper cleaning. Hard work had kept him from dwelling on the loss of his family. God willing, it would keep his mind off Willa, too.

"Max! Are you in there?"

He went to the door and found a dozen boys gathered in front of the workshop.

"No school today?" he teased.

Gabe held up a battered, yellowing baseball. "We need an umpire."

And he held up the hammer he'd just polished. "Sorry, guys. I am leaving for work soon."

"Not today," Marcus said. "Next Saturday."

Ben nodded enthusiastically. "For the Swan Meadow fundraiser. People pay to get in, and the money pays for stuff we need at the school."

Although Max had never attended, he'd heard about the

annual event, where people came from miles around to check out homemade baked goods and handmade crafts.

"Sounds good. Next weekend, you say?"

Twelve heads bobbed up and down. Twelve eager faces smiled.

"You don't work on Saturday, right?"

"No, Gabe . . . unless I have fallen behind during the week."

"You can catch up. We will help you!"

The boys cheered in agreement.

Ben ground a fist into his new catcher's mitt. "This day is special. Only happens one time a year."

"Yeah," his brother agreed. "Say you'll do it, Max!"

"*Please?*" the team harmonized.

"The coach from Lancaster won't play us if we don't have an umpire."

Gabe looked up at him. Not long ago, the boy was gaunt and pale. Now, he stood strong and full-bodied, pink-cheeked and confident, thanks in no small part to Emily, who'd arranged for the heart operation that saved his life. Gabe deserved credit, too, for following doctors' orders, even when they were tough.

"A week from *this* Saturday, you say?"

"Yeah, but we sure could use some practice before that," Ben hinted. "Are you working this Saturday?"

Day after tomorrow . . . Max had checked the calendar just this morning, and didn't recall anything written in either weekend box.

"Okay, I can give you a couple of hours. But it will have to be bright and early. I have wood to chop and stack."

The boys encircled him, shaking his hand, patting his back, issuing heartfelt thank-yous. Then they ran off, laughing and high-fiving one another, calling dibs on at-bat order and positions in the field. Max remembered the last game he'd umpired, during the festival. They didn't know it yet, but he had other ideas about how to make the most of their individual talents.

Back in the shop, he scribbled *Swan Meadow Fundraiser* on the calendar. Dropping the hammer into his tool kit, he walked to his truck. For the boys' sake, he hoped for good weather. For his own, too, because what bachelor wouldn't look forward to home cooking and baked goods?

And maybe, just maybe, Willa would be there.

Willa stood at Emily's side, doing her best to keep their patient from squirming.

"I just want to peek at your throat," Emily said, holding up a tongue depressor.

Willa reached behind her, plucked another one from the dispenser on the counter. "Here y'go, li'l guy."

Pudgy hands turned it over, inspecting it as carefully as a lab tech, looking for germs. It distracted the little boy long enough for Emily to shine a light into his mouth.

"It isn't strep," she told the worried mom, "but it is a little red. He doesn't have a fever, so it could be nothing more than fall allergies. Make sure he drinks plenty of water. If you have soup on the stove, that'll help, too."

The woman gathered up her son. "Thank you, Dr. Baker. Thank you so much. I am sorry . . . I cannot pay this time . . ."

This time? Like so many others, the woman had never paid for clinic services.

"I will bring you a pie. Phillip likes apple, yah?"

"That isn't necessary, Rebecca . . ."

"Oh, but it is. My husband and I do not believe in indebtedness."

Nodding, Emily smiled. "I've yet to see a pie that Phillip *doesn't* like, so any flavor will do."

The waiting room was empty, so Willa used the free time wisely. First, she typed the details of their last case into the computer. Next, she scrubbed down the exam room and prepped it for the next patient. Working here filled her with pride as few things in her life had. It was an honor to work with and learn from Emily, who'd used her inheritance to build the Baker Free Clinic, where anyone who walked through the door received medical services and peace of mind, whether or not they could afford to pay for them. Willa's friendship with Emily was yet another reason to love her life here in Pleasant Valley.

Emily stood in her office doorway, grinning at their babies, who tossed toys back and forth from one playpen to the other. "Aren't they adorable!"

"They get along really well." Willa laughed. "I hope that'll last."

Emily laughed, too. "Why? Are you entertaining the idea of an arranged marriage?"

"Good grief, no! They deserve to grow up, fall in love, and choose their life mates, the way you and Phillip did."

A wistful smile lifted the corners of Emily's mouth. "Yeah, God sure knew what He was doing, putting us together. I can't imagine being happier."

"You deserve it. Not only because you're terrific people, but because of all you've done for Pleasant Valley."

Emily looked confused.

"Your brother left you a lot of money, and instead of frittering it away on *stuff*, you built this place. Phillip could have insisted that you invest it in his shop. Or land. A new truck for his business. Instead, he cooperates with you in every way imaginable. And the beneficiaries are the people who live here."

"What a nice thing to say! But to be honest, I think both Phillip and I get more out of this place than we put into it."

The admission didn't surprise Willa at all, and she said so.

"What's this I hear about a *thing* between you and Max?"

"*Thing?*"

"Don't look so shocked. This is a tight-knit community. Sneeze . . . someone on the other side of town will holler, 'God bless you!'"

"I . . . I don't know what you heard but—"

"Actually, I didn't hear anything." Emily stood beside Willa, and resting both elbows on the counter, said, "I see it with my own eyes."

Willa knew she needed to be careful with everything she said about him, because like Dan, Max valued his privacy.

"He's a very kind, generous man. Without his truck, I couldn't work here."

"C'mon, Willa. Surely you don't think he gave you those keys so you could work here."

"To be honest, I don't know why he's so good to me."

"Really?" Straightening, Emily huffed. "He's crazy about you. If I can see that, why can't you?"

She wanted to ask what, exactly, Emily thought she'd seen. Because after the other night, when she'd made a spectacle of herself, he'd been strangely distant. *And who could blame him*?

"What's this?" Emily moved in close, cupped Willa's chin in her palm. "Tears? Why?"

It took less than two minutes to let it out, starting with

the way she'd invited him to supper, ending with that memory-making, dream-inspiring kiss.

"He knows about my background . . . the drugs, the rehab, unwed mother . . . The way I behaved, he probably thinks I have no morals at all!"

"You're way too hard on yourself. I'm sure none of that matters to him, not even a little bit."

"Then why hasn't he stopped by, not even to return Anki's bowls?"

"Because he hasn't finished the leftovers yet?"

She plucked a tissue from the box on the counter. "I wish it was that simple," she said, then dried her eyes and blew her nose.

"For years and years, Max and Phillip have been like this." Emily crossed index finger over pointer. "I don't know him all that well, but I know Phillip. If Max was a judgmental, self-righteous jerk, well, Phillip wouldn't think so highly of him. So it's *that* simple."

"I hope you're right. I really do."

"Have a little faith. And exercise some patience."

"Says the woman who turned her entire life around for a guy she'd known for two months." Willa blew her nose again, then laughed. "I hear things, too, y'know."

"That was different. While Gabe was in the hospital, we were together, a *lot*. Afterward, too. So the number of hours a normal couple spends together before saying I do? You can multiply that by a hundred."

"I'd give anything to spend more time with him."

The bell above the door jangled, and Max walked in, holding a bloody towel around his forearm.

"What happened to you!" Willa said, rushing to his side.

"Lost my balance on the ladder. Might have a concussion, too, if the nail hadn't caught me."

Emily joined them, and peeling back the towel, exposed

the long, jagged cut. Pressing the towel back into place, she faced Willa. "Take him to Exam Room One. He'll need stitches and a tetanus shot."

"You . . . you want *me* to take care of him?"

"Why not? You've watched me give injections and stitch bigger wounds than that." She gave Willa a gentle shove. "Get a move on. He's lookin' a bit green around the gills. Call me when you've finished so I can give it my stamp of approval."

Once Emily closed her office door, Willa grasped his elbow and led the way down the hall. Patting the papered seat of the exam table, she said, "Hop on up here while I get things ready."

After scrubbing up at the small sink, she snapped on a pair of blue surgical gloves and prepared a suture tray: lidocaine syringe, gauze, adhesive tape, antiseptic solution, hemostats, toothed forceps, scissors, needle driver . . . *Well, the supplies are here* . . . Now, all Willa needed was the courage to perform the procedure, all on her own. Eyes closed, she held her breath and asked God to guide her hands.

Willa set a stainless steel pan beside him on the exam table, placed a leak-proof pad across his thighs, and covered it with sterile drapes to absorb blood and cleaning solutions. Then, gingerly, she removed the blood-soaked towel and tossed it aside. The laceration was long—six, maybe seven inches—and at least half an inch deep. She picked up the bottle of iodine, and before upending it, said, "Does it hurt much?"

"Only my pride, for letting this happen."

Smiling, she warned him that the antiseptic might sting, and when he nodded, she drenched the wound. He cringed, but only a little. A good thing, because Willa didn't know how she'd react to seeing him in real pain, especially if she caused it.

Using sterile gauze pads, she wiped blood from the skin surrounding the gash.

"This is just a little anesthetic," she said, unwrapping the lidocaine syringe. "It'll numb the area, so you won't feel much more than a few tugs as I stitch you up."

She could tell that Max was about to say, as so many of Emily's male patients had, that he could tough it out without the numbing medication.

"It'll be over before you know it," she said, giving him the first stick. "I can't risk that you'll lurch or jerk while I work."

"I did not realize you were a poet."

Willa looked at him, just long enough to read the playful smile in his eyes, then depressed the plunger. It took five additional pricks to deliver the entire vial, and once she'd emptied it, she dropped it into the biohazard container beside her.

She tugged off her bloodied gloves and added them to the container. "It'll take a minute or two to do its job. And while it does . . ." She aimed the gooseneck lamp at the slash, then wriggled into clean gloves. ". . . I'll look for dirt, or anything else that might have worked its way into the cut." Using the smooth-edged forceps, she held the sides of the wound back. "Last thing you need is to get an infection, right?"

"Right." .

"I don't see anything. And you're lucky. That nail completely missed the radial artery. The ulnar, too." Touching the forceps' tip to his skin, Willa said, "Feel that?"

"No. Not really."

She exhaled a shaky breath.

"No need to be nervous. You will do fine. I just know it."

"Nervous? Me?" Willa laughed.

"Can you hem a dress?"

"Yes . . ."

"And repair a seam?"

"Yes . . ."

"This is no different."

Except that if I drop a stitch on a seam or a hem on a dress, I can rip it out and start over. . . .

"I trust you," he said. "One hundred percent."

"Well, then, let's get busy." *Start in the middle,* she reminded herself, *then work your way up, then down . . .*

"Gabe and his cousins, and a bunch of other boys stopped by my shop this morning."

"Why?"

"A team from Lancaster will be here for the Swan Meadow fundraiser and the boys want to play them. But only if they have an umpire."

"When is it?"

"Two Saturdays from now. This week, they want me to oversee a practice game."

"I'm not surprised."

"About . . . ?"

"First, that they asked you. You're patient. I know this from personal experience, because when you were teaching me how to drive Li'l Red, you never raised your voice. Not even when it sounded like I might grind the gears to dust."

Max laughed. "You remembered most of what your mother showed you. That made you a pretty good student."

"And second, you're one of the most honest, fair-minded men I know."

"Careful now, you will make me blush."

"Done," she announced, dropping the curved needle into the container. "Sixteen sutures. I probably could have gotten away with twelve, but the closer together they are, the smaller the scar."

Max inspected the work and gave it an approving nod. "Good work, Nurse Reynolds. Now I will not have to worry about scaring off marriage prospects."

Willa pretended she hadn't heard the comment. *He's joking,* she told herself. Better that than cope with the possibility that he had prospects in mind.

She rinsed the sutures with more lidocaine and patted the area dry with gauze pads. Using a cotton swab, she spread antibiotic ointment over the wound, covered it with a gauze pad, and wrapped it with an adhesive bandage.

"Keep it clean and dry," she instructed, "and come back day after tomorrow, so I can change the bandage and make sure infection hasn't set in."

"Will do." He stood, uncuffed his red-stained shirt-sleeve, and said, "How much do I owe you?"

She tore off the bloodied paper and gave the roll a jerk, until clean paper covered the exam table. Giving it a pat, she said, "We aren't finished yet. You scraped yourself on a nail. That could spell trouble. Big trouble. And that means a tetanus shot."

Another pair of gloves hit the trash bin before she rolled up the sleeve of his uninjured arm.

"Another pair of gloves?"

"Can't be too careful where my precious friends are concerned!"

Something flickered in his eyes, reminiscent of the way he'd looked the other night, when she'd thrown herself at him like a desperate maiden woman. *Be quiet, you nincompoop,* she scolded, *and just do your job.*

Willa spread a sterile mat on the rolling cart and pulled

it closer. After tearing open the alcohol pad, she rubbed it across his bicep and picked up the syringe.

"Relax, and you'll hardly feel it," she said. And when his muscle softened, she inserted the needle. Slapping the small, round bandage into place, she pulled down his sleeve. "*Now* we're finished," she said, and buttoned the cuff.

He squeezed her hand. "I have said it before, but it bears repeating. You are quite a woman, Willa Reynolds."

"Yes, she is," Emily said. "I don't know how I managed without her. And *that* bears repeating, too."

Max didn't let go of her hand. Instead, he said, "How much do I owe you, Dr. Baker?"

"No need to stand on formality, Mr. Lambright." Emily laughed. "As Willa can tell you, we have no set prices. Those who can afford to, pay what they feel is fair."

Standing, he pulled out his wallet and withdrew bills of several denominations.

"I suppose you cannot accept tips," he joked, pressing them into Willa's palm. When she laughed and shook her head, he faced Emily. "Will you and Phillip join Gabe at the school fundraiser?"

"I'm sure we will. I wouldn't feel right, letting him go that far on his scooter. Are you going, too?"

"That boy of yours coerced me into umpiring the baseball game, so yes, I am."

"I'll pack a few extra sandwiches, and you can eat with us after the game. Willa, what about you?"

"I need to ask about Dan and Anki's plans. If I can talk her into it, we'll be there, too."

"Wonderful! I'll make fried chicken, instead, enough for all of us."

"I'll bring potato salad. And lemonade. And pie!"

Max walked to the door. "You two are making me hungry." He held up his bandaged arm. "Thank you, Willa. I will be back. Two days, right?"

"Right. And remember . . . clean and dry . . ."

He winked, put on his hat, and closed the door behind him.

"See?" Emily said. "You handled that like a pro. Except . . ."

Willa hid behind her hands. "Oh no. I forgot to call you, so you could make sure I didn't make any mistakes!"

"It's all right."

"You won't get into trouble?"

"No. Students make little mistakes like that all the time. If anyone asks, I'll blame it on your overzealousness. And any state official who meets you won't have any trouble believing that!"

"Still . . . I'll be more careful from now on. A lot more careful. You have my word."

"How are things with Max?"

Emily wasn't referring to his emergency visit to the clinic. Her wily grin was a dead giveaway.

"Fine, I guess."

"What's that famous saying about fooling your friends?"

In junior high, Willa had written a paper about Abe Lincoln, and used the quote, verbatim: *You can fool all the people some of the time and some of the people all the time, but you cannot fool all the people all the time.*

"History wasn't my best subject," she said.

"He held your hand. And stared into your eyes. If you ask me, the love bug bit that man, *hard.*"

"No disrespect, boss, but I didn't ask."

"There's no shame in admitting that you're cap over apron crazy about him."

"So what if I am? He's Amish. I'm not."

"But you could be . . ."

"I wouldn't know where to begin."

"If people took Bishop Fisher at face value, they'd avoid him like the plague. He's all bark, no bite, as the saying goes, but believe me, if not for him, Phillip and I would still be ships in the night. Talk to him. What could it hurt? And a little tip? He loves apple pie."

"Wow. I don't think I've ever heard a sentence with that many clichés packed into it."

"Yeah, well, you want my advice? You'll stop beating around the bush. It's a waste of time, and unnecessarily hard on the shrubbery."

Emily laughed at her own joke, then said, "Be honest with me: Do you love Max?"

"Maybe." Willa shrugged. "Probably."

"Do you hate it here at Pleasant Valley?"

"The longer I'm here, the better I like it."

"Any hang-ups about the Amish? Things you think are weird, stuff you disagree with?"

She shook her head. "No. It took some getting used to, but I like the ease and peace of mind that comes from 'living Plain.'" Willa met Emily's eyes. "You've been here a while now. Do you ever regret becoming Amish?"

"Nope."

The simple, straightforward answer gave Willa hope.

"Was it hard, learning all the 'get baptized' stuff?"

"It might have been . . . without good incentive."

"Phillip and Gabe, you mean."

"Yup."

"But Em . . . you had something to offer these people. This clinic has made such a positive difference in their lives. What do I have to give?"

"What makes you think they expect something from you?"

"I don't know. It's just . . . that's how life has always been: You want something, you'd better be prepared to pay for it. I think maybe that's what put Max off."

"Put him off?"

"You say he held my hand, looked into my eyes. I can't put my finger on it, but something's 'off.' When I threw myself at him the other night, I might have given him the impression that I'm willing to, um, pay for services rendered . . . with my body."

"I told you before, Max isn't like that. But you disagree. There's only one way to find out which one of us is right."

"Ask him," they said together.

Willa laughed, then said, "Here's a cliché for you: Easier said than done!"

Emily was quiet for a long moment. "You asked earlier what you have to give," she said. "Soon, you'll be a bona fide nursing assistant. But even without the certificate . . . You're smart and personable. Caring. Dedicated. A good friend."

"Just call me Rascal," Willa kidded, "your loyal companion."

"See there? You can't even crack a joke without somehow including him."

Willa couldn't very well deny it.

"Have you ever considered leaving here? Pleasant Valley, I mean?"

"At first, I thought about it a lot."

"But then you met Max." Emily drummed her fingers on the counter. "Here's some food for thought: Are you thinking about becoming Amish, just for him? Or would you want to live the life anyway?"

"I . . . I never really thought about it."

"Well, you'd better." She scooped up Rafe, stuffed him into his woolly blue coat.

Emily was right. Oh, so right! Because marriage was a big, important, life-changing step, a lifelong commitment that would alter her life *and* Frannie's.

"I'm going home . . ." Emily put on her own coat, slung Rafe's diaper bag over one shoulder, her medical bag over the other. ". . . and pray that you'll figure things out before it's too late."

Too late for what? Willa wondered.

"I know exactly what you're going through. Want to hear what helped me most?"

Willa wasn't sure that she did. And yet she said, "Sure . . ."

"I just kept telling myself if He wanted us together, He'd make it happen. At the risk of over-cliché-ing, here's one more for the road: 'Give it to God.' It's that simple . . . and that complicated." She kissed Rafe's cheek, pushed open the door, and said, "See you tomorrow."

The bell above the door tinkled, and Frannie said, "Mama?"

Willa picked her up. "Yes, sweet girl, we're going home, too. Want to help Mama turn out the lights and lock up?"

They walked from room to room, checking window latches and flicking switches. It wasn't until she powered down the computer that Willa realized how dark it was outside.

"The days are getting shorter," she said, helping Frannie into her coat. "Winter will be here before we know it. That means we need to go into town, buy us some boots. Mittens. Scarves and warm hats."

"Hat!" Frannie echoed, patting her own head. She grew

serious and contemplative, and pointed toward the first exam room. "Max boo-boo?"

"Yes, Max has a boo-boo. But it's okay. Mama fixed it."

"Aww, Mama." Frannie hugged her. Hugged her long and tight.

"I love you, too, sweet girl. More than anything or anyone in the world."

"Max boo-boo," she said again.

The baby liked Max, and he liked her. But then, everyone in Pleasant Valley liked Frannie. "And why wouldn't they, when you're the cutest, sweetest, most precious baby girl in the whole wide world!"

Frannie giggled, and Willa locked the door. With the baby safely tucked into the car seat Max had found, Willa revved Li'l Red's engine.

Emily had given her a lot to think about. For starters, *could* she make a happy life here, with or without Max?

Chapter Ten

Emily had made it known that for Amish patients without phones, official clinic appointments weren't necessary. Some stopped by in person to schedule routine exams, and except for the occasional emergency, very few showed up before nine.

Willa made a point of arriving by eight o'clock. That extra hour gave her time to pay bills, order supplies, and add information to the computer files. Most days, Frannie seemed content to play quietly with the wooden trains and stuffed dolls in her playpen.

This was not one of those days.

She'd fidgeted and fussed half the night, thanks to new molars that were trying to break through. Willa tried everything from rubbing dampened gauze pads on the baby's gums to letting her chomp on a raw carrot to filling her bottle with chamomile tea. The only thing that worked was bundling her into a thick quilt and rocking her in the big chair near the window.

Peripheral vision told her that, right now, Frannie was gnawing on the protective plastic that covered the playpen's railing. She took care not to make eye contact, because that was sure to start the crying up, all over again.

She heard a soft thump, and knew that Frannie had

decided to sit and look for something new to chew. After a few minutes of blessed silence, Willa risked a peek over her shoulder, and could barely contain her laughter.

"*Now* you sleep," she whispered around a yawn. *Enjoy it while it lasts* . . . Letting Frannie doze for too long now meant forsaking an afternoon nap, and it could very well cause another restless night.

The mission-style wall clock said 8:15. She couldn't allow herself to watch the steady to-and-fro motion of the pendulum for fear it would have the same effect as a hypnotist's pocket watch. She could almost hear a bespectacled gent chanting past his thick mustache: *You're getting sleepy. You're feeling very, very—*

The door opened with a *whoosh*, and Willa tensed, hoping Frannie hadn't heard the bell above it.

"Did I startle you?" Max said.

"No." She nodded toward Frannie, snoozing contentedly in the playpen. "She was up half the night. I wish I could spare her the whole teething ordeal."

"She will forget all about it once she sinks her teeth into a good cut of beef."

Willa grinned, gestured toward the exam room. "I'm anxious to see how things are healing. Frannie was quite concerned," she said as he settled onto the exam table. "If she said 'Max boo-boo?' once, she said it twenty times."

He glanced toward the room across the hall, where Frannie and Rafe spent their at-the-clinic hours. "I am flattered. You told her not to worry . . ."

Willa donned a pair of surgical gloves. "I told her you were fine. Every. Single. Time."

Max smiled, watching as she unwrapped the bandage. Once the stitched-up cut was exposed, he gave a satisfied nod. "Now you can say it for the last time."

"It does look good, doesn't it?"

"You sound surprised. That surprises *me*. You must know that you have natural skills."

"I still have a lot to learn."

"Emily said you're studying online . . . how does that work?"

"Let me wrap this up again, and I'll show you." As she had two evenings ago, Willa used a cotton swab to spread antibiotic ointment over the sutures, covered them with a large gauze pad, and secured it with white adhesive tape. "Day after tomorrow, I think it'll be safe to take off the dressing, let the wound get some air. And the day after that, come back and I'll remove the stitches." Just for fun, she sketched a tiny portrait of him on the tape.

"Say, that is a pretty good likeness," he said, reaching for his billfold.

Willa held up a hand to stop him. "You paid the other night, remember?"

"But this is a new service . . ."

"No, not new. It's part of the package. Sort of the way contractors work. When the job's done, a customer might find a little something that needs attention. You wouldn't add to the bill for that, right?"

Quiet laughter rumbled from his chest. "No, touch-ups are part of the package."

He put the wallet away and she tossed her gloves into the biohazard bin, then led the way to the counter. It took just a few keystrokes to bring up the college website, followed by two clicks to reach her student page.

Waving him closer, Willa clicked a tab that said ASSIGNMENTS. "I read them, do what I'm told, and send the completed work back to the teacher, here . . ." She moved the mouse, until the little white arrow hovered over SEND. "If they have questions, or see that I didn't quite understand something, they'll leave me a note, right there." Pointing, she indicated the NOTES label.

When she turned to face him, Willa realized that he stood nearly shoulder to shoulder with her. Leaning over the keyboard, eyes riveted to the screen, he watched every move she made.

"Fascinating."

"You aren't using a computer at work?"

"Dan thought it a waste of time and money."

She signed out of the school's page and clicked a key that brought back the clinic's screen saver. "He's right . . . and wrong. It can cost anywhere from a few hundred to a few thousand dollars to buy one of these babies. And getting started can be time-consuming. But once you invested in the machine and the setup, you'd save time and money."

He looked interested but confused.

"Record-keeping is tedious work. Work that requires man-hours." She pulled her key ring out of her pocket, showed him a small thumb drive. "Everything that's in here," Willa said, patting the monitor, "is on here. Emily has one just like it. Meaning, we both have access to all the files, no matter where we are."

Max nodded, but she could tell that he still had questions. Willa slid the drive into a slot on the side of the computer, and explained, step-by-step, how the accounts could be accessed from anywhere, at any time. When the list of clinic expenses popped up, he said, "Ah-ha. And you have similar files for patients?"

"Exactly."

"So if—God forbid—there was a fire, your records are safe."

"Yup. It requires saving what's in the computer to the drive, but even if we forgot for a couple of days . . ."

"I can see how this would help a business. Any business."

Leaning an elbow on the counter, he said, "But I would not know where to begin."

"I'm happy to help you. We can go into town, explain how you'll use the computer, and the store will install the programs you'll need. I can show you how to type in your regular customers' names and contact information, companies you regularly buy materials and supplies from, then use spreadsheets to—"

Laughing, Max held up a hand, stopping her. "I think my brain is going to explode."

"Sorry. I shouldn't have hit you with all that stuff, all at one time." She removed the thumb drive and dropped the keys back into the pocket of her lab coat. "It sounds crazy. Convoluted. Nearly impossible. But only at first. Think of it this way . . . When you accept a new job, you do the work in steps: Meet with the customer. Find out what they want and need. Provide drawings and a cost estimate, and if they like what they see, you provide a contract that spells it all out. Right?"

"Right . . ."

"And *then* you ask for a deposit, so you can order wood. Nails. Windows and doors. Roofing materials. Probably from a bunch of different sources, right?"

"Right . . ."

"And then you have to figure out which of your employees are best suited to do the work, right?"

"I see where you're going with this. But I doubt I could ever figure out how to get all of that into *there*." He pointed at the computer.

"I said I'd help you, and I will. I love this kind of work."

Max blanketed her hand with his own. "Willa, you already have too much to do." He listed all the things that drained her time and energy. "I could never ask you to—"

She looked at their hands, flat on the countertop. It was

a small, seemingly insignificant gesture, but to Willa, it was proof that Max felt comfortable with her. "You aren't asking. I'm offering." She placed her free hand atop his. "I'm serious. I love this kind of work!"

"Still . . ."

"We've already established that neither of us need a lot of sleep. So we'll get you a laptop, instead of a PC. They're one-hundred-percent portable, but hold just as much information. That way, you can bring it to Dan's house, and we can get you set up after everyone has gone to bed." She was rambling and knew it, but didn't know how to stop the rapid flow of words. "I'll be nearby if Frannie or Anki should need me, and it's quiet work. It won't take long. I promise. And I'll be right beside you, every step of the way."

Willa sent a silent prayer heavenward: *Let him say yes, Lord. Let him say* yes. Because then maybe, just maybe, if she unconsciously threw herself into his arms again, he wouldn't think she was trying to repay his kindnesses with—

"How soon can you go into town with me?"

Thank You, Lord, Willa thought, and brought the computer to life again. She looked over the day's schedule and said, "There's nothing on the calendar after lunch . . ."

"Emily won't need you after that?"

"After what?" Emily said, entering the clinic.

Willa quickly brought her up-to-date, and as she placed Rafe into his playpen, Emily said, "There's only one appointment this morning, just a follow-up on Jacob's sprained wrist. It's okay with me if you go right now."

Max met Willa's eyes. "Is that okay with you?"

"I . . . well . . ." She glanced at Frannie, who'd roused from her nap when Rafe started babbling the instant his mother removed his coat and hat.

"Bring her. I can drive Li'l Red, so she will be safe."

"She's teething, and might be a little fussy . . ."

He chuckled. "I have worked with Dan for years, so I can handle a little fussing."

Willa looked at Emily. "You're sure it's okay?"

"I'm sure." She handed Rafe a pacifier. "Don't tell Phillip. He thinks it's time to wean him off the thing." Grinning, she added, "And don't worry. You'll be on the clock. Stop at a burger joint and bring lunch, and we'll consider it a wash."

Willa rushed over to hug her. "I couldn't ask for a better friend." She squeezed a bit tighter. "Or a better boss."

Frannie, sensing that something good was about to happen, squealed happily.

"Let me have a look at that cut," Willa said, walking into the exam room. "If it looks as good as it did day before yesterday, I'll remove the stitches."

He followed without question, and afterward, asked how he could help her get Frannie ready for the outing.

"Already done," Emily said, holding out the diaper bag. "I changed her, put a few snacks in here, and filled a bottle with apple juice. Put on her coat and hat, and she's good to go."

"Bye-bye?" Frannie said, reaching for Willa.

"Yes, sweet girl, you're going bye-bye. With Max!"

The baby's excitement was palpable. "Max!"

He held out his hand. "Give me the keys, and I will warm up the truck."

She dropped them into his upturned palm. "Aren't you a trusting soul, giving me the only copy!"

"Oh, I have a spare. At home. In the shop."

And with that, he left them.

"*You're* a trusting soul," Emily said.

"What?" She tucked the baby's arms into her jacket. "Why?"

"You're setting yourself up to spend hours and hours alone with the guy. . . ."

Buttoning the coat, Willa said, "You told me he's crazy about me. That it was written all over his face."

"It's rare, I know," Emily said, "but I might have been wrong. Maybe he suffers from heartburn. Or migraines. An ingrown toenail."

"Gee, that's a real confidence booster." Fastening the hat ties under Frannie's chin, she added, "All of those things make people look like they're in pain!"

Emily shrugged. "You know what they say. Love hurts."

She lifted Frannie from the playpen. "Well, it shouldn't."

"I'm kidding. It doesn't. In my opinion, anyway."

Rafe watched, wide-eyed, as Willa carried Frannie to the door. "Don't worry, little guy. I'll bring your playmate back soon." Meeting Emily's eyes, she said, "Whatever tools you use, just set them aside. I'll run them through the autoclave this afternoon."

"Deal. Now go. And have fun!"

"I can make up the hours tomorrow . . ."

"I know love is blind, but is it deaf, too? You didn't hear me when I said bring me lunch and we're square?"

"I did. Thanks. You really *are* the best."

"Besides, you can't come in tomorrow."

"Why?"

"Because tomorrow you're going to visit Bishop Fisher."

She'd forgotten about sharing those plans with Emily. "But that can wait."

"No. It can't. You saw the schedule. Not one single

appointment. Why should we both be stuck here, doing nothing?"

Willa thought of all the things she *could* do, like making sure the paper files were properly alphabetized. Re-scrubbing the exam rooms. The bathroom, too. And the kids' playpens. The apartment-size fridge and stove in the kitchenette.

Emily flicked her fingers in the universal *shoo* gesture. "It isn't polite to keep a man waiting."

She looked outside, where Max stood, arms and ankles crossed, leaning his backside against Li'l Red's driver's door. The instant his eyes met hers, his entire demeanor changed, from distracted to delighted. *I feel the same way,* she thought, shoving the door open. But the closer she got, the less Willa believed that *she'd* inspired his happy transformation . . .

. . . . because Frannie, hands flapping, said, "Max!" and he was just as enthusiastic when he replied, "Frannie!"

While strapping the baby into the car seat he'd found and installed in the extended cab he'd added to the truck, Willa thought of the prayers that had lulled her to sleep ever since she'd found out that Frannie was on the way: *Protect and provide for her, always, Lord.*

Was it possible that Max was part of the answer to those prayers?

He'd seen her up to her elbows in dishwater. Battling wind to get clean laundry hung on the clothesline. Pink-cheeked and perspiring after carrying armloads of wood inside and stoking the fire. First thing in the morning, when he'd stopped by to drive Dan to a jobsite and Willa was busy cleaning up breakfast and packing Dan's lunch

bucket. In every case, Max made note of her good looks.
But right now, with the laptop's screen lighting her face,
he thought she looked out-and-out angelic. He couldn't
say which distracted him more . . . that she'd so cheerfully
given him the scant free time left at the end of her days, or
the fact that she was just plain gorgeous.

Both, he decided as her fingers click-clacked over
the keys.

Tonight, like last night, she'd cooked a satisfying meal,
cleaned it up, got Frannie ready for bed and tucked her in,
then sat down beside him to explain—in detail—how to
create a spreadsheet to track his inventory. If Willa felt
tired or put-upon, she hid it well.

Max glanced around the tidy kitchen, at white stoneware stacked neatly on the shelves above the counter. At
jars of seasonings and spices, arranged in alphabetical
order, in the hanging rack Dan had made from scraps
of oak.

". . . so you just hover the mouse over the square that
will hold your data, like this . . ." she said, bringing him
back to the here and now. He forced himself to look at her
fingers, curved over the keyboard, and noticed the rough
redness that showed how hard she worked.

Impulsively, he grabbed her left hand, gently stroked its
knuckles with the pad of his thumb. "I feel guilty saying
this, since I am adding to your workload, but you should
take better care of yourself."

"You're a fine one to talk." She turned his hand over
and inspected the thick calluses beneath each finger joint.

"You got me."

Laughing quietly, she got up. "Let's swap seats. I've got
you all set up, but you need to learn to fill in the cells."
She dropped a hand onto his shoulder. "I won't always sit
beside you while you're working."

"But I wish you could!" The confession surprised him, and if her sweet, crooked little smile was any indicator, surprised her even more.

Willa aimed her pointer finger at the empty chair, and he wasted no time filling it.

Blanketing his hand again, she draped it over the wireless mouse. "See, if you click the right button, you can highlight, then move things. Or delete them. And if you click the left button, you can enter information to a new cell."

He shook his head. "I wonder if this will ever make sense."

"Sure it will. No one gets it on their first try. It's like anything else. Practice makes perfect."

Again, he shook his head.

"The very first time you hit a nail with a hammer, what happened?"

"I missed."

"And the next time?"

"The nail bent."

"And the time after that?"

"I hit the head, but it took a few whacks to sink it."

"See what I mean? You had to *do* it a few times before you figured out how to properly use the tool. That's all the computer is. A tool." She patted his hand. "If you can build a house where nothing stood before, you can do this!"

Willa moved a file closer to him and quietly gave step-by-step instructions for typing into the spreadsheet. And just as she'd predicted, he was catching on.

When the numbers from that folder had been transferred to the spreadsheet, she opened a new one, and he completed it in half the time. Max was feeling pretty good about himself when she explained how to save the file.

Something went wrong, and the screen went blank. All that work, gone in an eye blink. He ran a hand through his hair, sat back, and said, "*Dunner uns Gewidder!*"

"Um . . . what?"

"I am sorry. Should not have let frustration get the better of me."

"No need to apologize. I expect I've heard Dan say far worse things."

She was tireless, uncomplaining, with the temperament of a saint. If she had a flaw, Max hadn't seen it yet. As his father used to say, *If something looks too good to be true, it* is!

The baby monitor's receiver hissed, telling them that Frannie had turned over in her crib. Frannie—living, breathing confirmation that her mother had been with a man who wasn't her husband. To her credit, pretense and piousness didn't seem part of Willa's character. She hadn't tried to hide the life she'd lived. Max remembered well the way she'd blurted it out on the day they met. Announced that she'd been a drug-addicted alcoholic, too. And yet the reality of it hit him like a slap, leaving him more confused than anything related to the laptop. That, he thought, was just plain absurd, considering how much time he'd spent with her.

Willa got up and grabbed his mug. "Your tea is cold. Let me warm—"

She stopped, stared into his eyes. All his life, people had been telling him that every thought in his head was visible on his face. For the first time, Max wished he'd put a little effort into masking his feelings.

Sitting again, she said, "Max. What's wrong?"

"Nothing." He glanced at the clock, hoping that by looking away, he could hide the fib he was about to tell. "I just noticed the time. We both have to get up early tomorrow." Rising, he stacked the file folders she'd asked him to bring.

"Okay, but first, let me show you how to retrieve your work. It looks lost, I know, but looks are deceiving."

Leaning over the laptop, she pecked a few keys and the spreadsheet reappeared in its entirety. Straightening, she placed his hand atop the mouse again, guided it until the arrow moved to the FILE, put pressure on his index finger. "Choose 'Save As' from the drop-down menu," she instructed.

She said more, but Max's mind was elsewhere . . . On Willa, blindly obeying the orders of a mangy drug dealer; Willa, in the criminal's arms . . .

"There. See? All's well," she was saying.

She was smiling, too, and Max pasted a fake grin on his face to match it.

It didn't work, unfortunately. He could tell by the way she leaned in, eyes narrowed and brows furrowed.

"Talk to me, Max. All this . . ." Her hand drew a circle around his face. "This isn't because you thought the file was lost. And it isn't because the computer overwhelmed you a little, or because you're tired."

Did she really expect him to admit, straight-out, that her past had reared up like a wild bear, making him fear his feelings?

"You two are working late," Anki said, shuffling into the room in a thick blue robe. The white cuffs of her nightgown peeked out from its long sleeves, and she tugged at one, then the other.

"We are finished," Max said, closing the laptop. He unplugged its electric cord and began winding it up. "Sorry if we woke you."

"You did not wake me. In fact, I only heard you when I entered the kitchen."

Willa went to the fridge. "Thirsty?" She removed the pitcher of milk and filled a mug.

"No." But Anki accepted the mug and slumped onto a kitchen chair.

"Hungry? There's cobbler left from supper."

Long blond hair spilled over one shoulder as Anki shook her head. Max had seen her without a cap, but this was the first time she'd untied the tight bun that had always sat on the crown of her head.

Willa dished up a bowl anyway, placed it in front of Anki, and plucked a spoon from the drawer beside the sink. "The wind, then . . ."

"No," she said again.

"If noise didn't wake you, and you aren't hungry or thirsty, why *are* you up at this hour?"

Anki looked at the clock. A faint smile curved her mouth as she said, "It is five minutes after ten, Willa dear. Hardly the middle of the night."

Willa's gaze met his, and he read her pleading message: *What is going on around here tonight!*

Anything he said would only add to her worries. Max put on his coat and stuffed the laptop into the canvas briefcase she'd talked the salesman into throwing in for free. Sliding its strap over his left shoulder, he held out his right hand.

"Thank you, Willa," he said, grasping her hand, "for everything you did for me today."

Her grip was warm, and despite the reminders of hard work, comforting. He wanted to kiss the lips that had so patiently taught him about the laptop . . . kiss them until all traces of fear and uncertainty disappeared from her eyes. And from his mind.

Get your mind straight! he thought, releasing her hand.

"After all you've done for me," she said, "no thanks necessary."

She was referring to the truck again, and the changes he'd made to it for Frannie's benefit. Would he ever convince her that she didn't owe him anything for that?

"In case I forgot to tell you, supper was good."

"You thanked me three or four times."

"It was that good!" Did he sound as foolish and clumsy to her as he sounded to himself?

"Will you and Dan start the housing development tomorrow?"

"No, that will not get under way until spring." This wasn't the time to announce that because of Anki, Dan had agreed to oversee local jobs while Max managed contracts away from Pleasant Valley. "Between now and then, though, I need to file for permits, measure each lot, order materials. Which means I will spend a good deal of time in Frostburg in the next few months."

Had he shared all this with Dan? Why else would it sound like he was repeating himself? Max shifted his weight from right foot to left. "What about you? Working here, or at the clinic?"

Now her eyes widened, the way they had when the cat startled her in the driveway.

"Tomorrow is the day she will meet with Bishop Fisher," Anki said.

He looked from Anki to Willa. "A meeting . . . with *the bishop*?"

Anki started to tell him why, but Willa stopped her with, "I hope weather forecasters are wrong about the upcoming winter. It'll be dangerous for you, driving back and forth on those zigzagging mountain highways in the snow." She walked to the door and, resting a hand on the knob, said, "I know you're a careful driver, but unfortunately, you won't be alone on the road."

It had been a long time since anyone cared about his safety. It felt good, but he couldn't let it distract him. He had lots to think about before moving forward with her. Unexpectedly, a disturbing thought came to mind: What if he'd misinterpreted everything, and she wasn't interested in deepening their relationship? What if she'd been working two jobs, saving every penny, broadening her education in order to ensure she could provide well for herself and Frannie, anywhere? The questions upset him more than he cared to admit.

"Can I stoke the fire before I go?"

"Thanks, but I can handle it."

"I have no doubt that you can." And he meant it.

She opened the door, and as he stepped onto the porch, Anki's voice stopped him.

"I will tell Dan how early you left. He was sure you two would work into the wee hours and wake up late."

Willa grunted. "I have never, *ever* slept late. Or slacked off in any other way, for that matter." Grinning, she shook a fist in the air. "I have a good mind to burn his bacon tomorrow. That'll show him!"

Max didn't know how he'd feel about her—and her past—after a night of contemplation, but he knew this:

If a future between them was in God's plan, it would be anything but boring!

Chapter Eleven

Frannie, asleep on her tummy, had folded her knees and elbows under her. As Willa gently tucked the blankets around her round, raised bum, she sighed contentedly. *Oh, to enjoy the deep sleep of an innocent baby.* She resisted the urge to finger-comb curls from her daughter's forehead.

Dan's throaty snores filtered across the hall, so she pulled the door shut, making sure not to let the latch click against the strike plate. She tiptoed downstairs, avoiding the creaky step third from the top, and found Anki right where she'd left her, still unmoving, still expressionless. But as she walked farther into the room, what she saw stopped her: huge kitchen shears in Anki's right hand, a foot-long mass of blond hair in the other.

Willa took the scissors and whispered, "Anki . . . *why*?"

In the brittle silence that followed, Willa acknowledged that, even in the New Order Amish world, women followed most Old Testament tenets. One plainly stated "shorn locks are shameful." In this case, Willa agreed, because Anki's hair was exquisite. Dozens of times, she'd shampooed the lustrous, slightly wavy tresses that hung far past Anki's waist. Afterward, while Willa styled it into braids or buns or twists, they'd discuss the weather,

Frannie's antics, whether to serve chicken or beef for supper. And she'd wish aloud for hair *half* as beautiful. Amish rules about pride forbade Anki from agreeing, but Willa could tell . . . Anki loved her hair, too. The fact that she'd hack at it with shears designed to cut legs and wings from raw roasting chickens . . . Willa didn't understand that at all!

She dropped the tool into the sink and knelt beside the chair, and grasping Anki's free hand, repeated, "Why?"

The woman responded with a hesitant shrug. "I thought . . ." She gawked at her handful of hair as if seeing it for the first time. "I was still dreaming . . . about Abby."

Abby . . . Abigail . . . her twin . . .

Willa and Frannie had been with the Hofmans for nearly six months, and according to Max, Anki had lost her twin shortly before their arrival. Day by day, she'd become more withdrawn and less predictable. If she didn't get help soon, what might Anki do next?

Willa slid a chair alongside Anki's. "Tell me about the dream."

For a second, Anki made eye contact with Willa. All too quickly, though, she locked her gaze on an unidentifiable spot across the room.

"I was outside, helping Mama gather eggs, and when I came inside . . ."

Her voice, a dull monotone, was barely audible. Willa leaned closer, not wanting to interrupt.

". . . I saw her. On the floor. In front of the sink. The sun was shining through the window. It reflected from Mama's butcher knife. There was blood. So much blood . . ."

Tears filled Anki's eyes, and when she blinked, one slid down her cheek, and landed on her shoulder.

"I dropped the eggs. The whole basket. They broke. And mixed with the blood. Then Mama walked in. And fainted."

Willa knew that Anki's mother couldn't have witnessed her daughter's suicide, because according to Max, both parents had died soon after Abigail moved away. Anki couldn't have seen anything, either, since the shunning had taken place many months before her twin's death. With bare snippets of information, delivered by a well-meaning neighbor, Anki's imagination had drawn terrifying mental images of her sister's last hours.

"How awful," Willa said, squeezing Anki's hands. If only she could think of something more helpful to say!

"I hate her," Anki blurted out. "Hate, hate, *hate her*."

Willa wished she'd paid more attention during the suicide unit of her psych class. Should she encourage Anki to talk more about it? Or change the subject?

"I'm sure it was hard. Very hard. For all of you." The words sounded hollow and pointless. *Lord, help me to help Anki!*

"It was such a selfish thing to do. She was so much more than my sister. She was my dearest friend. We shared everything. *Everything*. When she went away with that . . . that *man* . . . she took part of me with her. But I had faith. I trusted God to answer my prayers and bring her home someday."

Oh, how she wished Max hadn't left. He'd known Anki for years. Surely he'd know how to comfort her. Then again, maybe she wouldn't have opened up at all.

Anki inhaled a sharp breath, let it out slowly. Shifting slightly in the chair, she faced Willa. "I am sorry. It was wrong of me to burden you with—"

"Shhh," Willa interrupted. "You listened to all my

troubles when I first got here. Friends share things. Good things. Bad things." She squeezed Anki's hands. "Hurtful things. Especially hurtful things. It's good to have someone you can trust, someone you can talk to." Another squeeze, and then, "I'll always be here for you, Anki. Always."

Knuckling her eyes, Anki took another deep breath and smiled. Not much. But the attempt gave Willa hope. She made a decision: Tomorrow, right after her visit with the bishop, she'd ask Emily's advice on the situation. If it made Dan angry, so be it. All that really mattered was getting Anki the help she so desperately needed.

"Dan will *really* hate me now."

"He doesn't hate you," Willa insisted. "He loves you!"

She shook her head. "He is angry with me. Always, so angry with me."

"That's *because* he loves you. He's worried about you, and you know how men are . . . always wanting to solve problems for the women they love . . . He wants to help you, and because he doesn't know how, he says things that hurt your feelings. The person he's really angry with is himself, because he feels helpless."

Anki slipped her hands free of Willa's grasp, stroked the hair still clutched in her hand. "When he sees what I have done . . ."

Willa got up, held out her right hand. "Give that to me."

Like an errant child, Anki dropped the hair into Willa's upturned palm. "Now I will be ugly on the outside, too."

"Too" . . . meaning the anger she'd been harboring made her feel ugly on the inside?

"Stay right there," Willa instructed, "while I get your sewing scissors. They're sharper than the kitchen shears, and I can use them to . . ." She almost said, *To straighten up this awful mess you've made!* She used her fingers to imitate scissors. "I'm sure with a few snips here and a few snips there, we can even things up."

"What I have done is sinful. A snip here or there cannot change that."

"I've read those Old Testament Scriptures. First of all, they only say that 'shorn hair' was unpleasing to God. *Was,*" she said, emphasizing the word, "because Jesus's death changed all of that. And secondly . . ."

Willa darted into the parlor, where Anki kept her sewing basket, and returned with the scissors. She opened, then closed them with a snap.

"He will hate me."

"He won't. He doesn't," she said again. Bending at the waist, Willa lifted Anki's chin and forced her to make eye contact. "Your hair will grow back, you know."

"It took thirty-three years to reach this length!"

Straightening, Willa chuckled. "Remember my hair when I got here?"

"Yes. It looked like little Rafe's."

Emily often lamented how quickly he was growing up, using his ringlets to measure the passage of time: The once-bald baby now sported a mop of curls that completely covered his ears.

Striking a model's pose, Willa used one hand to fluff her shoulder-length waves. "And just look at it now!"

In all the months she'd been in Pleasant Valley, Willa had never seen Anki look more enthusiastic. But as quickly as her happiness appeared, it disappeared.

"I will have to wear my cap inside and out."

"To hide your hair from Dan?"

She lowered her head. "It will be a sin of omission."

"Do you trust Dan?" Willa asked.

Frowning, Anki said, "Yes . . ."

"And you love him?"

"Of course I do. He is my husband!"

"Then trust him, Anki. Just . . ." She shrugged, feeling helpless, and a little bit stupid. ". . . just tell him the truth. About your dream. About how Abigail's shunning, and her death, hurt you." Willa paused. "And don't give me that nonsense about him hating you. He won't. Ever. Period."

"But . . . he will be angry . . ."

"Maybe, but you know what they say . . . all bark, no bite . . . He'll get over it. He always does."

"Yes . . . all right."

Willa tugged at the tablecloth and draped it around Anki's shoulders.

It was heartbreaking, watching the mound of hair grow near Anki's feet. But fifteen minutes later, at least it was all one length.

"There. All finished." Carefully, she removed the make-shift cape and carried it onto the enclosed back porch, where she added it to the laundry basket. On her way back inside, Willa grabbed the broom and dustpan, and began sweeping up the evidence of Anki's folly.

"My neck is cold," she said, pulling the robe higher. On her feet now, she said, "I will sleep in the parlor."

No need to ask why. Anki didn't want her newly shorn bob to be the first thing Dan saw in the morning.

From the doorway, Anki said, "You should stop playing hard to get."

"I should . . . *What!*"

"No need to pretend with me. Friends share things, right?" She paused. "Do you love Max?"

"I'm not sure. I think so."

"Then trust him, Willa. Tell him how you feel. I have a feeling he will echo your words."

It was almost word for word the advice she had just given Anki. Willa didn't know how to feel about that.

"It's that obvious, huh?"

"Only to those who can see."

She rounded the corner, and Willa could hear her, fluffing the needlepoint pillow—the only decoration in the plain room—before unfolding the quilt that always hung over the back of the bentwood rocker. *Lord, bless her with a restful night's sleep.*

Because something told her that come morning, Anki would need every ounce of strength it would provide.

"Max, how good to see you."

If Anki's dull voice reflected her feelings, he didn't believe her words.

"Why are you here? I thought Dan said you were going to Cumberland today."

"I am. Just thought I would stop by, see if you or Willa need anything from town."

"She is upstairs, getting Frannie ready for the day." Moving woodenly to the bottom of the stairs, Anki placed a hand on the newel post. "Willa? Can you come down here for a minute?"

"No need to interrupt her."

"It's no interruption," Willa said, joining them in the kitchen.

Their personalities were completely different. Anki's demeanor summoned thoughts of chilly gray skies. Willa, on the other hand, reminded him of springtime . . . warm and bright and inviting.

"Don't you look dapper today," she said, tucking Frannie into her highchair. "Business meeting this morning?"

"Yes. I have been instructed not to name the property owner, but he wants us to build a few one-room cabins near Lover's Leap."

"I don't know which story interests me more . . ." She slid two slices of bread into the toaster. ". . . his secrecy or how the place got its name."

"All he'll allow me to say is that he's an environmentalist. And a preservationist."

She tied a huge bib around the baby's neck. "And a guy who knows how to encourage tourists to spend their money," Willa joked.

He had to agree. Lover's Leap was a popular Wills Mountain attraction, mostly for the spectacular views from the cliffs overlooking Wills Creek, 1,700 feet below.

"People have leaped to their deaths there," Anki said.

Frannie tried leaping . . . out of her high chair. "Max!" she called out, smiling as she reached for him. He took her hand and said, "Why is she so gussied up this morning?"

"Because she and her mama will meet with the bishop this morning," Anki answered.

"Oh? Why is that?"

"Tell me more about Cumberland's Lover's Leap," Willa said, buttering Frannie's toast.

Clever, he thought, how quickly she'd changed the subject. No matter. Sooner or later, he'd learn why she was meeting with Fisher.

A quick glance at the clock told him he had plenty of time before his own meeting with the property owner. Taking a seat near Frannie's high chair, he began:

"According to the legend, there was a man named Jack Chadwick, who had a reputation for being a fearless hunter. During one expedition, he ran across a chief who lived on the creek with his white wife and their daughter.

Because he had sided with the whites, the Shawnee tribe shunned him. Soon, Jack and the chief's daughter fell in love and wanted to marry, but her father rejected the idea, saying that Jack was too poor. But even if he'd had the money to care for her, she'd been promised to an officer at the fort. It broke Jack's heart, they say, and on his way back to his cabin, he kicked a rock. A big shiny rock that turned out to be pure silver. No one would call him poor now! And he was right. The chief gave his blessing to the marriage . . . until the officer came to claim his bride. Jack tried to convince the chief to change his mind, but when the man refused to budge, Jack asked the daughter to run away with him so they could be married. But she loved her father and would not disobey him. 'I cannot live with you,' she said, 'but I will die with you.' So off they went, to the high cliff, and holding hands, they jumped."

Willa exhaled a long sigh. "How sad that the beauty of places like that can be tarnished by a few dumb choices."

"Dumb?"

"I'd *never* kill myself over a man." She met his eyes. "You wouldn't do such a thing for a woman, would you?"

"No!"

Anki had been paying close attention, and now she leaned forward. "When will work on these cabins begin? After the Royal Valley Overlook project is finished?"

"No, the man wants these cabins finished before the snows come. It can be done, easily, if we divert some of the crew from smaller jobs near here. It will provide a new cash source to see us through the winter."

By now, Frannie had nearly finished her toast, and Willa was packing apple slices and cheese cubes into a paper bag. "A healthy snack for later," she explained, zipping the backpack's flap. "In case she starts fussing while the bishop and I are talking."

"How will you get there? Li'l Red?"

"No, I thought we'd walk. It's a nice sunny day. There might not be many more of these."

"But Willa," Anki said, "it is more than a mile. You cannot carry Frannie *and* the pie that far."

She sent a grin in Anki's direction. "Sure I can."

"Of course you *can*," Max said, "but why not let me drive you? It is right on my way. You can walk home again, and won't have the pie to carry."

"What do you say, Frannie? Would you like Max to drive us to the bishop's house?"

"Max!" Frannie hollered. "Max!"

"All right then," she said, pouring steaming water into a mug, "thank you, Mr. Lambright!" After adding a spoonful of sugar to the cup, Willa turned toward Anki. "Let's get you set up in the parlor. I found a novel in my suitcase. It's the story of a heroine who survives a steamboat explosion and has to raise her deaf brother, all by herself!"

While she got Anki situated, he grabbed a clean dish rag, dampened it, and gently wiped butter from Frannie's face and fingers. "There now," he said, winking, "all clean, and no longer shiny. And we saved your mama a few minutes. Time enough, maybe, to inspire her to tell me *why* you're visiting the bishop today."

Frannie opened and closed one plump fist. "Bye-bye?"

"Yes, we are going bye-bye."

She puckered her lips. "Kiss?"

"How can I say no!" Max leaned over the high-chair tray and deposited a quick peck on her mouth. "Mmm!" he said. "What is in that butter?"

"Honey," Willa answered. "Sometimes I make honey butter. Sometimes I mix in a little cinnamon and sugar."

"You are blessed, little Frannie," he said, winking again.

Willa blushed a bit at his compliment, but hid it by grabbing the baby's coat from the rack. "What time is your meeting?"

After another glance at the clock, he said, "In just over an hour."

"Whew." They headed outside. "You'll have just enough time . . . if we don't dillydally."

"Or lollygag."

"Or shilly-shally."

Max held up a hand. "I give up," he said, laughing. Then he realized there wasn't a car seat in his truck. He hated to withdraw his offer, but . . .

"Don't look so worried," she said, opening the passenger door. "It's less than a mile. And it isn't likely we'll encounter another vehicle. Besides, you're a careful driver."

Sliding into the truck, Willa pulled the seat belt around herself and Frannie. "Well? What are you waiting for, Christmas?"

He returned her smile, then closed the door. Did she have any idea how much he enjoyed being around her?

"Anki was fascinated by your Lover's Leap story. Almost as if she hadn't heard it before."

"She often puzzles me, too." He sighed. "Dan does not have an easy life."

"That's true, in some ways. He's well regarded in the community and has many good friends. You're probably his best friend. *And* you're the best partner he could have. Why, if not for you, putting up with the moods caused by Anki's behavior, I don't know how he'd earn a living."

They'd almost arrived at the bishop's house, and Max still hadn't had a chance to ask her about the meeting.

"Do you think if I stop at the supercenter on the way home, pick up a few staples, I can earn my seat at the supper table? *Again*?"

"Why would anyone mind!"

"Because Dan is probably keeping a tally of everything I eat, so that he can flash the total next time I make a 'spend money for the company' suggestion."

Laughing, Willa said, "No, he wouldn't do that." She faced Max and made an *uh-oh* look. "Would he?"

Max pulled up in front of the Fishers' house and jogged around to the passenger side of the truck. "No," he said, opening the door, "he probably would not." After helping her exit the truck, he reached into the back seat, slid the pie onto his palm.

"You're not even interested in what's on the menu?"

"Every meal you have served so far has been a wonderful surprise."

"Wow." She shifted Frannie to her left hip and accepted the dish. "You make it really tough on a gal."

"Oh?" he said again.

"Because now I'll feel awful if I disappoint you."

She started up the walk, but he grabbed her wrist. "You could not disappoint me if you tried."

She blushed. Grinned. Rolled her eyes. "Do you say things like that to embarrass me?"

"The truth should not embarrass you, Willa." And then, for no reason other than he was tempted to kiss her, Max cleared his throat and said, "You should go inside, and I should get to my meeting. See you around five o'clock?"

When she glanced at the Fishers' front door, the blush disappeared. In its place was a wide-eyed, uneasy look.

"No reason to worry," he assured her. "Fisher is more

bark than bite." Gently, he turned her, until she faced the porch. "The sooner you get inside, the sooner it will all be over."

Nodding, she moved forward, and Max got in behind the wheel. He drove north, then stopped; if the Fishers didn't answer, he'd take her back to the Hofmans'.

This should be interesting, he thought as she climbed the steps. How would she knock with one hand steadying Frannie on her hip and the other holding the pie?

He watched as she bent one leg at the knee, swung it backward, then forward, until her knee thumped the door. Three times. Shaking his head as the bishop's wife invited her inside, Max laughed and took his foot off the brake. Oh, but she was a delight, and he'd like nothing better than to spend hour after hour in her company. If only he could forget that she'd been with another man . . .

Despite the unpleasant mental pictures, he drove away, chuckling as he imagined how the Almighty would react to tonight's prayer: "Erase the pictures from my mind, Father!"

"Willa!" said the bishop's wife. "What a lovely surprise!" She opened the door wide and gestured her inside. "Micah," she called over her shoulder, "come see who has paid us a visit!"

Charity leaned close and rubbed noses with Frannie, cooing in baby talk. And Frannie returned the affection, right down to the last giggle.

"Sit, sit!" the woman said, relieving Willa of the pie. "For us?"

"For you."

Pulling out a kitchen chair, she called for her husband again, then helped Willa remove Frannie's cap and coat.

After welcoming the baby into her arms, Charity said, "Come, little one, and sit in the grandchildren's chair." She dragged it closer to the table. "This was Micah's. Then, our son's. Now, his youngest uses it."

"What a treasure!" Willa said, meaning it. "The oldest thing I own is a locket that belonged to my maternal grandmother." But what a stupid thing to say. She knew perfectly well that the Amish did not wear jewelry. Not even wedding rings!

"The kind with photographs inside?"

Willa nodded and felt doubly stupid, because pictures were frowned upon here, too.

"I have seen them, in the shops in town. Very pretty." She met Willa's eyes. "Whose photographs are in it?"

"My mother and her mother."

"I see . . ." Then, "I can give the baby a snack, yes?"

"She'd love that."

Frannie's eyes opened wide when Charity held up a saucer-sized sugar cookie.

"You too?" she asked Willa, breaking Frannie's treat into bite-sized pieces.

"No, but thanks." She wanted to get right down to business, ask the bishop's permission and guidance about baptism, and get out of here as soon as possible. She had work to do, after all. And Max was coming to supper . . .

When the bishop entered the room, Charity filled four stoneware mugs with milk, and placed them around the table. "Sit," she told him, "and we will have cookies."

"Cookies?" He pointed. "When I see *pie* there on the counter?" Laughing, he rubbed his ample belly. "We must not insult Willa, who baked it just for us!"

His wife sent him a sidelong glance and, smiling, doled

out plates and forks. Her wide-bladed knife hovered over the crust. "How big, Willa dear?"

"Oh, none for me. There are two more just like it at the Hofmans'. I baked this one especially for you!"

"Two more pies?" Charity asked.

"For tonight's dessert and . . ." She'd made one for Max, but uncertain about how they'd interpret that, kept the detail to herself.

The Fishers bowed their heads and, eyes closed, prayed silently before picking up their forks. And when they did, Frannie pointed excitedly. "Pie, Mama? Pie?"

"How old is she now?"

"Almost fifteen months."

"She says much for one so young."

"That's my fault. I talk to her, almost nonstop." She tucked a lock of hair behind Frannie's ear. "She loves learning, and I'm happy about that."

Charity slid her chair closer to Frannie's, cut off the tiniest bite, and held it to the baby's lips. "Oh my!" she said, laughing when it quickly disappeared.

"Mmm," Frannie said. "*Denke*." Then, "Mo'e?"

Willa tensed, and seeing it, Charity said, "It is all right, Willa dear. In Old Order times, good manners were considered a symptom of pride. I for one am happy that the New Order way replaced the old custom."

She was being careful, Willa noted, not to look in her husband's direction. To his credit, though, it seemed that he agreed with her. So far . . .

He surprised her by saying, "Yes, it is a good thing that such kindnesses are an everyday part of life now."

After helping herself to a bite, Charity said, "Delicious! Is it a family recipe, Willa?"

"Yes. My grandmother's."

"The locket grandmother?"

"Mmm-hmm."

"You do not wear this keepsake?"

"Not since moving here. It's in a little velvet bag in the dresser."

"I would love to see it sometime." Avoiding her husband's eyes, she quickly added, "To see if you resemble your mother and grandmother."

Everyone said she was the spitting image of her mother, a compliment that had always been a source of pride. But the Amish and pride . . . Willa shook her head and hoped the subject was closed.

Charity speared another small piece of apple and fed it to Frannie. "You remind me of a baby bird," she said. Facing Willa, she added, "Tell me, Willa, what brings you here on this chilly fall day?"

"Baptism."

"Commendable," the bishop said, "but here, we do not baptize children. It is a momentous occasion. A choice not to be taken lightly. That is why we wait until a person is nearing adulthood, so that they fully understand that joining the church is a lifelong commitment. I hope this does not upset you, but little Frannie will have to wait."

"It doesn't upset me at all, but the fact is, I'm not here to discuss her baptism . . ."

The Fishers exchanged a wary glance. "Yours, then?" the bishop wanted to know.

"Yes."

"Mother, will you take this sweet child into the parlor, so that Willa and I can discuss things, uninterrupted?"

"Of course!" Charity rose, lifted Frannie from the high chair, and said, "Come with me, little one. We will take a walk. Would you like that?"

"Wa'k!" Looking over the woman's shoulder, she waved to Willa. "Buh-bye, Mama! Me wa'k!"

"Yes, you'll walk. Have fun!"

Once they'd left the room, Fisher folded his hands on the table. "Am I to understand that you plan to stay in Pleasant Valley?"

"Yes. I love it here. The majestic vistas. The friendly people."

"Will you feel this way after you become a nurse?"

She saw no reason to point out the differences between a nurse and a nursing assistant. Instead, Willa said, "Definitely."

"You enjoy your work at Emily's clinic, then."

"Oh, yes. Helping people is so fulfilling." And in the event he might see that as prideful, she quickly added, "I'll never be able to fully repay everyone for their generosity, sharing hand-me-down clothes with Frannie and me, making sure she has a crib and high chair, the playpen at the clinic, but it's a start."

"But . . . you are saving your money."

She didn't understand what he was getting at, and yet Willa said, "Yes . . ."

"I see," he said, nodding slowly. "Now, my next question may seem none of my business, but I must ask it."

Silence, Willa decided, was the best response.

For now.

"Are you fond of Maximillian?"

Fond was hardly the word she'd use! "Yes, I am. But . . . isn't everyone?"

That, at least, inspired a quiet chuckle. "I agree. He is a fine young man, as I have said before. Liked by many. But . . ." His expression grew serious. "His life has not been easy."

"Oh, I know. Anki and Dan told me some things about his past. Max shared a few things, too."

"Mother and I care about him. Almost as much as if he were our own son."

"I'm happy to hear that. Even a man Max's age needs the advice of a father now and then."

"We would not like to see him hurt. Life has already tested him enough."

And then Willa got it: The bishop knew just enough about *her* past to worry that she might revert to her old ways, and if she did, Max would pay the price.

Now, it was Willa who folded her hands on the table. She locked eyes with Fisher and said, "Yes, I care about Max, Bishop Fisher. I care quite a lot. But he is *not* the reason I'll never backslide. I'm well aware that I made a lot of mistakes . . . serious, stupid mistakes, because *I* was stupid. Self-centered. But Frannie changed all that." She leaned in closer. "*She* is the reason I'm on the straight and narrow . . . the reason I'll stay there."

The bishop pursed his lips, stroked his long, thick beard. "Yes. Yes." He inspected his fingernails. "Are you aware, Willa, that to be baptized, you will have to make a confession?"

So. He wanted details, did he? "If that's a requirement, I'm all for it. I'll answer every question honestly, no matter how difficult, no matter how many might judge me once they know the whole truth."

Fisher smiled, a gentle, caring smile that made it easy to understand why, despite his tendency to butt in where he wasn't wanted, the people here held him in high regard.

"Child," he began, "no one will know your answers. Only God, and myself. But even if they did, they would not judge you. In all my years here, I have many times seen evidence of this community's forgiving nature, and not only in my position as bishop."

She breathed a sigh of relief and hoped he hadn't heard it.

"Just one more question, and then you can relax." He patted her tightly fisted hands. "Would you want to stay here in the community, become one of us, even if there is no future between you and Maximillian?"

What did one thing have to do with the other? she wondered. Had Max sought his advice after she'd shamelessly thrown herself at him? Or were the bishop's *Max* questions subtle hints that he'd committed himself to another woman, but hadn't yet found a way to tell her about it? Willa couldn't very well ask, or the bishop would have reason to write off everything she'd said.

"Pleasant Valley has earned its name." She sat up straighter, placed both hands in her lap. "It's a good, safe place for Frannie to grow up, and I believe it was God's will that I ended up here, surrounded by people who are more family than neighbors. It'll be a good, safe place for me, too. *That's* why I want to stay."

"I see. Well, all right, then. We will meet again. Several times. So that I can ask again why you want to be baptized. Once you have demonstrated that your heart is true and your faith is strong, we will study the Bible. Together. I expect that in time, you will convince me you want to renounce the ways of the modern world and commit yourself to living Plain. And then *I* will convince the elders, and after they vote . . . you will become a true member of the community."

Six months ago, if anyone had asked whether she'd ever consider "becoming Amish," Willa would have laughed, called them crazy. *Me? In plain clothes? No TV? No cell phone? No Internet?* But now, after spending time among these warm, welcoming people . . .

"Wow. Man. I . . . I just . . . I can't wait!" she blurted out.

His bushy eyebrows rose, nearly disappearing under hair the color of steel wool. "You should consider adding more Pennsylvania Dutch to your vocabulary. That," he said, chuckling, "might prove harder than all the rest!"

Willa laughed, too . . . with blessed relief. So far, it seemed that Bishop Micah Fisher approved of her. Perhaps, in time, Max would, too.

He got up, said, "Wait right here . . ." and went into the parlor. When the bishop returned, he carried three books: the Bible, the *Ausband* hymnal, and *The Martyr's Mirror*. "I hope you will make yourself well acquainted with these."

"I will." She caught herself nodding, and it reminded her of the head-bobbing dachshund that sat for years in the back window of her grandmother's Oldsmobile. "I will take care of them and return them as soon as possible." She hugged them to her chest. "You have my word."

"No . . . they are my gift to you." He smiled again. "Emily has the same books. She took their words to heart. I have faith that you will not disappoint me, either."

It was high praise, coming from this man, and Willa knew the good feelings they called forth would stay with her throughout their lessons.

"We will talk soon about when the teaching should begin."

"Yes. Soon." She glanced into the parlor, and seeing Charity in the doorway, holding Frannie, realized that the bishop's wife had been listening in. The smile in her eyes said what words needn't: She, too, was pleased with the meeting's outcome.

Willa approached the bishop's wife. "I didn't hear a peep out of her, so thank you for keeping Frannie so happy."

"Ach." She gave the comment a dismissive wave. "She is a joy." Handing the baby to Willa, Charity added, "We want to help any way we can to make you into a full-fledged Amish woman!"

"I'm looking forward to that."

Because oh, how good it would feel to finally have a place to call home!

Chapter Twelve

It shouldn't have surprised her to find Anki right where she'd left her, but it did.

"How did your meeting go?" Anki asked. "Will you be one of us soon?"

Willa let Frannie down to crawl around, smiling as she toddled from chair to chair on chubby, unsteady legs, and provided Anki with an abbreviated version of what she and the bishop had discussed. "It sounds like a major investment of time and work, but it'll be worth it."

"We can hope."

What did *that* mean? Willa wondered. She noticed the novel beside Anki, right where she'd put it. "How did you enjoy the story?"

Anki picked up the book, glanced at its cover, at the back jacket, and put it down again. "I forgot it was there."

That shouldn't have surprised her, either, and yet . . .

Without a radio or television to keep her occupied, how had the woman spent the past hour? *Staring blankly into space, as usual.* More than ever, Willa wanted to bring her to the clinic, give Emily a chance to see and hear for herself that things were not normal in the mind of Anki Hofman.

"What did Dan say about your hair?"

Another shrug, and then, "He said it will be easier to wash and quicker to dry."

"He wasn't angry, then?"

"I think he has tired of me. So much that he no longer cares enough to get angry."

Something had to be done. Not tomorrow or next week, but *now*. And Willa knew that if she didn't start things in motion, Anki would continue down this dangerous slope until something horrible happened.

"Let's take a short drive, make the most of the sunshine while we can."

She tidied the lap quilt and shrugged. "I would rather stay here."

No doubt she meant it. Left to her own devices, only God knew how long Anki would sit there.

"Anki, get up. Get up right now."

At least the woman had the good grace to look a bit shocked at her stern, maternal tone.

"I told you. I would rather—"

"If you don't get up, right this minute, and come with me, I'll have no choice but to ask Dan to help me get you into the truck."

Anki rolled her eyes, and Willa knew the threat had fallen on deaf ears.

"Frannie," she said, "tell Anki to get up so we can go bye-bye in the truck."

The baby fast-crawled to the woman's side, and leaning on the cushion beside her, said, "Up, Anki. *Up!* Bye-bye? *Bye-bye!*"

Just as she'd hoped, the child got through to her. Anki wasn't happy about it, but she tossed aside the quilt and got to her feet.

Frannie clapped, and that, at least, inspired a tiny grin.

Willa held out her hand. "C'mon, sweet girl. Let's get Anki's coat and cap, and we'll all go bye-bye!"

Five minutes later, they sat in the clinic's waiting room. Anki hadn't said a word since leaving the house. She sat, sullen-faced and stiff-backed, staring at the rack of books above the toy box, where Frannie squealed as she tossed wooden cars, faceless dolls, and a small rocking horse over her shoulder. Willa didn't dare leave the room, not even long enough to let Emily know they were there. Soon enough, she'd hear Frannie, and—

The door to the second exam room opened, and Emily led the way into the waiting area. "You'll be just fine," she said, one hand on her patient's shoulder. "If you continue experiencing morning sickness, try keeping a package of saltines near your bed. Eat a few the minute you get up."

"I will. *Denke*," the woman said. When she turned to leave, she saw Willa and Anki, sitting side by side near the window wall. "Hello!" she said. "I hope neither of you are feeling poorly. . . ."

"Good to see you, Naomi." Knowing how private the Amish could be, Willa didn't mention the pregnancy.

"I am beside myself with joy," the woman said. "I must go quickly and tell Benjamin the happy news." One hand on her belly, she added, "*Two* more babies will arrive at spring's end!"

Anki stiffened, and Willa could almost read her mind: *Why have you blessed this woman with* four *children, Lord, but You haven't seen fit to give me* one?

"Congratulations," Willa said. "Frannie will soon have another playmate . . . *two* more playmates!"

Naomi hurried into her cape and out the door as Emily sat across from Anki. "I hope Naomi is right," she said, reaching across the space to pat the woman's hands, "and neither of you are here because you're ill."

Willa wished she'd had a chance to give Emily a heads-up on Anki's condition. The woman so rarely left the house that it wasn't likely the doctor had noticed anything awry.

"Anki has been a bit down lately." It wasn't the truth. Anki had been feeling down for as long as she'd known her. "She barely eats. Doesn't sleep well. Has no desire to do much of anything except . . ."

"Except sit and be left alone," Anki snapped.

Willa chose to ignore the angry outburst. "I thought maybe you could give her a quick examination, rule out anything physical that might be causing her symptoms."

Emily's brows drew together slightly—not so much that Anki would notice—but the action told Willa that she'd picked up on the subtle hints.

"Let's step into the exam room," Emily said, standing.

"Willa brought me here. She might as well hear whatever you have to say."

Willa noticed that Emily carefully avoided looking her way.

"I'm sure you don't mind if your good friend hears the details of the examination," Emily explained, "and you're more than welcome to tell her everything once we've finished. But I'm bound by certain regulations that demand patient privacy." She gently grasped Anki's elbow and helped her to her feet. "I won't keep you long. I promise."

Anki followed, but not without cutting a sharp glare Willa's way before stepping into the exam room. When the door closed, Willa said, "Oh, Frannie girl, I have a feeling we're going to hear some serious complaining during the ride back home!"

Hopefully, Anki would cooperate when Emily asked her to remove her cap, just as she always did when examining the community's women. Willa ran down the routine procedure: stethoscope, chest and back; pulse, neck and wrist; light into the throat and inner ears; tap to the knees to test reflexes. Would Anki protest when Emily suggested a blood draw? Willa hoped not; to make a proper assessment, the doctor needed every possible bit of information. With or without it, if Emily hadn't figured out by the exam's conclusion that Anki's problems were psychological, the blunt, chin-length haircut would cinch it.

The door opened, and there stood Emily, clipboard in the crook of one arm, Anki holding the other. "I'll send that blood sample off first thing in the morning, but as I said, I don't expect to find anything wrong."

It only took the quickest glance for Willa to read her friend's face: There was a problem, all right, but it wasn't physical. Fortunately, patient privacy protocols wouldn't keep Emily from sharing details with her nursing assistant. Willa needed every possible bit of information, too, if she hoped to help Anki at home.

"I wish you'd change your mind and let me give you a prescription."

Anki shook her head so hard that the cap shifted on her head. "I do *not* need pills, and I will *not* take them."

"Will you come back in a few days? Talk with me about what's bothering you?"

"You are a good woman, Emily, and I consider you a friend. But I will not waste your time or mine, talking about problems that do not exist."

Oh, Anki, Willa thought. *You're making a mistake. A terrible mistake.*

As predicted, the short drive between the clinic and the

Hofmans' house was anything but comfortable, and Dan was waiting for them out front.

"I was worried sick when I got home and no one was here!" he said.

Willa helped Anki hop out of the front seat. "Sorry, Dan. I should have left you a note."

"Where were you?"

She lifted Frannie from the car seat, thankful that for the moment, she didn't have to look into his angry face. "At the clinic."

"She thought I was coming down with something." Anki didn't even bat an eye at the blatant lie. "Emily gave me a checkup. I am fine."

Hearing that she wasn't sick seemed to dissipate Dan's panic somewhat. Willa hoped a good meal and conversation with Max would quell the last of his ire. He didn't know it yet, but the first chance she got, Willa intended to tell him exactly what she suspected was wrong with his wife: major depressive disorder. Anki had demonstrated every symptom, from a lack of interest to weight loss, sleep disorders and fatigue, difficulty concentrating, and worst of all, thoughts of death and suicide.

He held the door as his wife went inside, and as Willa stepped up onto the porch, Dan said, "You have invited Max to supper again?"

"Yes. It seemed the right thing to do. He drove Frannie and me to the Fishers' house, so I could talk to the bishop about baptism."

"Ah, yes. So you were serious about that, then?"

"I was. More accurately, I *am*."

He followed her into the parlor, where she stooped to remove the baby's hat and jacket.

"Good. Maybe that will motivate the man to do the right thing."

Willa carried Frannie into the kitchen and put the child onto the gleaming speckled linoleum. "The right thing?" She laid a chair on its side to keep the baby in the room.

"If you two were married, maybe he would stop looking like a long-lost lamb whenever you are around. It is enough to make a man lose his lunch, I tell you!"

He wasn't smiling, but Willa recognized the teasing glint in his blue eyes. The expression wiped years from his rugged face. If she and Max were married, could she—as a friend—tell Dan that he ought to smile more?

"Anki tells me that you did your best, straightening up the mess she made with the kitchen shears."

Willa groaned. "I only wish I could have prevented it altogether. That . . . and then maybe the dreams that drove her to do it . . ." She looked around him. "Where has she gone?"

"Where else? Upstairs. To bed."

And there it was again, the sad, defeated expression that so often darkened his face.

"Has she told you about the dreams?"

"No. She does not tell me anything. Hurts my heart, because once, we talked all the time, about everything. Now?" Shoulders slumped and head down, he exhaled a heavy sigh. "Now she stares. Silent. I thought it was because we have no children. But having Frannie around proved that is not the problem."

Willa thought of the way Anki had reacted, seeing Naomi's excitement over her latest pregnancy. If the Hofmans had been blessed with children, would they have been enough to divert Anki's attention from her twin's suicide? Or would she have slipped into that dark hole anyway and neglected them? *God's will,* she thought . . .

"If you get a chance to speak with Emily, I think she'll recommend that Anki see someone who specializes in depressive disorders. Her sister's suicide . . ." Willa filled a pot with water and placed it on the stove's back burner. "It affected her far more than she's willing to admit."

"She is angry with Abigail, still. We all were, when she chose that Englisher over her life here. But when we got that news?" He sighed again. "She had hoped and prayed for a reunion, if not in this life, in the next. When Abigail took that from her . . ." He ended with a helpless shrug.

"Mind if I ask you a personal question?"

Thumbs hooked behind his suspenders, Dan said, "You can ask . . ."

"How did she tell you about her hair?"

"By taking off her cap." He dropped heavily onto a kitchen chair and held his head in his hands. "I did not know how to react. Did not know what to say. So I said nothing."

"And Anki? What did *she* say?"

"She asked if I was angry. I told her the truth: I did not understand. When she said nothing, I said 'It is hair. It will grow back.' I have since asked the Almighty's forgiveness for that lie."

That couldn't have been easy for this big, always-in-charge man. Sharing his pain with Willa? She knew that couldn't be easy, either. After all these months under his roof, she'd come to love him like a brother. If the Amish weren't so opposed to displays of affection, she'd give him a much-needed hug, right now!

"Max will be here soon," he said, rising slowly. "I will be in the shed."

She carried the potato basket to the counter. "I'll call when supper's ready."

"Five o'clock?"

Oh, how it hurt to see him suffering this way! Willa crossed the room and threw her arms around him. "Don't worry, Dan. Anki will come around. She has to!"

He rested his chin on top of her head, absorbing her simple offer of comfort. A second passed, if that, before he held her at arm's length.

"You have a good heart, Willa Reynolds," he said, and hurried outside.

And although he couldn't hear it, she said, "You do, too, Dan Hofman."

"Dan?" Frannie echoed, hugging Willa's legs. "Dan bye-bye?"

"He'll be back soon, sweet girl." She handed the child a cracker and got busy scrubbing vegetables. The roast had been marinating since before her visit to the Fishers. Sliding its pan from the fridge, she poured the milk down the drain. "What do you think, Frannie, m'girl? Just cabbage? Or onions, carrots, and potatoes?"

The chair blockade had captured the baby's attention. Willa stood, hands on hips, watching Frannie squat and peer through the opening between the chair's legs. A cracker distracted her long enough to allow Willa to place a second chair on its side in the opposite direction.

"No!" Frannie complained. "No, Mama!"

"Sorry, sweet girl, but you'd be miserable in the high chair while I make supper, and I can't have you meandering hither and yon while I'm working."

Now Frannie whimpered, and lay facedown on the floor. "No," she wailed. "No . . ."

"What have we here?"

"Max!" Oh, but he looked handsome in his crisp white shirt and trim-fitting black trousers. "You're early."

"And a good thing," he said, picking up the baby. "Looks like this girl needed rescuing!"

"Max," Frannie said, laying her head on his shoulder. And patting his back, she added, "Aw, Max."

He looked even more handsome as his face lit up in reaction to Frannie's affectionate welcome. She deserved a father like him, Willa thought . . . and bit her lip. *You have to stop thinking such things. It isn't fair to any of you!*

Joining her at the sink, he said, "What can I do to help?"

"You're kidding, right? You're *already* helping! She's a bit grumpy tonight. I overstayed my visit with the Fishers. And then . . ." Should she tell him about her talk with Dan? No, that was a discussion best saved for later.

"And then what?"

"And then we got home." She looked up, saying without words that it had something to do with Anki, in the room above them.

Willa went back to scrubbing the vegetables as Max asked, "Where is Dan?"

"In the shed."

"If you'll help me get her into her coat, I'll take Frannie outside . . ."

"He wasn't in the best of moods when he left here."

"Why?"

"Anki cut her hair, for one thing. We weren't here when he got home, for another. And it scared him, I think."

"Why were you gone?"

"Because . . ." she began in a near whisper.

When he moved closer to better hear her, Frannie flung one arm over his shoulders, the other over Willa's. "Aw, hug," she said. "Hug!"

They laughed, but stopped when Anki joined them. "The three of you make a happy little family."

A crooked smile tilted his mouth. "We do?"

She answered with a sniff, then stepped up beside Willa

and shoved her hands into the sudsy water. "I will wash the vegetables. You peel and chop them. Okay?"

The woman was, after all, the boss. Willa wondered if it felt good, issuing an order for a change, instead of succumbing to the instructions of others. "Sounds good to me. With both of us working, we'll get this stuff in the pot in half the time!"

The woman replied with an indifferent shrug. "Where is Dan?"

"In the shed," Willa repeated.

"Because I have disappointed him. Again."

"No, Anki, he's organizing. Remember those baby food jars he found last week? Well, he said something about sorting his nuts and bolts and screws, and somehow fastening them to the pegboard above his workbench. And you know how he gets when a job is unfinished."

Willa didn't know why the reminder would upset Anki, but clearly it had. *If she keeps scrubbing the vegetables that way,* she thought, *I won't need to peel them!* Max must have noticed, too, because he raised his eyebrows and mouthed, "Uh-oh . . ."

"So what do you think? Is it all right if I take Frannie outside? I can push her on Dan's swing."

Willa pictured the square-shaped seat and back, flat arms, and thick rope that Dan had hung from the big oak out back soon after their arrival in Pleasant Valley. He'd retreated to his shed for hours then, too, and when he returned to the house after dusk, a sly grin had brightened his usually serious, dark-bearded face. Admitting it would have made him guilty of the sin of pride, but he'd been pleased with his work. Next morning, under the guise of testing the leather straps attached to hold Frannie securely in place, he'd put the little girl in his swing. Willa could count on one hand the number of times she'd heard him laugh out loud, and have fingers left over. As Frannie squealed happily during her first ride, he'd thrown back his head and roared. Maybe what he needed right now was a reminder of that day.

Moments after they stepped outside, Anki said, "You owe him the truth."

"Uh . . . what?"

She rolled her eyes. "Max cares for you. He cares for Frannie, too. He deserves to know . . . everything."

Willa clamped her molars together, buying time to think, because she didn't want to say anything that might upset Anki.

"The longer you wait, the harder it will be, because the more time that passes . . . he will care even more. And then it will break his heart when he learns that—"

Willa was agitated to the point of trembling. She put down the paring knife and plunged her hands into the dishwater. "Anki. Please. Stop."

"You must tell him. It is the right thing to do."

Willa grasped Anki's wrists. "He knows." *Most of it, anyway.*

Shaking her head, Anki blinked. "Everything?"

Don't make me tell a lie, Anki. Please don't!

"He knows about the drugs?"

Willa turned her loose. "He does."

"That you sold them *and* used them?"

"Yes."

Grabbing the red-checkered towel beside the sink, Willa felt the sting of tears in her eyes. When arranging the job with the Hofmans, Alice had been pretty up front about Willa's past. Thankfully, the social worker couldn't tell them what she didn't know. It wasn't likely that Max would ever hear the rest of her ugly story. A good thing, because Anki was right. If he ever learned about all the unspeakable things she'd done to ensure a steady supply of drugs . . .

"I will never understand," Anki was saying, "what God is thinking."

"No one can know the mind of God."

She continued as if Willa hadn't said a word. "Naomi already has children, and now, He will give her *twins*?" She threw up her hands, then watched, mesmerized, as the suds floated slowly, silently to the small braided rug under her feet, where they dissolved, one miniscule, shimmering bubble at a time. "Even *you* have a child." Shaking Willa's shoulders, she cried, "*Why. Not. Me!*"

Willa had asked herself that same question, dozens, maybe even hundreds of times, and knew better than anyone how unworthy she was of a gift so precious. It would be easy to lash out, make Anki sorry for every stinging word. But the poor woman had spent *months* lost in her lonely thoughts, reliving her sister's suicide, wishing for children . . . Willa couldn't hold Anki responsible for the hurtful things she'd said.

"Everything all right in here?"

Max . . .

How much had he heard? And why hadn't she heard Frannie?

"Mama!" Frannie said, arms extended.

Willa pulled her close. "Oh my goodness! Your fat little cheeks are cold!" She untied the knitted cap. "Did you have fun on Dan's swing?"

"Max . . ."

Willa interpreted that to mean Dan might have built the swing, but today, at least, Max made it fun.

A worry frown etched his brow. "Need any help?"

"No, Anki and I have things well in hand." She hung the baby's jacket on its hook, and after tucking Frannie into the high chair, placed a cracker on the tray. "So Max, was Dan able to put all the nuts and bolts in their proper places?"

He shifted his weight from one foot to the other, looked at the clock, out the window, into the parlor . . . everywhere but at her. His guilty look told her that he'd seen something out there in the shed—something that directly involved Dan—but he couldn't discuss it in front of Anki.

Anki's reedy voice broke into her thoughts. "I am tired."

"Supper won't be ready for a couple of hours," Willa said, "so there's plenty of time for a nap. Although if you sleep now, you might not be able to tonight." Knowing Anki, she'd be up half the night anyway, pacing from window to window, going up and down the stairs, opening and closing cupboard doors and drawers, as if searching for some missing treasure.

"Yes, you make a good point. Is the book you gave me still in the parlor?"

"Last time I saw it, it was on the sofa cushion." *Where I put it before Frannie and I left for the Fishers'.*

"I will go upstairs to read, then." She lumbered toward the stairs, stopping to kiss Frannie's forehead on the way. "Do you know how precious you are, little one?"

The baby's brown eyes widened, and she looked from Willa to Max, as if silently asking for help in understanding Anki's peculiar behavior.

"Once I have supper in the oven, I'll bring you some tea."

"If you like . . ."

No one spoke, not even Frannie, until the creaking floorboards overhead told them Anki was out of earshot.

"She is in a bad way today, isn't she." Max sounded

every bit as concerned as he looked. "Dan is a mess, too. Maybe it would be best if I left, so that—"

"Oh, please stay!" Willa didn't like the ring of desperation in her voice and tried to hide it by arranging potatoes and carrots around the roast. "Dan enjoys having you here." *Not as much as I do, but . . .*

"Traffic was light coming back from Cumberland. I should have gone home, killed some time before bursting in here early. And uninvited."

She added sliced onions to the pot. "I invited you, remember? So what if you were a little early."

Max leaned a shoulder against the doorjamb, folded both arms over his chest, and crossed one booted foot over the other. "Do you always serve supper at five?"

"As close to it as possible, because that's when Dan likes to eat."

"Ah . . . and this is Dan's house, so . . ."

"Exactly." She poured a cupful of water into the pan, and after turning up the flame beneath it, covered it. "If this was your house, what time would we eat?"

"Hmm . . ." Eyes narrowed, he gave the question some thought. "I suppose five is as good a time as any."

"Not too early, not too late," they said together.

They laughed together, too, and Frannie saw it as an invitation to join them.

Then, as suddenly as it began, the merriment ended when Max said, "I am sorry Anki was harsh with you earlier. She has no right to speak to you that way. No right at all."

"Oh, I don't mind. She has . . . issues. So if she's short-tempered from time to time, it's easy to forgive."

"Not everyone would be as forgiving." Now he stood, feet shoulder width apart, filling the doorway. "You have a good heart, Willa."

"You wouldn't say that if you heard the things I *didn't* say!"

"I suppose we are all entitled to a few choice words . . . in the privacy of our minds."

"Ah, privacy. I've almost forgotten what it is!"

As if signaled by a stage director, Frannie hollered a jubilant, "Mama!"

He stuck a forefinger into his ear. "For one so small, she makes a big noise! If you need help, just have her call me."

"I won't, but I will."

He opened the door and said, "Uh . . . *what*?"

Nervous laughter bubbled from her lips as he started down the back porch steps. "Go and tell Dan to relax. Anki is upstairs reading, so all is well in the Hofman kitchen." His boots had just hit the flagstone walk when she said, "And Max?"

He stopped, facing her.

"Please don't change your mind about joining us for supper."

A tender smile twinkled in his eyes, and knowing what it meant, Willa's heart thumped a little harder: He would stay, for no reason other than she'd asked him to.

It was reason enough to hope that someday, he'd stay with her . . . permanently.

Chapter Thirteen

"Sorry, boss. I looked everywhere. Talked to everyone who knew her, but no luck."

Joe threw the mug he'd been holding, narrowly missing Arnie's bearded face. It hit the wall hard, and rained glass on the grit- and grime-covered floor.

"I'm not paying you to hunt for four-leaf clovers, you idiot." He stomped across the room, stood nose to nose with the taller, leaner man. "Go to a barbershop, you long-haired freak, and maybe you'll actually be able to find some clues!"

Arnie shook his head, effectively shifting the bangs out of his eyes. "Look, Joe, she's been gone for what, seven months? How come all of a sudden you want her back?"

He put the final twist on a joint and growled, "She's worth a lot of money, that's why!"

"You never did say how much you owe Seamus . . ."

"Because it's none of your business. I'll tell you this much: If I had thirty thousand dollars right now, I wouldn't have to lick that fool's boots."

"Thirty grand? That's all you need?" Arnie's high-pitched snicker grated in Joe's ears. "That's chump change for a dude like you."

"Just . . . shut up, fool, and get back out there. And this time, you'd better bring her here." He hoped Arnie wouldn't make him spell it out: He had plans for Willa. For that baby, too. If Arnie came back without them—or at the very least, a solid lead to them—the would-be hippy would regret it for the rest of his minutes-long life.

"Awright, Joe, but it ain't gonna be any easier than it was last time. She's smart. Smart enough to hide someplace nobody would ever think to look for her."

"Then use your head for something other than a place to hang that smelly old baseball cap and start looking *there*."

Arnie tugged the hat lower on his forehead. "Okay, but I'm gonna need money. For gas and food, maybe a motel room or whatever."

Cursing under his breath, Joe tugged the stainless steel chain that hung from a belt loop and opened the wallet attached to the other end. "There," he said, tossing five hundred dollars at Arnie's feet. "But you're not getting another dime until you drag her back here, understand? So you'd better spend it wisely."

Stooping, Arnie picked up the bills and stuffed them into an inside pocket, then zipped his camouflage parka. "What number you want I should call? You know, if I find her."

Joe held a match to one end of the joint. "Not *if,* but *when*. Call the burner phone."

Once Arnie left, Joe took a long, deep drag and held it. Eyes closed, he instantly felt his jangled nerves calm. Free drugs and booze were the only perks of this job. Since Willa had run off, that is. Since then, he'd run the operation single-handedly, answering to no one but Seamus Hanrahan. So far, he hadn't given the man any reason to complain or question his judgment. A good thing, too, because cold hard cash, not loyalty, was the only thing of value to the burly Irishman. Mistakes could be costly. Or deadly. So Joe didn't make them. Ever. Aside from easy access to "product," it was a tough, scary job. Not that he'd admit it. To anyone. But then, no one had put a gun to his head and forced him to sign on with the crazy redhead. Fact was, it had been far too easy to get involved.

If only getting *un*involved was as easy. *Should've stayed in school, earned your accounting degree.* It wasn't likely to give him access to hundreds of thousands of dollars and all the drugs and booze he could handle, but at least he wouldn't have to sleep with one eye open, worrying that even a minor misstep could cost him his life. Literally.

Hanrahan's latest implied threats were one hundred percent Willa's fault. In the first weeks after she'd left, Joe had stayed so high that he barely noticed she was gone. *That's what a ready supply of drugs going out and money coming in will do for a man.* But now, the cops were watching. Watching closely. And that was bad, real bad, for business. If Hanrahan decided to conduct one of his impromptu audits, he'd take the missing money out of Joe's hide. Maybe even—how did he like to put it?—plant him face-down and six feet under. Unless she'd changed a lot, he could put her back to work and bank that thirty grand in a few weeks. And if he sold the kid, he could double that amount.

Smirking, he squinted into the sweet-smelling smoke that encircled his head. Because girls, even baby girls, commanded a high price in the right marketplace . . .

* * *

Anki sat in the rocking chair, staring out the parlor window. "Looks like a snow sky," she said, mostly to herself. "I hope Dan gets back before it starts."

She looked cold, sitting there hugging herself, so Willa draped a quilt over her legs. "And I hope the forecasters are right . . . strong winds and a drop in temps, but no snow."

"I love the snow."

Typical, Willa thought, of people who didn't have to deal with it. *Stop being so negative, Will. Anki would help if she could.*

Or would she? Willa thought of Dan who, until she and Frannie moved in, had spent every minute of his free time cooking and cleaning, because his wife couldn't.

Anki tucked her feet under her and pulled the quilt up to her chin. "Everything looks so clean and pure, covered in a blanket of white."

"It's pretty, I'll give you that."

Frannie, hands on the curved wooden arms of Anki's chair, leaned left and right, effectively rocking it as her sweet two-note song filled the room. "Wocky-wocky-wocky," she chanted, a baby-talk version of what Willa had crooned while rocking her to sleep. After a few seconds, Willa stood quietly, studying Anki's face. Even at her age, Frannie understood that Anki's mind was elsewhere, and the realization prompted a disappointed sigh. Something outside caught her attention, and she dropped to her knees and crawled to the low-hung window. Then, pressing her nose to the glass pane, she pointed. "Kitty!"

Willa dropped to her knees, too, and pulling her daughter into a sideways hug, followed her line of vision to the gray tabby that sashayed toward the shed. "Yup. Cute kitty!"

Now Frannie pressed a forefinger against the glass. "S'ing?"

"No, sweetie, we can't swing right now. Too cold outside."

Eyes wide, Frannie pretended to shiver. "Co'd!"

"Very cold!" This winter would mark the baby's first experience with snow.

On her feet now, Willa went to the woodstove, where Dan had loaded the old coal scuttle with kindling and stacked logs beside it. "God bless Dan! Thanks to him, we have everything we need for a fire," she told Anki.

No response.

Crouching, she wadded newspapers into tight balls, and upon hearing the crinkling sound, Frannie said, "Hot!"

"Yes, sweet girl." She forced a warning tone into her voice. "*Very* hot."

Still leaning into the windowsill, the baby nodded, and matched her mother's serious expression.

Willa reached for the matchbox that Dan kept on the top shelf of the cupboard beside the stove, lit one, and ignited the paper and tinder she'd layered in the stove's belly. Minutes later, after adding a few dry logs, she closed the door and adjusted the damper.

"There!" she said. "We'll be toasty-warm in no time!"

"Toe-tee!" Frannie echoed. And then she yawned. A long, lung-filling yawn that she punctuated with an exaggerated exhalation.

"Goodness!" Willa said, scooping her up. "We'd better get some lunch into your belly, then put you down for a nap." Standing beside the rocker, she said, "Would you rather have a ham or turkey sandwich, Anki?"

Still no response. "All right then, I'll feed Frannie and settle her into the crib, and then I'll bring you a plate."

She waited for a reply, and receiving none, looked into Frannie's lovable face. "Max brought some chocolate syrup last time he came for supper. How about I squirt some into your milk?"

"Mi'k!"

"And a sliced apple?"

"Ah-puh!"

The baby was talking more and more these days. Soon, she'd form sentences, and learn to pronounce every word properly. She'd walk without holding on to furniture, then run, and . . .

Tears stung Willa's eyes. "Oh sweet girl," she said, putting her into the high chair, "please don't be in such a hurry to grow up." Willa pressed a lingering kiss on her forehead. "Mama loves her baby girl!"

"Ah-puh?"

Laughing, Willa took an apple from the fruit basket centerpiece and then grabbed a cracker. "Munch on this while I cut and peel it for you."

After handing Frannie the cracker, Willa peeled and cut the apple into bite-size cubes, then did the same with a slice of ham. Piece by piece, the food disappeared as Frannie babbled happily.

Night before last, she'd chattered, too, and Max had responded as though every word made perfect sense. Oh, how Willa missed him! The feeling reminded her of last night's supper, which hadn't been nearly as enjoyable, thanks to Dan's straightforward announcement:

"No need to set a place for Max," he'd said, hanging his hat and coat near the door. "He will not be here tonight."

"Oh no. He's all right, I hope!"

Even now, Willa heard the almost-pleading, disappointed notes in her voice. She stood, absentmindedly stirring chocolate syrup into Frannie's cup of milk, picturing Dan's teasing smirk. "He will be fine once he plows through that mountain of dirty clothes."

Willa would gladly have offered to wash them . . . if he'd so much as dropped a hint about the ever-growing mound. But asking for help wasn't in his nature. She'd grown accustomed to his gentle smile. His soft-spoken voice. The way he locked his gaze to hers, whether she was asking him to pass the salt or describing her work at the clinic. He laughed easily—and oh, how she loved the sound of it!—and displayed a sense of humor that inspired her and Dan and even Frannie to laugh.

"Mama?"

The baby's voice—and the annoying clank of the spoon against the plastic sippy cup—roused her from her reverie. Stifling a chuckle, she popped on the cap. "Sorry, sweet girl. Mama took a short trip to la-la land."

"*Denke*!"

"English *and* Dutch," Willa whispered. "My *smart* sweet girl!"

"Mmm-mmm," Frannie said. "Mi'k!"

Winking, Willa said, "I'll be sure to tell Max how much you enjoy it."

The baby turned, and hanging slightly over the chair's side, looked toward the back door. "Max?"

Willa glanced at the place he'd chosen as his own, here at Dan and Anki's table . . . directly across from hers. Although all six chairs were identical, his looked more bare than the rest. She caught herself smiling, despite the gloom of missing him.

"Max is working, but he might stop by later."

Frannie yawned again, and this time, stretched both arms toward the ceiling.

"Aw, is my sweet girl sleepy?" She held a clean dishcloth under warm water, wiped the baby's hands and face, and lifted her from the chair. Upstairs, after changing Frannie's diaper and dressing her in one-piece pajamas made from old towels, she put her in the crib. The baby sprawled out, drowsy eyes watching as Willa tugged a colorful quilt over her.

"Tell you what," she said, leaning in to kiss her cheeks, "while you're sleeping, I'll bake some cookies." *And if Max decides to join us for supper, I'll send him home with some.*

After settling Frannie into her crib, Willa made her way back downstairs, smiling all the way. "What have you become?" she muttered, rounding the corner into the kitchen. Not all that long ago, she'd balked every time Joe insisted on a meal, a back rub, or some other self-centered favor. Although she'd hated being ordered around, Willa filled every demand to ensure a steady supply of drugs. At first, Joe was generous, handing out pills like candy; then controlled her supply once he was sure she needed them . . . needed them so badly that she'd do anything, no matter how repulsive or demeaning, to get them. If cancer hadn't taken her mother, seeing what her only child had allowed herself to become would have killed her. "Thanks, Lord," she whispered, putting a huge bowl onto the counter, "for protecting her from that."

Her mother had never relied on a man. Once, a fellow who considered himself her steady beau tried to tell her what to do. Not only did she read him the riot act, she kicked him to the curb, too. The memory made Willa smile. And then tears pooled in her eyes. When she lost her mom, she'd lost her sense of self, lost her way, lost all sense of right and wrong, and all chances of following in her mother's footsteps.

The baby monitor flickered, telling her that Frannie had rolled over in her sleep.

Frannie, who'd saved her life.

Frannie, who'd given her reason to live.

"I smell vanilla," Anki said, plopping onto Max's chair.

Willa wanted to tell her to get up and sit in her *own* chair. And then she remembered that here in her own home, Anki had every right to sit anywhere she pleased.

She turned the oven dial to 375 degrees. "I'm making cookies. Want to help?"

For a second there, it looked like she might say yes. Instead, Anki shook her head. "I will just watch."

"That's fine." Spreading parchment paper on the cookie sheets, she said, "It's still nice, having you here with me."

"Do you believe Dan is in town buying a print cartridge for the construction trailer?"

Willa dumped two cups of flour into the big bowl. "If that's what he said, sure. Why would he lie about something so silly?"

"To hide the facts. That he would rather be anywhere than here with me."

"He wouldn't be here at this time of day, anyway. He'd be on a jobsite. Or in his office, ordering supplies. Or delivering materials to one of the crews."

What were the chances, Willa wondered, that Anki might snap out of the doldrums if she had something—someone—to think about other than herself?

She added sugar to the bowl. "Mind if I ask you a personal question?"

Anki shrugged.

"How did you know Dan was the right man for you?"

Anki frowned. Stared at her hands, tightly fisted in her lap. And then the strangest thing happened . . . Anki's face lit up with a wistful smile.

"I saw him at the fall festival, standing with a group of young men, laughing at something one of them said. The sound of it . . ." Anki pressed a palm to her chest. "It warmed me to my core." She giggled. "I might have fallen in love, just a little bit, right then and there. He stood out, and not only because he was taller and more broad-shouldered than the others."

"So you didn't know him then?"

"Not on that day . . ."

"How did you get together?"

That inspired quiet laughter. "I dared my sister to tell him that I thought he was handsome."

"And she did?"

"Oh yes. Abby was never one to shy away from a dare!"

Willa suspected that if she didn't ask another pointed question, quickly, Anki would veer off track, probably far enough to mire herself in a rut of bad memories about her sister's death. After measuring out two teaspoons of baking powder, she added, "And she did it right way?"

"Immediately."

"Oh my goodness!" She mixed the dry ingredients together. "Did you hide?"

"I most certainly did not! We weren't identical twins, and she was the only one who didn't think she was the prettiest. I didn't want Dan thinking Abby was making up the story as a test to see if he was interested in *her*!"

Softened butter went into a second bowl, and as she cracked eggs into it, Willa said, "Let me guess . . . he came marching right over."

"No." The dreamy smile grew. "He was so shy and quiet. He caught me staring, and immediately looked away. But he kept peeking around Abigail. After a minute, she put her hands beside her mouth and hollered, 'Anki! Come here! This man wants to meet you!'"

"And you went?" Now, she added the vanilla, and a pinch of salt, and beat everything together.

"I tried, but I could not move my feet. I saw her shake her head. And grab his hand. And *drag* him to where I stood, stiff as a statue and dumb as a post."

"Oh, how I wish I'd been there for *that* introduction!"

Giggling again, Anki admitted, "We saw each other three more times after that, at the church social, at his cousin's wedding, when a neighbor died. I knew his name, and I suppose he must have known mine, but we were not introduced, officially, until Charity Fisher saw us, staring at one another across the headstones. She grabbed his wrist, and mine, and forced us to shake hands. And then she said, 'Daniel Hofman, this is Anki Nafziger. Say hello to Anki, Dan.' And he did. 'Now you,' she said to me. And once we had that out of the way, she turned us around and gave us a shove. 'Go. Take a walk. Talk about what a blessing it is that it did not rain on the day of Elmer Yoder's burial.'"

"And she just left you!"

"And she just left us." She looked at the wall, where the red, orange, and yellow fall foliage surrounding the photograph of Deep Creek Lake brightened the October calendar page. "We were married one month later, and one month from today, we will have been husband and wife for ten years."

"Ten years," Willa said, blending the liquid ingredients with the dry. "I envy you."

Anki's mood darkened. "Why?"

"A whole decade with the love of your life. What a beautiful blessing."

"God does not agree."

"Anki, of course He does!"

"Then why has He deprived me of children?"

"He must have other plans for you. Alice, the social worker who brought me here, has no children. Yet look at all the good she's doing for everyone in her care!"

A nearly whispered groan issued from Anki. "The only thing I am good at is driving my husband farther and farther from me. Even God has rejected me!"

"I disagree." Willa pinched off a lump of cookie dough and rolled it into a ball. "Just the other day," she said, placing it on the parchment, "I read Luke 23:29. It said something like, 'Blessed are the barren and the wombs that never bore and the breasts that never nursed!' He wouldn't reject you, Anki."

"No children. A husband who barely tolerates me. A sister who hated life so much that she took her own . . ." She groaned again. "If He hasn't rejected me, then *where* is *He*?"

"I'm going to be honest with you. Because I consider you a friend. A dear, dear friend." Willa plopped another ball of dough onto the cookie sheet. "You can't fix what's wrong with you all by yourself. You need help. Therapy. Medicine. Emily can tell you where to find both."

"Willa Reynolds, stop this!" Anki got up so fast, she nearly toppled the chair. "Stop it right now! Have I not made it clear that I will not talk to Emily again, that I will not take pills?"

"All right then. In that case, we need to find something *positive* for you to think about. Something that will make you feel healthy and whole and productive. Like . . . like your shop. They're predicting a long, hard winter. That will give us plenty of time to get it cleaned up and ready to reopen in the spring!"

She sat, hid behind her hands, and, voice muffled by

her fingers, said, "What makes you think that a woman who is too weak to seek help is strong enough to run a business?"

"You are stronger than you think."

Willa was a little surprised, looking at the straight rows of cookie balls that lined the parchment-covered cookie sheets. Had she been so distracted by her conversation with Anki that she'd mindlessly used up half of the dough?

She slid the sheets into the oven and washed her hands, then filled two mugs with milk. "Drink up, Anki. You need protein."

"Why? Taking care of my health will only prolong the inevitable."

Flustered, angry, desperate to find a way through to Anki, Willa dropped a fist onto the table, hard enough to rattle the salt and pepper shakers.

"You aren't deaf or blind, and you're surely not the only person who has lost a loved one. You're not the only woman who doesn't have children, either. If it's a baby you want, stop feeling sorry for yourself! Get your head right with God! Prepare your head and your heart and look into adopting one of the hundreds of children who need a loving home and caring parents!"

She sat, stone-faced and silent, staring into Willa's eyes.

Oh Lord, forgive me . . . I've said too much. She isn't strong enough to hear such—

"You are right. I do feel sorry for myself. I am weak and self-centered, too."

Willa grabbed her by the shoulders, pulled her into a standing position and wrapped her in a fierce hug.

"Now *you* stop it. What's wrong with you isn't your fault." Standing back, she bored her gaze into Anki's eyes, gave her a little shake. "Something in here," she said, gently tapping Anki's temple, "isn't working properly. Maybe it's hormonal. Maybe it's hereditary. Maybe it's the trauma of losing your sister in such a horrible, heartbreaking way." Pulling her close again, Willa said, "I'm sorry, Anki. Truly sorry. I had no right to speak to you that way." And holding her at arm's length again, she added, "In the months I've been here, I've come to think of you as family. I love you, and I'm worried about you . . . worried *for* you. But that's no excuse. I should never have spoken to you that way. Will you forgive me?"

Nodding, Anki whispered, "There is nothing to forgive." Turning from Willa's embrace, she sat down again. "I can smell the cookies. Do you think they have finished baking?"

"Omigoodness!" Willa grabbed a thick pot holder and, opening the oven door, peeked inside. "Whew!" she exclaimed, closing the door. "A minute, maybe two more, and they would have burnt. Thank you for being so observant."

"Is there ham enough for a sandwich?"

"Yes! Yes, of course there is!" Leaning into the fridge, Willa stacked the fixings in her arms, then placed them on the table. "I'm so glad your appetite is back," she said, assembling the sandwich. She cut it on the diagonal, plated it, and slid it in front of Anki. "Some crackers to go with it? Soup?"

"Soup sounds good." And then, smiling, Anki picked up half of the sandwich. "It has been a while since anyone scolded me like that." She bit off the point. "Who knew it would stimulate my appetite!"

Willa gave in to the urge to hug her again, from behind the chair this time. "Oh Anki, I didn't mean to scold you. I'd never do anything to hurt you, because I meant what I said: I love you like family!"

"I know."

Just *what* did she know? Willa kissed the top of Anki's head and went back to the stove. Once the cookies were out of the oven, she gulped down a glass of water, noticed that her hands were trembling, and she knew exactly why: If her outburst had sent Anki deeper into despair . . . Willa couldn't even bring herself to complete the thought. So she prayed, instead. *Thank you, Lord, for protecting Anki from my big, out-of-control mouth!*

"Will Max be here for supper tonight?"

"I don't know. I haven't talked with him since he was here the other night."

"Will you do me a favor?"

"Anything, Anki," she said, meaning it, "*anything*."

"After supper, once Frannie is tucked in for the night, take him outside. If he joins us for supper, that is. Take him for a long walk and tell him how you feel. One of you has to make the first move. Why not you, my outspoken friend."

By now, she'd moved the cooled cookies onto plates, and started a new batch for the oven. "If he joins us, I'll think about it."

Anki clucked her tongue. "What is there to think about?" She took another sip of milk. "Look at it this way: If I had not taken the bull by the horns, do you think my bashful Dan and I would be married today?"

"But Anki . . . what if Max isn't ready for such a big step? What if he likes living alone, where it's quiet and clean?"

"If you do not see the way he looks at you, if you do not hear the way he speaks to you, maybe *you* are deaf and blind!"

"It's definitely something to pray about . . ." Then, "So what do you think? Would you like some help, getting the shop ready to open again in the spring?"

"You are a good friend, a remarkable woman. But Willa, you already have so many demands on your time."

"I'd *make* time for something this important."

"I know you would, and I love you for it. Let us just leave it at this: We will pray about it."

"Yes. And if it's God's will, we'll do it!"

She took a cookie, handed one to Anki. "Are the Amish allowed to make a toast to good friends?"

Anki tapped her treat against Willa's. "To good friends," she said, and took a bite.

Willa wasn't so gullible or naïve as to believe that Anki's problems were all solved. But this was a start. A good start. And for the first time since moving to Pleasant Valley, she had hope that her friend could one day know peace of mind.

Lord, let Max visit tonight, because I want to tell him all about this scary, annoying, amazing afternoon!

Would she take Anki's advice, and admit that she'd fallen in love with him?

If it's God's will, I'll do it!

Chapter Fourteen

Over the next few weeks, Anki's disposition improved. Willa still noticed some of the old, worrisome symptoms of depression—slipping into periods of silence, separating herself from others, skipping meals, pacing instead of sleeping—but it seemed, on the surface, anyway, that she was making a sincere effort to climb out of the dark hole she'd dug for herself. Either that, or her acting skills could put Hollywood stars to shame.

Much as she wanted to, Willa hadn't been able to share what was going on with Max, because lately, she'd only seen him in passing. Dan explained his absence by telling her Max had been putting in long, hard hours to iron out the wrinkles between planners, developers, and Frostburg's Allegheny County officials. "I would carry half that load," he'd said, "but I do not have Max's people skills. He is much better suited to the job."

Silently, Willa had agreed. She could picture Max dealing with decision makers who felt college degrees and brass nameplates gave them carte blanche to intimidate a simple Amish contractor. By now, he'd taught them an unforgettable lesson: One quiet man could say more with simple honesty and know-how than they could with fancy words and bullying tactics.

"It will soon be Thanksgiving," Anki said.

Willa was surprised that she'd noticed, let alone mentioned it. "Do you think we should have a big dinner?"

"Of course. It is a perfect day to give thanks for our many blessings."

"A turkey and stuffing, then? And pumpkin pies?"

"Of course!" Anki repeated. "We have many things to be grateful for."

Willa waited, wondering *what* things. Instead of answering the unasked question, Anki said, "Do you believe we really could reopen my shop, come spring?"

Now, it was Willa who said, "Of course!" Hearing the word "we" pleased her.

"Will you go there with me, so we can see how much work we are facing?"

She thought of everything on today's to-do list: afternoon hours at the clinic, taking the CNA practice exam, laundry, helping Dan out by shoveling a path to the woodpile, meals . . .

"How about this morning, after I put Frannie down for her nap? I'll bring the baby monitor out there, a tablet and a pencil, and write down everything we'll need to do. That way, we can tackle one or two things a day without stressing ourselves out. And who knows . . . while we're there, you might find a few things to give as Christmas gifts . . . save yourself the bother of making or buying stuff."

"You are the only one in danger of stressing out." Anki rolled her eyes. "If only I had half your energy!"

More desperation than energy, Willa thought, *and you don't want that!* She was motivated by a desire to make a better life for Frannie. For herself. For Dan and Anki. She hadn't told anyone about what she hoped to do, come spring. Every time she looked at the bottom line on her bank statement, it seemed more and more as if she could make her dream come true.

"Did I tell you that Emily invited us to share Thanksgiving at their house?"

Anki's reaction was hard to read, so she added, "I wanted to run it by you and Dan before saying yes or no. What do you think?"

"I suppose it might be nice."

"It'll give us a chance to see the big addition Max built for them. Although Emily talks about it so much, I can almost see it in my mind!"

"She should not boast. It is sinful."

"Oh, I didn't mean to imply she brags. More like . . . 'Gabe loves looking out his window,' and 'Rafe sleeps more soundly in a room of his own.'"

Emily had shared her excitement about another important addition to their home, but Anki had been doing so well lately that Willa was afraid that mentioning it would move her backward.

"I'm planning to drive into town tomorrow—if this weather holds—and buy some of what we'll need for our part of the dinner. I offered to make the turkey and stuffing, plus a lot of other stuff. Why don't you come with me?"

"What time tomorrow?"

"Early. You know how the stores are on Saturdays!"

"We will see . . ."

In other words, if Anki woke up in a half-decent mood, there was a chance she'd tag along.

"I hope Dan gets home before I leave for the clinic, so I can ask how he feels about dinner at the Bakers'."

"He will not mind. Tell her we will be there." Anki paused, sent Willa a sidelong glance. "Did Emily invite Max, too?"

"I'm sure she did. He and Phillip are closer than some brothers."

Tidying the folds of her skirt, Anki smiled. "It will be a perfect day to tell Max how you feel."

"Maybe . . ."

"Ma-a-ay-be-e-e," Frannie copied. "Ma-a-ay-be-e-e!"

"Just look at you," Willa said, wiping bits of cheese and egg from Frannie's face, "wide awake and rarin' to go. I'm afraid morning naps will soon be a thing of the past."

"She is growing quickly," Anki observed.

Willa hoisted the baby from the chair. "Thanks to you and Dan, who provided a safe haven during one of the most difficult times in our lives."

Anki waved off the comment. "As Dan always says, you more than earn your keep around here. A little bit of me selfishly hopes you and Max never marry, because then you will leave me." Flushing slightly, she quickly tacked on, "I mean us."

Willa didn't have the heart to tell her that, first thing this spring, she planned to move into the Yoders' second house. During a routine exam of the couple's youngest grandson, she'd learned about the rental, and let it be known that she'd like nothing better than to become a tenant. Mrs. Yoder had made it clear that she'd like nothing better, saying, "I know you will care for the house as if it were your very own. Our last tenant was not so reliable!" Willa had offered a deposit, which Hope flatly refused: "You will need that money for furniture, because the place is as empty as the Hershbergers' heads!"

"When will you take your nursing test?"

"The week before Christmas. And boy, do I have the collywobbles!"

Anki's eyes opened wide. "The . . . the *what*?"

Laughing, Willa explained. "It was something my

grandfather used to say when anyone was scared or nervous. I looked it up once, and its origins go back to the days of cholera epidemics, when people would hold their stomachs as the symptoms began."

"A very funny word for a very serious condition."

Willa wrinkled her nose. "I suppose you're right. I won't use it again." She looked heavenward. "No disrespect, Gramps."

"Nap?" Frannie asked.

"Well, will wonders never cease!" Taking the little girl out of the high chair, Willa told Anki, "I'll only be a few minutes. Are your snow boots down here? Or should I get them from your closet?"

"Why would they be here, when I never go outside?"

Willa chose to ignore the cranky question, and at the top of the stairs, whispered into Frannie's hair, "Promise me you'll always take the advice of doctors, because it'd break my heart to see you sliding up and down the mood scale, like Anki."

"Anki?" Frannie said as Willa eased her out of the terry-cloth romper. "Anki nap?"

Reaching for a fresh diaper, Willa shook her head. "No, sweetie, today Anki will help Mama work."

"Wo'k. F'annie wo'k?"

Leaning into the crib, she rubbed noses with the baby. "If you take a nice long nap, I'll teach you to roll socks into a ball. How's that!"

Clapping, Frannie said, "Baw!"

Willa pictured the tidy parlor as it would look once Frannie started tossing balled-up socks around the room, laughing as she helped her lie flat. Then she rolled down the window shade, pulled the quilt up to the baby's chin, grabbed the baby monitor's receiver, and tiptoed from the room.

Just as she entered the kitchen, Dan walked through the back door.

"Where is your print cartridge?" Anki wanted to know.

He must have been thinking, *"What, no hello, good to see you, husband,"* because he looked slightly miffed. True to his nature, Dan sloughed it off and said, "I stopped at the trailer on the way home, threw out the old one, replaced it with the new one."

Willa dropped the receiver into her apron pocket and reached into the narrow drawer in the rolling cart and withdrew a pencil and tablet. "When did you last eat, Dan?"

"Breakfast."

"Let me fix you a sandwich, and then Anki and I are going to the shop."

Now, he looked genuinely surprised. "Anki's shop?"

"Mmm-hmm. To see how much needs to be done before she can open it, come spring."

He met his wife's eyes. "This was *your* idea?"

"No, Willa suggested it. And I decided . . ." She shrugged one shoulder. ". . . warmer weather is a long way off, so why not go along with it?"

From her vantage point at the counter, Willa could see them, and wondered who'd speak next. Dan, if she had to guess.

But it was Anki who said, "You are getting muddy snow all over the floor."

Looking down, he grimaced. "Sorry, Willa. Let me hang up my coat and I will sop up the mess."

"It's all right. I'll take care of it." She slid the sandwich onto the table, and he took his seat. And as she filled a mug with hot black coffee, Willa said, "Where's Max working today?"

"He's in Cumberland, checking on the Lover's Leap cabins."

She stooped to blot up the muddy mess. "I guess it's a good thing he pushed the crew so hard and got everything under roof before the snowstorm."

"It *is* a good thing." He bit into the sandwich, and chuckling, said, "A real forward thinker, that Max of yours."

That Max of *yours*? It was growing more frustrating by the day that everyone—Bishop Fisher, Emily and Phillip, Anki and Dan—thought of them as a couple. Everyone, that is, except for Max and Willa.

"Emily wants to know if we'll join them for Thanksgiving dinner at their house."

"I will eat here or there or anywhere," he said, and followed it up with a swig of coffee.

It sounded an awful lot like he'd picked up a few things, listening to her read Dr. Seuss to Frannie. She didn't know whether the "no children" problem originated with Dan or Anki—and since Anki refused to be tested, they probably never would—but in Willa's opinion, he'd be a great dad. Not as good as Max, but . . .

"Is it all right if I take Anki out back now? I need to put in a few hours at the clinic once Frannie wakes up from her nap."

"Sure, sure." He polished off the sandwich and washed it down with the last of the coffee. "I have a few things to do, and then maybe I will join you."

Willa helped Anki into her jacket. "You'll definitely want to wear your snow boots. I shoveled paths, but not from here to the shed."

Unless she was mistaken, Anki was about to change her

mind. All because she'd have to walk a quarter of a mile through six inches of snow.

"I'll go out first," she said, buttoning up her own jacket, "and clear the way." Tugging a woolen cap onto her head, Willa added, "You'll still need those boots, because I can't go all the way down to the grass. Not without disturbing the roots."

Dan leaned both elbows on the table, no doubt waiting to see how his wife would respond. Fearing his reaction might reflect the disapproval in his eyes, Willa said, "Next spring, I'll get the wheelbarrow and gather up every flat stone I can find, and use them to make a proper path to connect the house to the shop." She wiggled her fingers into mittens that matched her hat. "It'll make it easier for you to get back and forth, Anki. Easier for your customers, too."

"I like the idea. We have pavers behind the trailer," Dan said. "When the snow melts, I will bring them here, and help you put them down." He glanced at Anki, and grasping her hand, said, "I am sure you would like to help. It will be good exercise. And when we finish, you will be happy for all the hard work." He aimed a beefy forefinger at the ceiling. "And every time you follow it back and forth, you will be happy again, that you did not track mud into the house *or* the shop."

Seeing his excitement made *Willa* happy. Unfortunately, Anki didn't seem to agree. She'd sunk low in her chair and, arms crossed over her chest, stared at her hands, clutched on the table.

"You stay put, Anki. We can visit the shop anytime. It isn't like the snow will melt anytime soon. And if what's out there already is any indicator, we'll see more of the same before the robins start singing in the trees." *Be quiet, Will,* she told herself. *Why are you babbling like a ninny?*

"We'll have plenty of time to see what's what out there and get everything done long before the tourists start making their way up the mountain." She looked at Dan, hoping to see that he agreed. Looked at Anki when he didn't. "Right?"

Flustered, Willa fumbled with her parka's zipper. "Stupid mittens," she muttered, jerking them from her hands. She wriggled out of the coat, stuffed the gloves in the right pocket, the hat in the left, and jammed it on its hook. Why, oh why did she feel so *helpless* where Anki was concerned? She'd been so careful not to say or do anything that might upset her. And just when Willa thought it was safe to relax . . .

"I'll be in the basement, folding clothes." She didn't wait for a reply, but hurried down the stairs. At the bottom, Willa pulled the chain that lit the big bare bulb that flooded the laundry area with light. "You have studying to do," she complained under her breath. "Yet here you are, refolding towels." She'd stuff them into a basket and carry them upstairs . . . if it didn't require passing Dan and Anki in the kitchen.

At least she'd remembered the baby monitor's receiver. Reaching into her pocket, she stared at the arc of tiny red lights. Then, holding it near her ear, she listened to the sounds of her baby girl. Frannie's steady breaths were reassuring, and eyes closed, she concentrated on that, instead of Anki's chaotic behavior.

"You aren't being fair," she muttered, re-pocketing the receiver. For the past few weeks, Anki had behaved like every other woman her age. It was wrong, unreasonable, to jump to the conclusion that, for a moment or two, she'd regressed.

Something the bishop had said during their last lesson came to mind, a verse that he claimed had always comforted him: *"Have I not commanded you? Be strong and courageous . . . do not be discouraged, for the Lord your God will be with you . . ."*

These past few weeks had been blissfully calm. Her greatest challenge had been choosing between roasting a chicken or baking a ham for the Hofmans' supper. None of the clinic's patients had been seriously ill. Her savings account balance made her believe she could make it on her own. But she'd selfishly allowed Anki to fool her, because believing in the *positives* was easier than dealing with the *negatives*. If she'd been that wrong about Anki, had she been wrong about everything else . . . such as her ability to live on her own? To pass the CNA exam? Earn her right to baptism with a full confession? Give in to the love she felt for Max by making a full confession to *him?* For the first time since moving to Pleasant Valley, where she'd felt safe and whole, Willa was afraid. *Do not be afraid,* she repeated. Burying her face in a fluffy towel, she willed herself not to cry.

"Why are you smelling the laundry?"

Startled, she whirled around, and looked into Max's smiling face. His expression grew concerned, though, when he met her eyes.

He closed the gap between them in three long strides. "Willa, what is wrong?"

Oh, how she wanted to lean into him, absorb his warm strength. "Nothing. Really. Too much thinking."

"About . . . ?"

She risked a quick glance toward the stairs, where the light from the kitchen spilled down like a golden runner. In all the months she'd been here, Willa had never paid attention to whether or not voices traveled *up* the steps. She was afraid again, this time that Anki might be able to hear. "Just . . . things."

Hands on her shoulders, he said, "Dan is in the parlor and she is upstairs. You can talk to me."

"Really. It's nothing. Nothing a good night's sleep won't cure."

He tucked in his chin. "You realize it is barely past noon, right?"

His way of telling her that it would be hours before she could escape into the rest she craved?

If he kept standing there, looking concerned, offering comfort, she'd burst out crying. And only the good Lord knew what secrets she'd divulge if that happened!

"I was going to help Anki in her shop. Well, not help her *today*. We were planning to go inside, make a list of things that need to be done, so we can get them done this winter, and she can get back to business next spring. You know . . . things like cleaning. Painting. Rearranging display shelves. Restocking . . ."

Max laid a finger over her lips, halting her rapid-fire flow of words. When he removed it, she continued with, "I misjudged her behavior. She seemed so . . . so normal these past few weeks. Talking. Smiling. Laughing, even! But . . ." Willa shook her head. "She . . . I was just . . . Anki fooled me, because I let her. Because . . . because I was so fixated on my own petty problems . . . because selfish woman that I am—"

"Willa, you are many things, but selfish is definitely not one of them."

What did *that* mean . . . *you are many things* . . . ? Was he referring to her history? Her unwed mother status? Or that before her pregnancy, she'd been an addict?

"You are stubborn. You can be demanding, and a little silly sometimes. Now and then, you talk too much, and too fast. But selfish?" Tilting his head slightly, he wrapped a curl around his forefinger. "No. *That* you are not."

"Max, I've been meaning to talk to you about something."

"You have?"

He let go of the curl, combed his fingers through her hair. Hairpins clinked to the floor as he loosened her bun. He was different today. Bolder. More confident. Fearless. Was he aware how much she needed those things right now?

"This something . . . it has been on your mind for a while?"

"Almost from the day we met."

Tilting his head again, he took a step closer, flashed a crooked, mischievous grin. "Well?"

"Well what?"

"Are you going to make me guess?"

A Ben Franklin quote came to mind, and Willa decided not to put it off a moment longer . . .

"I've wanted to tell you, *so many times,* but I needed to be sure, because—"

"So this is where you disappeared to!"

Willa peered over Max's shoulder, and seeing Anki's stern expression, moved away from him.

"We need to put a bell around your neck," he said. "You are quiet as a cat."

Willa checked the receiver, and satisfied that it was working and Frannie was all right, said, "Are you okay?"

"I have changed my mind. I would like to go to the shop."

To fill her request, Willa needed to race upstairs, get into her winter gear, and shovel a walkway. If she'd done it earlier, both the path and the inspection would be complete by now.

"When you didn't want to go out into the snow, we decided to do it tomorrow, right?"

The furrows in Anki's brow deepened. "Oh. I did not realize it had been *decided*." Hitching up her skirt, she planted one foot on the bottom step. "Will we still go to town? After we visit the shop?"

"Yes, sure!" It would mean burning the midnight oil tonight, and again tomorrow, to make up for time lost from studying for her exam, but Willa would agree to just about anything to lift Anki's spirits. "We'll get outside early—it'll only take a few minutes to make our list—and once the shopping is done, we'll have lunch at Shorthorn's. The Yoders told me they make a mean burger platter."

"I have never been fond of burgers."

"Oh, I'm sure there's something on the menu you'll like!"

"Very well," Anki said, and continued up the stairs.

Once she was out of sight, Max pulled her close and pressed a kiss to her temple. "No wonder you are a nervous wreck." Another kiss, and then, "Just the other day, she was smiling, laughing, participating in the conversation, and now?" A raspy sigh escaped his throat. "I am sorry, Willa. I know how hard this is for you."

"Not nearly as hard as it is for Dan. And Anki!"

He leaned back, looked deep into her eyes, and said, "I have something to tell you, too. But I do not want to rush through it."

"After supper tonight, maybe?"

"I will be in town tonight, having dinner with the man we're building the Lover's Leap cabins for."

"Ah. Mr. Mysterious." Willa unconsciously smoothed his shirt's button placket. "Dan must be so pleased. You've pretty much single-handedly doubled your business in just a few months." Suddenly conscious of her wifely gesture, she snapped back her hand. And smiling up at him, added, "You're a remarkable guy, you know that?"

"I have been called many things, but never that," he said.

She could tell that he didn't agree, not because the Amish didn't believe in basking in praise, but because conceitedness simply wasn't part of his character.

"I know how the Amish feel about compliments of any kind, but Max, you deserve to see yourself through my eyes, at least when we're alone. And in my eyes, you're strong and tall and handsome enough to inspire great artists to paint your portrait."

His lips parted, no doubt to stop her, but Willa wouldn't allow it. "You have the most amazing eyes, bluer than the sky." Ever so gently, she drew a fingertip across his long lashes, inspiring a quiet chuckle. "And a beautiful smile. I can't decide which captivates me more."

"Willa, please stop. Women look beautiful when they blush. But me?" Chuckling, he shook his head. "I'll just look foolish."

"No, you stop. You need to know how extraordinary you are."

He was laughing when he said, "Oh, I do, do I?"

"Yes, you do. I was a mess when you came down here. On the verge of tears. Afraid. Worried. Confused. And when I saw you, all of it . . ." She snapped her fingers. "All of it was gone, just like that."

Max bobbed his head, looking embarrassed and ill at ease. *Just say it, Will. Why wait until tomorrow to tell him how you feel?*

"I don't know how else to say this except to just—"

"Max," Dan hollered down the stairs, "that mutt of yours is barking up a storm out there in your truck."

"Oh man! I forgot all about him. I will be right up," he called back. Then, facing Willa, Max walked toward the steps. "I had only planned to stop by and say a quick hello. He has been cooped up in that cab since before dawn. I need to take him home, then get back to Cumberland."

"Oh, poor Rascal. He's probably hungry. Or needs to do his business." *And maybe he's just lonely for you.* Willa knew how miserable that could make a body!

"Tomorrow, can we pick up where we left off?"

"Absolutely. Drive safely. And good luck with Mr. Mystery!"

"Enjoy your afternoon . . ."

And then, just like that, he was gone.

Willa couldn't say whether or not her clinic hours would be enjoyable, but she knew this:

She'd spend every spare moment asking God to send a sign . . . would He bless a union between her and Max? If so, she'd ask Him to prevent all future interruptions, and bless her with the courage to finally tell Max that she loved him.

While Willa loaded groceries into the truck, Frannie and Anki waited in the cab. Thanks to below-freezing temperatures, the perishables would be safe until they'd finished lunch. After parking out back, Willa led the way into Beula's and chose a table facing the front windows. No sooner had she buckled Frannie into a fifties-style Formica high chair than the baby pointed at the model train chugging along a track that hung near the diner's ceiling.

"See the train?" Willa said.

Anki surprised them both by leaning forward and saying, "Choo-choo! Choo-choo!"

The baby liked that and did her best to copy it. "Too-too! Too-too!"

"Close enough," Willa said, laughing. The moment was bittersweet, because at the rate Frannie was going, she'd be reading the big letters on the boxcars' sides anytime now.

The waitress handed them menus and gave Frannie three fat crayons. She used one to draw a big smiley face, right in the middle of the tray. "Now you do it, cutie-pie!" she said. She looked at Willa and added, "I'll be back in a minute to take your orders."

Anki hadn't even opened her menu, and Willa stifled a frustrated sigh. "They serve breakfast here all day. How about pancakes or waffles?"

"All right. Waffles."

"With bacon or sausage?"

"Sausage. And hash browns. Coffee, too."

If Anki ate half of it, Willa would be surprised, but she sent a silent prayer of thanks heavenward that the woman had at least *seemed* interested in eating.

When the waitress returned, she carried two coffeepots. "Regular or decaf?"

Willa stood the white ceramic mugs upright on their saucers. "Regular, just black, thanks." Then she ordered for Anki, adding, "I'll have the same, with chocolate milk for the baby."

"Gotcha. Back in a jiffy." The girl snapped her gum and hurried away.

"Looks like more snow on the way," Anki said, staring out the window.

Willa followed her line of vision, to where snow glowed bright bluish-white on the mountaintops. A thick stand of evergreens blanketed the lower elevations, and the low-hanging clouds cast ghostly gray shadows on the ragged cliffs.

"Oh, Anki, isn't it just beautiful!"

"I suppose."

"Mama!" Frannie said, and Willa leaned over to admire zigzagging lines of blue, red, and yellow that crisscrossed the white plastic tray.

"Frannie! It's so pretty!"

Pointing at each crayon, she identified the colors, and with no prompting whatever, the baby said, "Boo? Wed? Dallow?"

"That's right! Aren't you a smarty!"

As Anki continued staring into the steely sky and Frannie went back to doodling, Willa sipped her coffee and tried to visualize the trial exam paper she'd filled out last night. Eyes closed, she tried to recall topics that would be included in the test: nutrition, hygiene, psychosocial care, hands-on clinical skills such as recording blood pressure, assisting patients with bedpans and hand-washing . . .

"Who is that man?"

Again, Willa followed Anki's gaze, this time to the parking lot, where a blue-jeaned man leaned casually against the grille of a mud-spattered SUV. The wind whipped through his hair, tangling greasy-looking brown strands with his scruffy beard. It carried away hazy wisps from his brown-filtered cigarette, too.

"It looks like he is staring right at us," Anki said.

He propped mirrored aviator sunglasses onto the bill of a soiled Orioles cap and squinted into the smoke. "My goodness," Willa whispered, "it *does* look that way, doesn't it?"

"Do you know him?"

"No." But he reminded her of every emaciated addict

who had worked for Joe. Alice had told her that like most cities these days, Oakland had its share of drug problems. Unlike other similar towns, the social worker had stressed, it offered several top-notch rehab centers.

"He is making me nervous."

The waitress arrived just then, balancing two overloaded plates on one forearm, and carrying a lidded soft drink cup in her free hand. "Chocolate milk, just for you, cutie-pie! Brought you a little spoon, too," she said, putting both on the tray.

Frannie looked from the spoon to her drawing to the drink, and the waitress said, "Can't decide which to grab first, huh?"

Anki, frowning, nodded toward the window. "Who is that man in the parking lot?"

Bending her knees, the waitress peered outside. "Never saw the creep before in my life." Straightening, she added, "Thank goodness!"

Suddenly, he flicked the cigarette to the blacktop and crushed it underfoot. Pulling up his jacket collar, he pocketed his hands and sauntered away.

"Yeah. No kidding," Willa agreed.

Anki picked at her waffles, but Frannie ate with gusto. Willa poked at her meal, but only ate a few bites. She couldn't get her mind off the way that man had so boldly stared at them. *Stop being a big scaredy-cat,* she told herself. *He probably just didn't want to smoke in his car.* Besides, the radio DJ had warned listeners to bundle up, because today's high temps wouldn't reach twenty-five. "And if you factor in the wind chill," he'd added, "it'll feel more like seventeen!" Surely by now the stranger had found someplace warm and out of the wind.

After paying the tab, she bundled Frannie up and made sure Anki had buttoned her coat, then led the way back to

Li'l Red . . . searching right and left as they crossed the parking lot. If she saw that man again, she'd march right back into the diner and ask someone to call the police. *Who knows . . . you might prevent a purse snatching or a mugging!*

It wasn't until she backed out of the parking space that she spotted him, this time standing between two enormous pickup trucks. Thankfully, he seemed too preoccupied shaking another cigarette from the red and white pack to notice her. But Willa held her breath: To get from here to the road, she needed to drive right past him. What were the chances he'd still be too distracted to see *that*?

None, as it turned out.

He held up a cell phone, aimed it her way, and snapped a photo.

She could think of only one thing to explain why anyone would watch, then follow, then take her picture:

Joe.

Chapter Fifteen

"You will wear yourself out," Dan said. "No man can put in ten long, hard hours on the jobsite, and spend another five here, poring over the books. Keep this up and you will drop like a felled tree. And neither of us can afford that. Let it go, man. Just let it go, and have faith that once word gets out about the Royal Valley, a few dollars lost in Cumberland will not matter."

Max drove a hand through his hair. He should have been up front weeks ago, when he found the error that led to the low bid, a bid so low that the owner would have been a fool to hire another firm. It was no surprise that Dan's numbers hadn't added up; supervising fifteen smaller jobs while Anki slid in and out of depression was enough to distract anyone. But when Max pointed out the slipup, Dan misunderstood, and not wanting to add to Dan's burdens, Max had taken the blame.

Unfortunately, underbidding the Cumberland job was just one of many errors Dan had made lately. He'd delivered materials to the wrong site. Twice. Ordered eight yards of concrete instead of eighteen. But why torture either one of them by adding to the list!

Max picked up the full-color trifold brochure that Dan had ordered . . . without discussing it with him. It's what the corporate-type contractors are doing, he'd said; to compete with them, they had to *look* like them.

"Until we complete the development," Max said, waving it in the air, "and buyers see for themselves that our work is higher quality than the competition, *this* . . ." He threw down the pamphlet. ". . . is not worth the glossy paper it is printed on."

"We have spent years building a good reputation in the industry. No one will know about the mistake. And it is not as though we have cheated anyone . . . but ourselves. So let it go, Max. Just let it go."

It went against everything in him, but Max dropped his pencil into the big mug on his desk and grabbed his jacket. "You are right. Go home, Dan. That is what I am going to do."

"Come with me. It is suppertime. Willa has been a bit . . . *off* lately. I think maybe because she misses you."

Hearing it felt good, so good that he almost decided to take Dan up on the offer. Finding a way to replace the money lost to the low bid didn't look very promising. But he *could* find out what had been bothering Willa and help her through it.

Thanksgiving was only two days away. Two days to catch up on his sleep. To pray for God's guidance. She deserved the best of him.

And if she'd have him, Max intended to give it to her.

"Only one more call," Alice said, "and you'll be free of me!"

"I hope not. I've come to think of you as a friend."

"I feel the same way, but I'm not supposed to admit it. It's unprofessional, you know?"

Coming from the usually all-business social worker, that was high praise.

"So tell me all about school. You're about to wrap things up, right?"

"I take the CNA exam day after tomorrow."

"You don't sound nervous. That's good. Real good."

"I studied a lot, and Emily has taught me a lot."

"After your certification arrives, will you keep working at the Baker Clinic, or look for a job in the city?"

It felt good, knowing that Alice believed she'd pass the test. "Thanks for the vote of confidence. And yes, I'm staying. I love it there."

"Sounds like you love Pleasant Valley, period." Alice's gruff chuckle filtered through the phone. "What about that young carpenter you told me about? Anything developing between you two?"

"He's great. Terrific. I like and respect him a lot."

"A non-answer if ever I heard one!"

"I'm hoping that once I'm baptized . . ."

"So you're serious about staying in the community?"

"Hard to believe, isn't it, after the way I behaved when you told me about this place."

"The day I dropped you off at the Hofmans', I made a bet with myself that you wouldn't last a week."

"Oh?"

"You owe me a hot fudge sundae, girlie!"

The women shared a moment of friendly laughter, and then Alice said, "When is the baptism?"

"As close to New Year's Day as possible."

"I get it. New beginnings, fresh starts, and all that."

"Exactly."

"How's that adorable little girl of yours? Bet she's grown a bunch since I saw her last."

"I've had to let down the hems on all her dresses. And she's on the verge of forming sentences."

"I don't doubt it for a minute. Smart cookie, that kid of yours. How does she like it there?"

"She fits right in. Loves everyone, and everyone loves her."

"Including Max?"

It surprised her a bit, hearing that Alice remembered his name. "She adores him." *And so do I!*

"I'm happy to hear things are going so well for you. And . . . how's Anki doing?"

"We're all looking forward to Thanksgiving, when we can state out loud how grateful we are that she's having more good days than bad."

And it was true . . . mostly. But even if it wasn't, Willa had to be careful. After the first of the year, she'd complete her nine months of parental supervision, required to keep the state from taking control of Frannie. She was close, so close to complete freedom, and didn't want to say anything to give Alice the impression that Anki's instability might negatively impact the baby. Much as she'd like to tell her friend about the stranger lurking around the diner, Willa didn't mention that, either: If Alice suspected the man had been sent by Joe, she could view *that* as a threat to Frannie's well-being.

"I'm happy for you, Willa. You've worked hard, completely turned your life around. I hope things work out for you and the carpenter, because if anyone deserves happiness, it's you."

"Thanks, Alice."

"Well, better get back to work. I have a dozen check-in calls to make before I start my rounds."

"Surprise visits, eh? Tell me . . . why haven't you come

to Pleasant Valley since that first day? I mean, you said yourself that you didn't think I could make it here."

"I've been there. Four times."

"Really? Why didn't you stop by and say hi?"

"Didn't have time, for one thing."

Willa decided that if there were other things, she'd rather not know what they were.

"I'll call you after the first of the year, and we'll set things up so you can buy me that sundae, and I can hand-deliver the paperwork that says our professional association has come to an official end."

"I'm already looking forward to it."

"I have to tell you, Willa . . . I've been in this business for nearly thirty years, and it's rare to see a client succeed the way you have. I never met your mother, but from what you've told me, I know she'd be as proud of you as I am."

Willa carried the glow of those words with her for the rest of the day.

More than ever, she looked forward to Thanksgiving, when she could share her hopeful, happy news with Max.

"Hey. Dude. Are you Max Lambright?"

On his hands and knees, hammering deck boards onto a cabin porch, he said, "I am . . ."

"They told me at the bake shop where to find you. Name's Joe, by the way."

Standing, Max dropped a handful of nails into his work apron's pocket and met the man's eyes.

Somehow, he knew that this was Joe, the man who'd turned Willa into a drug addict. Who'd abused her . . . until she escaped from him. "What can I do for you?"

"I showed this picture around at Shorthorn's diner in Oakland. Guy at the register recognized her, said he works part-time at the medical supply place, and saw her in there with you."

A month or so ago, after hearing Emily complain about having to wait for a week for a delivery too large to fit in Li'l Red's bed, he'd offered to drive Willa to retrieve it.

"A picture you say?"

Joe took a step closer, handed Max a wrinkled photograph: Willa, wearing snug jeans and a form-fitting white sweater, a smoking cigarette between two fingers of her left hand, a bottle of beer in the other. She looked weary and troubled, nothing like the lively, happy woman who'd stolen his heart.

"Well? You know her or not?"

Tempting as it was to pocket the photo, Max handed it back. "Why are you looking for her?"

"She owes me. Big-time."

"Owes you what?"

"Thirty grand, not that it's any of your business. I'm here to get it back. Every. Stinking. Dime."

Max knew that after running away from Joe, Willa had been on the run for nearly a year before arriving in Pleasant Valley. He also knew that she'd worked assorted odd jobs . . . until Frannie came along. With a baby to care for, it wouldn't have taken long to spend the money inherited from her mother. But he didn't believe for an instant that she'd stolen that money. Despite being Amish, Max had heard about the dark underworld this man called home, a world where thirty thousand dollars could change hands in mere minutes. Joe must be desperate to tell such an outrageous lie to repay someone even more terrifying than himself.

"What will you do if you find her?"

"Not *if*, but *when*."

Max's heart pounded hard. "And then?"

Joe's eyes narrowed to slits. "She caused me a lot of trouble, leaving the way she did. So like I said, she owes me."

Max got the message, loud and clear. Yes, Willa had made mistakes. Big, serious, life-altering mistakes. But she'd changed, one hundred percent. After all the hard work she'd put into turning her life around, she didn't deserve to pay the price Joe would demand.

"How long have you been looking for her?"

Max read his surprised expression to mean that his money problems were fairly recent—and so was the idea of using Willa to solve them.

"That, *Amishman,* is none of your business."

Anger and fear burned in the other man's eyes, and Max knew he'd been right: Joe had double-crossed someone even more evil than himself, and stood to pay a high price if he couldn't make things right, and fast.

"What if *I* gave you the money you need?"

Joe snorted. "Why would you shell out thirty grand for some used-up broad who'd do anything, *anything,* for a fix?"

Max couldn't even picture Willa in that condition! "Because . . . she's a friend."

One brow rose high on his forehead. "Ah-ha. Is that so."

The words, the tone of voice, the look on Joe's face all said that he believed Willa had traded one addiction for another.

"Tomorrow is Thanksgiving. I will not be able to get the money until Saturday morning."

Frowning now, Joe said, "So . . . you're *serious*?" He pulled out a cigarette, squinted into the smoke as he added,

"I don't care where the cash comes from, long as I get it. So, your money, your timetable."

Max had always lived frugally, and despite Dan's low-bid error, his cut of the company's profits had added substantially to his savings balance. Withdrawing that much would still leave him with enough to pay his bills. Not much, but enough.

"Saturday, then. Right here."

"The bank opens at nine. I will meet you at ten."

"You're sure she's worth it?"

Of course she was, and he'd gladly pay double the amount—triple, even—if it meant getting this sorry excuse of a man out of Willa's life, once and for all.

A horrifying thought entered his head: What if Joe came back, again and again, demanding similar payments? Even if he wrote up a contract of sorts, he couldn't very well expect this criminal to honor it.

Between now and Saturday, he'd have to trust God to supply him with a rock-solid idea, one threatening enough to terrify Joe as much as he'd terrified Willa.

"I hear she has a kid now . . ."

Max wasn't about to provide this sad excuse for a man with any information about sweet little Frannie.

"Girl, right?"

He didn't deserve to know even that much about her.

"Guess she'd be, what, one? One and a half?"

Max shifted the hammer from his left hand to his right. Oh, how satisfying it would feel to draw back and land a good hard blow to the side of Joe's smirking, haughty face!

"Saturday, ten o'clock," he said, putting his back to Joe.

"I'll be here. And if you shortchange me, I'll make it my life's mission to find her and the kid. I won't get much

for her, used up as she is, but kids—whoa!—kids go for
big bucks!"

Max watched him drive away, then dropped to his knees,
held a nail in place, and drove it into the two-by-four with
one brutal hammer blow. By now, he was trembling with
rage. *I will ask Your forgiveness for the things I am thinking,
Lord, but right now . . .*

Another nail disappeared in just one ferocious whack.

Right now, he needed to get a handle on this rage,
because tomorrow, he'd spend most of Thanksgiving
with the Hofmans and the Bakers, and the last thing he
wanted was for Willa to know that Joe had come looking
for her . . . and sweet Frannie.

"I hope we're not getting here too early . . ."

"Willa, of course not. Come in!" Sarah said.

Emily, standing beside her mother-in-law, held out her
arms, and Frannie fell willingly into them. "How would
you like to visit with Rafe and Gabe, little miss?"

The baby repeated her friends' names, and tugged at
her bonnet straps. "Off!"

Laughing, Emily fulfilled the request as Willa said, "I
have some things in the truck. Soon as I carry them in,
Sarah and I will join you."

"Yes," the older woman said. "I could use a cup of
coffee." She looked at Willa. "It is good of you to help
with the meal." One bushy gray eyebrow rose on her forehead as she added, "I just hope you are a good cook!"

"We'll soon find out, won't we!"

Willa made quick work of carrying bags of flour and
sugar, vegetables, and canned goods into the kitchen. She'd
already been up for hours, baking bread and rolls, making

stuffing, and roasting the turkey so they'd only need to be warmed up once they arrived at the Bakers' house.

"It truly is good of you," Sarah said again. "Peeling potatoes and slicing carrots is not as easy as it used to be." She held out withered, arthritic hands. "The work gets done, but these old things pay the price. Phillip chose a bride just in the nick of time, if you ask me!"

She pulled out a chair and, as Sarah sat, Willa placed the package of green beans on the table. "Just snap a few, and if your fingers ache, I'm more than happy to take over."

"You will make a good Amish woman," Sarah said. "And if Maximillian ever gets up his nerve, you will make a good Amish wife, too."

Now really, Willa thought, *how am I supposed to react to that!* In place of a response, Willa poured Sarah a mug of coffee.

A quick scan of the room made her smile, because even on a gray day like this, the room felt bright and sunny, thanks to big windows and overhead lights. The pale blue stripes that trimmed Emily's stoneware caught her eye. Neat stacks of plates, bowls, and mugs gleamed on the shelves of the glass-doored hutch. Below them, on the sideboard, a matching soup tureen, butter dish, and gravy boat had been arranged on a rectangular white-on-white runner. If ever she had a home of her own, Willa would love to own a set just like it.

After refrigerating the perishables, she filled another two mugs with coffee. "Come sit with Emily and me in the parlor," she said to Sarah.

"You go. I will finish the beans."

Willa noticed that Sarah had barely made a dent in the pile, and as she made her way to the parlor, wished for a way to ease the older woman's aches. Rounding the corner, she found Emily sitting cross-legged in the playpen, helping Rafe and Frannie stack wooden blocks.

"I brought you coffee," Willa said, "but maybe you'd rather have a bottle of milk."

The women shared a moment of laughter as Emily climbed out.

"I can't imagine how much harder things like that will be in four or five months!"

Willa met her eyes, read the teasing glint, and said, "Are you saying what I think you're saying?"

Emily tiptoed to the low table between the padded wood chairs and waved Willa closer. "I'm just dying to tell someone, but you have to give me your word . . . you won't tell anyone. Especially not Phillip."

Hand raised as if taking an oath, she said, "Your secret's safe with me."

One hand on her belly, Emily said, "I'm pregnant. And it's . . ." She looked around, to make sure Phillip wouldn't overhear, and added, ". . . and it's twins!"

Willa leaped up from her chair and threw her arms around her friend. "What! Is there something in the water up here? Twins? Really?"

"I've suspected for a few weeks, but yesterday, my ob-gyn confirmed it."

"So *that* was the mysterious errand you had to run!" Willa returned to her seat. "Oh, Em. I'm thrilled for you. But why haven't you told Phillip yet?"

"I wanted to surprise him. He told me just the other day—don't let on that you know!—that he was going to wait until everyone had said a blessing, then make us all take turns sharing what we're most thankful for."

"What a sweet thing to do."

"That's my Phillip . . . sweet as they come."

"The timing couldn't be more perfect, now that Max is

all finished adding three new bedrooms and a bathroom to your second floor."

"Oh, no kidding. That's something else to be thankful for." She sipped her coffee. "I can't imagine how hard it must have been for Sarah, for all the people who once lived by Old Order rules. I mean really . . . no indoor plumbing, in the dead of winter, with little children in tow!"

Willa nodded. "I still can't believe it. *Twins*!"

"Shh! Sarah moves like a cat, and if she hears, the surprise is doomed!"

Again, the women laughed.

"You took your exam, right?"

Willa nodded. "Yes, yesterday. I think I passed, but we'll find out soon enough."

Emily waved away her uncertainty. "You passed. No doubt in my mind. Are you going to announce it today?"

"No." She felt the heat of a blush creep into her cheeks. "I'd kind of rather wait and share it with Max before I tell anyone else."

"So the Hofmans don't know?"

She shook her head. "Not yet."

"Well, aren't we a couple of secret-keepers!"

Now, the children stood up in the playpen and joined in their mothers' laughter.

"He has no idea what's coming his way," Emily said, winking at Rafe.

"Yeah, but he's walking pretty well on his own now. By the time those two are born," she said, pointing at Emily's stomach, "he'll be able to outrun them, easily!" She got to her feet. "I need to get the pies into the oven. Why don't you stretch out on the sofa, and when I've finished, you can help me set the table."

Emily sent a grateful smile Willa's way. "You're a good friend, Will, and I love ya to pieces!"

She found Sarah at the sink, rinsing the beans. "The smell takes me back," the woman said, "to when I was a little girl, sitting on a stool beside my *groossmammi*'s rocking chair. The woman could snap a peck of beans in an hour!"

During the next hour, the women chatted quietly, Willa asking questions about Old Order ways, Sarah only too happy to highlight the positives.

"Well, nothing to do now but set the table," Willa said, hands on her hips. "I'll get Emily. She said she wants to help."

Willa found her dozing on the sofa. In the playpen, Frannie and Rafe snoozed contentedly.

"Everybody's fast asleep," she whispered to Sarah.

"She is with child. I know it."

Emily had said the woman moved like a cat; had she overheard something?

"She behaved the same when little Rafe was on the way. Besides, there is a look in her eyes." Sarah untied her apron, hung it on a peg, and walked toward the hallway. "I will change my dress. Sloppy me! I got it all wet, washing the beans!"

"Take your time," Willa said. "We have things well under control."

She proceeded to open and close drawers until she found the one that housed tablecloths. After arranging the plates, flatware, and tumblers, she stood back. Everything looked lovely, she thought, admiring her work. When Max saw it, would he agree with Sarah . . . that she'd make a good Amish wife?

Stop it, ninny! You're not supposed to get all bigheaded

over stuff like this! And anyway, she still hadn't found an opportunity—or the courage—to tell him how she felt. "Well, you're not Amish yet," she said to herself, "so you can enjoy it for the moment."

"Talking to yourself, eh?"

Willa whirled around, thrilled and stunned and giddy at the sight of him, standing in the doorway. Beside him, sitting at attention, Rascal smiled.

"What're *you* two doing here?"

"We, ah, we were invited . . . right?"

"Well, sure. Yeah. Of course. I only meant . . ." She stooped to pat the dog's head. "You smell fantastic. Did your dad give you a bath today?"

"Not everyone approves of dogs coming inside, and since the Bakers have always welcomed him, I thought it was a good idea."

"Who *wouldn't* welcome this gorgeous boy!" Straightening, she glanced at the clock. "Oh wow! I can't believe it's already one o'clock!"

His tone was apologetic. "I am early, I know, but I made something for you, and wanted to give it to you while we were alone."

Until now, she'd been so distracted by his beautiful face that she hadn't noticed how he'd hidden one hand behind his back. Willa watched as he extended his arm and held out a small wooden box.

"It's beautiful, Max," she said, stroking the smooth, burled wood. On the lid, he'd engraved her initials. How odd that the cedar lining had been so precisely mitered that she'd need a magnifying glass to see the joints, yet the *W* and the *A* were off-center. "You made this? For me?"

"Yes, and yes."

"How did you know my middle name is Ann?"

"I asked Anki."

"Does it open?"

"Well, sure. Yeah. Of course," he teased, echoing her earlier comment. "A box that does not open would be of little use to you, now would it? And by the way . . . I would have wrapped it, if I had paper. A bow. Or a clue *how*."

As she lifted the lid, a faint woody scent wafted into her nostrils. She removed a slip of paper that fit perfectly inside and read aloud, "'Congratulations, Willa'?"

"I do not remember printing a question mark . . ."

"Congratulations for what?"

"You passed your exam, yes?"

Despite his crazy schedule, he'd remembered. *And* made a gift, specifically for the occasion. Tears of gratitude stung her eyes. "I think so, but I won't know for weeks yet."

"You passed. I am sure of it."

She put the note back where she'd found it and closed the box. "I love it. Thank you, Max. I'll treasure it always."

"Do you know what it is for?"

"Not jewelry, especially not after I'm baptized." She hugged it to her chest. "I know! Frannie loves putting coins into silly prize machines, turning the crank, watching the little toy fall out. I'll keep coins in it!"

He shook his head.

"No?"

"I will make Frannie a coin box of her own. This one," he said, pointing at it, "is for business cards."

"Business cards?" She stifled a nervous giggle. "What would someone like me need with business cards?"

"Someone like you? Caring, hard-working, precise . . ."

"Cut it out, Max. You're making me blush."

"So? Pink is a good color on you." He pointed at the

box again. "You'll give the cards to your patients, so they will know how to reach you when aches and sprains trouble them."

Emily's patients, she thought, *already know how to get in touch . . . by walking into the clinic. . . .*

"This must have taken hours," she said, opening, closing, then hugging it again. "You've been working from dawn until dusk on the jobsites. When did you find the time?"

He took a step forward and wrapped his fingers around hers. "People *make* time for what is important."

Could he feel her pulse pounding in her fingertips? Could he hear the breaths, rasping short and quick from her throat? He'd gone to a lot of trouble, painstakingly crafting this perfect treasure . . . had put a lot of thought into creating something meaningful, *just for her*. Willa had never been more certain of anything in her life: She loved this man!

"Max, I lo—"

"I thought you were going to call me so I could help you set the table," Emily interrupted.

It took a second or two for Willa to gather her thoughts. "You were sleeping so peacefully—the kids, too—that I didn't want to disturb you."

"You know what? You're one of the most thoughtful people I've ever known." Emily moved in close to see what Willa and Max were holding. "Oh, it's just gorgeous, Max. Did you make it?"

He nodded as Willa said, "It's for my business cards. After my certificate arrives."

Grinning, Emily said, "See there? Max believes you passed, too!"

He held her gaze. "Emily is right."

Was it her imagination, or was he looking at her as if seeing her for the first time?

"I'm sure you thanked him properly," Emily said.

"Properly?"

Emily slid an arm around his back, around Willa's, and pushed them together. "There now. Pucker up, girl, and show the man how much you like your present."

Max leaned down just enough to graze her lips with his. "I am glad you like it."

Overcome with emotion, Willa said, "Like it? Why, I *love* it, but not nearly as much as I lo—"

"It smells like Thanksgiving in here," Phillip said. Rubbing his palms together, he added, "When do we eat?"

Emily linked her arm with his. "Not for another hour yet."

He looked at the tiny box. "What's that?"

"Max made it for Willa. A graduation gift of sorts to hold her business cards once her CNA certificate arrives."

"*If* it arrives," Willa said.

But Phillip continued with, "A visible show of confidence, eh, Max, old boy?" Grinning mischievously, he said, "Good thinking, m'friend! That oughta earn you a thank-you kiss." He winked. "Or three."

Just then, Dan rapped on the back door window. "Are we late?" he asked, opening it wide.

A cold blast of wind blew into the room, and Emily quickly ushered them inside. "Get in here," she said, closing the door, "where it's warm."

As Emily and Willa hung the coats on the entryway's pegs, Anki asked, "Is this little alcove part of the work you did here, Max?"

"It is."

"I like it. Good way to keep the dirt and grit out of the kitchen."

"Come spring," Dan said, "I'll build one for you if you like."

One shoulder lifted in a half-hearted shrug. "A lot can happen between now and then."

Emily and Willa exchanged a worried look, and before anyone could pick up on it, Emily said, "Let me show you what else this talented carpenter did." Leading the way into the hall, she held a finger over her lips. "The kids are napping, so *shhh*."

"Where is Gabe?" Max wanted to know.

Phillip chuckled. "In his room, building a city with his blocks and trucks and trains."

Upstairs, as they walked from room to room, Willa complimented Max's attention to detail, noting perfectly mitered corners and nearly invisible nail holes.

"See, this is why I partnered with him," Dan joked. "His work makes us both look good!"

Laughing, they stepped into Gabe's room. The boy's face lit up as he wrapped Emily in an affectionate hug. "Happy Thanksgiving, everyone!" he told the rest of them.

Each adult returned the greeting . . . except for Anki, who stood near the window, staring out at the steel-gray sky.

"Snow is coming," she said, her breath forming clouds on the glass. "It will not be pleasant, I fear."

"But it'll be fun," Willa said, "watching the kids play in it tomorrow."

"Something for the memory book," Max agreed, tapping his temple.

What was going on in that handsome head, she wondered, to cause the worry frown on his striking face? She glanced at Phillip, at Dan and Emily, to see if they'd noticed, too. Seeing no visible evidence of it, Willa shrugged it off as a figment of her imagination. But half an hour later, as they gathered around the big round table, Willa wished her imagination would take a break!

The children, emulating the grown-ups, bowed their heads and closed their eyes, lips moving in silent prayer. When the blessings ended, Phillip stood and began slicing the turkey as Willa and Emily passed mashed potatoes, gravy, steamed vegetables, and home-baked rolls, and the children chattered. Once the plates had been filled, conversation between the men turned to work and the oncoming storm, while Emily and Willa discussed their plans to rearrange the clinic's waiting room furniture to make room for additional chairs.

And Anki sat, stiff and silent as a statue, staring out the window. When Phillip cleared his throat, she looked at Willa like a woman waking from a deep sleep.

"In honor of the day," Phillip said, "I think each of us should share something we're thankful for. Gabe, would you like to start?"

The boy squinted one eye and gave it a moment's thought. "I'm thankful Emily helped me get the operation that gave me a healthy heart." Turning, he said to his grandmother. "Your turn, *Groossmammi*."

"Ah, yes. I also am thankful for your healthy heart, Gabriel. And for myself?" She looked at Phillip. At her daughter Hannah and son-in-law and their sons. "I am thankful that each of you keeps God in your hearts."

Hannah, Eli, and their boys expressed gratitude for a safe home, enough work to keep the wolf from the door, and good health. Dan gave thanks for good friends, and Anki, much to everyone's surprise, gave thanks for Willa, who repaired the mess she'd made of her hair.

Max said, "Much as I hate to sound redundant, I, too, am grateful for good friends." And he was looking directly at Willa as he said it.

"Willa?" Phillip coaxed.

"I'm thankful for the Hofmans, who opened their home to Frannie and me, and made us feel like family. And now," she said to Phillip, "we get to hear from the man who put us all on the spot with his little 'why are you thankful' game!"

Once the good-hearted laughter ended, Phillip said, "I am surrounded by all that I'm grateful for . . . a loving wife, boisterous boys, and true friends."

That left just one person, and before she began to speak, Emily looked at Willa, and winked. "Like Phillip," she said, "I'm thankful for everyone in this room, and . . . and for the babies that will soon join us."

Phillip got up and, hands on her shoulders, said, "What?"

"I knew it!" Sarah shouted.

"We're going to have another baby?" Phillip said.

"No, sweetie. I said babies. Plural." She patted her belly. "Twins."

He repeated the word, but no sound came out. And then he said, "Twins?"

Drawing her close, he kissed her, and didn't step back until he heard Gabe say, "Two brothers?"

Emily knuckled tears from her eyes and returned to her seat. "Or two sisters. Or one of each!"

"Did you hear that, Rafe? We're about to get brothers. Or sisters." He looked at Emily. "Will they match?"

Laughing, she mussed his hair. "They might be identical, sweet boy, but they might not."

Phillip remained on his feet, looking stunned and

overjoyed, muttering things like "Babies" and "twins" and "I can hardly believe my ears!"

Max got up, too, and wrapped his friend in a fierce hug. "Congratulations, Phillip. I am happy for you and Emily."

Soon, Dan and Eli joined them, and the room pulsed with raucous laughter, good-natured shoves, and affectionate slaps on the back.

Willa had heard that the Amish preferred not to give in to public displays of affection. *Thank goodness these Amish believe in it!* Because watching the brotherly exchange was a beautiful thing to see. It seemed a shame that only the men were enjoying the Bakers' good news, so Willa got up, gathered Sarah, Hannah, Emily, and Anki by the hand, and led them in a merry circle dance. Rafe and Frannie sat, wide-eyed and fascinated by the adults' celebration. Gabe must have felt left out, too, because within seconds, he'd joined the manly merriment on the other side of the room.

"Enough foolhardiness," Sarah announced. "The workday begins early tomorrow, and we have much to do, right here, right now. Men and children into the parlor so we women can roll up our sleeves and get busy with the cleanup!"

Willa filled the dishpan with hot, soapy water. "Good," Emily said. "You wash and I'll dry."

"And I will supervise in the parlor," Sarah teased. Turning to Anki, she added, "Will you wrap up the leftovers?"

"I am happy to." Immediately, she walked to the opposite side of the big kitchen to focus on her assignment.

For a long while, Emily and Willa chatted above the steady *whoosh* of running water, the clatter of plates, the rasp of steel wool on pot bottoms, the clank of pans.

And then Emily leaned close to whisper, "I'm such an insensitive idiot!"

"Why?" Willa whispered back.

"I went on and on about the babies, and then we *all* went on and on, and poor Anki—"

"I have finished," she announced. "You will find the leftovers stacked in the refrigerator."

Emily slid an arm around her. "Thanks, friend. Please, won't you take some home?"

"No, no . . . our pantry and fridge are filled to overflowing."

"She's right," Willa agreed. "There isn't room for anything more!"

Anki flipped on the back porch light and peered into the yard. "I do not like the looks of this weather. I am going to ask Dan to take me home."

Anki started walking toward the parlor, but stopped halfway there, turned, and faced Emily. "I am truly happy for you. For Phillip and Gabe and little Rafe, too. News of your twins is a blessing, so of course you want to rejoice. That does not make you insensitive."

And with that, she left the room.

Despite lowered voices, running water, the clatter of plates, and the grate of steel wool against pot bottoms, Anki had overheard everything. Willa's heart ached for her, and judging by the look on Emily's face, she felt the same way.

"Stop worrying," Willa said. "She's stronger than she looks."

"Still . . ." Brow furrowed, Emily looked toward the parlor. "If she shows signs of backsliding, call me, no matter the time."

"Let's hope I won't have reason to call, because you need uninterrupted sleep, now more than ever!"

They joined the others in the parlor just as Dan burst in through the front door. "Tried to start up the truck and get the heater going," he said, dusting snow from his shoulders, "but either the battery is dead or the ignition is acting up again."

"Leave it here," Phillip told him, "and I'll have a look at it tomorrow."

"Good idea," Max put in. "I am happy to drive you and Anki home."

"But that will take you miles out of your way . . . in the opposite direction!"

"It is no bother, friend." He shrugged. "This house is bigger than it once was, but not big enough for overnight guests."

"Good point." Dan met Anki's eyes. "Are you ready to go?"

"I am."

Everything about her, from her stance to her facial expression to the wooden tone of voice told Willa that Emily's worries hadn't been groundless: Anki very well might be moving toward another downward spiral.

As Willa dressed Frannie for the ride home, Emily thanked her for all she'd done to make this a Thanksgiving to remember. She said her own thank-yous and good-byes and followed the Hofmans to the driveway.

The snow was coming down hard, burying the last stubborn black-eyed Susans and low-growing shrubs under a thick blanket that sparkled, diamond-bright, in the headlights' beams. Every tree branch, fence post, and roof bore the weight of it, and as it spewed steadily from the black sky, the frigid wind whirled it into spirals that skipped and bounced across the yard like white tornadoes.

Max brushed snow from her driver's-side window. "My truck has four-wheel drive," he hollered over the howling gusts. "Just steer into the tracks it will make, and you should have decent traction." His blue eyes glowed with concern. "Slow and steady," he said, "and you'll be fine. But please, Willa, be careful."

She glanced into the rearview mirror and saw Frannie's perfect, angelic face.

"I will."

An easy promise, because the future—for Frannie, for herself, and God willing, their life with Max—would depend on it.

Max led the way, dragging his feet through the powdery drifts, effectively plowing a lane that Willa could follow to the front porch. He held the door as she carried the baby into the parlor, where Dan, still in his overcoat, was down on one knee, stoking the fire.

She thanked Max for making the short trek easier, then said, "I've never seen snow like this."

"Some years are easier than others." He flicked snow from her shoulders, Frannie's, too. "You will stop shivering once you get out of these wet coats."

He started down the steps, and although she realized it was best that he get home before the weather worsened, Willa's heart ached a little. Dan and Max had utilitarian cell phones, used only for the business, but neither had home phones. At times like these, she wished that wasn't the case, so he could call and tell her he'd made it home safely.

"Be careful, Max. It's coming down like crazy."

"I will . . . once I leave here. Before I go, I want to shovel a path to the woodpile and bring in a couple arm-loads of wood."

The woodstove door closed with a metallic *clank* and Dan got to his feet. "I can do that," he said. "The longer you wait, the harder your drive will be."

"No sense in both of us getting soaked. Stay put. I will be right back."

"Thanks, friend," Dan said, closing the door behind him. He took off his coat, gave it a couple of shakes, and hung it on the wall peg. "Good man, that Max," he told Willa. "Good enough that he actually believes he can go home tonight."

"You think he'll have to stay?"

He looked out the window. "That footpath he made has already disappeared. So have the tire tracks in the drive-way."

Standing beside him, she looked outside. "This is a normal Oakland winter?"

Anki said, "A few years ago, two hundred sixty-two inches fell. And a few years after that, two hundred and five!"

Dan chuckled. "Anki! Just look at the girl's face—you are scaring her!"

"I am only stating facts."

Facing Willa, he said, "Changed your mind about making Pleasant Valley your home, eh?"

She could hear Max, stacking logs on the porch, then walking right back into the biting wind and swirling snow to make sure his friends wouldn't need to trudge through knee-deep drifts to stay warm tonight. Oh, how she loved that bighearted man!

"It'll take a lot more than the threat of snowstorms to make me leave this place."

Dan studied her face. "You know? I believe you."

Frannie, whimpering, rubbed her eyes. "Aw, are you sleepy, sweet girl? It has been a long, exciting day, hasn't it!" Scooping her up, she started for the stairs. "Anki, if you'll put on a kettle of water, I'll make us some cocoa just as soon as I put her to bed."

"Cocoa? From scratch?"

"The bottled stuff will do in a pinch, but a night like this calls for homemade."

Anki stood for a moment, hands clasped under her chin, and in that moment, Willa got a glimpse of the young, carefree girl Anki had once been. It gave her hope that with time and love and prayer, that kind of innocent joy might again light her features, often.

All too soon, the cocoa was gone, and as Max rose, Rascal followed him to the door.

When she asked, "Where do you think you're going?" Rascal looked up at her.

And looked at Max when he replied, "Why, home, of course."

"In the middle of a blizzard? Are you out of your mind!"

Rascal *woofed* softly, as if in agreement.

"Well, I cannot stay here all night."

"Why not? I'll make up the couch for you. Not as comfy as your own bed, but better than taking a chance on crashing into a tree—or worse—out there!"

"She is right," Dan said. "Only a madman would venture into this storm."

He stared out the window. "I can hardly believe how much snow has fallen in the past half hour." Facing Dan, he said, "Much as it pains me to admit it, you are right."

"I can get the linens now, if you're sleepy . . ."

"To be honest, I am wide awake."

"Not me." Dan got up, held a hand out to Anki, and said, "I hope you will get *some* sleep on that old thing."

Max tucked his thumbs into his waistband. "As Willa said, it beats sleeping in a snowbank."

"The highboy's bottom drawers creak something fierce, and the noise is sure to wake Dan and Anki. I'll just run upstairs now and grab your bedding." Willa started walking toward the hall, then stopped. "Can I get you anything before I go upstairs?"

"You will be back soon—especially since you plan to *run* upstairs—so I should be fine."

She wasn't sure which appealed to her more . . . his full-blown smile or that roguish grin. At the moment, she thought, stacking linens in her arms, it was the grin that lit up his eyes. Since he'd be sleeping just a few feet from the woodstove, a summer-weight quilt would do. She chose the one with almost-turquoise accents that reminded her of his eyes. She grabbed an extra one, just in case, and headed back downstairs.

Max had just added a log to the fire when she walked into the parlor, and once she'd put the bedding onto Dan's chair cushions, he said, "You are too kind to me."

Willa chuckled. "Says the guy who let a near stranger borrow his truck, volunteered to drive Dan and Anki home in a blizzard, then braved the wind and snow to make sure we had enough wood to last the night."

"I did what anyone would do."

"Trust me," she said, settling at one end of the sofa, "not everyone is like you."

Leaving a cushion between them, he sat on the other end. "How long have you known about the Bakers' twins?"

Give the man points for a quick topic change, she thought. "Not long."

"I thought maybe that was why you did the lion's share of the work today."

"Emily offered their house, and it made perfect sense, since their dining room is larger than Hannah's or the Hofmans', but I didn't think it was fair for her and Phillip to provide the house and the food and do the cooking, too."

"I can still taste Sarah's stuffing and candied yams," he said, patting his belly. "And Hannah's mashed potatoes. And that pumpkin pie . . ."

"It was a meal to remember, that's for sure!"

"Well," he said, drawing out the word, "all I can say is, I have not enjoyed Thanksgiving this much since I was a boy."

Tucking her legs under her, Willa sat, facing him. "At your grandparents' house?"

"Yes. We alternated holidays between my mother's family and my father's. Some years, more than forty of us shared the meal."

"Forty! Oh, how wonderful that must have been!"

"It was. Crowded, but wonderful." He paused. "What was Thanksgiving like in your family?"

"Quiet. Small. *Real* small." She shrugged. "I never knew my father or his family, and once my mother lost her mom and dad, we didn't celebrate."

"That seems a shame."

"Oh, Mom would have loved it, but she worked two and three jobs, and just didn't have time. But one year," Willa said, "I tried to surprise her. Saved up my pennies and went shopping, and after Mom left for her second job, I started cooking and baking. Turkey. Stuffing. Sweet potatoes. Rolls . . ." She laughed. "Burnt that bird so badly, I almost had to call the fire department!"

"Aw, what a shame. Were you able to salvage any of the meal?"

"Only to use the drumsticks as weapons against the rats in the alley!"

If he noticed that she'd just admitted having lived in a building that was home to people *and* rats, he gave no sign of it.

"How old were you?"

"Thirteen."

"You know what they say . . . it is the thought that counts. I am sure it left you with good memories, despite the charcoal bird."

Giggling, Willa said, "My favorite memory of that day was Mom's reaction. She didn't get mad, not even when she realized I'd ruined her favorite roasting pan. It went into the trash bag with all the blackened food, and she laughed so hard while tossing it into the dumpster that she actually wet her pants."

"She sounds like a remarkable woman, an outstanding mother."

"Oh, she was." The image of her mother brought tears to Willa's eyes, but she blinked them away. "She's the reason that I started making changes the instant I found out I was pregnant. I knew if I hoped to be even half the mother she was, I had to turn myself around."

"You have succeeded."

She was about to thank him for the compliment when Rascal whimpered and rested his chin on Max's knee.

"Patience, boy," he said, patting the dog's head. "I need to shovel a space for you out there."

The dog whined again as Max put on his coat and

boots, and whimpered yet again as his master closed the door behind him. Willa got onto the floor and, sitting beside the dog, wrapped her arms around his neck. "Don't worry, buddy, he won't be long." Leaning into her, Rascal exhaled a heavy sigh. "Yeah, I know how you feel. I miss him, too." She hugged him a little tighter. "And just between you and me? We *both* love him."

The minutes passed slowly, and when Max opened the door, his coat was caked with thick, heavy snow. "Let's go," he said, patting his thigh, and instantly, the dog followed him outside.

Once they returned, she dried the wet snow from Max's hair and Rascal's fur, then led them both toward the warmth of the stove. "You two stay put while I get us something warm to drink." She winked at the pup. "Water for you—not as good as cocoa, I know—but chocolate isn't good for dogs."

While warming the cocoa, Willa remembered telling Rascal that she loved Max. It was time, she decided, that he heard it for himself. And time that she knew, once and for all, whether or not he felt the same way. She'd put it off far too long!

First, she placed a shallow pan of water near the five-foot braided rug that Rascal had made his own, and while he lapped at it, she carried steaming mugs of cocoa into the parlor.

"While it's cooling," she said, placing them on the coffee table, "I have something to tell you."

And then the lights went out.

Coincidence, she wondered, or was the universe conspiring against her? Willa couldn't help laughing.

"The electricity is out, and you think it is funny?"

"No. *That* isn't funny at all. It's just . . ." *Tell him, you nincompoop! Just tell him!* "It's just that I've been trying to tell you, for months, it seems, that I'm crazy, head over heels in love with you. And every time I try to get the words out, something—or someone—interrupts me. I'm beginning to think maybe it's God's way of saying, 'Be quiet, you little fool, because this isn't My will!'"

"God would never call you a little fool."

That made her laugh harder still. "A *big* fool, then."

"No. Because you are not a fool." He drew her into a hug. "I have been wanting to say the same thing. And, as you said, there was a disruption of some sort, every time."

Max pressed both palms to her cheeks and looked deep into her eyes, and a sob ached in her throat when she saw tears clinging to his long lashes. "I love you, too."

Willa considered pinching herself, to make sure she wasn't dreaming, that he'd really said the words she yearned to hear.

She cringed.

"Well now, *that* is not the reaction I expected!"

"I'm just bracing myself."

"For . . . ?"

"A bolt of lightning. A meteor to land in the yard. Interference of some kind that—"

He silenced her with a kiss. A lingering, loving kiss that made her feel weak and powerless, like a marionette whose puppeteer had loosened the strings. She held on tighter, seeking his strength.

"It doesn't matter what happens now," he said. "It's out in the open, finally."

"Wait." She stuck a finger into her ear and jiggled it. "Am I hearing things? Did you just use . . . *contractions*?"

He blinked a few times, as if replaying his last words. "It seems you're rubbing off on me." Dropping a kiss onto her forehead, he added, "Do not look so worried. It isn't a bad thing."

She hoped not. Last thing Willa wanted was to change him, because in her mind, he was perfect in every way.

"I should light some candles. Lanterns. So that if Anki or Dan wakes up, they can find their way across the hall."

"I can help."

"But you won't. For one thing, you have no idea where anything is. For another, I know where all the squeaky boards are . . . and how to avoid them."

"I did not realize Dan is such a light sleeper."

"He isn't. But Anki is. And . . ." She stood on tiptoe and kissed him. "And I'd kind of like to be alone with you, so I can hear those beautiful words again. And again."

"I love you."

She rested her cheek against his chest, heard the steady beat of his big, loving heart. Much as she hated to leave the warmth of his embrace, Willa stepped back. "It won't take long. I promise. Sit down. Relax. Drink your cocoa."

Upstairs, Willa placed a small lantern on the bathroom vanity and lit it. She set another on the dresser where she stored Frannie's clothes. She tiptoed back down the steps, put a fat candle in the center of the kitchen table. Now, in the parlor, she struck another thick wooden match and held it to the wick of each sconce that flanked the woodstove.

"There. That didn't take too long, did it?"

He patted the cushion beside him. "Eleven minutes, if the grandfather clock is accurate." And when she sat down, he slid an arm across her shoulders. "Guess what?"

"You don't like scented candles?"

"As a matter of fact, I don't, but—"

"Neither do I. Just call me a purist."

"As I was about to say . . ." Touching his nose to hers,

he said, "If I had known how easy it would be to say it . . . how *good* it would feel to hear it . . . I never would have waited so long."

And then he said it. Three times in a row. And each time, she echoed the words.

Willa snuggled into his side. "Do you think that Dan and Anki felt this way, once upon a time?"

"Probably."

"I hope so." She remembered the way Anki had looked, listening as everyone cheered the good news of the Bakers' twins. "And I hope she doesn't slip back into her strange, private world, now that she knows about the babies." She sat up, met his eyes. "Just the other day, at the clinic, when Naomi was leaving Emily's office, she talked about *her* twins. Anki wasn't happy to hear that, either."

"Sad."

"Definitely." She nestled close again. "And it doesn't help when people tell her she should accept her childlessness as God's will."

"Who says that?"

He sounded annoyed, and she loved him all the more for his protective nature. "The women at church. The bishop. Dan. All clumsy attempts at comforting her, I'm sure, but it hurts her."

"Then we're all blessed to have you here, looking out for her. It was good that you suggested reopening the shop. Maybe if she concentrates on all that she has instead of what she *doesn't* have . . ."

And there it was again, that strange, troubled edge to his voice.

"Can I ask you a question?"

He lifted her chin on a bent forefinger, looking longingly into her eyes. "Anything. Any time."

"Is something wrong?"

His brows drew together. "What do you mean?"

"I don't know, exactly. It just seems . . . I feel like there's something on your mind. Something that involves me."

"No . . ."

That's what his lips said, but his eyes didn't agree.

"Is it my past? I haven't withheld the truth from anyone. So are you concerned that, even after the baptism, others will think you've chosen poorly?"

"The only opinions I care about are God's, and yours."

She had to smile a little at that. And yet . . .

"Are you worried that as time passes, I'll miss the modern world? That I might take my CNA certificate and find a job *away* from Pleasant Valley?"

"The thought never crossed my mind."

"Then Max, what *is* it?"

He shook his head, reached for the mug, and sipped from it. "Too much work, not enough sleep, constant intrusions . . ." He winked at her, then took another sip. His features had grown serious when he said, "You should stop looking for problems, because believe me, life will surprise us with plenty of them."

Like the buggy accident and fire that took his family? Willa wanted nothing more than to ease his mind. "You're right."

Satisfied—or so it seemed—he sat back and pulled her into his side. "We have a lot to talk about, don't we."

A wedding? Whether or not she'd continue working for the Hofmans? Would they encourage Frannie to call him Dad?

"You can say that again."

"But not tonight." Eyes closed, he kissed her temple. "I just want to sit here, basking in the knowledge that you love me, after all. And thanking God that you love me. *Me*."

After all?

Willa heard the edge in his normally smooth baritone and couldn't help but think it had something to do with her past.

It wouldn't be easy, keeping her doubts to herself, but the only way to prove she'd stopped looking for trouble was to silence every nagging doubt that continued to pummel her mind.

Chapter Sixteen

The baby monitor hissed and blinked.

Willa leaped up and grabbed it from its place on the mantel and said, "She never wakes up during the night."

He heard the concern in her voice, and thanks to the device's flashing red lights, saw it on her pretty face.

"I need to check on her."

As she dashed up the stairs, Max considered possible explanations for the baby's uncharacteristic fussing. Perhaps she'd sensed that the power was out. Or maybe, without electricity to power the furnace, Frannie had grown cold.

He got up and poked at the logs in the woodstove, squinting into the blazing heat emanating from its belly. Plenty of warmth, he decided, to float from the ceiling grate and into the floor vent into Frannie's room. When she'd leaned in to accept his good-night kiss, she'd looked more rosy-cheeked than usual, but Max had attributed it to the excitement of the day, and the snow that had dampened her face and hair.

Willa hurried into the room, holding the baby to her chest. "She has a low-grade fever. Will you hold her while I get some acetaminophen?"

"Sure," he said, and as soon as he held out his arms,

Frannie reached for him. As she snuggled close, Max admitted that he loved her little girl, too. A completely different kind of love than what he felt for Willa, but every bit as deep and abiding. And based on the trusting way Frannie clung to him, she felt the same way.

"Aw, my little angel girl," he whispered against her cheek.

Tiny fingers opened and closed on the locks of hair that curled over his collar. "Aww," she echoed. "Nice Max."

She'd said those very words, dozens of times. So why, this time, had they put tears in his eyes?

Willa returned just then, and seeing his reaction, pressed a palm to his cheek. "Don't worry, sweet man. It isn't a high fever, and she has no other symptoms." She unscrewed the cap of the bottle and poured half an inch of purple liquid into a tiny plastic cup. "We'll get this into her, and I'll feed her a bottle of water, and God willing, all will be well by morning."

Frannie and Rafe spent all day, every day at the Baker Clinic. No telling what sort of germs they'd been exposed to, inhaling the air over there! An intense need to protect Frannie overwhelmed him.

And as the baby dutifully swallowed the medicine, Max thought of Joe . . .

He hadn't thought to ask where the greedy, evil-eyed man would wait for his payment. No doubt the blizzard had trapped him, too. It would only take county officials a couple days to clear the roads. Would he wait until the bank employees could make their way to town? If not, would Joe find Willa, make good on his threat to drag her and Frannie away from Pleasant Valley? A reflexive shudder passed through him as he considered the dark and dangerous ways the evil man would use them to get back his money.

He couldn't let that happen, *wouldn't* let it happen, even if it meant draining his savings account or taking out a loan to satisfy the maniac.

Willa wiped the medication from Frannie's lips, and recapping the bottle, said, "There it is again . . . that *look* that tells me you have something on your mind."

She'd always been caring and perceptive. It was what made her a good mother, a good friend to Anki, a good nurse. It was also why she sensed he was keeping something from her.

"Frannie is not well. Breaks my heart to see her so listless." He hoped the half-truth would satisfy her.

Eyes narrowed slightly, she studied his face. "Okay. I guess that'll have to do . . . *this time.*"

Max returned her smile. But his heart wasn't in it. Sooner or later, he'd have to tell her about the deal he'd made with Joe. Would Willa agree it had been the right thing to do? Or would her pride and independence make her resent him for it?

It only took a few days for the county to make the roads passable. A blessing, Max believed, since it meant he could uphold his end of the bargain with Joe. Once the transaction was complete, he'd sit Willa down and explain what he'd done . . . and why: It didn't matter that the money had been earned by way of illegal activity. As long as Joe believed she'd stolen from *him*, Willa and Frannie were in danger.

Standing exactly where he'd been when the crook left him, he rehearsed his plan, and hoped *his* threat was menacing—and believable—enough to ensure that this was the last time they'd see or hear from Joe.

"I'm surprised you showed up," Joe said.

"Guess the people you usually do business with do not take promises seriously."

"Y'got me there, Amishman." He lit a fresh cigarette with the one between his lips. "So? Did you get the moolah?"

"I did. But before I give it to you, there are a few things you need to know."

Moving closer, he bored into Joe's rheumy eyes, and spoke slowly: "There is an audiotape of our earlier conversation." He pointed at the phony surveillance camera he'd bought at the twenty-four-hour discount store and hung earlier that morning. "It will back up what's on the film." Max slid the envelope from his pocket and held it aloft. "If I see you again, if you contact Willa, *ever,* I will take both to the police."

"Seriously?" He laughed, long and loud. "You actually expect me to believe an Amish guy used technology to—"

"I am a businessman, and use whatever tools are necessary." He took yet another step closer. "A friend in law enforcement explained that my, ah, *technology* will provide prosecutors with all they'll need to open a deeper investigation . . . which will turn up enough evidence to put you in an eight-foot cell for the rest of your life."

Eyes and lips narrowed, Joe swallowed. Hard.

Max waved the envelope in the air. "Do we have a deal, or not?"

"It's against the law to tape anyone without their knowledge or consent."

"My first offense," Max said with a nonchalant shrug. "If they issue a fine, I will gladly pay it."

Joe shoved the envelope into his jacket's inside pocket, and as he turned to walk away, Max added, "*This* meeting has been recorded, as well . . . for your information."

"Yeah? Whatever." Then Joe got into his car and drove away.

"Aren't you going to be surprised," Max said around a grin, "when you open that envelope."

He'd find one hundred one-dollar bills. Old ones, thickened by years of handling.

Tonight, he'd beg the Almighty's forgiveness for lying about the tapes, but right now, Max felt better than he had since Joe's shadow had fallen across his work before Thanksgiving. Since he'd be on his knees anyway, he might as well ask whether or not to bother Willa with the sordid details of his encounters with her ex.

Because the more he thought about it, the less he believed she'd react well.

The Pleasant Valley children put on a glorious Christmas pageant, singing songs and acting out adorable skits that had their families and friends laughing and applauding and singing along. They'd made hand-stamped cards, too, and passed their colorful flowers, stars, lambs, and ducklings throughout the building. After a chorus of happy well-wishes, the churchgoers left for their own Christmas celebrations.

Willa and Emily had talked about sharing the holiday, as they had on Thanksgiving, but when Hannah's boys came down with colds and little Rafe caught the bug, they decided separate, smaller celebrations might be better.

Before leaving for the service, Willa had surrounded a rump roast with potatoes and carrots, onions, and green beans, and slid the roasting pan into the oven. She'd promised to bake a cherry pie for Max—his favorite—and a chocolate cake for Dan. After the meal, they'd open presents, and she could hardly wait.

She'd hand-stitched a lovely yellow dress for Anki, a fat little doll for Frannie, and three oversized bandannas for Dan. Max's had been hardest to wrap, but it would be worth every painstaking moment to see his reaction to what she'd made for him.

The sumptuous aroma of the roast overpowered the scent of pine garlands she'd made to drape around the windows and candle holders. A simple, unadorned wreath hung on the front door, and one just like it decorated the back porch, too.

She'd set the table and stoked the fire, and now, with Frannie catching a quick nap before dinner, Willa didn't know what to do with herself. She tried reading, but couldn't pay attention. So she paced. Fussed with the decorations. And paced. Rearranged the tableware. And paced. Finally, the sound of tires grating up the gravel drive . . . Max's truck!

He'd barely shrugged out of his jacket when she welcomed him with hugs and kisses. "Merry Christmas, Max!"

"I love you, too," he said, laughing. "Dan and Anki will be home soon, so before they get here, I wondered . . . should we tell them about the engagement today?"

"No, I don't think so."

He looked even more surprised than he sounded. "Why?"

"Because you haven't actually asked me to marry you, for starters!"

"Ah," he said, laughing, "I suppose you have a point." Taking her hand, he led her to the table and pulled out a chair. "Sit, and let me tell you all about the way weddings happen here in Pleasant Valley."

He pulled out a chair, too, and facing her, sandwiched her hands between his own.

"Usually, people get married after the fall harvest. October, most often, because the weather is more predictable."

"Is it true that Amish boys and girls make commitments at the tender age of sixteen?"

"In some cases, yes. But they will not make things official until they are twenty."

"And they both have to be Amish. And baptized."

"Yup."

"No rings."

"Nope. But the man will give the woman a practical gift."

"Like a toaster?" she teased.

"Something like that. And once things are set in motion, the bride-to-be will tell her parents, and the bishop will announce their intentions at the end of a Sunday service . . . a service that the couple will not attend."

"Why not?"

"Because they are at the home of the bride's father, sharing a private meal . . . and talking."

"About?"

"To be honest, I am not sure."

"What happens to us? I mean, you can't ask my parents' permission. And we can't share that private meal at their house."

"We have friends. Good, trustworthy friends." He squeezed her hands. "They will be our family."

"Yeah, that makes perfect sense."

"You will wear a blue dress, and I will wear a bow tie."

"What, no tuxedo?" She laughed. "And no long wedding veil trailing behind me as I walk down the aisle?"

"There will be no aisle. Just a simple ceremony followed by a feast that might last for hours." He kissed the tip of her nose. "Tradition states that the newlyweds should spend their wedding night in the bride's parents' house. Since there is no such thing, we'll just have to go home."

"Home. I like the sound of that." She sighed. "Will there be a honeymoon?"

"Do you want a honeymoon?"

"Not really. I'd much rather jump right into the whole marriage thing with both feet. Besides, why spend money on a trip . . ." Willa paused. "Besides, if we *did* have a honeymoon, where would we go?"

"Pennsylvania. Ohio. New York. Indiana. Anywhere we might have relatives to visit."

"Oh no. Just . . . no!" she said. "We'll stay home." She wondered if he had relatives in other states. "Unless there's someone you'd like to see . . ."

He kissed her again. "I feel as you do. Let's jump right into this whole marriage thing with both feet." Another kiss, and then, "I hear Dan's truck."

"Rats. And this was just getting interesting."

Everyone enjoyed the meal. Even Anki took a second helping of Willa's roast. "Only one thing could make this better," she said. "Dill pickles, thinly sliced, on buttered bread, with a thick slice of this tender roast."

It was the most she'd said in days, so Willa hopped up to get the open jar of pickles from the fridge. She buttered two slices of bread, layered the sandwich with pickles and a hunk of beef, and handed it to Anki.

It shouldn't have surprised her when Anki shook her head, and yet it did. Surprised her, and disappointed her, too, that the woman couldn't hold it together, even on Christmas day!

"When can we open presents?" Anki wanted to know.

Willa made herself smile. "Let me put the perishables away, and then we can dig in. Sound good?"

"I suppose we have no choice, do we?"

"Anki, sweetie, if it means this much to you, the clearing can wait." Willa took her by the hand, led her into the parlor. "I'll get Frannie and tell Max and Dan it's time. Okay?"

"Thank you, Willa. You are always so understanding."

"No, Anki." She kissed the top of her head. "I love you, and I want you to be happy, whatever it takes."

Soon, the little family had gathered around the coffee table. Dan passed out presents, starting with Frannie. He helped her tear the shiny silver paper from what he'd carved for her . . . a sweet toy train. Engine, coal car, and caboose. Squealing happily, she sat on the floor, pushing it back and forth and singsonging, "Choo-choo-choo!"

Anki had sewn an adorable little apron for the baby and made one just like it for Willa. "I know how much you like the pockets," she said, "so I made them extra wide and extra deep."

Willa took off the apron she was wearing and replaced it with the new one. "I love it," she said. "Thank you, Anki!"

"This is for Frannie," Max said, and the baby quickly uncovered a box, slightly bigger than Willa's. Instead of initials, he'd engraved her name on its lid.

She was clearly torn between the train and the tiny box that opened and closed with a quiet click, and while she tried to spend equal time with each, the adults laughed.

Everyone but Anki, that is.

"Here," Dan said to her. "For you."

She peeled away the bright red wrapper, exposing a leather case. Inside was a set of brushes, arranged in an artful, upside-down *V*, each held in place by its own tiny leather pouch: Filberts, round and fan brushes, liners and pallet knives, and more. Willa held her breath, waiting for Anki to show emotion of some kind. When she didn't, Willa said, "They're wonderful, Anki! Think of all the beautiful paintings you can create with them!"

A faint smile lifted the corners of her mouth. "Thank you, Dan," she said, almost timidly. "Willa is right. They are wonderful." Then, reaching behind her, she pulled a thin, rectangular box from behind the throw pillow. "For you," she said, handing it to him.

Dan lifted the lid, held up a shirt. Collarless. Cuffless. Pocketless. "A man cannot have too many white shirts," he said, folding, then returning it to the container.

Max gave him a new, perfectly weighted hammer, and the men roared with laughter when Dan presented Max with an identical tool.

"Great minds think alike," Max said.

"And as my grandpa used to say, fools seldom differ!" And although Dan was smiling, Willa could see that he still hadn't shed the disappointment of Anki's reaction to his thoughtful gift.

She gathered the wrapping paper, wadded it up, and held it in her lap, hoping no one would realize that she was stalling, so that her gift to Max would be last.

He'd wrapped her present in the same pink paper he'd used for Frannie's, and inside, Willa found a soft, fringed scarf. Holding it to her cheek, she said, "It's gorgeous, Max. I needed one, but even if I didn't, I'd love it!"

"Hmpf," Anki said. "Who can *love* an article of clothing?"

Everyone, it seemed, had chosen to follow Willa's lead, and ignored the inappropriate remark.

"I hope it will fit," Max said, inviting a new round of laughter.

And then Willa got up, slid a package from behind the sofa, and leaned it against Max's knees. He lifted it. Shook it. Pretended to smell it. And feigning a frown, said, "A stack of architectural paper, for drawing house plans."

"Spoilsport," she said, going along with his guess.

Once the blue paper fluttered to the floor, he turned it around. "My view," he whispered. Then, meeting her eyes, he said, "This is the view from my porch. It's . . . I'm . . . I don't know what to say, except, thank you. And that seems sadly unsuitable, because it's perfect."

"When did you paint that?" Anki wanted to know.

"At night, while everyone slept, I'd come downstairs and worked in the laundry room. The light is good and bright in there. And I had access to water, and the laundry tub, and the folding table to use as an easel."

"Oil, or acrylic?"

"Acrylic. I didn't have the luxury of waiting for the oils to dry."

"Willa," Max continued, still gazing at the painting, "you only saw this once. How could you have remembered, right down to the old gnarled tree at the foot of Backbone Mountain?"

Her heartbeat doubled. It felt good, so good, seeing that he liked it.

"I will make a frame for it and hang it above the fireplace."

Soon to be our *fireplace,* seemed to be the message he was sending by way of those oh-so-blue eyes.

"It should be fine," Bishop Fisher said. "I will need to discuss it with the elders, though, and get their approval."

"Oh, thank you, Bishop. How long does it usually take? To get their approval?" She hesitated, then added, "Do you think there might be a problem? Because of my past?"

Fisher sent her a benevolent smile. "You speak as though

every member of the community, from the youngest to the eldest, knows about that. You have my word, dear Willa, that they do not."

"But . . . how did you explain why Frannie doesn't have a father?"

"People here are not as caught up with such things as they are in the Englishers' world. And even if they were, our way is to pray the questions away."

"You have no idea what a relief that is. I realize it isn't a guarantee . . . that the elders will approve of my being baptized, becoming Amish . . . but it gives me hope. For that, I thank you."

"You have only yourself—and the Almighty—to thank. You have worked hard. I have seen great changes in you during your time here. You have contributed much, be-friended many. These things tell me that you will be a good addition to our community."

"If they approve, do you think they'll make an exception, and allow me to be baptized on New Year's Day?"

"Pray about it. I will, as well."

Willa left the bishop's house feeling hopeful, elated, and excited to share the news with Max. Unfortunately, he was in Frostburg, ironing out some add-ons to the Frost-burg contract.

While waiting to hear the elders' verdict, she threw herself into work, at the clinic, at the Hofmans', on the surprise she'd been planning for Anki's upcoming birth-day. For that one, she'd made good use of the time she'd once spent studying. The gift was from both her and Frannie, who'd been her usual cooperative self, sleeping deeply all through the night. If she hadn't been such a deep sleeper, Willa never could have put in so many after-bedtime hours. Armed with cleaning rags, paintbrushes, and good old-fashioned elbow grease, she'd turned the once-dingy shop into a place that, if all went as planned, could open for business by April first.

She'd stayed late at the clinic, determined to complete the supplies inventory so that in the morning, Emily could place the order that would restock every shelf. The mother-to-be had left hours ago, and the only sound Willa heard was the *click-clack* of her keyboard. The peace and quiet felt good, and soothed her, took her mind off the deliberations that were probably taking place, even as she typed. Discussions that would help—or prevent—her from becoming Amish.

Loud rapping at the door startled her, and she walked cautiously toward the waiting room. When she saw Micah Fisher outside, waving under the overhead light, Willa felt optimistic, then terrified, because she knew he'd come here to deliver the news, good or bad.

"Stop looking so worried," he said when she let him in. "I am the bearer of good news."

"They said yes? I can be baptized?"

"Yes, and yes."

Willa threw her arms around him, and turning in a slow circle, said, "Thank you! Thank you! Thank you!"

Hands on her shoulders, he stopped her.

"I'm sorry," she said. "So sorry. I forgot that the Amish don't give in to public displays of affection. It's just that I'm so happy, well, I'm afraid I lost my head."

He was laughing when he said, "It is all right. No harm done."

"Please, let me fix you some tea. Or coffee. A glass of milk."

"No, no." He held up a hand. "I knew you were waiting for word, so . . ."

"Will you sit with me then? Tell me what happens next?"

"As it turns out," he began, taking a seat, "seven others have decided to make a fresh start this New Year."

"Seven!" Willa could hardly believe it.

Boys would sit on one side, he explained, girls on the other. "The service will last a few hours. We will read Scripture. In the High German. The focus will be living a humble and virtuous life, a life pleasing to God. We will pray, all of us together, and kneel in silent worship. You will promise to live by the *Ordnung,* and commit yourself to this life, for the rest of your life."

"The sweetest five words I've ever heard." *Not as sweet as hearing Max say I love you, but sweet nonetheless.* "It'll be the first day of the rest of my life."

When the bishop looked as pleased as she felt, Willa knew she'd said the right thing.

And that she'd made the right decision, for herself, and for Frannie.

Chapter Seventeen

After all she'd been through, it did Max's heart good to see her looking so content with life. "You look happy, Willa. Really happy."

"I am. I'm proud, too. I know that's a sin, so please don't tell the bishop!"

"Your secret is safe with me," he said, laughing.

"It feels *so good* knowing that I'm finally making choices that everyone approves of."

"Everyone?"

"Everyone who matters." She kissed him. "You, for instance."

He kissed her, too. "Feels good, hearing that my opinion matters."

While she rested her head on his shoulder, Max's mind raced . . .

She'd traded the conveniences of the modern world for the Plain life. Spent countless hours working toward a CNA certificate—even though she'd already earned a college degree—because she loved contributing to the community. Dedicated additional hours to win the right to become baptized. And she'd done it all in her usual *do it right or not at all* way. Still . . . if Willa had a loving family out there somewhere, people she could trust and rely upon, would she have made *any* of those choices?

"What do you suppose your mother would have thought about your becoming Amish?"

The question erased her happy smile. She didn't reply right away. It took her so long to respond, in fact, that Max didn't think she'd answer at all.

"Everything my mom did, she did to make my life better. So I think she would approve, wholeheartedly."

Her smile had returned, along with the serene expression that warmed it.

"You were with the bishop for a long time this afternoon."

"It didn't seem long at all. I've come to think of him as a friend. I think he's wonderful."

"Not everyone agrees, you know."

"I felt that way, not long ago. But working with him, one on one, helped me see him in a different light. It can't be easy, watching over everyone here in Pleasant Valley. And yet he does it without complaint, because like a doting parent, he loves and wants what's best for them." Her smile grew. "For *us*."

"You are right." Fingertips tracing the contours of her jaw, he said, "How long has Frannie been asleep?"

She looked at him as if he'd grown an extra pair of ears. "You were here when I put her down. An hour? A little more, maybe?"

"Long enough that you could take a walk with me?"

Leaning close, she kissed his cheek. "I'd love that. Just let me grab my coat. And the baby monitor."

Their boots crunched over hard-packed snow as they walked, arm in arm, toward the end of the driveway.

"I don't think I'll ever get used to that," she said, pointing up. "I mean, of course I *knew* there were billions of stars in the sky, but the bright city lights and smog made them hard to see. And that moon . . . Why, it's so big and bright, like our very own spotlight." A soft breath puffed from her lips. "God is quite an artist, isn't He?"

"When you talk this way, you make me feel guilty."

She looked up at him. "Guilty? Why?"

"I have lived beneath this same sky all of my life, but I didn't fully appreciate it until just now. See, that is an example of the many things you've taught me . . . taught all of us in the community."

It was too dark to know for sure, but Max had a feeling the compliment had inspired a blush. He stopped walking, took her hands in his. "You are a treasure, and more beautiful inside than out . . . and that's saying something."

If there had been any doubt in his mind about her feelings for him, they vanished as quickly as the snowflakes that had landed on her long eyelashes.

"Correct me if I'm wrong," he continued, "but in the world of the English, a man asks permission to marry the love of his life."

Willa laughed. "My orphan status got you off the hook, didn't it!"

"I would gladly—proudly—have done it. And promised to be your safe haven, always." Max took the neatly folded handkerchief from his jacket pocket, gave it a flap, and said, "And once they've received permission, they present their intended with a ring, yes?"

"Yes, but I know about the no-jewelry rule. I don't mind a bit. Honest."

"Nevertheless . . ." He stooped, spread the hanky on the ground, and got down on one knee. Looking up at her, he extended one hand, to show her the tiny circle of twine resting on his palm. "It's our secret," he said, slipping it onto her ring finger. "A bit too big, but see here?" He tapped the small knot on the top. "It symbolizes eternity, my way of saying I'll love you, forever."

Willa sat on his knee and threw her arms around him. "Now *I* feel guilty," she said, her voice raspy with tears. "I've made you violate the rules, and you'll have to ask forgiveness."

"There's nothing to ask forgiveness *for*. You won't wear this ring."

She held it to her heart. "Never?"

"Well, I suppose you can slip it on from time to time, if you need a reminder of what's in my heart."

"It's more beautiful, even, than silver or gold, and I'll treasure it always."

"So . . . you will marry me, then?"

She pressed her lips to his and mumbled, "I will. I do. Yes. And I love you."

What a peculiar time for the meeting with Joe to come to mind, he thought. If he told her about it now, he'd destroy this moment for her . . . for himself.

He had the rest of his life to explain, and if her stubborn pride caused her to disagree with what he'd done to protect her from the amoral drug dealer, he'd have the rest of his life to make up for it.

As winter gave way to spring, Anki's progress seemed to stall.

"I am at a complete loss," Dan said one afternoon as he and Max were reviewing construction plans.

He'd been pacing like a caged wolf for five minutes straight. "You will wear a path in the linoleum," Max said.

"Sit. Finish your coffee. Then we can go over the plans for those last cabins at Lover's Leap."

But Dan continued walking from one end of the construction trailer to the other, and back again. "I have never felt more helpless."

"Easier said than done, I know, but what can you do, except continue being patient?"

"She worries me, and—do not misunderstand—I love her. But I have never been more angry with her. Not even when she cut her hair. She behaves as if no other woman in history was barren. Why does she refuse to be satisfied with all that she has, instead of thinking only of the one thing she does *not* have!"

In Dan's shoes, Max would feel angry, too. Angry, and hurt that his life's mate seemed incapable of facing a future with just *him*.

"Willa seems to think Abigail has a lot to do with Anki's behavior. Seems she'd held fast to the belief that God would answer her prayers, find a way to bring Abigail home. But the suicide killed that hope as surely as Abigail killed herself."

That, at least, put Dan into a chair.

"I need some good news," he said. "Where do things stand with you and Willa?"

It took concerted effort not to grin from ear to ear. "She will marry me."

"And you are not concerned that someday, she will miss living the English life?"

"She is strong. And willful—so she's well named. I believe she has put her old life behind her, as much for Frannie as for herself. So my only concern is whether or not I can give her the good life she has earned."

Despite his show of confidence, the conversation shadowed Max for the rest of the day. That night, as

Frannie stacked blocks on her highchair tray and Willa washed dishes, he leaned beside her at the counter. "Why are you so determined to trade the freedom of your old life to live Plain?"

"Well, that came from out of the blue." Taking a moment to measure his mood, Willa dried her hands, led him to the table, and pulled out a chair. "I can see why you're apprehensive," she said, on her knees in front of him. "I mean, why would someone like me trade the so-called excitement of the English world for the restrictions of being Amish!" She kissed his knuckles. "But the real question is, why did I ever see that as freedom!"

Willa held up her left hand, showing him a faint rash on her ring finger. "Every chance I get, I put on that sweet little ring you made for me. It's scratchy and itchy, but I don't care." She giggled quietly. "Once, after wearing it all night, I woke up with a red splotch on my cheek. Dan said it must have been a spider bite, and suggested I try to find and kill it before it could bite Frannie, too."

Max laughed, although he couldn't quite connect his question with her story about the ring.

"It's almost as symbolic as the knot you tied at the top of the ring. Don't you see? I'm not giving up anything . . . I'm gaining the life I've always dreamed of!"

Heart pulsing with love, he pulled her into a hug. "I don't know what I ever did in my life to deserve a blessing like you, but if God ever sees fit to show me . . ."

He felt the prick of tears behind his eyelids, and to hide them, he kissed her. Kissed her as he'd never kissed her before.

Dan clomped into the room, and seeing them, spouted a nervous laugh. "Just wanted you to know I am going to the trailer," he said as they stepped apart, "to balance the company checkbook."

When he opened the door, Frannie waved. "Aw, nice Dan. Bye-bye!"

"I will be back soon, little one." He smiled, rolled his eyes, and told Max, "Feel free to finish . . . the *dishes* . . ."

The door closed, and he was gone.

"This is his house," Max began.

And Willa finished with, "I think we should do what he says."

As their lips met, Frannie said, "Max kiss Mama. Aww."

"Now really," Max said, laughing, "how is a man to do . . . *dishes* . . . with all these interruptions!"

It had been a quiet day at the clinic, and Willa insisted that Emily go home to relax and put up her feet. "You're not going to have a lot of opportunities to do it once those babies get here!" she'd said.

And Emily quickly agreed.

Willa had entered the day's log into the computer and was about to clean up the exam rooms when the phone rang. "Aw, nuts. Please don't let it be something that'll force Emily to come back," she muttered.

The phone rang a third time, and she answered with her customary, "Baker Free Clinic."

"You think you're pretty smart, don't you?"

She'd recognize that reedy, whiny voice anywhere. During those first months in Pleasant Valley, Willa had skulked around like a thief in the night, worrying that Joe would find her. But as time passed with no contact from him, she'd allowed herself to relax.

"How did you find me?" But no sooner were the words out than she remembered the scary man in the diner parking lot, who'd stared . . . and taken pictures.

"Here's a better question for you . . ."

She could almost see his watery gray eyes, eyes that appeared smaller because of thick nearsighted lenses, and cringed.

"How many times did I say if you ever left me, I'd find you, no matter how long it took?"

Hundreds . . .

"And yet you ran off like a junkyard dog, after all I did for you!"

After all he'd done? *Like turning me into a common junkie? Using me as a drug mule? Raping and beating me whenever the mood struck?*

"I put a roof over your head, you ungrateful witch. Put food in your belly . . . Speaking of which, where's my kid?"

Willa looked over her shoulder, toward the spare exam space that she and Emily used as their babies' playroom. She could hear Frannie back there, chattering happily to each of the three tiny dollies that went everywhere with her.

"She isn't your kid. Never was. Never will be," she said through clenched teeth.

"Easy now, *Willa,* better climb down off your high horse, and think about this: If I found you, I've found her, too."

How had he learned that the baby was a girl? *Calm down,* she told herself. *He doesn't want you* or *Frannie.*

Willa looked at her framed CNA certificate, hanging above the computer. "I have a good job now," she said. "How much do you want?"

He laughed. *Laughed*!

"Silly Miss Nurse's Assistant. I need the money now, not in ten or twenty years . . . which is how long it'll take you to . . ." He faked a cough. ". . . to *earn* it. And I'm going to need a whole lot more than I got the last time I went to Pleasant Valley."

She didn't understand, and said so.

"Your hardworking Amish boyfriend handed me a fat stack . . . a hundred one-dollar bills, strutted like a suspendered peacock, and said if I showed up again, he'd go to the cops with video and audiotapes. Proof that I intended to sell you, if I could find anybody dumb enough to buy you, to get my dough back. Sell your brown-eyed kid, too." A sinister snicker filtered through the phone line. "Y'know, it feels kinda good that she looks so much like me."

Had he seen her? How else would he know that she resembled him? It seemed totally out of character for Max to reveal so much personal information, especially after learning Joe's identity and what he wanted. But if not Max, who *had* supplied Joe with so many details?

Yet again, she remembered the stranger at the diner. Joe had sent him. She was sure of it now. But how many times had he watched her? And how long had he been watching?

From the sound of things, Joe was desperate, so not long.

Later, she'd find answers. Right now, she gave in to fear. And a measure of anger. Joe said he'd met with her Amish boyfriend, that Max had outsmarted him. It meant he'd made a decision that put himself, Dan and Anki, and Frannie in danger. If he'd discussed it with her, Willa would have reminded him that before moving to Pleasant Valley, she'd taken care of herself, that she could have done it this time without endangering anyone . . . except maybe herself . . . if only he'd given her the chance. Why hadn't he given her the chance?

"Don't worry your drug-fried brain over that money, Willa. Like I said, I found other ways to earn it back."

Earn, indeed, she thought, and immediately pitied anyone involved in his evil plot to make it happen.

"Wasn't easy, on account-a you, but I did it."

Thank God she'd had the foresight to lock the door after Emily left, because for all she knew, he was right outside, high on cocaine and loaded for bear. If she riled him, he'd just follow her home, and only the good Lord knew what he'd do after that.

Oh, Max would hear from her about this, that much was certain!

"If you *earned* back the money," she said, "why are you calling me?"

"Well, Willa, it's like this . . ."

She pictured him, straddling his black Harley's saddle, squinting into cigarette smoke while inspecting his long, oval-shaped fingernails. Had he cut his shaggy hair? Shaved his scraggly brown beard? Worn something other than chains and black leather? What had she been thinking, getting involved with a man like Joe? *Thank You, God, for saving me from that life!*

"Yeah, I got my money back, but that doesn't mean I consider us even. One way or the other, you're gonna pay for leaving me, for making me look like a fool. You won't see it comin', but trust me, li'l Amish girl, it's comin'."

He hung up, and for a long time, Willa stared at the now-silent phone.

"Mama," Frannie called. "Bye-bye?"

"Yes, sweet girl. We're going home." *For as long as we can, every chance we get, we're going home.*

On countless occasions, Max had witnessed her frustration with Anki. She'd looked worried on the night Frannie spiked a fever. Anxious as she studied for the CNA exam, and fretful while memorizing Bible verses to impress the bishop. But he'd never seen her angry, at least, not at him, and Max didn't like the feeling one bit.

"I was going to tell you, that very day, and many times since. But it just never seemed to be the right time. Sort of the way you and I tried and tried to share our feelings for one another, and life kept interrupting."

"No, Max, this is different. This is about our *lives.*"

"Saying I love you, planning a future, protecting you from that animal is not?"

"I know it makes me sound like a melodramatic female, but I learned the hard way that Joe is a dangerous man, with dangerous friends. If he decides to make good on his threat . . ." Willa heaved a shaky sigh. "If anything happened to Frannie, to Dan and Anki, to *you,* I'd never forgive myself."

He tried to hug her, right there in the parlor with Dan and Anki witnessing everything, but she shied away. "I need some time to process things."

For purely selfish reasons, everything in him told Max to talk her out of that mindset. What if while she was *processing,* she decided that what he'd done was proof he couldn't be trusted?

"How much time?"

She turned away from him, not completely, but enough that Max felt the chill all the way to the soles of his feet.

"I don't know." Looking into his eyes, she said, "You're busy, I'm busy, let's just see how things play out."

"But Willa, what if during this *time* you say you need, he comes back? How will I protect you and Frannie if you are here and I'm . . . not?"

"*Now* you're starting to get it. He can't be trusted. It's better for everyone concerned if I go somewhere for a while, until he forgets about Frannie and me."

"Are you listening to yourself? You've been here the better part of a year, and in all this time, he hasn't forgotten about you. What makes you think that going somewhere will make that happen? He found you once; he can find you again."

He was pacing now. Ranting. Flinging his arms in the air. Max knew he must look like a raving lunatic, but he didn't care.

"Where would you go? How would you support yourself and Frannie? And . . . and how long is long enough?"

"I can take care of myself!" she shouted. "I did just fine on my own. I don't need you to make choices for me. Okay? Let me take Frannie and we'll go where he'll never find us. And when *I* believe it's safe, we'll come home."

"You are not going anywhere," Dan said. "You will be safe, you and Frannie both, right here in Pleasant Valley."

"Stay at my house. You and Frannie can have the entire second floor. People will not judge. They will understand. And if they don't?" Max raked his fingers through his hair. "If they don't, *damn them*!"

"He is right, Willa. What good can come from you leaving this place?"

"No good can come from it," Anki said. "You must stay."

In the wake of her simple statement, everyone fell silent.

"He will not come for you," Anki added.

"You can't know that," Willa said.

Shrugging, she said, "I have no explanation, except that as soon as you told us about this man, I prayed. Prayed as I have never prayed before." She shrugged again. "You are safe now. It is something I feel in my heart."

Anki sounded calm, self-assured, and completely at peace with what she'd said. Max wanted that for himself, and so he prayed. Prayed that Anki's perfect, peaceful demeanor had been heaven-sent, and that soon, he'd feel it, too.

He left the Hofmans' parlor and joined Willa, who stared silently out the back door, as if by sheer willpower, she could keep Joe away. "He isn't out there," Max said. "I saw how right you were about him. He's a despicable, wicked man. Which is why he planted those terrible thoughts in your head. He wants you to be as miserable as he is. Don't let him do that to you, Willa. Please. Don't let him do it to Frannie. To *us*."

Again, he tried to hug her, and again, she stiffened. He'd broken two bones, falling from a tree. Nearly sliced off a thumb, using the chain saw. Caught his arm on a protruding nail. Buried beloved family members. It made him feel guilty, admitting it, but none of it hurt as much as having her turn away from him.

"I am sorry," he said. "Nothing like it will happen again. From here on out, we'll be partners, you and I, partners in life. I will never keep anything from you again. You have my word."

She continued staring into the yard, so he added, "How can I make this up to you?"

Willa faced him, rested both hands on his forearms. "I want to stay here in Pleasant Valley. But I need a little time. If we marry, it won't be until October, so can you give me that? Time, I mean?"

If they married? Max could hardly believe what he was hearing. There were tears in her eyes when she'd said it, and knowing that he'd put them there hurt like crazy.

"All right. Take as much time as you need. I'll wait. However long it takes, I'll wait."

Willa lifted the corner of her apron, wiped her eyes, and said, "Thank you, Max."

She left him then, and he watched as, step by step, she made her way toward the stairs. On the landing, she turned and smiled, and he memorized the look of love in her eyes.

Yes, he'd wait, and trust that God would bring her back to him.

Because Max didn't know how he'd face life without her.

Chapter Eighteen

"I hope I can count on you to help with the wedding plans."

Anki put down her coffee cup. "I thought you put the marriage on hold, indefinitely?"

"I did. But . . ." Willa groaned quietly. "I'm praying that between now and October, Joe will find someone else to torture, and it'll be safe for us to marry. I want to be ready when the time comes, so that nothing will interfere with our plans."

Anki nodded. "I understand. But you might want to ask someone else. My memories of my marriage to Dan have grown dim."

Willa stood the steam iron on its end and sat across from her. "You don't really expect me to believe you've forgotten the most beautiful, wondrous day in your life, do you?"

Now, Anki's fingertip drew invisible figure eights on the tablecloth.

"Maybe you need a reminder of just how much you're treasured. By everyone. Dan, Frannie, me . . . and Max . . ."

At the mention of her name, the baby held up her empty cereal bowl. "Anki eat?"

How anyone could sit there, sullen and silent, with this

precious child in the room, Willa didn't know. She gave in to the impulse to hug the sad-eyed woman, then gave her a gentle shake. "I need you, Anki. I'm new to all this . . . this *Amish stuff.* Without your input, I'll probably do something stupid and get the bishop all fired up. You don't want to be responsible for him taking back my baptism, do you?"

The barest smile lifted one corner of Anki's mouth. "Only a grievous sin would cause him to do that." She looked away. "I will try to help you."

I will try. So why did Willa get the impression Anki had wanted to add, ". . . *if I am still here"*?

Turning her loose, Willa tried another tack. "Will you pray with me, Anki?"

"All right."

And why had *that* sounded like she wanted to say, *"If I must . . ."*?

Willa grabbed her hands and jumped right in:

"Oh God, I pray that You will bless my dear friend Anki with the gift of Your peace. Deliver joy into her heart, Almighty Father. Let her feel Your presence in this room, see it in the memory of the winter we've just survived, in the bloom of every spring flower You have delivered, hear Your voice in the songs of the crickets and sparrows, and in the words of her loving husband and friends. Amen."

"Aye-*men!*" Frannie said.

And when Willa looked up, she saw that her little girl had perfectly copied her own pose . . . eyes closed and head bowed, and hands clasped under her chin. Oh, how she loved this beautiful, big-hearted, brilliant child!

The words Max had spoken when he proposed fit this moment, perfectly. *I don't know what I ever did to deserve a gift like Frannie,* she thought, *but if You ever see fit to show me what it was, I'll do it again and again!*

"Is it true I have to wear a blue dress?"

"Most women do, but not all." She took another sip from her mug. "When Lydia Bontrager married Abel Hochstetler, she wore pale pink. Her sister wore light green. I have seen lavender and yellow, as well."

"What color was your wedding dress?"

"Gray."

Her voice was as gloomy as the hue, and it told Willa that Anki's mood swings had likely begun long before the community shunned Abigail . . . and before her twin committed suicide. If that hadn't been the source of Anki's misery, what *was*?

"Max says that he and Dan are making great progress on the cabins at Lover's Leap. Why don't we go and see for ourselves? I'm not scheduled at the clinic today . . ." Thanks to Anki's erratic attitude, she and Dan had decided to make sure one of them could always keep an eye on Anki. "I'll pack a picnic lunch for all of us, and afterward, you and I can go shopping."

"Shopping? For what?"

"As you pointed out just a few days ago, now that winter is over and Frannie is running everywhere, she needs shoes with hard soles. I saw an advertisement in *The Budget*. They are on sale at the supercenter this week."

"That place!" Anki groaned. "You do not need me. I will stay home. Besides," she said with a dismissive wave, "Dan already has a lunch. I watched him pack it this morning."

Willa had watched, too, offered to do it for him, as she had on so many other mornings. "Oh, now she asks," he'd teased, "when I have almost finished!" But not before shooting a disappointed glance in Anki's direction.

Perhaps she should view dealing with Anki's surly

attitude as practice for when Frannie became a teenager and began testing her talent for sassing and pouting.

The past four Sundays, Anki had blamed headaches for her refusal to attend services, but offered no reason for rejecting offers to enjoy the warm sunny weather from the comfort of the porch swing. Breathing nothing all winter but indoor, woodstove-heated air had taken its toll, slowing her pace, draining color from her face. *What will you do when Frannie's old enough to behave like a spoiled brat?* she asked herself. *You'll put a stop to it, that's what!*

"We're going, and that's that." Last time Willa tried a similar approach, Anki had flatly reminded her that she was an employee in the Hofman house, and as such, had no right to issue orders or ultimatums. With thoughts of the stinging barb fresh in her mind, she added, "You need fresh air, so if you stop whining, we'll go to Page's Ice Cream afterward." She softened things with, "I'd love a hot fudge sundae, wouldn't you?"

The treat was Anki's favorite, and Willa hoped it would lure her out of the house.

"I can't recall the last time I had one. What time will we leave?"

"As soon as I get the breakfast mess cleaned up, I'll see if Frannie will take a nap—she's almost outgrown the morning one—and start the laundry. Once I have the bedsheets on the line, I'll throw the leftovers from last night's supper into a basket, and off we'll go."

Anki looked into her lap, tidied the folds of her skirt. "I am not changing my clothes."

"Neither am I."

"I do not want to wear a bonnet, but . . ."

Translation: *Who might see my still-short hair?*

"We'll only wear them in the ice cream parlor." Willa

laughed. "Wouldn't want the bishop revoking *both* of our baptisms, now would we?"

"Silly Willa."

And there it was again, that hint of a smile that fueled the flicker of hope in Willa's heart.

"Things are lookin' great, Max."

Coming from the stoic Steve Leventhal, it was high praise.

"The wife loves the way you've positioned all the cabins in a semicircle around the lodge, and overlooking the Alleghenies. She thinks people will make reservations just for the photographs."

And Max loved the way he called the building—slightly more than twice the size of the cottages—a lodge.

"She loves the poured concrete registration counter you made for her, too. I thought it'd look cheap, but I'm surprised by how classy it looks."

Other contractors that Steve had interviewed about the development had passed on contracting. "You'll be sorry," they said, "because like every other son-of-the-boss, he's an arrogant gasbag, and he'll drive you to the poorhouse, demanding add-ons and changes."

At first, Max had written off the slurs, and blamed it on Englishers' tendency to resent those more well-to-do than themselves, especially when that wealth came the easy way . . . inheritance . . . as in Steve's case.

"We aim to please," he said.

"I want you guys to switch the asphalt shingles for metal. Green, so the roofs blend into the tree line."

"My crews are completing other contracts," Max explained. "Once a few men are freed up, we will revisit the change order."

"Change order? You mean . . . extra charges?"

"Good one," Max said, smiling. "You are a business-man, so I know you realize that metal roofing is triple the cost of asphalt. Plus, removing what is there, then replac-ing it with metal will require additional man-hours." He shrugged. "But we appreciate your business, and we are happy to write up that change order for you."

It looked to Max as though Steve couldn't decide whether to return his smile . . . or frown. In the end, he extended his hand. "Sounds fair to me," he said as Max grasped it. "Let me know how soon your men can get busy, because until the change is made, the little woman won't give me a moment's peace."

He'd heard it before, many times. Since he'd always run the customer service side of the business, it wasn't likely his partner could make the same claim. But trying to ease his worries about Anki by telling him that even their most affluent clients had similar marital issues would only invite a recitation of why the Plain life was preferable to any other.

Steve had just driven away when Dan's pickup rolled onto the site. "What did *he* want?"

"Just stopped by to ask us to replace the roofing material with metal."

Dan slammed the driver's door. "You told him no, I hope!"

"I told him the truth: Our crews are involved with other projects right now, but when we free up a few men, we're happy to write up a change order."

Snickering, Dan dropped a hand on Max's shoulder. "You are a better man than me. I would have told him no. Period."

Max believed that's exactly what Dan would say. But that wouldn't be good business. Steve owned properties throughout Western Maryland; burning that particular bridge didn't make fiscal sense. *Not when I'm about to take a wife and start a family!*

Family. The notion made his pulse pound. He and Willa hadn't discussed having children of their own, but based on everything she'd done to protect her little girl, Max believed Willa wouldn't want Frannie growing up an only child. Besides, why waste all that maternal love!

God, please tell me enough time has passed!

"I can't stay long," Willa whispered, "because Anki is in the truck with Frannie."

Emily stopped typing and peered over the top of the computer monitor. "Why?"

"She's stuck in a really weird mood, so I thought we'd take a picnic lunch to Dan and Max. A two birds with one stone thing: Get her out of the house, give the guys a treat. Afterward, we're going shopping to get Frannie some nice new walking shoes . . . or should I say running shoes," she said, grinning. "Last stop, ice cream at Page's."

"If you're here to ask if I'd like you to bring something back for me, the answer is yes!" She patted her quickly rounding belly. "Hand-dipped chocolate malt. M-m-m-m."

"I'm happy to do that. But the real reason I stopped by was to ask your advice about something."

She glanced out the window and saw Anki, staring straight ahead, despite the animated gestures of Frannie, in the back seat. "My advice? Unceasing prayer. Because unless she's willing to submit to medication and therapy . . ."

"I was just hoping that maybe this weekend, we could get the families together, and—"

"And you want me to take her aside, give her a good talking-to?"

"Well, I wouldn't have put it quite that way, but yes. Dan is beside himself with worry, and frankly, so am I. If she doesn't get help soon, only God knows what she might do."

"I'll talk with Phillip and let you know whether Saturday or Sunday is best."

"Friday night, even," Willa said. *The sooner, the better, because suicide tendencies run in some families.* "The other day, I was outside with Frannie, getting the flower beds ready for new planting. I'd left her in the parlor, reading another romance novel. She seemed perfectly content, so I was surprised, when we came back inside, to find her in her room. With the door locked. What a fright that gave me!"

"With her sister's history, I can see why." Emily paused, slowly shook her head. "I hate to say this, but it's beginning to look like her only hope is hospitalization. Garrett Regional has a great inpatient mental health program."

"Yeah, I was afraid of that." Willa glanced toward the truck again. "We'll definitely need Dan on our side to make that happen."

"You don't think he'll go for it?"

She thought of her one-on-one conversation with him yesterday morning, when he'd come so close to sobbing as he shared his concerns about Anki that she'd almost cried, too. "I'm really not sure. He's sick with worry, so maybe. On the other hand, he's a very private man."

"I'll talk with him first, then express my concerns as Anki's doctor. That way, when I broach the subject with her, she'll know he's onboard."

"Thanks, Em. You're the best."

She wiggled her eyebrows, then said, "Are Max and Dan expecting you?"

"Nope. This'll be a complete surprise. I owe Max an apology."

"Uh-oh. What did you do?"

"Oh, Em, you wouldn't believe the awful things I said to him."

"Because of the Joe thing?"

"Exactly. And after all he's done for me, I feel just horrible." Willa shook her head. "I can't wait to see him!"

Emily gasped and her eyes widened as she read the crawl at the bottom of the computer screen. "Willa . . . is this Joe and yours the same guy?"

Joining her at the counter, Willa leaned in as Emily double-clicked a small window in the upper right-hand corner. She was about to say "He isn't *my* Joe" when Emily turned up the speakers.

The young reporter announced that the state police had raided a local motel, one well-known for drug deals and numerous other illicit activities. In addition to confiscating multiple weapons, ammunition, and several pounds of cocaine and marijuana, five people had been taken into custody. The suspects' mug shots filled the screen, but Willa zeroed in on just one: Joe. Pending trial, the reporter said, the group would be held without bond at the Garrett County Detention Center; thanks to ample evidence found at the scene, each detainee faced up to forty years in prison. And because Joe and two others were also linked to an unsolved triple homicide case, they were looking at consecutive life sentences.

"I . . . I don't know what to say." Willa slumped into a waiting room chair. "I can hardly believe it. Is it possible that it's over, really over?"

Emily sat beside her. "Looks that way to me." Pulling her close in a sideways hug, she said, "Oh, thank You, Lord. Thank You!"

"I can't wait to see how Max will react to this!"

"If he looks anything like you do right now, he'll positively glow."

"I'd better get out there," she said, standing. "Don't lock up too early. I'd hate to eat all that chocolate malt by myself, especially after devouring a hot fudge sundae!"

During the drive between the clinic and Lover's Leap, Willa's thoughts wavered between the news that Joe would spend the rest of his life in a federal penitentiary, her need to repair the rift she'd caused between herself and Max, and the sight of Anki, stiff as a statue and staring through the windshield. Wouldn't life be grand if, in addition to every other blessing they'd received, Anki agreed to intensive inpatient therapy! Again, she pictured the way Dan had looked during their talk . . . shoulders hunched as if they carried the weight of the world. In a way, she supposed they did.

"Here we are," she announced, parking between Dan's truck and Max's. She saw them, a hundred or so yards away. Heard their power saws, too. "Oh, Anki, just look at those cabins. Didn't they do a beautiful job!"

"They always do good work."

Rather than react as she wanted to—by exhaling a sigh of frustration—Willa waved in the hope of catching Max's attention. But he was too preoccupied with the long board on his sawhorses to notice. She was about to turn away when he looked up, and even from this distance, she could see his bright smile.

"Here, Anki," she said, handing over the picnic basket. "Will you spread the blanket? I want to let Max know that we've brought lunch. Frannie and I will only be a minute, promise."

He met them halfway, grinning with every step. "What are you doing up here?"

"I wanted to see the cabins, and thought why not bring lunch while I was at it. A four birds with one stone sort of thing."

"Four?" He touched noses with Frannie, whose giggles seemed to bounce from every nearby tree.

Counting on her fingers, she said, "Cabins, lunch, an apology, and wonderful news."

He looked curious, and a little bit uneasy.

"You didn't do anything to deserve the way I treated you, the things I said. I have no good excuse for behaving like a grouchy old crone when I learned about the whole Joe thing. I'm sorry, Max, truly sorry."

He removed his hat, drew the back of his hand across his brow. "I am sorry, too. I never should have—"

"Shh," she said, shaking her head. "Let's just call it even."

"And the good news?"

She listed the highlights of the news story, ending with, "Joe is going to prison for the rest of his life. We'll never have to worry about him again."

Relief softened his features. "Do I sound like a beast for saying the news is the answer to prayer?"

"You sound human. And for your information, I feel the same way."

"You are one of a kind, Willa Reynolds, and I thank God for you every day."

Until that moment, she hadn't given much thought to her surname.

"Willa Lambright," she said, mostly to herself. "I like the sound of it!"

"It is a good strong name, one I have been honored to carry. But it has never sounded better than when paired with yours."

"Max!" Dan bellowed. "We have too much to do for you to stand there, staring like a moony-eyed boy!"

Willa leaned in close. "For your information," she said again, "Frannie and I love moony-eyed boys."

"Ah, Willa," he breathed, "thank you."

"For what? You don't even know what I packed for your lunch!"

He kissed her forehead. Kissed Frannie's, too. "Moony-eyed boys are not picky."

"Once things are ready, I'll holler."

She watched as he returned to his sawing, then made her way to the blanket. It surprised her a bit, seeing that Anki had fallen asleep. Rather than disturb her, Willa put Frannie down and let her toddle across the grassy expanse that separated them from the men. The baby squatted, poked at a blade of grass, then picked up a small pebble and inspected it.

She extended her hand. "Give it to Mama, sweet girl."

And Frannie said, "Mine!"

Willa pulled a doll from the diaper bag, grabbed the rock, and quickly replaced it with the toy. She had a hard time stifling her laughter when Frannie looked none too pleased as her gaze flitted from her hand to the doll and back again. "Aw, give your dolly a hug . . ."

The baby gave it a moment's thought, then grinned and echoed Willa's words.

"Look at the pretty trees," Willa said, pointing skyward.

But Frannie seemed distracted by the airplane that buzzed overhead. "Ooh! Mama!"

"Plane," Willa said.

And just that quickly, Frannie's attention returned to the toy. Pressing her fingertip into the doll's face, she said, "Eyes?"

While some Amish dolls had faces, most did not. "We

are all alike in the mind of God," she'd learned. But what harm could come from drawing simple features on the white cloth?

Willa found a pen in the bag, got to her knees. "Eyes," she said, drawing small black dots on the doll's face. Three strokes of the pen gave each eyelashes, another two provided tiny brows, and when Frannie saw it, she cut loose with a joyous squeal. "Eyes!"

Now, Frannie pointed again. "Hoppy?"

"Yes, sweetie, she's very happy, just like you!" And to prove it, Willa drew a minuscule semicircle, prompting another gale of gleeful laughter.

Anki sat up with a start. "What is wrong with her!"

"She's just excited." Willa carried Frannie to the blanket. "Show Anki your pretty dolly, sweet girl."

Pointing and babbling excitedly, she said, "Eyes! *Happy!*"

Anki's deadpan expression matched her voice. "Unacceptable. If the bishop sees this . . ." She shook her head. "I would not let him see it, if I were you."

Frannie, reading the woman's mood, looked to Willa for solace. But what could she say to a child not even two years old?

Opening the picnic basket, she handed the baby a sugar cookie. "I can't do this often!" she told Anki. "Food is not a smart substitute for emotional relief."

"Emotional relief? What does *that* mean?"

"I should have found another way to comfort her, because if she grows accustomed to eating when something or someone hurts her . . ." Willa smiled, despite the subject matter, because Frannie looked so precious, chomping on the treat. "Let's just say it isn't healthy, physically or emotionally."

Anki's response was an uncaring wave of the hand. "What time will we eat?"

"Very soon. If you like, we can set things up right now."

Frannie, sensing Anki's frame of mind, climbed into her lap. "Happy?"

"Yes, I suppose."

But she didn't mean it, and Frannie sensed that, too.

First chance she got, Willa intended to talk with Dan about bringing Anki to Garrett County's mental health center.

Because every day, it seemed, Anki withdrew further into the dark recesses of her own mind. How long before she stayed there, permanently?

Max ate heartily, and savored every bite. What he enjoyed most was Dan's reaction to the women's surprise visit. He ate with gusto, laughing, cracking jokes, playing peekaboo with Frannie, even teasing Anki in a good-natured way.

Much better to focus on the good things, he decided, than on Anki's aloof reactions. Good things like the sun's rays, slicing through slow-moving clouds that hung over the Alleghenies like a snow-white canopy. Thick stands of hemlock, beech, and pine trees grew from the crags and bluffs and absorbed the drone of cars and tractor trailers that hissed and beeped along Old National Pike below.

The panorama reminded him of the painting Willa had given him as a Christmas gift. He'd used weathered beech to frame it, and it now hung above the mantel where he could admire it on a daily basis. This vista had nothing in common with her painting, really, except that she'd taught him to see every facet of God's creation with fresh, appreciative eyes.

Removing his hat, he drew a forearm across his perspiring forehead, and caught sight of the faint red scar that reached from his wrist to his elbow. She'd taken tiny, closely placed stitches, and promised that the extra time it took would result in little to no reminder of the accident that had sent him to the clinic that day. Then, as now, he hoped she was wrong, because he liked looking at the scar and remembering the tender loving care she'd administered.

He'd run out of two-by-fours, and walked toward the stack they'd piled at the edge of the temporary dirt-and-gravel drive. A week from now, a layer of crushed stone would cover everything, helping with water runoff and keeping mud to a minimum.

As he shouldered a long board, Max glanced toward the women. From where he stood, he saw Willa, back resting against the trunk of a tree, hugging Frannie to her chest. The sight was enough to make his heart pound with love. Oh, how blissful would life be when, finally, she'd sleep beside him! First chance he got, Max intended to speak with the bishop, and ask about scheduling the wedding before October. The sooner, the better.

But wait . . . where was Anki?

Turning in a slow circle, he scanned the entire area, from the tidy semicircle of amber-wood cabins to the row of dusty pickup trucks parked nearby, and when he didn't see her, a sense of foreboding snaked up his spine. Pitching the board aside, he jogged toward the blanket. During lunch, Dan had mentioned a field of wildflowers growing alongside Wills Mountain Road. He wouldn't be the least bit surprised to hear that she'd taken the short hike alone, instead of waiting for Willa and Frannie to enjoy it with her.

And then he saw her, standing dangerously close to the cliff that overlooked Wills Creek. It was a nine-hundred-foot drop from where she stood to the ground below . . . with dozens of jagged, ragged outcroppings between the precipice and the rocky shore. What was she thinking, getting so close to the rim?

If he shouted her name, he might startle her badly enough to send her over the edge. But if he didn't . . .

A mere seventy-five yards separated them, and he ran it full out, praying with every footfall that he'd reach her before she fell . . . or jumped. "Don't do it, Anki," he called out. *"Don't do it!"*

Whether she heard his frantic voice or the sound of his boots pounding over the grassy knoll, Max would never know. She turned, slowly, and as she met his eyes, Anki sent him an eerie, almost serene smile. Then, arms raised like a swimmer preparing to dive into a calm, crystal-blue pool, she leapt as Max thundered, "No-o-o—!"

Chapter Nineteen

Shuddering from hat to boots, Max forced himself to look over the edge, and what he saw hit him hard enough to send him to his knees. A dozen thoughts flitted through his mind: What had she been looking at? Why would she do such a thing? Was it possible she'd survived, despite the way she'd landed, arms and legs bent at abnormal angles? He didn't see how, but he prayed for a miracle, anyway; if she was alive, it would *be* a miracle.

Dan, who'd no doubt heard his bloodcurdling bellow, was quickly making his way closer.

Max got to his feet just as Dan reached his side.

"Are you out of your mind, man, standing so near the edge? Did you not hear about the people who plunged to their deaths, almost from that very spot?"

Max didn't want to be the one to break the gruesome news. *Better he hears it from you than one of the paramedics, total strangers . . .*

"I ran out of two-by-fours," he began. "Went to grab a few, looked up and saw her, standing right here." He pointed at the ground. "Didn't want to risk shouting, scaring her so she'd lose her balance."

"Her. You mean . . . ?" He swallowed. Hard. "Where is Anki?"

But Dan already knew. Max could almost feel the fear, pulsing from him.

He took a step forward, as if to look over the rim. But Max grabbed his forearm, and stopped him. It wasn't like Dan to submit, no questions asked.

There were tears in his eyes when he said, "Max. Please. I have to."

If Max allowed his partner to look down there, Dan would have to live with those images for the rest of his life. He tightened his hold. "We're standing on shale, Dan. You know as well as I do, it breaks easily."

"She was standing here . . ." His sob-thickened voice cracked. ". . . when the shale shattered?"

If he admitted what he'd witnessed, Dan would have to live with *that* every time he closed his eyes. *Lord forgive me,* he thought, and said, "Yes."

Dan made another attempt to see for himself. Max said, "Don't . . ."

From the corner of his eye, he saw Willa, who'd bundled Frannie in the blanket before joining them.

Standing on his left side, she stood on tiptoe and whispered into his ear, "Where is your cell phone? I'll call for help."

Her eyes said it all: She knew that Anki had jumped . . . and hadn't survived. "In my truck," he managed to say.

"Dan," she said, "let's get away from the edge, okay?"

Somehow, her soft, soothing voice reached Dan, and he allowed Max to lead him toward the trucks. He opened the glove box and handed her the phone, and she wasted no time dialing 911. After buckling Dan into the pickup, Max closed the door and listened as she provided a quick, concise report, concluding with, "A friend will make sure her husband meets the team at the ER."

She started to hand him the phone, then withdrew it.

"Just let me call Emily real quick, ask her to see if Phillip and his brother-in-law will pick up Dan's truck."

While she made the request, Max recalled a day, several years earlier, when the state police had blocked traffic on the highway to enable the high angle team to rescue a hiker. The helicopter crew had lowered a basket, then flown the body to the hospital. That accident, according to all reports, had been an accident. When they asked what he'd witnessed—and Max was sure that they would—he would not say the word "suicide." To protect Dan, he'd carry that ugly secret to his grave.

Willa returned the phone, and he said, "I should go, so we're sure to be at the hospital when the helicopter gets there."

"Of course. We'll be thinking of you."

We, meaning Willa and Frannie. It seemed that even the baby understood the gravity of the situation. Wide-eyed and silent, she looked back and forth between her mother and Max. Oh, how he loved her!

"Don't worry, little one. Everything will be all right." He kissed her round pink cheek. "I promise."

"Aw," she said, smiling a bit, "nice Max."

Eyes on Willa again, he said, "I have no idea how long this will take."

"Then it's good you'll be with him. But . . ." She glanced at Dan, shaking his head in the passenger seat. "I'm not sure it's a good idea for him to be at the house. At least not just yet."

"Too many reminders?"

"Exactly."

"Good thinking," he said again. "I'll bring him home with me." Max kissed her forehead, let his lips linger there for a moment. "Thanks for being *you,* sweet Willa. I'll be thinking of you, too."

Chapter Twenty

The soft shimmer of sunlight slanted in through the stained glass and painted a rainbow swath from the windows to the altar. A shard of light haloed Dan's head and fell across his shoulders like a cobalt cape as he sat, elbows resting on knees in the front row.

They'd been alone in the hospital chapel for nearly half an hour, and in that time, neither Dan nor Max had said a word. Here, surrounded by flickering votive candles and glossy-leafed green plants, it seemed unnecessary to speak.

Somewhere behind them, a woman wept softly. Up ahead, a gray-haired man knelt on one of the padded kneelers, head bowed and hands folded as he sent silent pleas for a loved one heavenward.

"I have racked my brain," Dan said, "and cannot come up with an answer . . . why was she there?"

Guilt throbbed in Max's heart as he thought, *She was there to end her life*. But he couldn't say it. Not now, not ever.

"When we first began working this morning, I saw an eagle fly over the narrows. Maybe it came back, and she wanted a closer look."

Dan only shook his head. "You need not stay here with me, Max."

He had to give it to the man, who'd stood straight-backed and somber as the doctor delivered the heartrending news: During the emergency exploratory surgery, they'd discovered that in addition to numerous internal injuries, Anki had suffered a shattered spine, a broken neck, and multiple compound fractures. "No need to worry that she suffered, Mr. Hofman," the surgeon had said, "we believe your wife died upon impact." If the words hit Max like a punch to the gut, he could only imagine how hard they had hit Dan.

"I am staying. For as long as you need me." When it seemed he was about to protest, Max quickly added, "You would do it for me . . ."

Nodding, Dan stood. "I can pray at home."

At some point during the drive between Oakland and Pleasant Valley, he'd need to talk Dan into staying with him, instead of going back to the house where he'd shared *everything* with his wife of ten years. It wasn't until he approached his own house that Dan said, "Max. Where is your mind? You just passed my driveway."

He could have told the truth, that he was thinking about those disturbing seconds as she smiled, then went sailing toward the creek. Instead, Max said, "Stay at my house for a few days. There is plenty of room, and you will have complete privacy."

But Dan shook his head adamantly. "You are kind to offer—and I understand what prompted it—but I belong in my own home."

Making a U-turn, Max headed for the Hofmans', hoping that during the short drive, Dan would picture Anki's things in their closet, her favorite quilt on the bed, the flowerpot on the table, and realize it was too soon to be surrounded by reminders of her.

He parked between Dan's truck and Li'l Red, and sent a silent thank-you to Phillip and Eli. But seeing his pickup wouldn't be enough to ease his friend's mind.

Facing Dan, he said, "I remember how hard it was, walking into our house after the buggy accident, seeing my father's work hat near the back door, his boots and my brothers' lined up beneath it. For days, they had the power to turn me into a sniveling mess."

"You were just a boy."

"I was not a boy when my grandparents' house burned, yet I felt the same way every time I saw my mother's and sisters' things."

Dan snorted. "You were still a boy. An older boy, but not a man, either." Dan opened the passenger door. "I am a man, and as such, I must have faith that God will see me through this." He started to close the door, but hesitated. "Can you come in?"

"Yes." He wanted—*needed*—to see Willa and Frannie, partly to remind himself that despite the nightmarish thing that had happened today, God answered prayers.

Dan said a cursory hello to Willa and Frannie and went directly into the parlor, and sitting in his favorite chair, picked up his Bible.

Willa grasped Max's arm. "He seems so . . . composed. I don't know what I expected, but not that."

"The calm after the storm. And perhaps before it." Max slid an arm across her shoulders, rested his chin on her head. "He is exhausted. Once he's upstairs, asleep, I will explain."

Max crossed the room and leaned over Frannie's high chair. "Just look at you," he said, kissing the tip of her nose. "Every inch of your pretty face is covered with strawberry jam."

"'Tawbewwy!" she said, inviting him to share her cracker.

He pretended to nibble at a corner. "M-m-m! Thank you!"

"When was the last time you had anything to eat?" Willa wanted to know.

"Lunch."

The word hung between them like a sooty spiderweb, and woke images of the wonderful hour they'd shared . . . and the life-altering event that had happened afterward.

"Let me make you a sandwich."

He shook his head. "Thanks, but I'm not hungry."

"Later, maybe."

"Maybe."

She poured him a glass of lemonade, and as he sat chatting with Frannie, Willa began making a hearty sandwich. He didn't ask, and she didn't offer the information, but Max knew that in minutes, she'd deliver it to Dan.

As expected, she filled a second tumbler and carried both into the parlor. "I'll just put it here," he heard her say, "and when you're ready, it'll be there."

Willa didn't wait for a rejection or a thank-you. And when she stepped back into the kitchen, Max saw that she was fighting tears. He went to her, held her close, and turned her so that the sight of her mother crying wouldn't upset Frannie.

As in the chapel, no words were necessary as they clung to one another, seeking and giving comfort.

Willa hurried upstairs and did her best to remove obvious signs of Anki's presence in the Hofmans' bedroom. Dresses and undergarments that had been tossed over chairs and bedposts now hung neatly in the couple's closet. Shoes and boots stood in a tidy row beneath them, and bonnets and hats were lined up on the shelf above. After changing the sheets, she turned down the bed and pulled the blinds, then left a bedside lamp glowing to light Dan's way. Across the hall, she placed Anki's soap and shampoo into a basket on the linen cupboard floor. With fresh towels on the hooks, the bathroom was ready, too.

On her way downstairs, she noticed the sandwich, delivered soon after Max had brought Dan home from the hospital. He hadn't taken a bite. Not all that unusual, under the circumstances; after losing her mom, Willa didn't eat for nearly a week. Tomorrow, she'd make his favorites . . . shepherd's pie and applesauce cake, and God willing, he'd feel like nibbling at it, at least.

"Can I get you some pie?" she asked, retrieving the plate.

Dan put down his Bible and, shaking his head, got to his feet. "No, I think I will go to bed."

But he didn't. Instead, he began pacing, pounding a fist into his palm. He stopped suddenly and, facing her, grabbed her shoulders. "Look me in the eye. I can handle the truth. Do you think she fell? That her death was an accident?"

In truth, Willa believed quite the opposite, and yet she said, "Yes, Dan. A horrible, heartbreaking accident."

Tears pooled in his eyes as he walked away. "I pray you are right." He dropped onto the seat of his chair. "I could not bear thinking she would deliberately leave me."

"She loved you, Dan. Cling to that. Remember her as she was before her sister died."

Eyes closed, he leaned back against the cushions. "Yes. Those were good times. Blessed times."

Standing again, he sent her a trembly smile. "Thank you, Willa." He was halfway up the stairs when he added, "I will see you in the morning."

"Good night, Dan." Wishing him sweet dreams and peaceful sleep seemed hypocritical, because she knew he'd enjoy neither.

When she turned toward the kitchen, she saw Max in the doorway, holding Frannie in his arms. "I was just on my way upstairs to get her into her nightclothes."

"That's so sweet of you, but I can do it." Taking the baby, she said over her shoulder, "Do you have to leave right away?"

"I can't leave. Not just yet."

As soon as she'd readied Frannie for bed, Willa returned to the kitchen and found him seated at the table, shaking his head.

She poured them both a cup of coffee and sat beside him.

"I hope he will get some sleep," Max said.

"He's exhausted, so I'm sure he will. Off and on, anyway."

He took her hands in his. "I haven't even had the pleasure of sharing life with you yet, but if I lost you . . ."

"I feel the same way," she admitted. "Do you feel like talking about what happened at the hospital?"

A heavy sigh prefaced his words. "It was awful. The helicopter pilot told me Anki was dead when they got to her, that she probably hit an outcropping on the way down."

"At least she didn't suffer."

"I could not bring myself to tell Dan the truth of what I saw."

So she'd been right . . . Max *had* witnessed the whole thing. Willa's heart ached for him. She remained quiet. If he wanted to share details, she'd listen. But if he didn't, she'd accept that, too.

"I cannot think of anything more selfish," he began. "What she did . . ."

The anguish in his eyes told her that he was picturing it, all over again.

"What she did," he continued, "freed her from her own misery, but what about Dan?"

He was on his feet now, walking from the table to the sink and back again.

"It's all right, Max. As long as he believes it was an accident . . ."

Max met her eyes. "I am not sure he does believe it."

"In this case, uncertainty is less painful than reality."

"The paramedics, the police, they all asked me questions. And I lied. Willa," he said, his voice cracking, "I lied to all of them. The bishop will also ask what happened, and I will lie to him, too."

She went to him, held him tight. "I'm angry with her, too," she admitted, "because she put you in this position! If anyone knew the pain suicide causes, it was Anki. But in good conscience, I can't be too hard on her."

He met her eyes.

"'There but by the grace of God,'" she quoted.

Taking her hand, he led her back to the table, where he sat and patted his thigh. "What do you mean?"

"There were times when I felt desperate enough to end my life. I'd become a criminal. An addict."

"That was Joe's doing."

"I love you for saying that, but every choice I made . . ." She sighed. "Let's just say that I could have made wiser decisions. After a while, staying seemed easier than leaving. But the longer I stayed, the more alone and hopeless I felt. And I gave serious thought to taking a handful of pills."

"Shh," he said, brushing the bangs from her forehead. "Don't talk like that."

Willa studied his face, every angle and plane, every smile and frown line. "I haven't felt that way, not even a little bit, since I learned that I was pregnant."

"I have said it before, but it bears repeating: Thank God for Frannie, for so many reasons. She saved you from that life and led you to me."

Her heart swelled with love for him, and she searched her mind for words that would relieve him of the guilt associated with having misled everyone about what he'd witnessed at the cliffside.

"Worst part is," he said softly, "wondering if Anki's final act doomed her to hell."

"What she did is a tragedy, but I don't believe it's unforgivable. From everything I learned while getting ready for baptism, the only sin God can't forgive is rejecting Him. He knew Anki's heart, and that mental instability clouded her judgment. He's a God of love and mercy, so He realizes—better than any of us—that she wasn't fully responsible for her actions."

Max nodded, and gave her words some thought. "I agree. But my sins were deliberate, and I was completely in control of my mind when I committed them."

"Your sins? *What* sins?"

"Lies. So many lies . . ."

She pressed a palm to his chest. "God knows *your* heart, too, Max, and He's aware that the truth would have hurt Dan in deep and lasting ways. He'd spend the rest of his days blaming himself, wondering what he might have done to prevent the suicide. And, he'd have to cope with the judgment of the community. Plus, the bishop couldn't allow her to be buried near family and friends. What you did, you did out of love for Dan. How could God disapprove of that?"

Max drew her closer and said, "God saved my soul, and you saved my heart. I only have one regret."

Willa stiffened, wondering which of her past sins he might mention.

"I regret that He didn't bring you to me a long, long time ago."

His words felt like a healing balm, a bright light on this dark, dreary day, and moved her to tears. For so long Willa had wondered . . . would she ever know deep and abiding love? The answer was right here, in her arms, and she answered in the only way she could:

"Thank you, Lord, for this loving, bighearted man!"

When Willa heard rumblings about which church women would prepare Anki for the viewing, she insisted on doing it herself.

"You do not know how," Rebecca said matter-of-factly.

It was true, and although she knew the ladies' intentions were good, she felt duty-bound to perform this last act of service for her friend.

The bishop's wife said, "Do not look so disheartened, dear Willa. I know what to do, and I can teach you."

She nearly gave in to the temptation to show her gratitude by throwing her arms around the woman. Instead, she simply said, "Thank you, Charity."

Several of the women's husbands had already moved the furniture out of the Hofmans' parlor and positioned the long kitchen table in the center of the room. Step by step, Charity explained that first, they must bathe Anki, then dress her in white. They worked in silence, and after Willa arranged the bonnet ribbons on Anki's shoulders, they stood side by side.

"She looks at peace," Charity said, smoothing Anki's apron hem.

Knowing how much she'd suffered these many months, Willa hoped it was true. It was good that no one, not even Dan, would see her battered, broken body, and she thanked God that her face hadn't been touched by the fall.

"She was blessed to have you at her side for so long."

Since leaving Lover's Leap that day, Willa had turned it over and over in her mind: Could she have done more? Said something? Spent additional time, one-on-one with her friend? And the answer to all three questions had been yes . . . but that, as her grandfather used to say, was water under the bridge. On the heels of the old adage, he'd added, every time, "What will you do next?"

She'd continue working at the clinic, caring for Pleasant Valley's residents. She'd be the mother Frannie deserved, and a true partner to Max. She'd live an upright, Plain life, in Anki's memory . . .

. . . and thank God every day for Alice, who'd brought her here in the first place.

She heard the men in the parlor, rearranging furniture to make room for the simple pine coffin that friends would pass as they paid their last respects.

Chapter Twenty-One

Dan seemed sad from time to time, of course, but he'd returned to work and was eating and sleeping almost as he had before Anki's death. Max was spending more time at the Hofmans' these days, and few things could have pleased her more.

On the one-month anniversary of the suicide, Willa made all of Dan's favorite foods, no doubt hoping to distract him from the fateful date. After the meal, he decided to take a walk, and when Max offered to go with him, Dan said, "If it is all the same to you, I would rather be alone."

"Then my thoughts will be with you."

Frannie, stretching and yawning in her high chair, whimpered, "Bed, Mama?"

"Just as soon as I finish up the last of these dishes, sweet girl."

"Let me do it."

"Max . . ."

He picked up the baby and handed her to Willa. "But nothing," he said, turning them toward the parlor door.

"You're very sweet but . . ."

"Not so sweet that a little dishwater will melt me. Now

get the child into bed before she falls asleep right there in your arms."

He made quick work of the job, and when Willa returned, she thanked him with a kiss.

"It is a beautiful night." He took her hand. "Come sit outside with me."

Seated beside him on the porch swing Dan had made and hung for Anki, she said, "I love this time of day. Just listen to all the soothing night sounds . . ."

In a nearby tree, an owl hooted, and from one of the shrubs planted along the flagstone walk, they heard the plaintive cry of a whip-poor-will. Crickets and tree toads chirped all around them, and in the distance, eerie high-pitched coyote howls. Hearing them, Rascal got onto his feet and, head down, the hair along his spine stood up and a low growl rumbled from his chest.

"It's all right, buddy," Willa said, smoothing the ruffled fur. "They're too far away to hurt us."

He sent her a grateful doggy smile, then once again settled onto the braided mat in front of the door.

"Where do you suppose Dan went?" Max asked.

"He's probably in the shed. Ever since we painted and reorganized it, he spends a lot of time out there."

"Your touches are everywhere." He hugged her to his side.

"My touches . . . ?"

He pointed at the roses in the flower bed that hugged the porch. "I can't recall the last time they bloomed. And those little white flowers along the walk . . ."

"Candytuft," she said. "Not the best-smelling flowers on the planet, but they sure are pretty, aren't they?"

Moonlight angled down from the starry sky and touched each bud and blossom with silvery light. "Yes, pretty," he agreed. "And inside, you helped Anki rearrange everything, from dishes in the cupboards to clothes in the closets to furniture."

"She never asked for much. I couldn't refuse."

"Still, I have a feeling Dan is going to miss all the things you did that turned his little house into a home."

Turning, she said, "Why would he miss it? It isn't as if I'm going anywhere."

"*Yet*."

She combed slender fingers through the fringe that edged one of the swing's throw pillows. He waited, expecting an upbeat, typically Willa response. When none came, Max said, "How long do you think we should wait to talk to the bishop about our wedding?"

"I've wondered that, too. Because how would it look, if right in the middle of Dan's deepest grief, we get married and celebrate?"

"I suppose we could ask the bishop to do it quietly . . ."

"He doesn't strike me as the type who'd bend the rules. But you know him better than I do. . . ."

Max nodded. "I suppose you are right. He will likely tell us to exercise patience."

"Patience," Willa echoed. "I'll never forget what my grandfather used to say about it. 'Why is it that the thing I'm worst at is the thing I'm most often asked to do!'"

Chuckling, Max said, "I think I would have liked your grandfather."

"And he would have loved you!"

Rascal got up again and trotted to the far edge of the porch, and when Max went to see what had so completely captured the pup's attention, he saw light, blazing bright from the shed's windows.

"You were right," he said, returning to the swing. "Dan is out back. I'm going out there. I shouldn't be long."

"Take as long as you need," Willa said. "And if the opening presents itself, tell him I love him."

A minute later, Max walked into the shed, and found Dan seated on the long bench that once had held folded quilts, embroidered tablecloths, and other for-sale linens that Anki had made.

"Willa says there is pie . . ." Another lie, he said to himself. *Better take care, because you are getting far too good at it.*

"I was about to head back inside," Dan said, standing. As he closed the gap between himself and Max, he added, "Is she all right? Willa, I mean?"

"She's fine."

"She and Anki had grown so close. No doubt the . . . the accident has been hard for her, too."

"She's a strong woman."

"I envy you, partner. It was not Anki's fault, I know, but she never was the wife your Willa will be."

"Willa is stubborn . . ." He had to say *something* negative to soften the comparison.

"Small price to pay for her strength."

Not knowing what to say, Max hooked both thumbs behind his suspenders, and prayed for godly wisdom.

"You are a good friend, Max, but you need not worry about me. I will mourn. I will nurse feelings of guilt. I will question myself, and God, too, but I will do it in private, and in time, I have faith that the pain will lessen. Because I have prayed. Oh, how I have prayed! And although I will miss her, I must thank the good Lord that my Anki is at peace. Finally, at last, after all her heartache and misery, my sweet wife is at peace."

Dan dropped a hand onto Max's shoulder. "Now go.

Spend time with your bride-to-be and that precious child. Talk about your wedding. Plan your future. And trust that I will be fine. We are still partners, after all, and if I know Willa, I will join you for meals. Many meals."

Chuckling quietly, he gave Max a brotherly shove. "Let's go now, and have that pie."

Nodding, Max led the way back to the porch, where Willa still sat on the swing.

"You know," Dan said, climbing the creaking, gray-painted wooden steps, "I have changed my mind about that pie." On his way inside, he patted Willa's head. "Leave a slice out for me. I have a feeling I will wake in the middle of the night. It will be a sweet distraction from the . . . darkness."

With that, he bid them good night and went inside.

Once Max settled beside Willa once more, she said, "What happened out there?"

He didn't trust himself to speak, and so he said, "Maybe later."

Willa leaned her head on his shoulder, exhaled a shaky sigh. "I wish there was something we could do for him."

"We are doing it. Remember the way Dan had behaved during supper . . . smiling at Frannie's antics, eating heartily, asking for a second slice of cake, just as he would have on any ordinary night?"

Willa whispered, "Yes. I suppose he's slowly coming around, isn't he." She paused, then added, "But then . . . he hasn't really been alone since . . ."

Max heard the worry in her voice. How long, he wondered, would they have trouble saying *since the suicide*?

"I don't think the full impact of what happened has hit him yet." She paused, drew a long, slow breath. "Grief is a funny thing and affects everyone differently. You know that better than most. After my mom died, it took me months to accept the ugly reality that she was *gone,* that I'd never see her or talk with her again. And when that truth hit me, the sorrow would come in waves. One minute I'd be going about my business, talking and laughing, and the next I'd start bawling my eyes out."

"Yes . . ." It had been that way for him, too, following the buggy accident, and again after the fire.

On his feet now, Max said, "I have something for you. For us, really. It's in the truck. I'll be right back."

When he returned, Max handed her a small leather pouch, held shut by a matching drawstring.

"Go ahead," he instructed. "Open it."

She loosened the drawstring and removed the wooden box he'd given her on Thanksgiving.

"So that's why my initials were off-center," she said, stroking the intricate, hand-carved lid. "You were leaving room for the *L*!"

He shrugged it off. "Because someday, soon I hope, your last name will be Lambright."

Smiling, he wondered how long it would take her to open the box. When she did, he sat back, so that he could better see her reaction. Her face, lit by the moon's glow, looked excited and curious and expectant, all at the same time.

"Oh, Max," she said, palming the strawberry-size heart he'd carved from a scrap of Brazilian cherrywood. "It's perfect. And so smooth!"

Suddenly, Willa frowned slightly. "But . . . how did you get the box? It's been in my top dresser drawer, and nearly every day, I take it out to admire it."

"Then I guess you haven't admired it this week."

Her frown dimmed. "No, between work and . . . everything else that's been going on . . ."

"Night before last, when I carried Frannie up to bed, I snuck into your room and took it."

"So *that's* why you were so insistent about leaving your jacket on, so you could pocket it, and I wouldn't notice."

He answered with a smile, then said, "I felt a little bad about the rash caused by the ring of twine. Now, instead of wearing it when you're contemplating our future, you can hold my heart. Makes perfect sense, since you've had it almost from the first moment I saw you that day on the jobsite."

"I love it. And I love *you*."

"Why do I hear a 'but' in your voice?"

"Not a 'but.' I just feel a little guilty. I'm so happy, Max, happier than I've ever been, and Dan . . . well, Dan isn't."

"We have the rest of our lives to see him through this, you and Frannie and me."

"You aren't worried, even a little bit, that someday the English world will call, and I'll answer?"

"Nope. And you are not worried that you will tire of living the Plain life?"

"Surrounded by all the reminders of the loving things you've done for Frannie and me? I couldn't!"

Willa pressed the wooden heart into his palm, folded his fingers around it. "Know what I want?"

Max couldn't begin to guess, so he said, "What . . . ?"

"I want you to engrave your initials onto the box, along with mine, because the treasure it holds should be *ours,* not mine . . . a constant, tangible reminder that I love you with all my heart, that I've finally, *finally* found a home."

Willa snuggled close, and he felt her warm breath against his neck—felt her tears, too—as she added, "I'm home, Max. I'm home to stay."

Don't miss the first book in Loree Lough's
A Little Child Shall Lead Them series,
available now!
Please read on for an excerpt.

ALL HE'LL EVER NEED

A Little Child Shall Lead Them

**Among the New-new Order Amish of Oakland,
Maryland, children bring precious hope, joy—and
sometimes an unexpected second chance at love . . .**

For Amish widower Phillip Baker, providing for his
family in the wake of his wife's death means back-
breaking work and renewed dedication to his faith. Still,
his strength can't help him relate to his little son's
struggles. It seems a godsend when new doctor Emily
White is able to treat Gabe's shyness and fear even as
she helps heal him. But no matter how strongly Phillip is
drawn to the caring Englisher from the city, their
differences may be too great to overcome . . .

Reeling from her own tragic loss, Emily keeps
loneliness at bay through her clinic work. Somehow,
though, Gabe and his gentle, sad-eyed father are making
her want to risk opening her heart again. But can she
find acceptance in their Plain world—and a way to turn
their separate lives into a family forever?

"Is your little boy all right, Mr. Baker? He's as white as a bedsheet."

Phillip glanced down at his son, the light of his life . . .

. . . and watched as the boy sank to the floor of the auto supply store like a marionette whose strings had been cut.

Heart pounding, he dropped his billfold on the counter and, gripping Gabe's upper arms, went down with him. Phillip cradled the boy to his chest and did his best to ignore other patrons who had encircled them. Gently he combed his fingers through his son's golden-brown locks, searching for a bump—or worse, blood. Finding neither, Phillip breathed a sigh of relief.

The clerk hid behind her hands. "Oh my. Oh dear. Oh goodness gracious!" She peeked between two fingers. "Should I call nine-one-one?"

"I already did," barked the man to Phillip's left.

An ambulance . . .

Phillip remembered the day, several years earlier, when Gustafson fell from the barn loft. His wife called an ambulance, and without insurance, it had taken the elderly couple more than a year to pay the invoice. Like most residents of the community, he didn't have health insurance, either. But that was a worry for another day. He'd find a way to pay the bill, even if it meant working eighty hours a week instead of fifty. Anything for his Gabe. *Anything*.

"Why does he look upset?" the wife asked. "He should be thanking you for your quick thinking!"

From the corner of his eye, Phillip saw the husband frown.

"He's *Amish*, that's why," the man said. "Those people will spend big bucks to care for their cows and horses, even pigs! But their kids?" He expelled an angry snort.

Those people, Phillip wanted to retort, did *not* care more about livestock than their children. Living Plain was a concept very few Englishers fully understood. The lifestyle was, at times, difficult for *him* to understand. Phillip shrugged it off, as he had every other time someone in town passed judgment on his way of life. It didn't matter what others thought. Gabe mattered, and nothing else.

The ear-piercing wail of a siren grew louder, and so did the murmurings of those gathered. Then, silence as the boxy red-and-white vehicle lurched to a stop out front.

Two burly first responders leapt from the cab, raced around to the back, threw open the doors, and shoved a gurney into the auto supply store.

"What's the trouble here?" the taller one wanted to know.

"I'm the one who called you guys," the big man offered. "This kid here." He pointed at Gabe. "He fell, just like that." He snapped his fingers.

"Fainted is more like it," his wife corrected.

Phillip wished they'd both just stop talking. "He's my son," he said. His voice trembled, exactly as it had on the night he'd lost Rebecca. He cleared his throat. "He . . . he collapsed."

The men made quick work of easing Gabe onto the gurney. It wasn't until they unbuttoned his dark wool jacket that tears filled the boy's eyes.

"What are they doing, Dad?"

"It's okay, Son. These good men are here to help you."

A shallow, shaky breath issued from Gabe's bluish lips as he blinked the tears away.

"What's his name, sir?" The man's name tag said MATTHEWS. His partner's read WHITE.

"Gabe. Gabriel Baker."

Stethoscope in place, Matthews listened to Gabe's chest while White gripped the child's pale, narrow wrist.

"Thready pulse," White said. Then, leaning closer to Gabe's face, "Gabriel? Can you hear us?"

The boy nodded.

Matthews clamped a device onto Gabe's forefinger.

"What is that?" Phillip asked.

"An oximeter. It measures the oxygen in his blood." He turned to the boy. "How old are you, Gabe?"

"Four."

Phillip's heart clenched when his boy held up four tiny fingers and sent a wan smile his way.

"Wow. Four, huh! I have a five-year-old daughter." He held a thermometer under Gabe's tongue. "Ninety-nine point five," he said after it beeped. Then, "When will you turn five?"

"July fourth."

"No kiddin'! Lucky kid! Fireworks *and* a cake!"

A slight furrow creased Gabe's pale brow. Was he remembering last summer's community celebration, when his aunt Hannah tripped over a tree root, carrying the birthday cake, and splattered it across the lawn? No, it had probably been the baseball game that inspired the frown. Gabe, so busy waving at his grandmother during the ninth inning that he'd nearly missed the ball. It bobbled in the tiny, made-by-Phillip mitt, and when at last he got control, the ball sailed right past the first baseman. The error cost his team the win, and it had been pretty much all Gabe talked about for the remainder of the day, even as bright, colorful fireworks painted the inky sky with star- and waterfall-shaped explosions.

Matthews pricked Gabe's finger. The boy flinched, but only slightly. "Sorry, kiddo. I should have given you a heads-up about that." He met Phillip's eyes. "This is just to rule out diabetes, sir."

"He isn't diabetic."

"It's a disorder that can present itself quickly." He touched a small card to the dot of blood and directed his attention to Gabe. "Are you thirsty a lot, Gabe?"

The boy shook his head.

"Headaches?"

"Sometimes . . ."

He looked over at Phillip. "Has he lost weight lately?"

"No. Not that I know of. Gabe has never been . . . hefty."

"Noted. So tell me, Gabe, do you find yourself feeling tired easily?" Meeting Phillip's eyes again, Matthews said, "If he is diabetic, it could explain what happened today."

"Yes, I do get tired, but only if I run a lot."

White stepped up. "So who's your favorite superhero, kiddo? Spider-Man? Batman? Ant-Man?"

"We're Amish," Phillip said. "He doesn't know anything about those—"

"I know about Snoopy. Can he be a superhero?"

"Sure he can." White wrapped a colorful bandage around Gabe's tiny finger and squeezed his shoulder.

Matthews met Phillip's eyes. "Has he had a cold lately? The flu? Any long-standing medical issues we should know about?"

"Issues?" Phillip echoed.

"Like heart disease. Cancer. Diabetes."

"No, no, thank the good Lord. Nothing like that. He's never been as sturdy as other boys his age, but until recently, he hasn't been weak and pale, either."

"Are you in pain, Gabe?" White asked.

"No, just dizzy."

"Dizzy, huh? How often do you feel this way? Every day?"

"Yes, but not the whole day. As I told you, usually just when I run, or climb the stairs too fast."

The paramedics exchanged a glance. Phillip didn't like the concern on their faces.

"Well," Matthews said, "you're a brave boy. Your dad must be real proud of you."

Gabe zeroed in on Phillip's face.

"Yes." He gave Gabe's hand a light squeeze. "As proud as a father can be."

Matthews covered Gabe with a blanket while White fastened the security straps over the boy's chest, waist, and thighs.

White asked, "Did he hit his head when he fell?"

"No, I don't believe so. I checked for a bump, and blood, but didn't find either."

White turned Gabe's head, just enough to comb gloved fingers through the boy's hair. "I don't see anything, either. But don't worry. They'll have a closer look in the ER."

With that, the small crowd parted as the partners wheeled the gurney toward the exit.

"We're taking him to Garrett Regional." Locking the gurney into place on the ambulance floor, Matthews added, "You can meet us there, sir."

Phillip and his neighbors in Pleasant Valley were New Order Amish, and many drove gas-powered vehicles. His '99 pickup looked every bit its age and had earned its nickname. Yes, Old Reliable would get him to the hospital, but he had no intention of following the ambulance. "I promised not to leave him alone," he announced. "I'm going with you."

Matthews perched on the narrow bench beside the gurney. "Okay, but it's gonna be tight in here." He pointed at the other end of the seat. "Park it and try to stay out of the way."

The clerk raced up to the still-open rear doors. "Mr. Baker!" she hollered, an oversized bag dangling from one hand, waving Phillip's wallet with the other. "Mr. Baker, don't forget these!"

Phillip could have hugged her. "Thank you. I totally forgot."

"Under the circumstances, that's perfectly understandable." She handed him the plastic bag of spark plugs, air and oil filters, and other assorted parts he'd purchased to repair the assortment of lawn mowers, small earth movers, and miscellaneous farm equipment awaiting his attention at the shop. "Your receipt is in the bag. Good luck with your little boy."

"Thank you," he said again, and climbed in beside Matthews.

From the driver's seat, White called over his shoulder. "Puttin' her into gear and headin' out. Everybody buckled up?"

Seconds later, siren blaring and lights flashing, the vehicle maneuvered in and out of traffic on Route 219.

"I think we set a record," White said, parking alongside the hospital's ER entrance. "Six minutes flat."

Seemed more like an hour to Phillip, especially as he watched his nearly unconscious son struggle to keep his eyes open.

Inside, the first responders wheeled Gabe into an exam cubicle, and Phillip dogged their heels.

"The ladies at the desk are gonna want some info from you," White said, nodding toward the admitting counter.

"It can wait. I promised to stay with him, remember?" There wasn't much to tell, anyway: name, age, birth date. Besides, he couldn't risk having them turn Gabe away when they learned he was uninsured.

"By law, they have to treat your boy, even if you're not insured," Matthews said reassuringly.

White added, "They'll see him sooner once they have what they need."

Torn between setting things in motion and leaving Gabe alone, Phillip shifted his weight from one foot to the other.

"Okay with you, Gabe, if we hang out with you while your dad fills out some paperwork?"

A weak nod was his answer.

Phillip squeezed his son's hand again. "I won't be long."

It took less than five minutes to provide the necessary information, and to his great relief, the woman barely reacted when he explained his lack of insurance. Upon returning to Gabe's cubicle, White greeted him with a grin. "You're in luck. My sister's on duty. She's one of the best diagnosticians in the state."

A *female* doctor? Phillip didn't know how to feel about that.

All it took was a pathetic moan from Gabe to shift his attitude: If she could help his boy, it didn't matter that she was a woman.

Right?

Connect with

Visit us online at
KensingtonBooks.com
to read more from your favorite authors, see books
by series, view reading group guides, and more.

Join us on social media

for sneak peeks, chances to win books and prize packs,
and to share your thoughts with other readers.

facebook.com/kensingtonpublishing
twitter.com/kensingtonbooks

Tell us what you think!

To share your thoughts, submit a review,
or sign up for our eNewsletters, please visit:
KensingtonBooks.com/TellUs.

More by Bestselling Author
Hannah Howell

__Highland Angel	978-1-4201-0864-4	$6.99US/$8.99CAN
__If He's Sinful	978-1-4201-0461-5	$6.99US/$8.99CAN
__Wild Conquest	978-1-4201-0464-6	$6.99US/$8.99CAN
__If He's Wicked	978-1-4201-0460-8	$6.99US/$8.49CAN
__My Lady Captor	978-0-8217-7430-4	$6.99US/$8.49CAN
__Highland Sinner	978-0-8217-8001-5	$6.99US/$8.49CAN
__Highland Captive	978-0-8217-8003-9	$6.99US/$8.49CAN
__Nature of the Beast	978-1-4201-0435-6	$6.99US/$8.49CAN
__Highland Fire	978-0-8217-7429-8	$6.99US/$8.49CAN
__Silver Flame	978-1-4201-0107-2	$6.99US/$8.49CAN
__Highland Wolf	978-0-8217-8000-8	$6.99US/$9.99CAN
__Highland Wedding	978-0-8217-8002-2	$4.99US/$6.99CAN
__Highland Destiny	978-1-4201-0259-8	$4.99US/$6.99CAN
__Only for You	978-0-8217-8151-7	$6.99US/$8.99CAN
__Highland Promise	978-1-4201-0261-1	$4.99US/$6.99CAN
__Highland Vow	978-1-4201-0260-4	$4.99US/$6.99CAN
__Highland Savage	978-0-8217-7999-6	$6.99US/$9.99CAN
__Beauty and the Beast	978-0-8217-8004-6	$4.99US/$6.99CAN
__Unconquered	978-0-8217-8088-6	$4.99US/$6.99CAN
__Highland Barbarian	978-0-8217-7998-9	$6.99US/$9.99CAN
__Highland Conqueror	978-0-8217-8148-7	$6.99US/$9.99CAN
__Conqueror's Kiss	978-0-8217-8005-3	$4.99US/$6.99CAN
__A Stockingful of Joy	978-1-4201-0018-1	$4.99US/$6.99CAN
__Highland Bride	978-0-8217-7995-8	$4.99US/$6.99CAN
__Highland Lover	978-0-8217-7759-6	$6.99US/$9.99CAN

Available Wherever Books Are Sold!

Check out our website at
http://www.kensingtonbooks.com